We'd like to offer you a fantastic new job in
Australia: your office window has a view over
Sydney Harbour—blue sky, glittering waters
and luxurious sailboats look tempting.
And, best of all, straight after work
you have a date with your hot new boss!

AUSTRALIAN BOSS: DIAMOND RING
by Jennie Adams

Sparkling talent Jennie Adams brings you
a story that is as unique and vibrant as it is
heart-wrenchingly emotional. Jennie writes
'…feel-good fantasy with [an] edge…'
(*RT Book Reviews*)

LIGHTS, CAMERA…KISS THE BOSS
by Nikki Logan

Sydney, Australia: sparks fly between
hot-shot TV producer Dan and his latest star!
Nikki Logan's debut book is contemporary,
sassy, and captures the butterflies and the
rush from first date to first kiss…to *'I do'*!

GW00356702

Dear Reader

Fiona Donner is talented, insightful, open and giving. She is determined to reach her full potential as an artist, and is unaware of her beauty and appeal as a woman.

A man full of strength and shields, honour and vulnerability, potential and giving, Brent MacKay has faced abandonment and a physical condition that is his gift and his challenge. He is successful and grounded, has built a family with his brothers, but he will never marry or commit to a woman. That simply isn't a place Brent can go.

How can these two people find their way to a happy ending when the odds seem impossible?

When I wrote this story, I needed to put Brent and Fiona together and let them explore family and support networks, disappointment, hope, ambition and guardedness. Together, can they discover that wonderful connection and excitement and relief that comes from finding a soulmate and realising that, despite all the odds and obstacles, there is enough faith inside and enough love in each other to overcome all of it?

Do you believe a man and a woman can find a deep, calm happiness that is simply unbreachable, that all the world can see is for ever? I do, and I think Brent and Fiona will too. But I'll let you look for yourselves…

With love from Australia

Jennie

AUSTRALIAN BOSS: DIAMOND RING

BY
JENNIE ADAMS

MILLS & BOON

DID YOU PURCHASE THIS BOOK WITHOUT A COVER?

If you did, you should be aware it is **stolen property** as it was reported *unsold and destroyed* by a retailer. Neither the author nor the publisher has received any payment for this book.

All the characters in this book have no existence outside the imagination of the author, and have no relation whatsoever to anyone bearing the same name or names. They are not even distantly inspired by any individual known or unknown to the author, and all the incidents are pure invention.

All Rights Reserved including the right of reproduction in whole or in part in any form. This edition is published by arrangement with Harlequin Enterprises II BV/S.à.r.l. The text of this publication or any part thereof may not be reproduced or transmitted in any form or by any means, electronic or mechanical, including photocopying, recording, storage in an information retrieval system, or otherwise, without the written permission of the publisher.

This book is sold subject to the condition that it shall not, by way of trade or otherwise, be lent, resold, hired out or otherwise circulated without the prior consent of the publisher in any form of binding or cover other than that in which it is published and without a similar condition including this condition being imposed on the subsequent purchaser.

® and TM are trademarks owned and used by the trademark owner and/or its licensee. Trademarks marked with ® are registered with the United Kingdom Patent Office and/or the Office for Harmonisation in the Internal Market and in other countries.

First published in Great Britain 2009
Harlequin Mills & Boon Limited,
Eton House, 18-24 Paradise Road, Richmond, Surrey TW9 1SR

© Jennifer Ann Ryan 2009

ISBN: 978 0 263 86981 1

Harlequin Mills & Boon policy is to use papers that are natural, renewable and recyclable products and made from wood grown in sustainable forests. The logging and manufacturing process conform to the legal environmental regulations of the country of origin.

Printed and bound in Spain
by Litografia Rosés, S.A., Barcelona

Australian author **Jennie Adams** grew up in a rambling farmhouse surrounded by books, and by people who loved reading them. She decided at a young age to be a writer, but it took many years and a lot of scenic detours before she sat down to pen her first romance novel. Jennie has worked in a number of careers and voluntary positions, including transcription typist and pre-school assistant. She is the proud mother of three fabulous adult children and makes her home in a small inland city in New South Wales. In her leisure time Jennie loves long, rambling walks, discovering new music, starting knitting projects that she rarely finishes, chatting with friends, trips to the movies, and new dining experiences.

Jennie loves to hear from her readers, and can be contacted via her website at www.jennieadams.net

For David. For the sound of your laughter,
and your un-caffeinated morning voice.
For the memories we're building,
for the teasing and for your strength and your love
and your vulnerabilities.
For the best hugs in the world and for bringing me
home the piece of my puzzle that I needed so much.
I love you with all my heart. This one is for you.

CHAPTER ONE

A LITTLE tingle went down Fiona Donner's spine. It came from the impact of a pair of particularly appealing green eyes fringed with thick black lashes, focused utterly upon her as Brent MacKay made his job offer.

To compensate for that odd, unexpected reaction, Fiona used her best professional tone as she responded. 'Thank you. I'm thrilled to accept your offer and yes, I can start Monday!'

The famous, fabulous, talented, highly private and intensely focused millionaire landscape designer Brent MacKay wanted *her*. That was reason enough for a shiver or two, wasn't it? Fiona would be working with Brent for the next twelve months, with an option to extend if they were both happy with things by then. She knew already she would be happy. She'd just been offered the ultimate dream job!

Brent shifted in his executive office chair and

his lean, tanned face creased into a smile. 'You may find the pace challenging at first. I work hard across multiple projects at once and you'll be providing input into all the major jobs I handle.'

'I'm not afraid of hard work. In truth, I can't wait for the challenge.' She meant that with all her heart. 'A chance at a job like this doesn't come every day. It makes the past two and a half years of graphic design study worth every moment.'

And his offer was a true shot in the arm for her confidence in her artistic abilities. He wouldn't want her if he thought she lacked the talent. She would work on computer graphic design for work proposals and job outlines. Original landscape paintings for the walls of his clients. Specialised photography for advertising and more. Fiona couldn't wait!

See, Mum? I do *have what it takes to survive in this field.*

Fiona straightened in the comfortable black leather visitor's chair and tugged at the hem of the pink and white checked jacket that covered her generous—well, okay, *quite generous*—curves, and tweaked the matching skirt into place.

She was five foot eleven in her stockinged feet, and Junoesque to go with it. Well, at least in this outfit she looked as good as she could look.

'Here's hoping you still feel as enthusiastic

after your first week or so here.' Brent's glance lingered on her for just a moment before it moved to the bench-top storage that covered two of the walls in the room. Regimented rows of work covered their surfaces.

Fiona followed his glance, and followed it further, to the view of a busy outer Sydney suburb business street outside the ground floor window. A view of working class Australia going about what it did best. Working, and living.

If he wanted to, Brent could be in the heart of the city in a suite in a high-rise building with Sydney Harbour spread before him like an offering.

Instead, he was here in Everyman's territory. A place Fiona knew *she* would be very comfortable because she loved its reality. Fiona murmured, 'I will do everything possible to please you in every way.'

A beat of silence followed in which she realised her words could have been chosen a bit more carefully, and heat started to build at the base of her neck.

She hoped the blush stayed where it was and didn't give itself away all over her peaches and cream face. Fiona's hand rose to her high ponytail of blonde hair. She smoothed it in a nervous gesture before she could stop herself.

Her new employer stared at her intently before

he dropped his gaze and said a low, deep, 'I'm certain you will be everything that's required.'

The fingers of his right hand drummed out a rhythm on the desk for a moment before he stilled them, became utterly still, and cleared his throat. 'To date I've worked very privately on my projects at grass roots level, but I'm ready for this step now. You come highly recommended from the graphic design centre and, now that we've discussed the work, I very much want to bring you on board.'

To share in his creative process. It *was* a rather intimate thing. 'I'll respect your privacy, Mr MacKay. However you want us to work together, I'll do my best to fit in.'

'That's appreciated, though I'm sure we'll get along…fine.'

A few words followed by a calm glance that gave away absolutely nothing of his thoughts and yet somehow seemed to reach inside to a core part of her and find a connection anyway.

There was no reason for gooseflesh to break out on her skin, but it did. What was the matter with her? 'I'll work hard—whatever you feel will be helpful to the business.'

'Thank you.' He drew a breath. 'I'd like to introduce you to everyone now. It's a small office staff. Only about twenty people. Most of my employees are out on ground teams turning my designs into reality. You'll meet one of the teams Monday, others as time goes on.' Brent rose to his feet, crossed to her side and when she also stood, cupped her elbow to lead her to the door.

He was a tall man. Around six foot two, and all of it honed without an ounce of fat to be seen. Broad shoulders, slim hips, dark hair cropped short and with a distinct wave in it. His mouth was wide with a full lower lip, his teeth even and white. He had a straight nose that flared at the end.

And those gorgeous green eyes beneath winged brows. Eyes that seemed to watch the world with a combination of intensity and guardedness that Fiona found…compelling.

Employee to employer, that was. She found him compelling as a *brand new* employer. 'It will be nice to meet everyone, Mr MacKay.'

'They'll all be excited to hear you're coming on board,' he said. 'And please call me Brent. You're going to be all over a work site with me Monday morning getting grubby, so I think we can do away with the formalities. I suggest you wear jeans for that, by the way.'

As he spoke, a worker stepped through the front door of the building. A brisk May wind followed the woman in. Winter would officially arrive in another month. Out here in this suburb, further from the Sydney coast, it would get cold. For now, the weather just had a slight edge.

Fiona glanced at her employer. He had dressed for that edge in a tan button-down shirt over charcoal trousers. Business-casual. He should have looked less compelling than he did, but an aura of leashed strength and intensity came from him, was stamped on his face.

Please let me be equally strong and focused so I can do well here.

At almost twenty-six years of age, it shouldn't still matter so much to Fiona that she be able to prove herself. Perhaps if her family had been a little more supportive, or believed in her at all, it wouldn't have.

'Thank you…Brent.' Fiona breathed in the sharp blue tang of his aftershave and tried not to notice the warmth radiating through her clothing from his fingertips.

Brent led her deeper into the open-plan office area. 'You'll want to move out here to live, I assume, rather than try to commute? From the address on your résumé, I gather you lived in central Sydney while you attended your course.' He paused before the first desk, introduced Fiona and waited while she exchanged a few words with another employee.

As they moved on again, Fiona nodded. 'That flat-share in the heart of the city was convenient while I attended the graphic design centre. But I'd prefer to live close to my work here.' She liked the idea of migrating to this outer suburb. It would be an adventure.

It would bring her closer to several of her friends who came from out this way, too. And of course it would take her further from her family, who were all based on Sydney's North Shore, but she couldn't do anything about that.

The thought gave her a hint of something rather close to guilty relief. 'I'll start searching for a place immediately. Hopefully there'll be something available through a local real estate agent, or a listing in a shop window—'

'We'll discuss that once you've met everyone.' Brent guided her through the room, pausing at this desk and that desk to present her to his other employees.

She did her best to remember names and position titles as each person was introduced.

Finally Brent led her to the kitchenette at the rear of the open-plan area. Two men stood almost shoulder to shoulder there. The youngest wore a business suit, the older outdoor clothes. They both watched Fiona and Brent's progress across the room.

'Fiona, meet Linc and Alex MacKay, my brothers.' Brent gestured to each of the men in turn. 'Boys, I'd like you to meet Fiona Donner, the company's new graphic artist as of about—' he glanced at the watch on his wrist '—ten minutes ago.'

The way he addressed the men held pride and deep affection. She hadn't known he had brothers, but then her research for this job application had yielded very little of a personal nature about Brent MacKay.

'I'm pleased to meet you.' Linc shook Fiona's hand and let go. 'I run the chain of nurseries that, among other things, acts as Brent's key supplier.'

Linc was a tall man with dark hair, grey eyes and the same lean build as Brent.

No. Not the same build. He was deeper through the chest than Brent, thicker set all over. The impression of a shared leanness actually came from something in his expression, in a measure of guardedness in the backs of his eyes that Brent had also revealed.

Fiona murmured a greeting. 'I'm having trouble guessing who's the eldest. You seem very close in age.' As she said so, the lack of true genetic similarities between the men occurred to her.

'Brent's the eldest. Most people don't pick up on how close we are in age…' Linc gave her a slightly surprised look as he trailed off.

Before she could think about that, the youngest brother extended his hand.

'I'm Alex. I run an export business near here, but I'm also a shareholder in Brent's company. I hope you enjoy working here.'

'I can't wait to start.' Fiona shook the young man's hand and released it. The third brother was substantially younger than Linc or Brent. Early twenties, she'd have guessed, though that was young to be running a business.

Blue-eyed like Fiona herself, Alex had a square-cut jaw, broad forehead and mid-brown hair and looked nothing like either of his brothers. He also had a glint in his eyes that probably had women chasing after him.

Fiona wanted to know the nature of this family, how they all fitted together.

As for eyes, and glints therein, she only had eyes for her employer.

Well, she meant she was only *focused* on him. She was focused on her new job! She didn't have 'eyes' for men generally, anyway. Her role was that of 'everybody's friend' and she liked that just fine. It was much less stressful than getting into a relationship that would only end up disappointing her. Or, worse, disappointing the man involved. Been there, not interested in repeating that. It was enough having her mother's criticism of all the faults in her ability to appeal.

Fiona turned to Linc. 'Maybe I could take

photos at one of the nurseries some time soon. I'd love to get some background material to use when I start working with my computer designs for Brent.'

Linc's shrewd gaze examined her as he inclined his head. 'That can be arranged for you.'

'When there's time for us both to go,' Brent inserted, and fell abruptly quiet. His head twitched to the right and a frown swept over his brow.

Linc's eyebrows lifted and Alex stared at his older brother before both he and Linc looked quickly elsewhere.

Brent's entire body seemed to freeze then.

Uncertain of what she was sensing in him, Fiona said slowly, 'I don't need to visit the nursery if that's not convenient. It was just a thought.'

'It's not a problem.' Brent pushed his hands deep into his trouser pockets. 'I was just—'

'Distracted,' Alex put in.

'He lost his concentration,' Linc said at the same time, and clamped his lips together.

'I was just *thinking,*' Brent stated, and frowned again. 'I'll make a day for us to visit Linc's nursery, Fiona.' Brent seemed to make a conscious effort to move on from whatever that reaction had been. 'I'll make sure you get to do that. It's a good idea for you to take those photos, and I visit the nurseries regularly anyway to inspect the stock, keep the inventory fresh in my mind and see what new things Linc's managed to find for me. It'll be convenient for us to go together, that's all.'

'Well, thank you. I'll look forward to that when it happens.' Fiona nodded and relaxed a little. She hadn't committed a faux pax...

Which meant Brent's reaction had been—?

Something she wasn't going to be able to figure out right now.

So leave it alone, Fiona. You don't have to understand everything about him.

In truth, she tended to want to delve too deeply into what made people tick. Well, her mother said so anyway.

A short silence fell before Linc cleared his throat and addressed his brother. 'Have you discussed accommodation options with Fiona yet?'

'That was next on my list.' Brent turned to her. 'You're welcome to do whatever you like about your living arrangements, but Linc owns an investment property you might be interested in renting. It's a one bedroom flat about a ten minute drive from here. The complex it's in has courtyard parking for a car, if you own one.'

'Are you serious? I thought I'd be looking all

weekend and maybe end up staying in a pub or hostel before I managed to pin something down.' Fiona tried to stifle her grin, and failed.

A smile lurked in the backs of Brent's eyes in response, a beautiful, lovely smile. The man was lethal, and she didn't understand the connection she felt towards him.

Fiona drew a steadying breath and turned to Linc. 'How much are you asking for the flat per month? I'll have to stick to a budget.'

Linc named the figure.

'I'll be able to afford that rent.' That was a relief, and she simply needed to concentrate on the tasks and necessities at hand. Not on eyes that smiled at her through shields that made her think of her own life, its hurts and triumphs, and what Brent's might have been and might be now. 'When can I sign a lease agreement? I don't need to see the place first. If you recommend it, that's all I need to know. I don't want to miss out on the opportunity to pin this down, if that's at all possible.'

She smoothed her hands over her thighs and told herself to stop babbling.

Though Brent had remained silent during this interchange, his gaze followed the movement and she thought she heard him make a soft sound in the back of his throat before he glanced away.

If so, it was probably because she had drawn his attention to just how non-slim those thighs were.

On this lowering thought Fiona suppressed a sigh. Her body was what it was. There was no changing her build, or her height, or what she preferred to refer to as her curviness but her mother said was the result of far too much self-indulgence and couldn't Fiona try to eat less?

She didn't overeat. Her tiny mother couldn't see that, though. To Eloise Donner, Fiona was the stork among the pigeons and someone needed to shrink her somehow. Preferably while shrinking her into a far more practical mould at the same time.

And Brent had simply followed her movement with his gaze. It was completely meaningless. It wasn't as though her employer would be noticing her in that respect.

Which was a good thing, she reminded herself.

Linc drew a folded document and a set of keys from his back pocket and handed both to her. 'Once you've read the lease, you can go ahead and sign it and leave it with Jaimie. She'll pass it on to me the next time I'm here. Brent will explain where the place is and about getting you moved in, if you need help with that.'

The two brothers excused themselves and left then, and Fiona curled her fingers around the keys and lease and turned to her employer. 'That was generous of you and your brother. Thank you.'

'It was no trouble. Linc deals in a lot of that kind of property investment.' Brent watched his brothers exit the room and the building before he allowed his gaze to return to his new employee. He hadn't meant to follow the slide of Fiona's hands down her thighs moments ago.

He hadn't meant to notice her at all, but he had. She was a striking woman. Tall, beautifully built and curvy in all the right places. A woman who wouldn't blow away in a strong breeze, who a man could hold in his arms without fear of crushing her.

She was also femininity through and through. From the dark blonde hair tied back from her face in a high ponytail to the robin's egg blue eyes and fine arched brows, the straight nose and generous mouth, she looked softer than a flower, and equally as sweet.

The thoughts surprised him. Not the appreciation of her beauty. How could any man fail to notice that? But the intimacy of where his thoughts had taken him—thoughts of how it would be to hold her, of wanting to protect her from harm. Brent's life had been all about protecting himself, his brothers. His father had put him in a place where he'd had no choice but to be strong. To hide his flaws from the world so they wouldn't judge him as Charles had done. Brent hadn't reached out to a woman for the kind of intimacy that would result in wanting to protect her as well as protect his own interests in a long time. Actually…he never had.

He never would do that. His limits would forever prevent that. And Fiona looked the kind of woman who would deserve exactly that kind of…care.

Which simply reminded him that he needed to appreciate her attractiveness from the distance of an unconnected observer.

Right. And he did. He'd simply become distracted for a moment. The same thing applied to the head twitch he'd experienced earlier. It wouldn't happen again in front of her. He'd make sure of that as he did in all other circumstances.

Brent nodded in a completely concise, controlled manner as he came to this conclusion. If he felt somewhat relieved to have arrived back at a more known, comfortable place in his thinking, he told himself this was a good thing, anyway. 'Let's take you to Jaimie so you can sign your employment agreement and leave the lease with her.'

Once Fiona had done that, Brent gestured to his office area. 'Would you like to hear about some of the projects I've got going? Some preliminary information to give you an idea of what's in store for you?'

'Oh, yes, please. That will give me a chance to think over the weekend before I start work officially on Monday.' Fiona half-reached one hand towards him, dropped it self-consciously to her side, and her face pinked slightly.

His gaze locked onto that blossom of colour and his breath caught…

He pushed the door of his office open and stepped through to open the adjoining door. 'You'll be working in here. It's a decent-sized room. I hope it'll suit your needs.'

His voice was deep. Too deep. He cleared his throat.

Fiona's gaze tracked around the long room, dodged his. 'I'm sure it will. It's a generous working space. There's good light for my easel work, and plenty of desk space for computer monitors.'

'I imagine there'll be times when you'll need all of that space.'

'Is it okay to dress casually for when I'm painting? I realise there'll be times when I need to look smart. Client discussions…' A little ridge formed between her brows. 'Perhaps I should just dress smart all the time, and wear a smock or something when I paint. I'm inclined to be a bit messy during that process, but I could try to change that.'

'There's a dressing room. I keep clothes here. You can do the same. Messy is fine, anyway.' The thought of her using his changing room, shedding clothes and putting on new ones, wasn't a place he needed to go.

So get on with it, MacKay. 'On Monday we'll be helping to finish up a landscaping project, and I'll want you to take photos and think about a painting for the clients. They're an elderly couple, very agreeable. They'll be happy with whatever you put together. The photos will go into a Progress Album for the clients and our stock here for showing clients how we work. Nothing for newspapers or magazines, though. I accept the occasional interview to keep the media off my back but I'm selective, so if you're ever approached I expect you to shoot the enquiry straight to me.'

'I will do that.' Her expression showed she didn't understand the 'why' of it, but her acceptance was enough. 'And I can certainly take the photos and also use them to help me create an appropriate painting for the clients.'

Fiona gave him a pleasant but firm look. 'It's not ideal to come in partway through and need to produce a painting in that way, but I'm sure that won't happen in the future.'

Brent liked a woman—correction, a *person*—with enough spunk to say what they wanted.

From the distance of an observer. You like it from that distance. 'Don't worry. You'll be included in future planning. In fact, I have a project that's been driving me mad for the last three weeks. The client won't settle on a design. I'm hoping if I pull you in on that one it might get me the breakthrough I need.'

'Okay, well, that's good then, and I'll be happy to try to help with your project.' Her expression held the slightest sheepish edge before she squared her shoulders and seemed to decide it was best she'd been clear about her expectations.

Brent went on to explain the problems with the project he'd mentioned, and to discuss some other issues. Work was easy. He always felt at home with his landscape projects.

An hour later Fiona stood at the door of his office once more, bag in hand, and thanked him for his time. 'I can't wait to start work Monday. I'll have some photographic equipment to bring out to the landscaping site, if that's okay.'

'That's fine. Anything you bring will be safe there, though we should get your equipment added to the business's insurance cover.'

'Shall I phone the details in later today? Model numbers and so on?'

'Do that. You can leave them with Elizabeth, my receptionist.' With this issue resolved, Brent went on, 'If you need help to move into your flat this weekend—'

Fiona smiled her thanks, but shook her head. 'I can get Tommy to use his delivery truck to help me shift the larger items. My friends all knew I was coming for this interview, so they've been on standby, half-expecting this.'

So 'Tommy' was simply one of those 'friends'? Brent couldn't explain why he suddenly felt…lighter than he had a few seconds ago. 'Okay, then I guess I should let you go so you can start making arrangements.'

Fiona made a little bouncing motion on the balls of her feet. 'A new home, a new job and a new part of the city to live in. I can't wait to take it all on. Thank you again, Mr MacKay—*Brent*—for this chance.'

'You're more than welcome.' Brent said his goodbyes and then watched her leave the building, hips swaying with each step she took.

And then he immersed himself in landscape plans, where he could line up his ideas in neat rows and spend as long as he needed on each aspect of his work. His head twitched sharply to the right, but he was by himself now. He didn't worry about trying to conceal the action.

At least the condition he lived with was good for helping him to focus on his work, and he had every right to keep knowledge of it from the world at large. It was in his best interests to do so. His father's past behaviour had made that abundantly clear.

Brent dug into his plans and put thoughts of Fiona Donner's lovely smile—of *his new employee's smile*—right out of his mind…

CHAPTER TWO

'A DOZEN shrubs for you, Russ.' A worker placed the shrubs on the ground and moved away to collect another load.

It was Monday afternoon, towards the end of Fiona's first day at the new job. Spending it out of doors helping to complete an actual work project as well as gather photographic resources for her painting and for the company to use to showcase its services had been a thrill. She smiled to herself as words continued to flow around her.

'Hey, Phil. Can I use that mattock for the next ten minutes?'

'Great job with the bougainvillea, Chelsea.' This was Brent's voice as he turned his head to check on one of the more junior members of the ground team. 'Keep up the good work.'

The sun was shining and the ten-acre work site on the edge of a newish Sydney suburb was abuzz with activity. Brent was motivated and positive and determined, and the ground workers responded to his authority and encouragement by giving their absolute best. He was at home in this, and Fiona…found that knowledge of him perhaps a little too appealing.

'We're going to finish this job on time.' The site boss, a man in his mid-thirties with a shock of carroty hair squashed under a baseball cap, paused beside Fiona to murmur the words. 'I knew we would. The company hasn't missed a deadline yet, even when things have gone pear-shaped, as they did with this project when some of the goods we ordered didn't arrive three days ago.

'That never would have happened with Linc's nursery supplies. I'm guessing in future Brent will refuse to buy from anywhere else, even if it means asking his brother to import or source what it is that he needs.'

Brent had pulled in about a dozen extra workers from other job sites to work on this project. Fiona had done her share of carrying and carting and planting and fetching throughout the day, too. She was 'grubby', as Brent had predicted would happen. Mostly around the knees and seat of her jeans, and it was all good honest dirt. She'd learned so much about his process by getting her hands into it, and she'd had a ball getting dirty at the same time! 'There doesn't seem to be a lot left to do now.'

'I'd say another half hour of work for everyone, if that.' The boss moved on, and Fiona planted the last shrub in her allotment and dusted herself off.

She watched as Brent lifted a plant from a wheelbarrow and placed it in a prepared hole a few metres away with an efficient movement. In the early days of his business he had probably spent a lot of his time on this kind of thing.

He worked with a focused, economical efficiency. Her camera lens had tracked that focus again and again throughout the day. She itched to photograph him again now.

For their office files, Fiona justified. She glanced guiltily at the other nearby workers, but none of them seemed to be taking any particular notice of who or what she was studying.

Right now she needed to study landscape photo angles. She gathered her equipment. There should be a nice sunset soon, if she could find the right place on the property to photograph it. She fished her iPod out of her jeans pocket, placed the earphones in her ears and let the music and the lighting and the mood absorb her.

She truly was all about the work.

She was!

Brent found Fiona in a far corner of the property site, camera carefully placed on a tripod. She was waiting for something, he wasn't sure what. And, while she waited, her body moved unconsciously to music only she could hear.

In her jeans and fitted red shirt, with dirt smears on her legs and other places, and her hair ruffled and half-falling from her ponytail, she looked… lived-in, girl-next-door.

He almost managed to convince himself she looked quite ordinary, in fact, until she made a small sound in the back of her throat, leaned in and took several photos before she straightened with a satisfied sigh, pulled the earphones from her ears and began to dismantle her equipment.

Because the truth was Fiona dressed in this way was anything but ordinary, and with the flush of achievement on her face she was anything but comfortable or girl-next-door.

Brent drew a deep breath and stepped forward. 'Finished? Did you get the shots you wanted?'

'Oh!' Her hand rose to splay over her chest. 'I didn't realise you were there. I was photographing the sunset. I've taken around two hundred photos today. Not all of them will be used, of course, but I think I've gained a good overview of what a team of people can achieve on a site in a single session. But please tell me I wasn't muttering or singing while I worked.'

'You were soundless, I promise. I didn't want

to disturb your concentration so I waited, that was all.' Their fingers brushed as he reached to take the tripod from her.

Just that, and Brent's focus slipped. He froze on that slip. Came to a complete stop with his fingers closed over Fiona's. Only a beat of time passed before he moved his hand, but that one beat was a beat out of his control and that concerned him.

That Fiona now studied him with her head tipped to the side and curiosity stamped on her face bothered him more. There were certain things about him that he kept to himself. He'd learned from a master instructor that doing that was necessary.

Most of all it bothered him that this one woman set off in him things to do with his condition that very few other people could make happen, no matter how much they impacted on him. His need to protect his privacy about that rose even in the face of his awareness of her. It wasn't a comfortable combination.

'I think I got a couple of great shots just now.' She glanced up into the branches of the lemon-scented gum tree that towered over them. 'Ones with the light spearing down creating a dappled effect. I hope to base my painting on that concept.'

'That's good.' His thumb rubbed over and over

against a ridged edge on the tripod. Brent forced the movement to a stop. 'I'm glad you got the material you wanted.'

'It only took a little while, a bit of waiting for that perfect moment.' Fiona seemed about to ask him something.

Brent braced, but her glance shifted around the vacant lot, past him, swung left and right and finally moved to the outside perimeter where all the work vehicles had been parked.

'I guess maybe I took longer than I noticed. The work's finished.' She seemed chagrined. 'They've all left. I was so focused on what I was doing that I didn't notice. How long did I keep you waiting?'

'Not long, and I didn't mind waiting.' He growled it in a tone that quite likely made her believe the opposite. The truth was, he'd got value out of watching her work. 'If you're done here, we can leave now.'

'Yes. I'm done. Thanks.' She hustled towards his utility truck.

Brent joined her, opened the passenger door for her and climbed in behind the wheel. 'The office will be closed by the time we get back, but we'll get anything from inside that you need. Then, if you're not too tired, I'd like you to join Linc and Alex and me for dinner so they can hear your impressions of your first day on the job.'

They'd planned for this—to get Fiona's impressions without giving her too long to think first and maybe fall back on more PC answers rather than simply giving her true impressions.

And it would be fine. Taking her to his brothers would be exactly what he needed to bring this—whatever it was that he experienced when he was near her—back into perspective.

It had probably just been too long since he'd spent time with a woman. There were always offers. They never meant anything more than what they were, and maybe he was starting to feel a little jaded about that.

Brent pushed the thought aside, because there was nothing else for him. And he wasn't jaded, anyway. 'Linc and Alex and I all hold shares in each others' companies. So you'll be reporting to all of us.'

'I'd be happy to discuss the day with all of you. Actually, I'd like a chance to bat my reactions around with you, particularly.' Fiona glanced down at her jeans. 'I'm grubby, though.'

Brent drove into the traffic. 'That won't matter. We'll be eating at home, and Linc and Alex know we'll be coming straight from the site.'

'Then I'm happy to come to dinner and "report in".' Fiona smiled. 'Thanks.'

And Fiona was. Happy. Cheerful. Chatting

about the other workers and Brent's work projects generally as they made their way back to their suburb, where she collected her car from all day parking and followed him to his warehouse home.

'It's this way.' Brent waited while Fiona exited her car in the large ground floor parking area and led her into the foyer of the converted warehouse building he and his brothers shared. It felt good to bring her into his home, and that was one more reaction he didn't want to have to deal with.

Fiona stopped in the centre of the polished floor and her glance darted this way and that. 'Oh. How gorgeous. And it's so big and very private. I never imagined from the outside…'

'That was what we hoped when we bought the place and converted it. An illusion of it being nothing special, but inside there's space and…we know we're not on display.' He cleared his throat. 'We like it, anyway.'

Brent laid his hand on the curved handcrafted staircase that led to the upper level, and watched her look her fill in this place where he felt…comfortable, where he owned his space.

One end of the foyer held a leather sofa and chairs. The art on the walls was bold and bright— blues and whites, yellows and greens and pinks on canvases large enough not to get lost on the huge walls.

Fiona's gaze settled on those artworks for a long moment. Finally she said, 'The colours and designs of those are fabulous. I don't think I know the artist…'

'Alex'll be pleased you like his work.' Brent was pleased. And proud. And way too conscious of her reactions altogether. 'Let's go find my brothers.' He led the way up the staircase. 'We all have separate homes within the warehouse. For tonight, we're meeting in the courtyard area upstairs.'

'I think it's wonderful that you're all so close.' Her tone held a wistful edge she didn't quite manage to conceal.

Yet she had a family, had referred to parents and sisters on the drive to the site this morning, and obviously, if they'd raised someone like Fiona, her parents must be special people.

Before Brent could consider that further, his guest made a beeline for the youngest of his brothers. 'Alex. Your paintings are beautiful—'

'Thanks.' Alex turned from the barbecue with a modest smile and a wry twist of his mouth. 'Brent brought your portfolio home over the weekend to show us. Your work is far better.'

'Different,' Fiona corrected. 'Not necessarily better.'

Linc placed a bowl of salad on the long table. 'Hiring a graphic designer was a big step for our brother. He's accustomed to working his designs through on his own, but he felt the company was ready for it, that it would be a good thing.'

'I hope it will prove to be.' Fiona's gaze encompassed all of them.

Brent glanced her way. 'I've seen enough of Fiona's work, and now seen her in action, to have no doubt I've made the right choice.'

At least she had managed that while she'd fought her reactions to this talented and complex man. And surely, in a day or two, when she'd settled into the job and become used to her employer, she would move past this consciousness of him.

'I appreciate your faith in me, Brent.' In truth it touched a deep place in Fiona's heart that had been chilled the day she'd told her family she'd decided to follow her dream career, rather than the logical, safe one they'd steered her into when she'd first left high school at eighteen.

They'd been equally unenthusiastic when she'd phoned to say she'd landed this job and moved out here. She might as well have said she'd got a good bargain on bread this week at the supermarket for all the level of excitement or support she'd received in response.

So Brent's attitude was a boost, even if her

reaction to it didn't exactly help her to feel blasé towards him.

'It's easy to have that faith. You're talented, enthusiastic.' Brent's gaze lingered on her for a long moment before he gave a deliberately relaxed grin that soon became a natural one. 'The company can only benefit from your input.'

'Thank you.' For the generosity of his words and the sincerity in his eyes as he delivered them.

He was a complex man—there was so much beneath the surface. She'd sensed that from the first moment of meeting him. Now, she simply wanted to know him all the more.

And, because Fiona felt a little emotional about that, and about his praise, she quickly cleared her throat and smiled. 'It means a lot to work for someone who has such faith in me and who I can have total faith in as well.'

Fiona drew a deep breath and glanced at the feast spread on the table. 'The food smells wonderful. I confess I'm a little hungry!'

They all took their seats at a picnic style table with bench seating. Linc and Alex sat on one side. Fiona ended up seated beside her boss on the other.

Focus on the meal, Fiona. On being an appropriate guest, or talking about work.

There were vegetable kebabs made of cherry tomatoes, courgette, onion slices and button

mushrooms marinated in a wonderful herbed
Italian dressing and cooked to perfection. Steak
and sausages—Fiona left those to the men. Whole
potatoes cooked in foil and served with sour
cream and fresh chopped chives. And delightful
seasoned ground beef patties.

'Which of you is the chef?' The outdoor area
was set up with potted small trees and plants
everywhere. It was enclosed, no view, and the
overall feeling was one of security and...intimacy.

In a purely familial context!

'I did the easy stuff. Rosa did the kebabs.'
Alex's glance dipped to his plate. 'Rosa's our
cleaner, mostly, but she does other things for us
as well.' He hesitated and his brows drew together
as he considered the matter. 'Sort of like a mother
would or something.'

A mother these men didn't have? Alex's
words made it sound as though they hadn't ever
known that.

Fiona's thoughts returned to how dissimilar
the men were. She shifted her gaze to Brent's
face but his eyes were shielded with those long
silky lashes again.

Perhaps they'd all had different mothers? Or
fathers? Or some of both? Perhaps family life had
been a little complicated for them? Well, she knew
all about that from her own family. Though she

was the only one who would say that situation was complex. Her parents and sisters would say it would all be just fine if Fiona would simply make an effort to fit in better. 'My compliments to Rosa, then.'

'So tell us your impressions from today.' Linc carved another piece of meat from his steak as he waited for her response.

'I have some photos now that I believe will be good for general marketing purposes.' She explained the thoughts behind those concepts, and was pleased when Brent started to nod and approval showed clearly on his chiselled face.

'I also have photos for the idea I want to use for a painting for the clients.' It was a great idea to add a painting into each landscape project, and Fiona was keen to get started on this one. 'If the clients hang the painting in their home and talk to their visitors about the landscaping work Brent's done for them, that can only be good for business. Working with my hands, helping to do actual planting, really helped me to get a feel for what Brent's work is all about, too. I…valued that.'

She felt as though she'd been given an insight into him. Fiona glanced his way and for a brief moment their gazes met and she wondered if he sensed that connection in the same way she did.

Seconds later he blinked and looked away and the moment was gone.

'I'd like you to create a better business logo for us, too.' Was Brent's voice a little deeper than usual as he said this? 'I think we're due for a change there. I've never been entirely happy with the logo we have. I want something timeless, with a style that won't date, but what we have now feels a bit too pedestrian.'

'I'm sure I can come up with some viable possibilities. You might want something with just a few bold lines. It's surprising how effective that can be.'

Brent's gaze narrowed as he considered the idea. 'Yes. I can see that.' Again, that smile kicked up one side of his mouth. 'I like the way you think.'

'Thank you.'

They ate and they talked and Fiona lost her over-consciousness eventually and relaxed and, before she knew it, they were batting ideas back and forth. So fast, in fact, that she was almost breathless with it.

The scent of barbecued meat and vinaigrette dressing and city in the evening filled the air around them and she leaned close to her employer and he leaned in close to her, two heads bent together in an almost conspiratorial huddle, until she realised just how close they were and her consciousness of him sharpened again.

As they fell silent and his gaze tracked over her and came back to rest on her eyes, a shiver similar to that very first one she'd felt tickled over her senses. There was warmth in his expression, and frank male interest...

Before he shut the latter down.

It stung. More than Fiona wanted to admit because she'd had this experience enough times in her life. She'd had it the one time she'd trusted a man enough to get truly close to him. That had been years ago now, but it had left its mark, had made her wary, and that wariness had proved accurate over the years.

And now her employer was doing the same thing.

But he *was* only her employer and that was what she needed to remember.

'I'm looking forward to tapping into your vision.' That was what they needed to talk about, to focus on. She swallowed. 'For your work. Tapping into it and learning how to present it in its best light for each project. The emotion you convey...'

His expression became a mask and the fingers of his right hand drummed out a staccato rhythm on the table.

Moments later that rhythm stopped.

All of Brent stopped, frozen in time for a long moment as his gaze searched hers.

Finally he said, 'All I do is make the best I can out of each project I take on. That's just…work. Any emotion you put into it will be your own.'

His belief in this was in his eyes, in the closed conviction on his face. Belief and self-protectiveness.

Why wouldn't he acknowledge that he poured himself into his work? It was so obvious to her.

She'd examined a lot of his projects over the past two years. Landscape design had fascinated her from the start of her course, and *his* work had held the most appeal to her purely *because* of what she sensed in it.

Strength and conviction, imagination and reaching out and…protecting himself. Oh, she had responded most of all to that. It was one of the things that drew her to him, even when she knew she shouldn't and mustn't allow herself to be drawn. She'd only get hurt and, anyway, he was the boss, out of her reach and her league!

'I want to draw out what you've seen, your vision for each project.' Fiona spoke carefully, took the diplomatic route in her reply. 'But I'm certainly happy to add my own layering to that.'

'That's the best way to look at it.' Brent seemed satisfied with this and the conversation moved on then, expanded to include all three brothers again.

After a time, Alex got to his feet. 'I have phone calls to make to one of the company's overseas contacts before it gets too much later. If you'll excuse me?'

Linc stood beside Alex and a frown creased his brows. 'I might head out to Cecilia's. I wasn't really satisfied with the discussion we had earlier today on the phone.'

Fiona watched the brothers disappear and turned to Brent with the quirk of one eyebrow. She asked lightly, 'Woman trouble for your brother?'

Brent stood and began to gather dishes and utensils together. 'Cecilia manages Linc's largest plant nursery. Who knows what the issue is this time? They're two strong personalities. They clash sometimes.'

'Ah.' Fiona got to her feet and helped gather the remainder of the dishes. 'Where are we headed with these?'

'My place.' Brent led the way out of the court-yard area and along a hallway until they came to a recessed door. 'It can all go in the dishwasher.'

'And then I'd better leave.' Fiona held the plates carefully and waited as he opened the door to his home within the warehouse building. 'I enjoyed the meal and our talk. I hope your brothers were happy with my first day reactions.'

She'd all but forgotten the presence of the others at times as she'd focused her attention on her boss. Fiona knew she had to do better than *that!*

'I think we were all more than satisfied. Kitchen's this way.' Brent strode at a brisk pace past a large living area and into a slate and white kitchen.

Was it the rich aroma of percolated coffee that drew him along so fast? She didn't get the chance to more than half-glance around her.

Fiona stopped at the edge of the kitchen and then she did let her gaze take in the sight of three different coffee machines on the counter, and a myriad of other gadgets beside them.

Her lips twitched. 'I take it you *really* like coffee. And gadgetry.'

'Different blends for different times of the day. The coffee is on a timer, so I can make sure it's ready for me when I want it. My evening dose is decaf.' A slight smile creased his lips. Then his expression sobered as he examined the rest of the gadgets. 'The way they all work interests me. I probably have bought more things than I really need.'

As though he'd said too much, he drew two coffee mugs from an overhead cupboard and raised them in question.

'Yes, please.' If it was decaf, it wouldn't hurt to have it. She was intrigued by this small revelation into his personality, too. She would have liked to pursue the topic, maybe tease him a little about having an obsession about the way things worked.

A small memory flitted through her head as she thought this, of someone with similarities to her employer, but she lost it before it could fully form. 'The coffee smells far too good to be caffeine-free, you know.'

'It's an imported blend. A bit self-indulgent of me all up, I suppose. Overall, my curiosity hasn't always been welcomed, but I tend to indulge it nowadays, in my own setting, at least.' He cut off the words and then seemed to relax out of whatever place they had taken him. He poured the rich blend and passed her one of the cups.

'You're hardly self-indulgent, and I think curiosity is a good thing. How else do we learn?' The words emerged without her conscious volition. But he'd earned the money he had. If he wanted to import coffee and invest in gadgets he didn't necessarily use, why shouldn't he? Those things seemed very *small* indulgences and if he enjoyed exploring them at the same time… 'I mean great coffee is worth investing in.'

She put the mug to her lips and sipped, and the rich thick liquid slid down her throat so smoothly that she had to close her eyes and let a small sigh of satisfaction escape. 'Oh, that is *good*. I think for the pleasure of that taste alone, all your curiosity has been well worth it in this case.'

'You have a unique way of looking at things. Calling it that…' Brent fell silent.

'What else would it be?' She opened her eyes and caught his gaze on her. Unshielded in that first instance, and somehow almost vulnerable.

And…edged with a consciousness of her that brushed across her senses like a touch.

This time he didn't shut it down. Oh, he looked away, but the awareness was still etched on his face when he did that.

It echoed inside her, too. Fiona dropped her gaze to her cup again while her heart inexplicably pounded. It was a foolish reaction. One that she needed to quash because, even if he did find her attractive right now, that could change. In any case, he was her boss and it would be really far less than sensible for her to allow feelings towards him or to start believing he had any towards her.

Maybe he simply found her opinions interesting and she was imagining anything else.

They sipped their coffee standing right there, leaning against the kitchen counter. When the silence stretched, Fiona turned her gaze to Brent's living room, to squashy chocolate leather sofas and chairs and long rows of magazines lined up like soldiers across a set of three coffee tables.

There were neat stacks of library books set exactly so, and other books and pieces of paper arranged carefully all through the area and beside armchairs positioned around the room.

'I see you like to bring your work home, and you're very orderly.' Was this why he had rushed her past the area? Because there was something quite *different* about the way he'd laid out all that work?

His office space was similarly regimented, and it *was* different.

He rubbed his hand over the back of his head. 'I sometimes have to work on projects until they're finished, whether that means bringing things home or not. Once I get started, I get very focused and I can't stop. I've always been that way. Some people…find that objectionable but it's how I am. Core me. It's not something that's going to change.'

'Nor should it.' If he changed, he might lose some of the intensity that made his work what it was. Why on earth would he even consider such a possibility—? 'I imagine there'll be times when I'll do the same. Get deeply involved in the work, I mean.'

He shifted on his feet, passed his empty coffee cup from hand to hand.

'It's time I went.' One part of her didn't want to leave, wanted to stay in his company longer.

To talk about work issues, she told herself. Instead, she put her empty cup down on the counter top and made her way towards the front door.

'I enjoyed our talk this evening.' Brent paced beside her. His words brought them back to business, and of course that was a good thing.

As she approached the door she noticed the photomontage on the wall. It was positioned so it would be the last thing he looked at as he left his home each day.

Photos of him and his brothers.

Fiona looked, and looked again. And the story embedded in those images hit her so deeply her breath stalled in her throat and for a long moment she couldn't speak. She simply stood there, unable to shift her gaze.

When she finally found her voice it wasn't to state the obvious. Not, *You were all institutionalised.* Or, *There are no parents, are there?* At least not for a very long time. Or, *You're not biologically related.*

But, oh, they had created themselves into a family, first in that cold building in the background of several of the pictures, and later as they'd found their freedom and relocated here.

They were three men who'd *become* men

before their time, and had stood up for each other. It was all there, captured in the stark stares and guarded expressions of young boys and the determination of young men, and the laughter and wry smiles and inner shields of the men they were now.

How had they all ended up alone? Parentless? In Brent's case, extremely private, and she imagined the others had their issues with privacy, too. Just look at where they all lived.

His brothers must have changed their names through legal channels, or perhaps they'd all chosen the last name MacKay and adopted it at some point? 'I thought from the beginning that you and your brothers were close. I hadn't realised all the reasons why.'

Fiona didn't have that closeness in her own family. It was a knowledge she lived with and tried not to think about. Right now it felt very blatant to her. Blatant and sad, and yet Brent and his brothers must have been through so much more. Indeed, the two things were incomparable.

'We're there for each other. The few people who've looked at those photos didn't even realise—' Brent opened the door.

'That you're a chosen family, not a "by birth" one?' They were proof the former could be as strong as any example of the latter.

'Yes. "Chosen" is the right word for it. For us, that's better than where…we came from.' He stepped out into the corridor with her. 'I'll see you back to your car.'

End of discussion, and fair enough. Though she might want to know more, he *was* a private man and this was obviously very private business to him.

They walked in silence. Moments later she stood beside her small car.

'We have a meeting with a client at her home tomorrow.' Brent rubbed his jaw with his hand. 'It's the troublesome client I told you about on Friday.'

Fiona mentally reviewed her wardrobe. 'I'll be ready for it.'

'Perhaps between us we can get her to stop blocking the plans at every turn.' Brent waited while she seated herself, and then he pushed her door closed.

She started the engine and rolled down the window.

He leaned in. 'Drive safely. I'll see you to-morrow.'

'Goodnight, Brent.' He'd given her some things to think about. The family he had built and her questions about where he might have come from. His emotional guardedness. That regimented work lined up in his living room and in his office. The privacy he sought in his home and his work.

'Goodnight,' he murmured.

With a final wave and an odd reluctance to leave him, and with myriad questions flitting through her mind and no answers anywhere in sight, Fiona drove away.

CHAPTER THREE

'MRS FULLER will either have to get on board during this visit, or we cut our losses and dump the project. The work is interchangeable with a dozen other projects that all need my attention. At some point I have to assess what's going to be best financially for the company overall and, right now, letting her mess us around further isn't.' Brent murmured the words as he and Fiona waited in the formal sitting room of the woman's ritzy Sydney home.

They'd been kept cooling their heels here for twenty minutes now with no sign of their hostess.

'I agree. This isn't a smart use of your time. The woman's behaviour is insulting to you.' And that insult made Fiona feel...protective towards her boss.

Which was fine, because she was his employee. She had the right to feel that way. Even if she had been somewhat too personally conscious of her boss initially.

The door to the room swished open and a maid entered with a tea tray.

Rose Fuller swept in behind her. 'Thank you, Lilly. You may pour and leave us.'

Mrs Fuller waved a slender, well-tended hand towards the maid before she turned to greet her guests. 'Oh, I see you've brought an assistant, Mr MacKay?'

A very lowly one, her tone seemed to suggest.

'Mrs Fuller, meet my graphic designer, Fiona Donner. We were about to leave but, since you've managed the appointment belatedly after all, we'll do what we can in the limited time we have left.' Brent's voice held just the right amount of firmness. He got to his feet to shake hands with the woman and stepped back so Fiona could do the same. 'Fiona, meet Mrs Rose Fuller.'

The familiarity of name and face clicked into place when Fiona received a very practised smile and a rather limp hand to shake, though the woman had looked slightly chagrined by the end of Brent's speech.

Husband in politics. Big aspirations. Lots of media coverage as they did their best to climb the ranks.

Ah...

'It's nice to meet you, Mrs Fuller. I've been studying the project plans Brent has drawn up for you.' Fiona towered over Mrs Fuller by an entire head and shoulders. In the dainty room, with the maid pouring cups of tea into translucent china cups, Fiona had to fight off feeling oversized and, subsequently, unfeminine.

The two assessments did not necessarily have to go together, no matter what her mother may have said to the contrary at various times through-out Fiona's life. 'You must be pleased to have Brent on board for your landscaping work. He's the best in the city.'

'Well, of course I know Mr MacKay has a decent reputation, though he can be extremely elusive about contact outside of his work channels.'

'I apologise for turning down the dinner invi-tation, Mrs Fuller.' Brent's smile didn't quite reach his eyes. 'I saw the write-up in all the major papers the next day.'

'Yes, we made quite a splash.' Mrs Fuller went on, 'I'm afraid I just can't decide on any one of the plans we've discussed. My husband is very exacting and everything has to serve our lifestyle and our business interactions perfectly.' Their hostess gestured for them to take their seats, did so herself and waited while her maid handed out the teacups and left the room.

'Of course.' Fiona took a deep breath and

turned her attention to the view from the bay windows for a moment.

The house was elevated and the grounds rolled away to a seemingly endless stretch of Sydney coast. The scene from this window once the design work was completed in the grounds below would make an ideal painting for the client. If they could get the woman to start cooperating.

'Mrs Fuller, you've expressed what you want out of this landscaping project. Now it's time to trust us to provide it for you.' Brent placed his tea, untouched, onto the small table beside his chair and his fingers curled against his thighs as though he wanted to do something with them but was stopping himself.

Fiona took up the conversation where Brent had left off. 'The exciting news for you, Mrs Fuller, is that you'll be one of our first clients to have the benefit of an original artwork gifted to you at the completion of your project. I think a two metre by one metre canvas would work here. Of course, if you're unable to settle on our plans we'll need to move on. You'll understand my employer is highly sought after, and my paintings are award-winning works that will always find a welcome home…'

'That's a substantial-sized painting. I wasn't aware— What awards have you won?' The woman's eyes gleamed.

And Fiona ran with that. Just a little, and only because she truly did want her boss to get something back for the time he'd invested in this project so far. She named the prestigious awards.

Brent knew of them, of course. They'd been listed in her curriculum vitae and she'd included copies of the works in her portfolio.

'I recall now.' Mrs Fuller straightened her perfectly straight back even more. 'You're *that* Fiona Donner. One of the paintings was a landscape…'

'Yes. They both were. It's a favourite medium of mine.' Fiona could almost see the cogs turning in their hostess's brain.

She smiled at the woman. 'At this stage we are utterly one hundred per cent informed of your needs, Mrs Fuller. You've discussed them in detail with my employer, and he has explained everything to me. Now you can let it go, take that burden off shoulders that no doubt have many other responsibilities. Your husband, your social engagements.'

A suppressed hint of sound came from Brent that *could* have been a snort, though a quick glance his way revealed nothing but the blandest of facial expressions.

'It will be our pleasure to take care of the hard work and stress and decisions for you, Mrs Fuller.' Brent offered this assurance with calm confidence. 'All you need to do is enjoy the finished product when your landscape design is in place. Shall we discuss the original plans? I truly still believe they are what's going to be best to meet your needs.'

They talked. Or, rather, Brent did most of the talking in a firm, determined way. Mrs Fuller occasionally tried to get off track or waffle about some aspect or another she wasn't quite certain about. Invariably, Brent pulled her back.

Fiona sipped her tea until it was all gone while Mrs Fuller did the same.

Eventually, with all of his case put forward again as succinctly as possible, Brent leaned back in his chair. 'Well, Mrs Fuller. What do you say? Do we have a plan, or do we leave this here, cut our losses and both move on?'

'I'd like you to begin work, using the plan you originally produced, and providing a painting.' Mrs Fuller replaced her teacup in its saucer with a small click. 'It's a pity you weren't able to articulate things so clearly the first time…'

Several beats of silence passed.

Fiona didn't know she'd moved until she realised she was on her feet.

Brent whispered into her ear, 'Remember, the client is always right, even when she's not.' He'd risen with her and leaned in casually to give her those words while giving Mrs Fuller a business-like smile.

Fiona bit her lip and bit back the words that wanted to pour out, telling Mrs Fuller exactly how offensive she had just been.

It would be unrealistic, Fiona supposed, to expect a *complete* turnaround from the woman and, in the end, Brent had achieved what he wanted.

So score one for Brent MacKay Landscaping Designs. With brief—and, Fiona thought in the circumstances, very constrained—goodbyes to their hostess, they took their leave.

Brent led the way back to his utility truck, opened her door for Fiona and got behind the wheel himself.

'You have excellent people-handling skills, Fiona.' A grin kicked up one corner of his mouth and spread until it reached his eyes. 'I had a much easier time of it with you there to help me out.'

'Oh, I didn't do much. You're the one who produced the ideas Mrs Fuller should have leapt at in the first place.' Fiona brushed aside her part in things and did her best to brush aside her annoyance at the same time. 'In the end it all worked out, I guess, and I think Mrs Fuller is someone who, despite all the difficulties with her up to this point, will talk your work up to the skies once it's done for her.'

Fiona was doing quite well being upbeat and positive until she added a muttered, 'I didn't appreciate her insulting attitude to the importance of your time or the way she insinuated that her mucking around for weeks was somehow your fault!'

Brent laughed. 'I caught that, and I appreciate you caring.'

He set the vehicle in motion. 'You *were* very diplomatic with Mrs Fuller. I think you'd even manage to tame the crowd of people just like her who attend the Landscaping Awards nights.'

'That's one event you do attend each year.' The words slipped out before she could consider how telling he might find them. 'I mean, naturally you attend whatever functions you're interested in—'

'And I protect my privacy the rest of the time.' He made no apology, simply stated it as fact.

'The Deltran Landscaping Awards are prestigious.'

'Yes, and I'm nominated for an award this year.' Brent glanced her way. 'I'd like you to attend the ceremony with me. It will give me a chance to showcase you as part of the company.'

'I'd love to go.' The invitation was unexpected, but her acceptance was instantaneous. Too fast, really.

Because she was a little *too* delighted. Because the thought of an evening out with him appealed a little too much. She wasn't supposed to be feeling that way about him any more. Not since she'd thought that all through and concluded that she wouldn't.

'Then you can consider it a date.' The moment the words left Brent, a frown creased his brow. He drummed his fingers on the steering wheel. 'Consider it a business arrangement, I mean.'

Right.

'I think it will be a very useful evening for the company.' And, for that reason, it would be good to attend the evening with her boss.

'Maybe I should do something similar for this dinner Mum's roped me into attending with the family.' There. That was good. A segue into a different topic by commenting on something that bore similarities to the first topic. 'I could go for "safety in numbers" and take a friend along.'

'It sounds like an obligatory family event?' This seemed to surprise him.

No doubt because his interactions with his brothers contained none of the difficulties Fiona encountered at family functions. Her family tended to find her far too different and 'out of the box' for their tastes.

Ironic, really, when Brent was the one with the unusual 'family' structure.

'I didn't mean to make it sound as though

family events are a chore for me. Even if they were,' she added, and couldn't keep the doubt from her tone, 'the evening might be fun.'

Extremely doubtful, but in the end you never knew, right?

Brent drew the truck to a stop in its space behind their office building and turned to face her. 'I'll trade. You come to the Awards night with me and I'll be your "extra" for your family gathering. Assuming both these events aren't scheduled at once. When is your family get-together?'

Not the same night, as it happened.

Fiona was still shocked by his offer, even as she answered him. 'Th-thank you. I'd love to have you come along.' She stuttered out the details while Brent climbed out of the truck and led the way into the building and through to his office.

His face was tight. Maybe he regretted making his offer. Should she try to let him off the hook? 'If you don't really—'

'It'll be a chance for me to meet your family.' He picked up a handful of mail from his desk and began to sort through it. 'I'm planning to have you working for me for a long time, so it's strategic for us to do this.'

'Oh. Of course. Well, that's lovely, then.' And it was. Absolutely. Lovely, and practical and, for goodness' sake, why would she kid herself it was anything else? She would enjoy Brent's company as her boss meeting her family for a one-off occasion. That would be no biggie. Not at all.

This might provide a chance for your parents and sisters to see you actually have a serious job working for Brent, not some 'dangerously unstable artsy thing' as your mother dismissed it on the phone when you rang to tell her the good news that you'd got the position.

And maybe they'd see that she was making progress in that job. Yes, it was still very early days but Brent seemed pleased enough with her so far. It was about time her family acknowledged that her choices and decisions in life, though perhaps not right for them, were right for her and could even be quite successful.

As for the fact she hadn't entirely managed to quash her consciousness of Brent as a man…well, she would quash it.

Fiona hustled to the door so they could get on with some work.

'You're staring into space, Fiona! Do concentrate.' Eloise Donner's voice grated across Brent's nerve-endings as she addressed her daughter. 'You're holding things up.'

'I'm sure Fiona's just taking time to think through how she wants to answer the game question.' Brent battled to keep his tone unremarkable, polite.

He wanted to walk out, taking Fiona with him.

Her mother's niggling wasn't overtly vicious. In Brent's opinion, it was worse than that because it was subtle, ingrained and would be very difficult for Fiona to fight.

Particularly if she didn't want to get into an argument with her mother and have Eloise tell her she was overstating the problem or making much out of 'nothing'.

Something told him Eloise Donner would be good at saying things like that.

It was Wednesday night, just over a week after Fiona had first started working for him, and they were at that obligatory family gathering he'd invited himself along to.

As her employer, he had wanted to meet her family. But curiosity had also motivated him.

He had wanted to see what her family were like. Maybe he'd wanted to be around a family that had parents in it, full stop?

You got over missing that a long time ago, MacKay.

His father had made that easy. Just dumped him and walked away...

Well, the answer to what Fiona's family were like was 'nothing he'd expected'.

With Fiona being so kind and sweet, he'd thought her family would be the same, people who would have brought out those things in her by their own example. Instead, they were clinical, critical, super-practical and unemotional people who almost seemed to lack…soul?

They certainly *looked* nothing like Fiona. Her mother and sisters were petite and brittle, where Fiona was tall and lush and vibrant. Her father was a 'medium' man. Medium height, build, medium brown hair, medium interest in life, it appeared. Fiona's inner beauty was something that had obviously come from the core of her and flourished *against* the odds of her family influence.

Fiona glanced at the card in her hand. They were playing a board game. A particularly stultifying one, Brent thought. There were eight people at the table. Fiona's family, Fiona, him, and a couple of extras.

Fiona cast an uncomfortable glance his way before she pinned on that smile she'd worked so hard to hold all night. 'I don't think I know the answer to this one, Mum. I'll have to pass.'

'You must know.' Terrence Donner cast a slightly impatient glance his daughter's way. 'None of the questions in this game are unanswerable.'

'For people who enjoy documentaries and nonfiction reading, perhaps.' Brent's knee brushed against Fiona's as he shifted in his chair.

The jolt to his senses shouldn't have happened. He'd made the choice not to notice Fiona in that way.

So why had he?

You've noticed her from the start. You've simply been avoiding your awareness of her.

Well, then, he could go on avoiding it. He had to go on avoiding it because she set off behaviours in him that he had worked hard for decades to subdue, and he wasn't about to reveal those short-comings to her. He guarded those things.

'Nope. Sorry, Dad. I truly don't have an answer to put up at this point.' Fiona shrugged her shoulders and indicated they should move on to the next player, but her words were slightly breath-less.

Brent reacted to that knowledge more than he wanted to.

The game ended. Brent got to his feet. He might not have all his answers, but he knew he'd had enough of this. And so had Fiona. 'It's been nice to meet you all, but we have a long trip to get home. I think it's time we left.'

When they emerged outside the family's house Brent breathed in the night air and thought of Linc and Alex and how lucky he was to have them. A chosen family, not a blood one. As if that mattered. He wouldn't trade them. The thoughts helped him regain perspective and that put him in a better place to care for Fiona.

As a colleague and someone he'd begun to admire in that capacity…

He helped Fiona into his truck and talked about this and that as they made their way back towards her home.

If he talked, maybe she would forget the unpleasantness of the evening. And maybe *he* would forget how much he wanted to draw her into his arms and kiss her to take her mind off the fact that her family didn't treat her the way they all should. *That* desire was not businesslike.

Words pushed past his lips anyway. 'What's wrong with them? They don't—'

'I'm glad you got to meet my family, that they got to meet my boss and hear a little about the work I'm doing.' Fiona spoke over the top of him. Her words were deliberately upbeat as he turned the truck into an empty parking space in the apartment complex's courtyard. Upbeat but edged with that same breathless quality as earlier, when their knees had brushed beneath the table.

She went on, 'I hope that will have made my goals a little more real to them, a little more understandable.'

A little more *acceptable?* Her family made her feel abnormal when she was a great person in her own right. And that was clearly something that had been going on for a long time. *That* was Brent's assessment and it was one that was…a little too close to the bone for comfort.

Brent turned off the truck's ignition and strode around the front to open her door and help her out. 'You have a good start in a job that's in your chosen field. There are plenty of people out there who never manage to say that much. Your family should be proud of the way you've pursued and begun to obtain your goals.'

'Thank you and…maybe they are.' She spoke in a way that seemed to try to keep the uncertainty out of her tone. And gave a soft smile, no doubt aimed at easing the moment. 'Well, I promise you I will do my utmost to support you in return when it comes time to go to the Awards dinner.'

'Your company on the night will be more than enough.' Brent all but growled the words. 'I'll walk you up.'

See her into her apartment safely and then leave. That was what he needed to do, not linger here wanting nebulous things he didn't want to name but knew would get him into trouble if he went after them. Things that had to do with odd notions, such as comfort and closeness and acceptance.

What was the matter with him tonight? Where were these deep buried thoughts coming from?

When they reached the top of the staircase and made their way to her front door, Fiona put her key in the lock and turned to face him. 'They didn't pry too much into your business, I hope. When I was in the kitchen clearing away dishes.'

He pushed his hands into his pockets, frowned and took them out again. 'They didn't pry too much.'

She seemed to relax a little at that. 'Would you like a coffee or something before you drive on? I've only got instant—'

'No. Thanks. But I'll see you inside.' He had to know she was safely secured behind these walls. That was only common courtesy.

'O-okay.' She pushed the door open and walked inside.

Brent followed, closed it after him and glanced around.

A hand-woven rug brightened the floor. Those splashes of orange and sky-blue and red and green were echoed in throw cushions and the table lamp and an abstract Fiona Donner original on the wall.

She'd made a beautiful home, welcoming and individual and full of her life and vitality and sweetness. Brent wanted to sit on her sofa and just…be there among these things that held meaning for her. As though, if he did that, he'd…belong.

The inexplicable feeling washed through him, so much more than a simple awareness of her, even if that awareness had been causing him enough problems all by itself.

It took him enough by surprise that he hesitated in the centre of her small living room.

He should go.

He wanted to stay.

Since when had his emotions reached for such odd things? He didn't even do that whole 'feelings' arena. Linc and Alex—he loved them, but that was it. His inability to maintain a relationship with his father had taught him what his limits were. The autism—he hadn't been able to get past that. With Alex and Linc it was different, but they'd all come up together, had faced down their demons together.

With Fiona, Brent wasn't even prepared to let himself be attracted to her. He wasn't in the market for a relationship, and Fiona was someone who should be given that if a man was interested in her.

So say goodbye and leave. Do it now before any other temptation comes over you.

'Well, thanks again.'

'I should go.'

They spoke at the same time.

Fiona paused and her lashes fluttered over eyes the colour of the sky in the mountains on a warm summer day. Clear, sweet blue.

So lovely. He could appreciate the pure aesthetics of her, couldn't he? Just appreciate that?

Yes? And where was the distance to go with that kind of remote appreciation?

Brent didn't know the answer and, because he didn't, and because he couldn't quite make his feet take him to the door and through it, he addressed another issue that he did want answers to.

'Your family made tonight all about themselves.' Maybe she didn't want to discuss this, but what if she needed to? What if *he* needed to talk with her about the way her family had treated her?

His fingers reached out and brushed the back of her hand. She had smooth, soft skin like the petals of a rose. Too late not to touch her now. He'd done it. 'Your parents could have tried to be a bit accommodating of your tastes in terms of entertainment.'

'They think I need to fit in, be more like them, but I'm just…not. I tried that. It didn't work.' Her soft sigh was a whisper between them. 'But I love them, and they don't mean to make me uncomfortable.' She gestured with her hand to dismiss the topic. 'Thank you for your company, anyway.'

'You're welcome.' And he *had* to go.

Brent walked to the door and tugged it open and, with a low, 'Lock it after me,' he stepped through. On the other side, he waited until she did as he had asked, and then he walked to his truck and drove away.

What he thought about her family, about all this, didn't matter in the end. Whatever he now knew of her, whatever empathy he felt for her, he had nothing to offer anyone, and especially not someone like Fiona.

That was what he had to remember.

CHAPTER FOUR

BRENT parked his truck and made his way into the club. Fiona had left her flat keys on her work desk, half-hidden away between two separate messy piles of paper. He had discovered this fact as he'd cleared chocolate wrappers from her work area.

Not wrappers from chocolates his graphic designer had eaten from the stash in her bottom desk drawer.

But wrappers from the chocolates *he'd* eaten his way through while he'd examined her design program. He hadn't planned to eat the treats. He'd opened the drawer in search of a notepad and, though he'd told himself not to be tempted, somehow his hand had ended up in the drawer and the rest, as he focused all his attention on the nuts and bolts of her program and then on the work she'd done within it, had been, as they said, 'history'. He'd have to replace the candy stash before she got to work on Monday.

She was on the dance floor. His gaze locked onto her and he quickly forgot his thoughts. Dear God, she looked magnificent. A black skirt that came to just above her knees, high-heeled boots and a scoop-necked cream top that clung to her curves as she moved all combined to make her a highly irresistible package of appeal.

When the number ended, Fiona smiled at her partner and moved off the floor with him. She stood half a head taller than the man. At just about the moment Brent forced himself to acknowledge he felt jealous of that man, they joined a large group of people seated at some tables pulled close together.

The fellow put his arm around one of the women in the group and dropped a kiss on her cheek.

'Brent.' Fiona's exclamation came as he approached the tables. 'What brings you here—?'

'You.' The word was low, husky and far too intimate, reflecting thoughts that poured through him, pushed past his defences.

In her boots with the three-inch heel, she stood almost nose to nose with him. Brent wanted to trace all her dips and curves with his fingertips.

It had to be his autism speaking, a need for a tactile exploration to feed his thought processes the answers they sought.

Sure. You believe that, MacKay.

'Your flat keys. I found them on your desk after

you left.' *That* was his reason for finding her here. Only that. 'You might have spares somewhere, but I didn't know.'

'I do have a spare set. *In* my desk at work. Oh, of all the silly things for me to do!' Her gaze searched his face. 'I'm so sorry you had to chase me down. I don't have my mobile turned on, either. It's a waste of time in here because I wouldn't hear it ring. How did you know—?'

'I heard you mention the name of this place when you were on your mobile phone as you were leaving. There's no need to apologise. I couldn't have left you without your keys to get into your home.'

Fiona's mouth softened. 'Thank you.'

Just two simple words, and he leaned towards her. Brent straightened and his head tipped to the right. 'Ah—'

She was returning his glance, was as aware of him in this moment as he was of her, and Brent's need to protect his privacy fought with his need…for her.

But for what? To explore physical attraction with her? Because that was all he could want, wasn't it? For him, intimacy—true intimacy that involved opening up and letting someone else in was…out of the question.

And have you asked yourself why that is,

*MacKay? Why you're so determined to keep
people at arm's length?*

Brent knew the answer. He was different, and
his 'different' wasn't something people, generally,
would be able to accept. So he kept it to himself.
He was happier that way. Comfortable.

Safe?

It wasn't about that. And he had every right to
value his privacy, for whatever reasons he wanted
to. And there was *nothing else* behind the way he
felt. Nothing.

Fiona's gaze searched his eyes.

Brent stared into deep blue irises until he felt
the stares of some of her friends *on him.*

She looked past him and seemed to force a casual
smile. 'Everyone, this is my boss, Brent MacKay.'

A round of introductions followed. It gave
Brent a chance to settle his reactions to her.

So why did they continue to simmer beneath
the surface of every word, every exchange and
glance? Rejecting those reactions should be as
easy as deciding they weren't in his best interests
or, in fact, in hers. Brent had already decided that,
so why…? 'I should get going.'

'Would you like to—?' She stopped, clamped
those soft lips together.

Brent drew her keys from his pocket and, when
she held out her hand, dropped them into it.

'Thank you.' Her fingers curled over the keys before she snagged her bag from the back of a chair and dropped them into it. 'Please, let me at least…I don't know… Can I buy you a drink or something? I feel awful, putting you out this way. We could go to the bar. I see a few spaces over there. Most people are on the dance floor right now, I think.'

The bar stretched across the entirety of the far wall beyond the dance area. It was further from the music than the tables here. Brent's voice emerged as a low growl of sound. 'A drink would be…nice.'

He'd led her halfway around the dance floor before he registered that his choice might not have been particularly smart.

When they reached the bar, they ordered drinks and Fiona watched Brent from the corner of her eye in the bar mirror and saw the way they looked together.

A dark head and a fair one. A lean, strong face and a soft womanly one. They looked right to her, side by side this way.

The image reached past her defences, left them in the dust, left her wanting deep silent things she couldn't want, couldn't let herself admit.

What did Brent want?

Nothing you can pin hopes on, Fiona. Remember that.

'I hope chasing me down with my keys hasn't interfered with other plans of yours.' She didn't quite meet his gaze. 'That is…it's none of my business of course… I simply didn't want to take you away from—'

A girlfriend? A lover waiting for him somewhere? The thought stung, yet it wasn't her business, was it?

'You might have come here with someone—?'

He spoke almost when she did, and then stopped, and their gazes met and held and the atmosphere between them thickened into silently acknowledged curiosity and a certain comprehension.

'I don't…'

'There's no one.' Fiona's heart began to beat more heavily in her chest.

They both lowered their gazes to their drinks, sipped.

Brent's face tightened as he looked up at her again. 'This—'

'I've been thinking about the Doolan project.' Fiona rushed the words out and took another fortifying sip of her lemon mineral water. If she made it all about work they could forget those moments looking into each other's eyes in a mirror.

Could forget the warmth and consciousness in their eyes, the desire that when they faced each other in reality, they both worked hard to hide.

A part of her wanted to see it again, even though following that path with him could only lead to hurt for her because he would do what every other man had done.

He would go cold on the idea of her sooner or later. He'd already shown the capacity for that.

So talk about work, Fiona, and ease through these moments and then let him go. 'I know the couple are at loggerheads with each other in their personal lives, but I thought I might have an idea to keep both of them happy with our project plans.'

'Go on. I'm interested in any contribution you want to make.' It was clear he meant this.

And perhaps equally clear that he welcomed the change of topic to a work-related subject as much as she told herself she must take the conversation there.

The little sting of hurt was foolish and incidental, and she did her best to ignore its impact. 'If we use either of the couple's suggested overall ideas for the project, one of them is likely to resent the result.'

'It will be one more thing for them to argue about, and our company might get caught in the middle of that altercation.' His lashes formed thick crescents against his cheeks as he briefly dipped his gaze.

There was something almost vulnerable in that sight, and that made Fiona vulnerable as she softened towards him.

Maybe *they* needed to be at loggerheads so she could stop being so conscious of him as a man. Because, whether she wanted to be or not, she was, and, though she felt that same vibe back from him, he *was* her boss and he seemed determined not to notice her even if he *was* noticing her.

Oh, she had to stop this analysing!

Brent cast a wry smile her way. 'So do you think you and I could agree on something that might satisfy both of them?'

Far too easily.

So much for her idea of being at loggerheads for her own salvation. Fiona straightened on the stool. 'Yes. I think we could do it, for the sake of the project and for the company's overall good. It's simply a collaboration of minds, after all.'

'I couldn't agree more.' His nod was pure professionalism. The warmth in his glance was not, but he masked that quickly and she told herself to stop noticing. They sipped their drinks in silence before she spoke again.

'To answer your question from earlier, I caught a lift here with Stacey but I think she'll end up at Caleb's place later.' The couple had been one of her 'fix it' projects and had got back together after not speaking to each other for three months. 'I'll head off myself soon. I don't want a really late night.'

They'd finished their drinks. Somehow they were both on their feet.

'Thanks again for bringing my keys to me, for taking the time to do that.'

'Do you need a lift home?' He asked it in such a level way, yet his gaze was not level. It was thoughtful and cautious, offering and…almost braced for her to say no?

As if Brent MacKay would care whether she rejected or accepted him in anything. He was a self-made, very wealthy, highly eligible and extremely talented man. If anything, he had the whole world at his feet.

Yet that's not what you see in the backs of his eyes at times when he drops his guard a little. That's not what you saw in those photos with his brothers.

Well, what Fiona looked for and believed she 'saw' in those around her were things *she* had to guard. Her family's discomfort with that side of her had proved that. She tried to respond in kind. 'I left my car at Stacey's place. I just need to get a taxi that far.'

'What suburb?'

Fiona told him.

Brent nodded. 'I'll drive you.' Decision made.

'It's on the way. It would be silly for you to wait around for a taxi and have the expense of it when there's no need.'

'Thank you. I just feel guilty for bringing you out when you must have had far better things to do with your time than chase after a designer who can't even keep track of her apartment keys.'

'You're an artist. It is okay for you to forget things sometimes, you know. Some people would say it was almost obligatory.' They drew near the tables of her friends and Brent waited while she bade them all a quick goodbye.

Once they were outside he quickly hustled her to his truck and got them on the road. They didn't speak much at first. In the quiet of the night the truck's cab felt isolated and enclosed and... intimate.

If only she could be a little less conscious of him, but that didn't seem to be an option for her at the moment.

As he drove them towards her friend's home, she turned to him and searched his shadowy face. 'Were you at work late before you discovered my keys?'

'Yes. I got...caught up there.' His slight hesitation seemed to hold perhaps a hint of embarrassment. Or some kind of chagrin?

'Well, now I'm going to owe you twice as

much of an effort when I attend the Awards night with you tomorrow night.' Fiona gave him directions as they neared Stacey's home.

He drove the truck into an empty space on the street and killed the engine.

It was a quiet residential street and she'd parked her car underneath a street light.

'Talk about your work for the company if that chance comes up. That's all I ask.' He climbed from the truck, crossed in front and opened her door for her. 'Let's see you to your car.'

When they got to her car she had her key ready and she turned to him and thanked him quickly and maybe that would have done it, except her nose bumped the side of his neck as she did that because he moved, and she moved, and she didn't anticipate his closeness and suddenly all the resistance seemed pointless because all the awareness was there, wasn't it?

He smelled good. Did she press her nose to his neck for the slightest split second?

Did he tip his head towards hers, encouraging that act?

Two deep breaths, one from him, one from her, and they were apart again, the silence an endless consciousness until his gaze met hers and she saw what had to be rare indecision inside him.

'I shouldn't do this. It's not smart.' His words were an echo of her thoughts.

And she wanted to know… 'Why do *you*—'

He shook his head. 'Maybe it's those long, tall boots. They're as good to blame as anything.' His hand closed around her upper arm. His lashes swept down over glittering green eyes that had gone from indecision to determination in…the blink of green eyes.

And Fiona's senses stalled and her heart stalled and inside her the war hit a new level of anticipation and concern, of need to engage and need to retreat and she thought, *Now. He's going to kiss me now.*

And it *was* what she'd waited for, hoped for without wanting to admit it to herself. Would it be such a bad thing, even if it might cause complications for them?

But he stood there very still, and his fingers tensed where they held her. And his head twitched once, hard, to the right and the moment was lost.

Brent uttered a harsh, 'Goodnight,' and dropped his hand, and left her standing there while he walked away.

CHAPTER FIVE

'IT'S the autism playing out. Having that happen as much as it has lately in front of…other people makes me tense.' Brent muttered the words to Linc as the two men stepped out of his home the following night and into the communal corridor.

He tugged at the collar of the starched white dress shirt. 'You know how I feel about being in the public eye with that kind of thing.'

The loss of control of his condition in Fiona's company—he'd known it was happening from when he'd first met her. Because of that fact alone, he could forget any chance of being intimate with her. Not that he would have tried to pursue that. She worked for him, for starters, and she deserved better than he could give her.

Why was he thinking this way at all, anyway? He didn't want to examine his motives.

'Your autism is barely noticeable. Even when it does "play out", most people wouldn't figure out the source.' Linc drew a breath and his gaze searched Brent's. 'Are you sure that's what this is about?'

'What else would it be?' Brent spoke quickly, a little too loudly.

A murmur of voices sounded in the foyer below. Voices Brent recognised. His brother Alex.

And Fiona. Alex must have met her on the way in, before she had a chance to hit the buzzer.

He told himself he wasn't relieved to end the discussion with Linc.

'Good luck tonight, anyway.'

'Thanks.' Brent bade Linc a quiet goodbye and headed down the staircase.

When Alex spotted him, Brent's youngest brother excused himself from his guest, shared a brief word on the staircase with Brent and disappeared.

That left Brent and the woman at the foot of the stairs.

She was stunning. Utterly and completely stunning. The dress was creams and pinks and greys with a fitted top that left her arms bare and nipped in at her waist, then flared over shapely hips and thighs and fell to her calves in a soft swirl of fabric. It dipped into a discreet V front and back, caressing the curves of full breasts to perfection and revealing a lovely hint of the dip between her shoulder blades.

The dress showcased her beauty, but her beauty

itself was what stopped his heart for a moment before a deep, warm feeling washed through him.

He couldn't explain it. Only that Fiona was soft and curvy everywhere. He wanted to immerse himself in that softness, body, mind and…something even deeper that he didn't fully understand that had something to do with all the softness there *hadn't* been in his lifetime.

Okay. So that was fine. Any man would want that softness anyway. It didn't need to mean anything particularly deep. Brent's body tightened.

'Good evening. You look wonderful.' Husky words, his gaze locked probably too intimately and directly on hers as he battled to pull his thoughts and reactions into place.

'Good…good evening, Brent. And thank you. I thought about not wearing heels but you won't mind if I'm eye to eye with you?' She stepped forward on the killer high heels in question.

Her hair was piled onto her head and pinned back with some kind of butterfly clip. Wisps kissed her nape, and she looked tentative and a little uncertain of herself, and the way she walked in those heels…

Why would she see herself as anything other than stunning? Brent's gaze rose slowly to her face and locked there. 'I won't mind.' He might go mad from the results of all that not minding, but no. He wouldn't mind.

Some of the tension seemed to leave her and her gaze shifted to encompass all of him in a swift examination.

Brent had just started to relax himself when she did that, and the blue of her eyes deepened. Her smile wobbled and she hesitated there in his foyer while a delicate flush rose in her cheeks. Desire flared, a small flame burning brighter, back and forth between them.

'*You* look wonderful, Brent.' Her quiet words held conviction, and unease, and a wary consciousness. 'I hope I'm not too early. Alex let me in. I've kept the taxi waiting, as you suggested.'

'The timing is perfect.' Everything about her right now was perfect and, because that was so, it seemed a good idea to get out of here and get his focus onto the business of the evening. 'I'm sure tonight will be a good PR exercise.'

'I'm looking forward to it.' Fiona chatted on about it as they made their way outside, almost as though she too felt the need to distract herself. 'The guest list should provide some opportunities to mingle both with industry professionals and also members of the public who appreciate what we do.'

'Those contacts will make the night worth it,' Brent agreed.

Worth stepping outside his usual guardedness,

worth letting people see past his privacy and defences to a little of the man beneath.

Brent guided Fiona to the outer door with a hand on her elbow. She trembled beneath his touch, just slightly, just enough to make it impossible to think of anything but touching her.

When they climbed into the back of the taxi, closed themselves into the confines of that rear seat that somehow seemed so isolated despite the driver right in front of them, Brent noticed that intimacy again.

It was there in the knowledge of his body close to hers, their thighs touching where his legs sprawled and hers were folded neatly in front of her.

'I'm excited to have the chance to attend the Awards ceremony with you.' Fiona smiled as she turned her head to search his gaze. Smiled with an edge of awareness that he should have wished wasn't there.

Instead, a part of him that just didn't want to obey him revelled in her reaction, even as he thought of all the things he wouldn't like about the evening. 'I don't exactly adore public events, but this one is important for my work.'

'I could take them or leave them most of the time myself,' Fiona admitted, 'but I'm excited about tonight. I want your nominated design to win. I've studied all the candidate works and yours is by far the best.'

Her faith in him made him smile. 'I appreciate your confidence in me, though there are several other very talented contenders.'

They discussed the other works and their designers for the rest of the journey. Brent talked, but he never lost his awareness of her. She smelled of soft woman's skin, of subtle perfume that made him think of a tropical stretch of beach at midnight at the height of summer.

As they arrived at the converted mansion that would house the Awards ceremony, Fiona vehemently assured him there was no chance anyone else would be the winner tonight.

Brent wanted so very badly to lean forward and kiss the passionate declaration right off her lips. He allowed himself one brief touch of her forearm with his fingertips instead and they climbed from the taxi and made their way past several function rooms to the largest one, reserved for the ceremony. He had to do better than this and yet, with each passing moment, his determination to keep at arm's length from her became more and more difficult to follow.

The venue was busy, with multiple functions taking place in a variety of rooms. Brent turned his attention away from all of that and focused on the woman at his side. *On their joint interest in the night's events, he meant!*

'Oh, why can't he stop droning on and hurry up and just announce it?' Fiona couldn't hold the words back any longer. She whispered them against Brent's ear where they sat at the table with a number of other guests.

Yes, she shouldn't have leaned in so close and let her lips touch him that way, and no, she simply couldn't care about that fact right now.

They'd done all the right things all night, had mixed and mingled and every other thing they had to do. And all the while, through everything, the awareness of each other had simmered. Something had changed. Maybe it was Brent, maybe it was Fiona herself. Or perhaps it was both of them, striking sparks off each other in this different setting.

If he truly was attracted to her, if he was the exception rather than the rule…

A short bark of stifled laughter came from her employer's lips. He turned to smile at her, turned his head quickly enough that her lips brushed fully across his ear before she pulled back.

His smile turned to sensual consciousness between one breath and the next.

Fiona's senses fluttered as their gazes caught and held. A moment later she sat straight in her seat again and Brent sat straight in his and the keynote speaker continued his spiel about the history of the award. There'd been no break in proceedings, but her heart was pounding. That expression in Brent's eyes...

'The award.' She murmured the words beneath her breath. That was what was important right now. She shouldn't have said anything about the keynote speaker going on too much. She should have waited patiently and then she wouldn't have ended up with her mouth pressed to Brent's ear.

Well, right now patience wasn't her strong suit. Her senses were all out of whack because of what had just happened. And she wanted that award for her boss!

Are you sure you don't just simply want your boss?

Tonight, in formal suit, white shirt and bow tie, he looked better than James Bond. She could attribute his impact on her to the flattering clothing and the tie that exactly matched the colour of her eyes.

Her eyes. As though he'd chosen to wear it to complement her, not himself.

That's rather whimsical, don't you think, Fiona?

And attributing his appeal to any of those surface things simply wouldn't be honest, and she knew it.

Brent bent his head to hers and whispered, without getting too close to the shell of *her* ear, 'Whether I win the award doesn't matter one way or the other, you know.'

To a degree he was right. He would still be the highly successful landscape designer he was. But she wanted the industry recognition for him, believed he'd earned it, and wanted his peers and the various connections here tonight to see him win.

Fiona was about to explain those things when he reached out to cover her hand where it rested on the snowy linen of the tablecloth.

His deep voice whispered into her ear again. 'Don't stress, okay? We're fine here and look on the bright side. Whatever the outcome, we got a nice meal out of it.'

'We did, didn't we?' She laughed, as he had no doubt expected she would. And her hand turned. Her fingers curled around his and held on.

'For luck,' she murmured, and knew it was far more than that.

Brent made no attempt to break away from their joined touch. Instead, his fingers repeatedly stroked over hers as the speaker finally announced the third place, and a runner up, and finally, after a pause in which the whole room seemed to wait breathlessly…

'And the winner of this year's Deltran Landscaping Award is… Brent MacKay of Brent MacKay Landscaping Designs, for his design of Tarroway Gardens!'

'Oh, I *knew* they'd give it to you. I'm so proud, Brent. Congratulations!' Somehow Fiona ended up with her arms around Brent's shoulders.

By itself that would have been okay, but his arms closed around her in return and she felt the touch of his fingers against the flesh between her shoulders, the press of strong forearms covered in suit cloth against her upper arms.

The scent of his aftershave and his skin filled her senses and his mouth pressed against her hair. The moment of congratulation and excitement became something more, became a promise of what she had wanted all through this public night.

But people clapped, and the room and their surroundings came back. Brent got to his feet and gripped her hand and used that grip to tow her onto the podium with him. He introduced her and her role in the company, said a little about his work as he held their tucked hands at his side.

His acceptance speech was short and succinct and witty and wry. He stopped once in the middle and his shoulders tensed. His hand squeezed around hers before he seemed to relax and every-thing seemed all right again.

And then, award gripped in his other hand, he returned to their table and to a round of congratu-lations as the formality of the evening dissolved into industry talk, mingling and people drinking one last glass of wine while others lingered over pungent coffee served by waiting staff in smart grey coats.

There *were* some people like Brent's difficult client, people with certain aspirations, who now suddenly found Brent's business most interest-ing indeed.

Brent handed them business cards and let them know that if they wanted to book appointments to see him they'd be waiting at least a month. Fiona stayed at his side and simply gave herself the pleasure of watching people acknowledge his success. Pride in him joined other feelings and blended together inside her.

Finally they left the function room and made their way through the building's long winding corridors towards the front exit.

The doors to another of the function rooms just ahead swished open. Two men stepped through, one garrulous and talking a mile a minute, the other with his face turned half away, doing his best to ignore that man's effusiveness if his body language was anything to go by.

Fiona observed this and leaned on Brent's arm to peer across his body at the award statuette. 'It's a rather elegant tree, really. Sort of "eternal life-ish" in appearance, don't you think? I'd like to display it in a glass-fronted cabinet in the reception area at work.'

Brent seemed distracted by the men before them, but he forced a nod. 'We'll put *your* awards up at the same time—'

The men in front of them glanced their way as they drew closer. Probably they heard every word being said, but they weren't private words really so it hardly mattered, did it? So why did Fiona feel uneasy suddenly?

'Displaying all the awards would be nice,' Fiona murmured.

She would simply have walked on, but something about the stillness of one of the men drew her attention and she looked his way just as Brent drew a deep breath and did the same.

As they all drew level, Brent wrapped his free hand around her wrist, a gentle touch that guided her to a stop, yet his expression when she looked into his eyes was not gentle, but oh, so determined and guarded and…braced. For what?

Fiona left her wrist in his hold. She wasn't sure if he even knew he had it clasped there.

Brent could have done without this, but he looked into the face of one of the two men before him and waited for recognition to dawn. Oh, not for himself. He'd recognised Charles immediately. But for the older man—God, for his *father*—it was apparently taking longer.

Memory hit Brent. Of his father frowning, pushing Brent into a car, muttering that he couldn't be the father of a freak. Brent had tried so hard as a child to control the outward signs of his condition. He couldn't remember any other way. Even now he could feel his body tightening, trying to make sure nothing of the autism showed.

Well, it had been too late then. Tight-lipped and silent, his father had taken him to the orphanage, signed him over and walked away.

'It's been a long time.' Brent was proud of the flat, even tone of his voice. He hoped that calm extended to his expression, even if his body was braced.

Charles was older, his hair was grey, but the dawning expression in his eyes was the same. Displeasure, discomfort, rejection.

For a moment Brent thought the older man might simply walk on, not speak, and in that moment Brent knew he would not allow that. This time he wouldn't be ignored, brushed off. He opened his mouth to speak again.

'If I'd realised you'd be here—' Charles broke off, glanced at his companion and his frown deepened.

Brent recognised that look, too. It was amazing just how much came back to him. He'd thought it almost all forgotten. A twitch built at the base of his neck. He banked it down.

Fiona's glance made him wonder if she'd sensed that tension building. Her hand turned and her fingers closed around *his* wrist, and he thought she murmured, 'I know now where I've seen that before...' before she leaned into his side.

Then she gave a polite, plastic smile and said in a normal tone, 'Won't you introduce me, Brent?'

'Fiona Donner, meet Charles MacKay.' He didn't explain Fiona to Charles. He didn't explain his father's identity to Fiona.

Fiona's nostrils flared and the sparkle in her eyes flattened out until they were pure blue, expressionless chips. Her gaze turned to his and came back to his father and a thick silence fell.

Into that silence, Charles's companion spoke.

'You've won an award. Congratulations.' The man stepped forward and leaned in to examine the award, either oblivious at this point to the tensions in the air, or convinced he could actually do something about them. 'Oh, I see that's the landscaping industry award. I read about that in the club notices a few weeks ago. What do you think, Charlie?' He turned to address the question to the second man.

And what did 'Charlie' think? Was he surprised by Brent's success? Pleased by it? Discomfited by it?

Why care? His opinion means less than nothing. It's meant less than nothing for a long time now.

'The family resemblance is strong.' Fiona's words were low, the unspoken words written all over her.

This was the man who had given his son away. Somehow she understood so much. That knowledge hit Brent while a raft of emotions washed through him.

Old rejection. A need to understand.

His father's rejection, Charles's inability to love the child he'd helped create?

Brent pushed it all away before it could go any further. It was all past news. There was no point revisiting, though he couldn't be sorry this meeting had happened. At least he could say it was done now, and let go of the feeling he'd carried around of waiting to stumble across this man.

Yeah? So why didn't Brent feel any better or more resolved?

Because Charles was acting just the same, and some deep down part of Brent had maybe hoped, just the tiniest bit...

'Yes, we should be going, Fiona. I think we're done here.' As he spoke the words, Brent became truly aware of the curl of Fiona's fingers around muscles that had set like concrete. His free hand came up to close over Fiona's, to register the tension in *her* fingers.

She gave a sturdy tug, as though to shepherd him away from there, and her entire body pressed into his side.

The level of protectiveness he sensed in her in that moment stunned Brent and touched him in ways he couldn't define.

'Wow.' The jolly man's mobile face worked.

No doubt in another moment he would voice his conclusion that Brent and Charles were 'father and son'.

How would Brent's father explain that? He'd done such a good job of ignoring the fact that Brent had ever existed.

How *had* Charles MacKay dealt with that? An inconvenient accident that had taken his son so soon after the death of the older man's wife? If so, Brent was rather inconveniently 'resurrected'.

'If you'll excuse us.' The blandest of bland phrases. Brent decided it was somehow fitting.

He steeled his muscles to keep under his command. There would be no twitching of his head to the side, no drumming of fingers or anything else. Not in front of this man. No exposure. Brent started to turn away.

'Surely you'd have realised the major industry event in my calendar year was at this venue tonight.' His father's words stopped him. The displeasure and self-centredness in them was clear. 'You should stay out of the limelight altogether. I can't have—'

'I do what suits me. I've been in charge of myself for a long time now.' Anger made its way through Brent's reserve. That, too, he squashed down. It really wasn't worth it, was it?

Charles couldn't be proud of his success. The older man couldn't see past the shame he felt in Brent's existence.

You let Charles's shame impact on you, on how you live, how you present yourself.

Had Brent done that? Would he have looked at his autism differently if Charles had done so?

Well, Charles hadn't done, and that hadn't changed. Brent spoke with that thought fresh in his mind. 'If that doesn't appeal to you, you're welcome to stay clear of anywhere you think I might show up.'

As for Charles's business activities, Brent had little clue and planned to keep it that way. If they crossed paths again, so what? Brent wasn't about to actively keep away from anything for the sake of avoiding this man. What could Charles do, after all? Reject his son?

Been there, lived that, got the new and better, loving, close-knit family with Linc and Alex to prove it.

With that thought calmness came back to him. He *did* have Linc and Alex and they were what he wanted. Not the cold stranger in front of him.

'Good evening. Don't feel it's necessary to speak the next time we meet—'

'You must be highly medicated to succeed at hiding your flaw, even temporarily, for something like this evening.' His father's words held ignorance, accusation, harshness and confusion. 'I didn't know autis—'

'Obviously you don't know much.' Brent spoke over the top of the older man. 'Goodbye.'

He whisked Fiona away then. And he noted with some almost detached part of himself that his body responded perfectly to each of his commands.

Grip Fiona's hand. Lead her around the two men. Nod politely at the goggle-eyed companion in passing.

Stride away, relying on the length of those beautiful legs of Fiona's to allow her to keep up with his pace until they got outside and he sucked in a deep breath of cleansing air.

'There's a taxi. We're going. We're getting right away from here and from that—' Fiona's words were shocked, shaken. She flagged the cab forward with a hand that visibly trembled.

Brent turned his gaze to her and something deep and protective came to life in him. His voice was soft as he spoke, deep and gentle… 'Don't worry. Everything's fine—'

'No. It's not.' She shook her head, a decisive shake that said she wasn't about to be convinced.

And what else had she registered? Charles's final word? That Brent had autism?

Moments later they were ensconced in the back seat and her shoulder was pressed to his, their bodies tucked as close as she could get them as she gave her address to the driver without sparing him as much as a glance.

All her attention was for Brent. In part that made him uncomfortable, and yet…

'I should explain.' Brent cleared his throat. 'He's not…I don't…'

'What? He isn't important? You don't care that he rejected you because you're autistic?' The words burst out of her and then she chewed her lip. 'I'm sorry. I heard him, but I'd already wondered.'

It shouldn't surprise him that she'd come halfway to figuring it out. But now, thanks to Charles, Fiona completely knew the one thing that Brent had worked to keep to himself, where he could guard it and control it…and no person could judge him for it.

'Yes, I have a form of autism. It's less of a challenge physically or in other ways than many people live and deal with daily, but it's still an inherent part of me.'

The mix of emotions he felt as he told her this was difficult to define.

Fiona's face tightened and she whispered, 'How could he treat you like that?'

And Brent realised that for all he'd believed he'd resolved this in his heart and mind long ago, there was still…something there. 'I—don't know. I don't know how he could have done that.'

The glitter in her gaze was anger and other emotions mixed. It made something inside him clench. He curled his fingers because suddenly he wanted to lace them with hers.

'This explains your ability to concentrate your focus so intensely when you're producing those amazing landscape designs.' Fiona drew a determined breath, deliberately seemed to calm herself. 'I've thought that was amazing. Now I understand it.'

She turned Brent on his ear by addressing his condition as though it were of benefit.

God, she was amazing, even if she wasn't

seeing the whole picture. 'Well—' Brent realised he was simply sitting there, soaking in her warmth. He would have drawn away from Fiona then. He had to get this back to some kind of ordinary footing before his body started leading the rest of him, short-circuited what his brain knew he had to do, namely leave her alone, and got him in trouble.

'Please don't…shift away yet. I need…' Her words were low, a blend of anger and hurt and heart.

She had a generosity in her nature that Brent couldn't seem to help responding to.

'I know…that man revealed something about you that you obviously feel wasn't my business.' Her words were low, careful. 'He had no right to do that, but you can trust me with the knowledge. I'm just…furious about…'

'It doesn't matter.' Yet he couldn't deny his anger and old resentment. 'I don't need Charles MacKay's approval.'

'Maybe not, but you deserved his love and acceptance.' Fiona turned to fully face him and all her fury was in her eyes. Her fingers gripped his once again. 'You probably don't even want to think about him. We'll talk about the award. The night we had. It was a good night. You deserved to win. I said you'd get it, didn't I?'

She probably would have kept going, but he

squeezed her fingers and laid them against his thigh and covered her hand with his. Set the award on the floor of the taxi so he could focus solely on her. 'I dealt with my father dumping me a long time ago.'

'What happened so that it was only your father making the decision to…stop parenting you?'

To reject Brent? Pass him off into strangers' hands because he didn't want to deal with a child who was different? 'My mother died. I was young. All I remember was he couldn't cope with my issues. Now he's got the problem that I grew up, made something of myself, and he doesn't want to have to acknowledge my existence.'

'He's the one who should be ashamed to exist.' Fiona uttered the words and let him see in her gaze all she was feeling. Her protectiveness towards him that was so sweet when he was perfectly capable of looking after himself.

Yet something down inside him admitted it would be nice. To have a woman's care.

Well, he couldn't do that, could he? He couldn't let himself care or wish to be cared for. Brent could take the hard knocks of life. But setting himself up for the embarrassment of rejection because of his condition—

That was one 'been there, done that' he didn't want to repeat.

Are you sure it's only about that, MacKay?

Tension pooled at the base of Brent's neck and he frowned. Of course he was certain. What else would there be?

'Here we are.' The driver's voice interrupted Brent's thoughts and he realised they'd arrived at Fiona's block of flats.

Brent still had Fiona's fingers pressed to his thigh, could feel their warmth. Her body remained pressed to his. Consciousness of her swept over Brent then, and pushed past his guardedness about his condition. His instincts took over and at this moment his autism didn't come into it. Brent's hand caressed over Fiona's. His fingers stroked hers.

A dozen different thoughts buzzed in Fiona's head, with as many accompanying emotions.

When Brent instructed the driver to wait, climbing from the taxi with her to start the short journey to her flat, those thoughts distilled into pure feeling. The touch of his fingers at her elbow as he guided her along the path, up the staircase and along the balcony that led to her flat.

The beat of her blood in her veins as she tried to decide whether to invite him in, say goodnight, talk about their night, the award, the good parts of the evening.

Of all of it, the trip back here in the taxi with their bodies close to each other had been the best. And for her, she had to admit, the most emotional.

His father had rejected him, abandoned him, all because Brent had a condition he had learned to live with and, indeed, to use to his advantage in business, in his work. His uniqueness only made him all the more appealing.

And right now he had his hand at her elbow and Fiona's heart was beating a little faster because…she liked that touch.

Liked it too much for her safety? Attraction, that was easy to deal with, but was she more than attracted? Were her emotions involved? Because she really mustn't let that be the case.

He was her boss. She should say goodnight and walk inside… 'Brent, thank you for tonight—'

'Thank you for attending the Awards ceremony with me.' He paused. 'You got more than you bargained for with our exchange of a family night for the Awards night.'

'My family situation isn't even worth words in comparison to what happened tonight.' She shook her head. How could she even think her paltry difficulties with her family mattered now? 'Brent, I just don't know how to comfort—'

'Don't feel sorry for me.' Though he interrupted her, he did it gently, wrapping his fingers around hers where she'd been toying with her keys. 'My past is what it is. I've moved on from it.'

'Maybe, but you went on trying to conceal a

part of yourself that you shouldn't worry about that way.' She bit her lip. Her breath stuttered in her throat and she whispered, 'I can't talk—'

About it any more? Brent certainly didn't want to.

'Then we won't talk.' He uttered the words with an accepting edge. 'I'd rather do this, anyway.' He bent his head to hers.

Touched his lips to hers.

A soft, seeking, giving and taking exchange. Lips to lips. How could it be all of this between them? And yet, somewhere inside herself, Fiona had wanted and needed his kiss and not even known how much she did.

Now she knew.

A taste of delight and sweetness and desire and pleasure. Her fingers wrapped around his forearms, and his hands were about her waist.

It felt good and right to have his mouth over hers, his fingers pressing into the soft flesh of her waist. For a few wonderful moments, she lived in the sensations of kissing him.

His mouth caressed hers as though he needed and wanted to kiss her this way. Their gazes were locked, his lashes dusky crescents that fanned against his cheeks as he focused wholly on her. And then those lashes swept down fully and her eyes closed too, and it was all sensation and feeling and the beat of her heart in her breast and the spread of such warmth all through her.

That warmth told its own story. She *had* invested emotionally in him, at least to a degree, even when she knew that was dangerous. A little hint of panic surfaced as Fiona made this realisation.

And the moment that panic hit, she realised something in Brent had changed as well.

He ended the kiss and dropped his hands away from her. Stepped back, and some kind of regret showed in his eyes. 'I shouldn't have done that. It can't go anywhere. You and I can never—'

He cut off the rest of the sentence, but he didn't need to finish it. Fiona could do that herself.

Now that he'd felt the reality, had *touched* the reality of her generous curves, he did not want her. The house of cards that had been desire and pleasure and closeness and a hope she should never have allowed, crumbled down.

Fiona tipped up her chin and told herself it didn't matter. It absolutely, fiercely did not matter. 'Goodnight, Brent.'

'Goodnight. I'm—'

Sorry.

At least he didn't say it.

With one last glance from a troubled green gaze, Brent walked away.

CHAPTER SIX

REPEAT after me: I am a professional, I am a professional, I am a professional. I'm focused on my work, my career, my 'five year plan' and my goals for success…

Fiona attempted, yet again, for the umpteenth time, to figure out what was wrong with the feature plants in the painting she was working on. If she could feel settled or focused about anything at all, it might help her make a decent assessment of the problem.

And how could she feel settled when all of her was utterly distracted and had been since the night Brent had kissed her and walked away straight afterwards?

'Stupid thing.' She grabbed the open container of ochre paint from her work shelf.

Perhaps, if she blended a little white into it, she'd overcome the toning issue she had going on. If indeed the problem actually was a toning issue.

The colour wasn't right. That much she'd known from the start. She just wasn't certain if that was the entire problem.

'I shouldn't call the painting names. I'm the problem, not it.' She muttered the words, set the container on a small work table and set about mixing the white in.

Overall, this painting was *not* going well. That much she could say for sure, and that was a problem because the client expected to receive this artwork on Monday.

Brent was in the next room, working on something. Well, she assumed so. He'd had the door pushed across all morning so she couldn't be certain of anything, really, but she doubted he was having the same difficulties concentrating as she was.

In fact, he seemed just fine ignoring what had happened between them after the Awards night dinner. All of it. The revelation of his autism. The meeting with his father. Their kiss. His regret and rejection after it. Maybe it had been a sympathy kiss—for her sake. She had been very upset on his behalf and he was a kind man.

The thought made her cringe because to her it had been anything but that.

But he'd backed away from it, had clearly been put off by it. What other conclusion could she draw?

Fiona gave her paint one last vigorous stir. She would simply have to get on with her work, that was all. Take a leaf from her boss's book and only focus on the responsibilities they shared here. That was smart anyway. The only sensible thing to do, really, in the face of the fact that Brent didn't…want her.

So there. That was decided. Fiona snatched up her newly blended paint, briefly admired the glossy consistency of it and swung about to carry it to her easel.

'I need to go up into the mountains. This project—'

'I'm going to just focus on work… Oomph.'

As their words crossed each other, Fiona came up against a solid wall of chest. Paint hit that chest in a broad, gooey blob, slopped over her hand and splashed its way down until drips hit the floor.

'Oh, no.' The paint container wobbled in her hand. Fiona got it upright, but that was pointless now.

'I guess I should have knocked first or something.' Brent spoke in a slightly dazed tone while his fingers rose to his chest.

'It's my fault. I should have been looking at what I was doing.' Fiona's hand rose, too. She brushed at the dinner-plate sized splodge soaking into his shirt, sticking it to the firm muscles of his chest.

And then she stilled as Brent's fingers explored the paint, sliding back and forth through it, not to clear it off, but to get the full tactile experience of it.

The sight of that exploration was one of the most beautiful, sensual things Fiona had ever seen. Maybe he caught her staring because his fingers came to a standstill and very green eyes searched her gaze while heat coated his cheekbones.

Embarrassment, but why?

Because that's his condition speaking.

'You must think I'm strange—'

'I'm sorry I stared. It was just that you looked so—' She couldn't complete the words. Couldn't tell him that his expression had made her imagine his hands stroking her skin that way.

'I…um…I've ruined your shirt.' Her mouth pointed out the ridiculously obvious while the rest of her tried to catch its breath. 'I was trying to fix a problem with this artwork. The colour change probably wouldn't have fixed it, anyway. I need to *see* the particular seed pod that grows on the plants I've used in the painting. The trouble is they don't go to seed pods until they're quite mature. I won't find what I need at any young plant nursery.'

Brent's glance moved to the half finished painting. 'What you have there looks…okay.'

'Yes, and that's the problem. Okay is synonymous with "average". It isn't good enough.' Fiona frowned at the painting. 'I need the real thing.'

He looked from her to the painting and back again. 'If you can't fix this it's going to drive you crazy, isn't it?'

'Yes, but how do you—?'

'Know how that feels?' He shook his head. 'Because I've just spent all morning working on a project and not getting it where I need to because the one part of it that's vital to the design I can't perfect until I study rock formations in the mountains. And, as it happens, the rock formations I have in mind are the only place I know of where you'll find your plants, complete with seed pods. It's where I spotted the plants before I incorporated them into that landscape design in the first place. They aren't normally stocked in nurseries. Linc sourced some young plants for me when I needed them.'

'If you could get me a look at some…' Without thinking about it, she took his hand in hers and used the base of his shirt to wipe as much of the paint off his fingers as she could. 'I hope that shirt didn't have sentimental value. I'll replace it, of course.' Her fingers worked at the buttons on the shirt. She got through three of them before he shackled her wrist.

'Don't—' He broke off. 'You'll get it all over yourself.'

'It's too late to worry about that.' It was too late to worry about a few things, Fiona realised, including the impact of revealing his chest to her gaze, even if she could only see a little of it. She dropped her glance so he wouldn't see the expression in her eyes.

He probably liked petite women with dainty feet who didn't have issues about plants, with or without seed pods on them... 'You should shower. There'll be residue soaking through onto your skin. At least it's not the most expensive brand of paint, but I'm sorry it got wasted.'

'Don't worry about that, and don't worry about the shirt.' Brent hesitated as he searched her face again. 'You've been putting in long hours, trying to get this painting pulled together. I shouldn't have asked you to produce something on demand for a project you weren't in on from its conception. I said I wouldn't let that happen more than once.'

'It's all right—'

'No, it isn't, but we'll make it right.' He wiped his hand on his shirt again. 'I came in to tell you I'm going into the mountains to study rock formations. Maybe you should come with me, see these seed pods, take photos, draw them, whatever you need.'

'A day trip.' A day to spend time with him. No. It wasn't about that. It was for work, had to be for that reason only. And Fiona had to look at it from that perspective. 'I'm a professional. I *have* to be able to produce the goods on demand, without special trips or anything else.'

'No. You don't have to be able to do that. I'd never expect that of myself and I don't expect it of you.' Brent's gaze became very focused as he said this. 'Finish up here in the office while I take my shower. When I'm done, we're going to swing by your place and my place for clothes and then we'll go. Bring the work boots you wore on site. They'll do for the trail I want to take you on.'

'O-okay.' What else could she do but agree? And be grateful, Fiona added silently as she glanced once again at her stalled painting.

'Good.' Brent gave a nod and turned away to head for the shower. 'Oh, and we'll be gone overnight.'

He walked off before she could even collect her thoughts.

An overnight stay in the mountains with her boss...

'And that's a square-tailed kite. See it?' Brent pointed into the branches of a tree to the left on the trail in front of them.

They'd been flora and fauna spotting for the

past hour, indulging in guesswork when they didn't know what they were seeing, though in Brent's case he recognised most things, right down to a gold and white daisy Fiona hadn't seen in exactly its type anywhere before.

Fiona had photographed and sketched her seed pods. More importantly, she'd spent time simply studying them. Examining them from every angle, exploring the texture with her fingertips, feeling their weight and the roughness of their shells.

Brent's response to bush walking like this was very tactile, too. He would stroke his fingers over the spiky leaves on a bush, or stop to carefully examine a bottlebrush or some other native flower. That attention to detail carried through into his work as much as Fiona needed to carry it to her work. Fiona didn't doubt it was part of the reason his designs were so successful. She shouldn't wonder if that tactility would carry through into other more personal parts of his life, because those thoughts were adding to her consciousness of him.

His autism made him unique and special, and yet he seemed determined to dislike it and hide its existence from the world if he could.

And Fiona needed to hide the existence of how attracted to him she was. She truly should have turned down the offer of joining him on this trip but, once decided, Brent had been set on the idea, convinced it would be good for both of them. And so far it had been. They were…enjoying themselves. It just worried her how much she struggled to do that without letting her emotions and feelings for him carry her in directions she shouldn't go.

'Is it really a square-tailed kite or are you making that up?' She was proud of the slight teasing tone she produced, the relaxed humour as she went on. 'I *think* I've heard of those, but I'm a city girl…'

'It really is one.' Brent's mouth quirked up at one corner, as though he understood that edge of humour and enjoyed it.

But their gazes caught in that moment and she lost herself in moss-green irises and in an instant the relaxed state of their interaction changed.

Part of her welcomed that, was fiercely glad that he hadn't managed to completely lose his awareness of her, after all.

The other part warned her not to think like that. She would only open herself to hurt from him all over again, though she knew he hadn't set out to hurt her.

Brent's head twitched to the side. It was only a little twitch in the scheme of things, but his gaze searched hers after it happened and suddenly every feeling she'd had the night they'd run into his father rushed to the surface to join with the rest of her confusion and interest in him that she needed to stifle, yet couldn't seem to.

'Families should love each other unconditionally.' The words burst out of her. 'There shouldn't be any question about it. That should simply happen as a matter of course. Your father was very wrong to reject you the way he did. He should have seen that you were unique and special, not less in any way.'

'Not less, perhaps, but I *am* different.' A lookout appeared on the trail to their left. He led the way down to it over steps hewn from dirt and rock and leaned his arms against the chest-high railing to look out over the gorge spread before them. 'I made a family for myself with Linc and Alex and I'm happy in that.'

Happy with his brothers—yes. Fiona believed that, and it was wonderful. 'It's just that you're very guarded—'

'An institutional training ground will do that. Linc and Alex are the same. I'm afraid that's something all three of us are going to be stuck with.'

'I can understand why that would be true, but people can change…' She was stepping over the line again, wasn't she? It happened because she cared about him, and that in itself was a cause for concern. Fiona turned back towards the trail and couldn't help her one final comment. 'Well, I believe your autism only makes you more special, and your work richer and more amazing for all you bring to it. I think that's something to celebrate about you.'

'You have…a very open heart and I appreciate you saying that.' Appreciated and felt disconcerted by her openness, if his torn expression was any indication.

They continued their walk in silence. Her outburst had probably been too much, she supposed, but his situation hit a particularly raw spot with her.

Because aspects of it bore an unpleasant likeness to her treatment at the hands of her family. She'd said there was no comparison, but she couldn't ignore the similarities.

Fiona listened to the swishing of grasses and shrubs and the leaves of trees in the wind. Small birds and insects making their sounds, larger ones filling the air with clarion calls and sharp cries and warbles.

And she glanced at Brent and let the conversation move on because there didn't seem to be much choice. 'Thank you for this. I think I'll be able to do what I need to with my painting now.'

'I'm happy with my rock formation study, too. I consider the time well spent. We'll head to the house now.' As they completed their circuitous walk and approached his truck, he explained how he'd purchased the house in the mountains that he and his brothers now visited whenever they wanted to get out of the city.

'I'm looking forward to seeing the place.'

Brent started the truck and turned to face her while the engine idled and, oh, those beautiful deep green eyes were guarded and interested and thoughtful and self-protective all at once. Fiona longed to break through every barrier he had erected and know the man inside.

Yes, she wanted that even if it was dangerous to. Even though he had kissed her and then not wanted to be near her that way again.

'Seat belt.' Brent waited while Fiona strapped herself in. Her knowledge of his autism made him uncomfortable. He couldn't deny that. In his adult life, his brothers had been the only ones who knew of it. He didn't want Fiona to know of it, yet she did.

But it was more than that which had put lead in his stomach. The sinking feeling came from a very old, very deep conditioning that his father had handed to him.

Brent forced himself to admit it. Charles had done a number on him and Brent hadn't managed to process and deal with that in the way he'd wanted to believe he had done.

'Sorry. I'm ready now.' Fiona gave a wry smile. 'I guess I was sitting there daydreaming.'

'It's no problem.' Brent's thoughts turned back to the woman at his side. Strands of hair lay in soft wisps against Fiona's face and neck. Their walk had put a soft flush in her cheeks.

She was lovely inside and out, and that *was* an ongoing problem for him. He'd helped her along the pathway and known he would have found some excuse to touch her even if there hadn't been a practical reason to do so.

Even choosing to bring her on this trip, he could have done things differently. He could have told her to forget about the painting...

He'd been a repeat offender where resisting Fiona was concerned. After the Awards night he'd kissed her. He hadn't even thought about not doing that at the time, let alone given himself a chance to decide against it. He'd simply leaned in and covered soft, warm lips and taken what, deep down, he had wanted from the first day they'd met.

He still wanted her. That was his problem. He wanted her and her gentle attitude about his autism, her determination to be accepting, even if she didn't truly understand the issues, didn't help him to resist. Brent's fingers drummed out a rhythm on the steering wheel.

'Is it far to the house?' Fiona gazed out of the window as they made their way along the road.

'Not far, but it's just as well we finished our

walk when we did. Night falls earlier here, and there's often thick fog late in the afternoon. It's best not to be on the walking trails then.' He drew a breath. 'There's a small township between here and the house. We'll stop there and buy some groceries, and something ready to go to have for dinner tonight.'

They had to eat. It was too late to return to Sydney now. All he needed to do was treat the situation as though it were nothing out of the ordinary, and that was what it would be.

With this decision made, Brent drove them to the township. They shopped in one of those 'all things for all occasions' long narrow stores with foodstuffs lined along each outer wall and a single row up the middle. A barbecued chicken, a creamy potato bake and a big fresh salad air-sealed in a bag all made their way into the shopping basket. Breakfast items and fresh milk, and a glazed fruit and custard flan followed.

'I'll put on a hundred pounds if we add any more food like that.' Fiona made the comment half jokingly, but her eyes weren't laughing. 'Mum would have a fit if she saw—' She cut the words off.

But she'd said enough. Her mother had made a comment on the night he'd met her family.

I hardly think that's appropriate clothing for someone your size, dear.

Brent had assumed the comment was ill-thought out and something to do with fashion choices and Fiona being tall.

But it hadn't been that at all, had it? Fiona's mother had been criticising her *size*. As though Fiona could do anything about being voluptuous.

As though she should want to!

'You don't need to worry about food intake. You obviously eat appropriately. Your size is right for you.' He growled each of the words more harshly than the last. And he piled apples and bananas into the basket, and some high nutrition, slow energy release snacks.

Fiona gave him a thoughtful, slightly arrested glance and then walked ahead of him through the store.

Brent dragged his gaze from the view of her bottom swaying in form-fitting jeans, tossed a few more items into the basket and followed her to the cashier's counter. His fingers drummed on the counter as the cashier processed his payment.

This time, he didn't even try to stop the incessant movement. Let Fiona look at it, think about what it meant.

She needed to start seeing his condition for what it was, not through rose-coloured spectacles, even if it was very kindly meant.

CHAPTER SEVEN

'I SHOULD set up my easel and have another go at this painting now.' The enthusiasm and inspiration was there inside Fiona, but she was also relaxed and mellow from the meal and the time spent chatting about nothing while they'd eaten.

She'd thought they'd be tense together but somehow they'd drifted into relaxation. Drifted in such a way that it was more dangerous than consciously thinking about it. 'I *think* I know where I want to go with the painting now. It'll mean starting over and I'm still considering a couple of aspects, but I brought a blank canvas—'

'Not tonight.' Brent's words were low, but firm. 'Rest tonight. Tomorrow you can paint.'

'What about your work?'

'I've got what I need.' He tapped his temple. 'It's in here. I'll let it churn in there for a day or two before I try to do anything more with it.'

And, when it had finished churning, something

amazing would come out. His creative ability was something Fiona found extremely…appealing.

Brent seemed relaxed himself right now. Really relaxed. Maybe that was because they'd done nothing but potter in the kitchen and get settled into their rooms before they stared out of the living room windows and watched the fog roll in until it obscured everything. Maybe Brent had relaxed because she'd stood back and left him to it while he'd organised their foodstuffs into regimented lines in the pantry and refrigerator just so.

Yet she got the impression he was deliberately allowing himself to do some of those things to prove something to her, rather than simply giving himself the freedom of them because he didn't need to keep secrets from her any longer.

'We could put on that MP3 disc you brought with you, listen to some music.' Brent raised his brows. 'If you want.'

'I would like that. I'll go get my music. I left it in my room in case I wanted to listen later when I'm going to sleep.' A little music, a little more relaxing. That would be a…nice way to round off the day.

A nice safe way.

She walked the length of the living room and corridor and went into the bedroom she'd been given, with its deep maroon and pale gold curtains. Fiona collected her music and went back out.

They sat on the sofa and listened and talked in a desultory fashion for the first hour. Made tea and drank it, and then the songs segued into a selection of dance tunes.

Two things happened. Fiona, who'd just carried their cups to the kitchen and left them there, danced her way back without thinking about what she was doing.

And Brent, who'd followed her with an opened package of cookies he'd placed away in the pantry cupboard, locked his gaze on the sway of her hips and a wave of male awareness rolled off him and over her.

'I…well…did you want to listen a bit longer or go to bed?' She uttered the words and then could have bitten her tongue out.

Oh, good way of putting it, Fiona! Heat blazed in her cheeks as she looked everywhere but at him.

She sank onto the sofa and lowered her gaze away from his. She didn't know whether to feel awkward for putting on that unplanned dancing display, or unsettled because her boss appeared to have enjoyed it. Or just purely embarrassed by what she had blurted afterwards.

'What I'd like is to dance with you to some of these tunes.' His words seemed to surprise him as much as they did her. He cleared his throat and

took his seat on the sofa again and pushed his
hands into his pockets.

Fiona understood that action now. If his hands
were contained he wouldn't drum his fingers on
things. How much self-control must it take *not*
to do those things that must want so desperately
to be done?

'I'd love to dance with you—'

'I don't often dance—'

Because of his autism? Did it cause problems
with coordination? She hadn't seen that in other
circumstances. And she shouldn't have made it
sound as though she was begging for him to dance
with her. 'You don't need to—'

Brent stared at her for a long moment through
a screen of silky lashes before he got to his feet
and held out his hand.

Fiona rose and put her hand in his.

For starters she kept her hand in his while they
moved a little to the music.

It was…nice. A thread of excitement ran
beneath the calm and she let that be there and
relaxed without meaning to because, in the
scheme of things, what more was this than Brent
enjoying himself and not seeming stressed and
Fiona just wanting to enjoy the moment, too?

'I'm guessing you probably danced with
several of the men in your group that night at the

club.' His words were a quiet murmur. 'Really danced, that is. Not…like this.'

'I'm lucky that group all enjoys dancing with anyone rather than sticking to partners only.' She did feel lucky—and safe. Accepted for herself. Well, for herself and for lending a friendly ear to all their lovelorn problems.

But she didn't want Brent to think this experience was second rate. It was not. 'I'm enjoying this, too.' The words were perhaps a little breathless, a little more revealing than they could have been.

His fingers tightened over hers. That was all, and yet it felt like a complete change from where they'd been, to the promise of something more.

Brent left her for a moment to close the curtains. A moment later her hand was back in his—both her hands were in his and they were swaying to the music.

'The night I brought your keys to you, I thought you were with the guy on the dance floor.' As Brent spoke the words, the light overhead flickered once, and again.

They both glanced up just as the bulb died. The music kept going, but now the living room was nothing but shadows.

'I don't know if there are any spare light globes here.' Brent's words sounded deeper in the near darkness. 'I don't remember seeing any in the cupboards.'

'It might make more sense to search for them in the morning, anyway.' When it was daylight. Fiona went on. 'It's ages since I've danced in the dark.' A very long time, and never like this. She worked hard to hide the breathless edge in her voice that had nothing to do with exertion. 'I used to do it with my girlfriends sometimes in the "silly" teenage years. It was a way to dance however we wanted with nobody to judge or see.'

'Then dance in the dark.' He drew her closer until his hands were around her waist. 'And I'll…be here with you while you do it.'

Fiona's arms rose naturally to his shoulders. It felt…right to move closer, to sway in his arms while he held her. She let herself have the moment.

Brent's eyes had adapted to the shadowy dimness. Enough that he could read the dreamy quality in Fiona's eyes and the softening of her mouth that told him they had taken this to a place he shouldn't have allowed it to go. He knew what he could and could not have with her. This… closeness didn't come under the 'could have' category.

He should release her—now—and leave the room.

He didn't do that.

He didn't *want* to do that and, for once, he was going to give himself what he did want. For a little time, a safe amount of time. Five minutes. Ten at the most. What could that hurt? Just to hold her while she danced? That wasn't the end of the world. That didn't have to get them into any trouble at all.

And if his urge to hold her was more need than want—

It wasn't.

Of course it wasn't.

A twitch built at the base of Brent's neck, and that was something else he didn't want to think about right now. The manifestation of his condition that made him different from others. Instead, Brent focused his attention on the feel of Fiona's waist beneath his hands. He held her close and breathed in her scent and felt her softness and they danced. For that period of time Brent set aside his issues and just…*was*.

They danced for hours, or at least it felt that way to Fiona. Brent's gaze held hers in the dimness, unmoving, so focused.

The music slowed to a dreamy number and Brent took a step closer to her and murmured, 'You put your whole heart into it when you dance. It's…beautiful.'

His hand rose from her waist, up, until he had

her hand clasped in his. He lifted her hand from his shoulder, moved it to his chest and cupped it there.

And, oh, it was the most wonderful feeling to have that one small connection with him and know he'd sought it, that he wanted it. That here in the shadowy room, for just a moment, he wanted this.

She curled her fingers into his and let the beat of his heart guide her while they swayed to the music.

Just trust me, Brent. Dance with me and trust me so you can be all of yourself with me.

Her heart ached with the need for him to do that. To relax with her and not modify anything about himself. And maybe she ached just as much for her own need.

'You dance beautifully, too.' She wanted him to pull her even closer so their bodies were flush against each other.

Yet keeping a little distance held a certain safeness for her because, even though she knew herself, knew her body size and her shape and her height and all the times she'd accepted she wasn't the build most men found appealing, if she and Brent didn't get *too close* then he wouldn't be too confronted by those things about her this time…

Oh, what a way to think!

The song ended and another began. A slow song from a popular romantic movie. Brent tugged her

forwards and their bodies brushed and she
couldn't think. Not while they were chest to chest,
thigh to thigh and his arms were around her. They
danced for real. Two people on a polished board
floor in a living room in a house in the middle of
nowhere in the mountains, dancing as potential
lovers would.

How could she think of work in this moment?
How could she see him as her boss when his arms
held her and all she wanted was to lay her head
against his shoulder and feel those arms close
around her even more securely?

They danced like that through one song and
another and another until Brent finally lifted one
hand to the back of her head and spoke. 'I meant
to stop after ten minutes. I didn't know I could do
this at all. I thought—'

He'd thought he would do something that made
him feel uncomfortable or embarrassed?

'I like the way you dance.' *I like the way you
do so many things.*

He pressed her cheek to his and swayed with
her to the music. 'I like this with you. *You*
dancing.'

'Us dancing. Together.' There. She'd said it.
Named it. And they were. Body to body, her heart
to his heart as the music swept them away and she

had what she had wanted. More closeness. A deeper closeness with him.

Fiona couldn't say just when they ceased to dance, or whose arms rose first to change the dance to an outright embrace.

It just happened and it felt right. Fiona didn't want to think about any of it or all the negative things her family had fed into her mind over the years about her size and her personality.

When she lifted her gaze to search his eyes, Brent let her see the glitter of need and awareness and attraction in their depths. There was a question, too, and she answered it in the tilt of her chin as his mouth lowered to hers, in the angle of her head to accommodate that melding of lips upon lips.

He stood perfectly still and kissed her.

His fingers dug into her back in a kneading motion, and he kissed her.

The pads of those fingers rubbed across and back over her upper arms beneath the loose sleeves of her shirt, and still he kissed her.

These were the reactions he worried about, that slipped through his control now, perhaps because he *wasn't* controlling himself.

To Fiona they were pure beauty because they told her he enjoyed touching her. She melted into his embrace and his arms and his mouth and his attention and loved all of it.

She lifted her hands and cupped his face with her fingers and breathed in the scent of him and wanted his kiss to never end.

When he drew her closer still, his body unashamedly craving hers, Fiona melted all over again.

'Let me…I need…' His words were deep, disjointed, hungry.

Anything. Whatever he wanted…

'Fiona…' He said her name and buried his face in her hair where it lay against her nape, and he breathed harsh and deep while a wave of tension built in his body, locked his muscles, even as he locked her to him.

'Brent.' She raised her hands to his back, rubbed them across those locked muscles and tried to soothe the tension from him.

His neck twitched. Once. Again.

He sighed and his hands tightened on the balls of her shoulders and he straightened and put distance between their bodies, and dropped his touch away from her.

Brent's guard went up, even as she watched him.

He closed his eyes and took in a single deep inhalation and held it. When his eyes opened again it was to look deep into hers before he spoke.

'You think you can accept my autism, but to you it is nothing more than a few random things that don't seem so unusual.'

'They're *not* so unusual. Lots of people have similar things about them.'

'You haven't seen what my father saw.' As though his words had surprised him, Brent stopped abruptly. 'I have nothing to offer in a…normal relationship. For my brothers I've found affection, appreciation, caring, but they have all of me that there is to give. I don't want to hurt you. That would happen if I…let you close and then couldn't give you those things. You deserve those things. This isn't because of you…'

But wasn't it? Oh, it was clear Brent believed what he was saying about himself, his capacity to care for others. Given his upbringing, the guardedness she'd seen in his eyes, in his history, Fiona could understand that. It was good that he could see this much of himself, that it went deeper than purely the fact that he had autism.

But in the end Brent was rejecting Fiona in the same way his father had rejected him. She had no defence against that, other than to walk away from that aspect of him and her and…try not to look back.

'You're right. We wouldn't be suited. I can see that now. I'm…grateful you put a stop to things when you did. We'll both be careful to keep things strictly on a business footing from now on. That's all we need. And…to stay away from this kind of situation.'

She whispered goodnight, left him to worry about the stereo system and walked away through the darkness to her room at the end of the corridor.

At her door, she turned and spoke through that darkness to him one more time, with all her effort focused on how she needed to come across to him, whether she hurt down inside right now or not. 'I think I'll be ready to paint in the morning. That's why we came here, after all. That and for you to study rock formations so you could nut out your new design in your head. Maybe you'll get a long way with that now, too.'

In fact, Fiona knew she would be ready to paint in the morning. She was no longer blocked. Because she'd found what she needed. She'd found the emotions that needed to go into her painting.

She'd found warmth and pleasure and hope and connection.

Brent had tried to shut them all down, but they hadn't gone away for her. So she would take them to her art and release them there.

CHAPTER EIGHT

FIONA did get up and paint. She painted her heart onto the canvas and painted Brent's heart as she perceived it without censoring herself or trying to understand all of what it was she believed she knew of him. Only that he was complex and giving and guarded and restless and still and so many things all rolled into one, and that he had made his choice against intimacy with her, at least *believing* it was in both their best interests for him to make that choice.

He had probably saved her from a great deal of hurt further down the track by taking this step now.

Right. She should feel very resolute at this point. So why didn't she?

Fiona handed the painting to the clients and they seemed more than pleased. A week passed. Brent spent much of it shut in his office or, when he wasn't sequestered in there, working from his home and leaving Fiona to her own devices.

Their personal situation was one thing. A good, workable business relationship was another and currently that relationship was suffering.

That side of things had to be addressed and Fiona was about to address it.

Well, if indeed he was actually ignoring her and not simply busy and focused and home surroundings were working best for him at the moment...

Fiona parked her car, hefted her half-finished painting in her hand and walked the short distance to the front of the MacKay brothers' warehouse home. She reached for the buzzer.

As she did so, her mobile phone rang.

'I've been working on my ideas for the project we discussed on the phone on Friday.' Brent's low voice filled her ear. 'I have the results spread out at home and I...would like you to take a look. Are you on your way to the office? Could you swing by here first?'

'Well...yes.' Most of Fiona's whipped up determination to force Brent past avoiding her evaporated. He'd probably just been busy thinking through project ideas anyway. Rather arrogant of her to put it down to him trying to stay away from her!

'I have a painting started that I want to show you for the same reason.' She cleared her throat. 'Actually, I'd decided to stop by with it. I'm standing outside your door now. I was about to press the buzzer.'

Given she felt a little silly now, she hoped he would assume it was nothing more than enthusiasm for the project that had driven her actions this morning.

There was a short beat and then Brent said, 'Good. I'll come down.' He let her in moments later and for one brief second his gaze searched her face and seemed to take in all of her at once.

'Come upstairs. I should have brought you in on this last week.' He kept walking, didn't meet her gaze as he went on. 'I've needed your input.'

'We need to maintain a good working relationship.' Fiona forced the tentative edge from her tone. 'Anything else aside.'

'Exactly.' He nodded. 'All the rest…aside.'

And, that easily, Fiona felt so much better. Even though feeling better because he sounded as unconvinced as she felt wasn't exactly sensible.

They climbed the stairs and entered his home together. Brent had the materials for the project spread in a long, neat line from one end of the floor space in his living room to the other.

He stopped abruptly and ran his hand over the

back of his head, frowned and then dropped his
hand to his side. 'It makes the most sense this
way.'

'And that's perfectly fine. It looks the same as
the work laid out in your office.' She said it
without inflection and was rewarded when his
shoulders lost some of their tension.

'Let me take that for you. I want to see it, too.'
He took her painting from her hands and propped
it onto a lounge chair he turned to face them.

Then he stared at the work she'd done while she
gave her explanation and the more she explained
and he looked, the more he nodded and comprehension sparkled in his gaze.

He touched her for the first time in days, then.
Pressed his fingers to her forearm as he smiled
finally and turned her to look at the first of the materials spread across his floor. 'I *thought* I'd
handled the concept the right way. Now that I've
seen your painting, I'm certain of it. We make—'

He didn't complete the sentence, but Fiona
looked at his work and knew what he'd been going
to say.

They made a good team.

And they did. If only…

No. No *if onlys*. There was this, and it had to
be enough. Fiona dropped to her knees on the
floor to look at his drawings, the images he'd

taken from books and arranged into a collage with notes between.

His entire vision was there, and her vision was there with it, the perfect complement to his work, and somehow that was just as intimate to her as anything that had passed between them.

She pored over his plans. That led to questions, lively discussion, and to her forgetting for a moment her other concerns as she immersed herself in the work, until finally she understood the entire concept—and was so impressed by his vision for it.

'I'm glad you can see where I need to take this, that you saw the same potential I have.' Brent held out his hand to draw her to her feet.

Fiona stifled a second set of *if onlys* and clasped his hand. She tried not to think of it as anything other than a courtesy to help her rise.

Her knees were all but numb and she glanced at the clock on his wall. 'I didn't notice so much time had passed. They'll be wondering at work where on earth we both are.'

Brent's fingers tightened around Fiona's hand as he helped her to her feet. She'd been crawling around his floor, automatically respecting his need to have his plans laid out in that long straight line he hadn't even thought about when he'd decided he needed her to come and look.

Had he really needed that so desperately this morning? Or had he needed this? He glanced down at their joined hands. This touch of her? This closeness to her? This reconnection through their work, through the emotions she took to her work and claimed he took to his work? He was starting to think maybe she was right about that, that he did, indeed, give parts of himself to his creative process that he otherwise tried to hold back elsewhere.

And here was Fiona, respecting his autism and the ways it affected him. And putting her whole heart out there as she always did, even while she tried to protect it.

He had to stay emotionally detached from her. He'd let down his guard enough with Fiona that he hadn't considered what she'd think of the way he prepared his materials, of his obsession with the project overall. That knowledge unnerved him.

It also didn't help him fight his growing attraction to her, and he didn't know where to go with this. The consciousness of each other remained, a constant ripple of unspoken thoughts and responses between them. They were both doing their best to ignore it. He'd told her he was determined to ignore it, but his actions weren't proving out those words right now.

He'd wanted to make love with her when they'd been away in the mountains. With Fiona it would definitely be too intimate and intense for him to be sure he could manage and control his responses.

And why was he thinking of making love with her anyway? That wasn't something that could ever happen.

Brent's lips tightened.

'We should head into the office.' He should probably not have asked her to come here, shouldn't have spent so much time with her, utterly absorbed in this one project and oblivious to anything else in existence. Except Fiona herself, and that was even worse. 'You'd probably like to get some other work done before the day disappears completely.'

'I think you're right.' She dusted her hands over her knees and gathered her painting. Perhaps she realised belatedly, too, just how distracted they'd allowed themselves to become, how easily they'd fallen into an intimate rapport with each other.

Yet they had to work together and do that well. Where did that leave them? He couldn't keep avoiding her the way he'd done in the past week. 'Fiona—'

'It's good that we're back on a better footing.' Her smile was full of determined good cheer that didn't quite erase the tinge of…sadness in her eyes? 'After getting slightly…off course while we were away. Circumstances, surroundings, can put people in that place, but we've sorted ourselves out now, haven't we?'

Right. And yet the attraction was still there between them. Still just as strong.

It would go away eventually as they both accepted what their roles with each other needed to be. Wouldn't it? He should be grateful for her determination, not feel as though both of them were somehow being short-changed in this.

'I'll head away now and see you when you get to the office.' Fiona moved towards the door and Brent…let her.

This was best, after all.

His mobile phone rang then. It would have been easy to ignore it but he'd trained himself to always check the number in case either of his brothers needed him. Brent checked and quickly answered. 'Linc. What's up?'

'There's a warehouse fire. I saw it on the TV Cecilia had on in the staff area at the nursery just now.' Tension edged his brother's tone. 'I couldn't tell for sure, but it *looked* like Alex's warehouse. The street and the location—I'm headed back to the city now, but it's going to take time for me to get in.'

'I'll go straight there.' Brent snatched his keys

from the stand inside the front door and strode forward still talking. 'You've tried to contact him?'

'Yes, and I can't get him either at the warehouse or on his mobile.' Linc cursed. 'Look, I have to end this call. There's fog here this morning and I've already had one closer encounter with a kangaroo on the road than I would have liked. Even speaking on hands-free, I can't afford to be distracted.'

'Keep safe, Linc.' They ended the call and Brent was out of the door before he realised Fiona was right on his heels, painting clutched in her hands.

'What's going on?' she asked. 'We'll go down while you tell me.'

They hit the stairs at a ground-eating pace as he explained the situation. A ball of tension had lodged in his gut. 'I have to find Alex. I have to make sure he's safe.'

Nothing can happen to my brother.

The thought came to him uncensored, an outpouring of how much he needed Linc and Alex. Of how much he loved them both. They may not have been born of the same blood, but they were bonded in all the ways of family. There were two people in the world who hadn't rejected him, condition and all, and who let him love them just as much, and Brent…*needed them.*

Fiona doesn't want to care about your condition, either, and you know your hesitations go deeper than that.

Because, in the end, could Charles MacKay have rejected and abandoned Brent solely because Brent had what was for him a manageable condition that shouldn't have mattered to a parent? That in fact should have made that parent care for him all the more?

Something deep inside Brent shifted as he absorbed this thought.

And Fiona's history—her family not caring for her the way they should have? *She* was perfect…

'Hurry, Brent. We have to make sure Alex is okay.' Fiona climbed into the utility truck beside him and tossed her painting into the back with scant concern for its care.

He hadn't anticipated her company. Hadn't taken the time to think about it at all. Now, he turned to her while his heart seemed to soften at the expression of concern on her face. And his fears for Alex came back full force, driving, for now, everything else out. 'You don't have to—'

'Yes. I do.' Fiona interrupted her boss without any compunction whatsoever. She had to be here with Brent, to be at his side while he located his brother. That was all there was to it. She couldn't change what she needed. She wasn't about to be denied this, either. So he could just get over that idea! 'Drive, Brent.'

Brent drove, his hands gripped around the steering wheel.

There was such love for Alex in Brent's focus, and Fiona couldn't help but be moved by that.

Any time Brent was focused intently it seemed to come back to things that touched his emotions. Her boss might not want to admit that, but its truth spoke for itself. He *was* a man capable of deep feeling. This morning, for reasons she wasn't sure she should try to define, Fiona needed to know that.

'Alex caused me a few grey hairs when I first got him out of the orphanage. The moment he turned sixteen, he came to me. To me and Linc, but I was the eldest, and a bit better set up at that stage.' His mouth turned up in wry remembrance. 'Alex and his bags of attitude. He settled down, though. I've got used to things being easier the last few years. Financial security for all of us. Safety…'

Both those things would have been hugely important for three men who'd had little control over their destinies for many years. And they'd no doubt used their earliest resources to buy a home they could all share, so they could stick close.

Yes, they were a true example of how family should be and for Brent, at least, he'd built that new world over the top of some very unhappy ashes.

Fiona thought of her own upbringing. 'I wish I could say my family were like you and Linc and Alex, but they're not.'

Her family did lack what should be there for her automatically, simply because she was theirs. But couldn't it be there, simply hidden away? Maybe they needed a little more encouragement to come to realise she needed them to love her simply for herself? Maybe she just hadn't tried hard enough, reached out to them enough? If she poured out her love to them, surely they would respond?

Brent parked the truck and they climbed out.

They'd had to park some distance back. He wrapped his fingers around her upper arm and guided her at a half jog past bystanders, through the crowd of inevitable onlookers.

As they drew closer, he sucked in one long, deep breath and blew it out. 'It's not his building that's on fire.'

He pulled his mobile phone from his pocket then and speed dialled it again as they hustled along. 'Still no answer.'

They reached the cordoned-off area in time to see several soot-smeared fire personnel emerge from the burning building. It was a terrifying sight. Men in full hazard gear, two of them with warehouse workers in their arms. Flames crackling, the roaring sound of a burning blaze as it consumed a path of destruction.

'There he is. Thank God. He could have been killed.' Brent uttered the words as he strode forward. 'This isn't the same as him listening for the rush of wind that comes before a train roars around a blind corner in a tunnel, giving you just seconds of warning to get out of the way. There's no predicting fire.'

He grabbed Fiona's hand and plunged them beneath the cordon.

'Alex did that?' she asked, but, from Brent's 'grey hairs' comment, she already knew the answer was yes.

Someone called for them to stay back, that they weren't allowed in.

If Brent heard, he ignored it. His focus was on his brother.

Alex had just finished giving water to a woman prone on the ground. His suit, face and hair were covered in soot. He laid the woman's head gently back down, spoke a few words with her and, when an ambulance officer approached, stepped back.

'You know most people undergo training before they start rushing into burning buildings.' Brent's words were low, gentle and raw at once, though Fiona could see he was working very hard to hide the latter emotion.

Even so, he clasped Alex into a bear hug for a long moment before he held him at arm's length and searched his brother's eyes, face. 'You're not injured? How did you end up in there?'

'Should have figured you'd find me before I had a chance to clean up.' Alex gave a lopsided grin. 'At least you're not hauling me away from trains and tunnels—' He broke off, glanced sheepishly at Fiona.

'I just mentioned that to Fiona, actually.' Brent shook his head, but his eyes were warm as they searched Alex's face again.

Certain aspects of Alex's paintings, colour choices, style came to Fiona's mind—came together with those comments about trains and tunnels. Graffiti art… 'I think you gave your big brother some tough moments while you were exploring your…er…talents, Alex.'

'Something like that.' He ducked his head with a self-conscious cough that quickly turned into the real thing.

Brent gave the younger man's shoulders one firm shake. 'Have you been checked out by the medical staff?'

'Yes, and they said I have to take today off work, which is stupid. It's just a cough. All I need is a shower and change of clothes before I go back to it.' He paused and gestured towards the building. 'They have everyone out now, at least. They got the last two just as you arrived.'

'And now you need rest and…' Brent hesitated and his brows came down. 'Rosa. You need Rosa. She'll know what to do to look after you.'

A short debate followed about how much Alex did or didn't need to be off work or babysat. That took them all the way to Brent's truck, where Fiona climbed into the back so the brothers could be together in the front.

Brent made the call, so whatever Alex wanted was apparently, at this point, irrelevant.

Fiona hid a smile.

She looked at the backs of those two heads; saw the set of Brent's shoulders and the way his head ticked to the right as he glanced once again at Alex, as though to reassure himself the youngest MacKay really was okay.

And emotion welled up out of nowhere and flooded through her. Emotion for this man who had made a family out of nothing, and made it work better than her 'real' one ever had. She didn't have a 'work only' attitude to Brent. Somewhere along the line that had changed, despite her belief that she couldn't allow that to happen.

And maybe she needed to at least admit that fact to herself, even if doing so couldn't change anything between them.

'Tell me how the fire started.' Brent dropped the topic of Alex's health as he headed for their warehouse home. 'And how you ended up in the middle of things like that. I'd like you to say you weren't even in the building but, from the look of you, I'd say multiple trips without any safety equipment or protective gear is more likely.'

'Half a dozen trips. I was careful.' Alex explained he'd spotted the start of the fire from his own office window, called it in and headed straight there.

And Brent listened and nodded and was clearly trying very hard not to let his head explode over all the things that could have happened to his brother and, thankfully, hadn't.

He drew the truck to a stop inside the warehouse's garage area and turned to Alex once again. 'I understand you couldn't have done anything differently. You no doubt saved lives today. How can I chide you for that? I'm just glad you're okay, that's all.'

As they all got out of the truck, Brent drew out his mobile phone and hit a speed number. 'Linc. Yeah. I've got him. He's got a chest full of smoke fumes and a couple of singed patches, but he's okay. Meet us at home, okay?' He ended the call.

Fiona hesitated as the two brothers headed for the staircase. 'I can head to work now, put in a belated showing for at least one of us since we haven't been in yet. I don't want to intrude on your family time—'

'Stay.' Alex uttered the single word while his gaze shifted from her to Brent and back again. There was something in his expression—a question and perhaps even hope—that Fiona didn't understand.

Brent's mouth tightened and he headed for the stairs. To Alex he said, 'Fiona and I were *working* on a *landscaping outline* here earlier this morning, so neither of us has been into the office yet.' He turned to Fiona and added, 'We might as well go at the same time when we do go.'

'At least my car's in all day parking.' Even if it hadn't been, Fiona would have forgotten about it one way and another this morning!

The change in Alex's expression was subtle.

The statement in Brent's was a little less subtle.

Fiona caught on at last and her face heated as she realised what their exchange had been all about. Alex had thought she and Brent had spent the night together and, from his expression earlier, he'd hoped that might have been the case.

Why?

Well, bachelors being bachelors, maybe she was better off not knowing why!

They went straight to Alex's home. He tipped out

his smashed mobile phone from his trouser pocket. That explained the lack of communication earlier.

'Did you get cut when that happened?' Some deep ingrained mothering instinct rose up in Fiona as she waited for Alex's answer. She wanted to insist he go check on that right this moment.

Brent turned his head when Fiona asked this question and sharp eyes examined Alex once again.

Alex shrugged his shoulders. 'I'll check it when I clean up. Shame about the phone, though. I really liked that one.'

The door pushed open and Linc stepped through. He strode straight to the living room where they stood. 'Reminds me of the time we got locked into the orphanage while that fire raged next door. I thought we were all going to burn, shut in there, before they decided it was "safe" to let us out.'

As he talked, he examined his brother through shrewd eyes. 'You're all right, then?'

'I want him through the shower, cleaned up to get the smoke off him.' Brent uttered the words before Alex could respond for himself. 'When she gets here, Rosa can go in there and check—'

'No. Rosa can *not* go in there and check. Anything,' Alex added, and sighed as the door pushed open yet again and a middle-aged woman bustled through it, shaking her head all the way. 'And yes, Linc,' Alex added, 'I'm all right.'

'Alex, Alex. You look a mess.' Rose made a tutting sound. 'Get those clothes off and take a shower!' She had a large carrier bag in one hand and headed for the kitchen with it while the men all sort of shuffled their feet and stood there. 'Well? Get going, Alex. I want you back out here by the time I've heated the chicken soup.'

Fiona stifled a smile in her chin, but Brent caught the edge of it as she turned her head.

'Rosa lives close to here,' he said, as though that explained everything. And then he fell silent.

Alex dutifully disappeared to shower. Linc filled the silence with his questions. What had happened? Was Alex truly okay? Had he honestly had appropriate medical attention?

When the youngest brother reappeared, Fiona couldn't help her words, either. 'Were you cut?'

'No cuts, just some bruises and, like Brent said, some singed bits. My hair, mostly.' He gave a weary, cheeky grin. 'I hate that. I have to look good for the girls, you know.'

Fiona laughed.

Rosa got a glint in her eyes and said she'd take care of Alex's hair problem. She fussed until Alex sat on the couch, and then put a bowl of fragrant soup into his hands with the promise that she would wield a pair of scissors on his behalf shortly.

The woman was a treasure. Fiona could understand why all three men valued their 'cleaner', who obviously had a wonderful mother's heart towards all of them.

'I'll be fine now.' Alex's embarrassment at being fussed over was clear on his face. 'Really. You should all go back to work, and Rosa, you don't have to stay. I might…I'll have a sleep or something.'

Somehow, Fiona doubted that, but she understood from his expectant expression that he hoped they would all clear out of there now.

'I will stay all afternoon.' Rosa indicated her cavernous bag again. 'I brought my knitting. I'll call you at the office, Brent, if anything worries me.'

'Right. Thank you. It's been a few years since we did this, hasn't it, Rosa?' Brent smiled and gripped his youngest brother on the shoulder. 'Just put up with being fussed on, okay? At least Rosa knows how to do that properly.'

'Yes, do take care, Alex.' Fiona turned with Brent.

As she turned away, Linc took his brother in his arms and dropped a kiss on the top of his head, as though he were a small boy, and as quickly pushed him away again.

It hurt, somehow, observing the love they all

shared, the depth of it. The guardedness that went with it, and the reasons for that guardedness…

Because they'd been institutionalised. Because they'd been abandoned by the ones who should have loved them.

Brent had more to contend with than being autistic. His father's rejection, a whole history of things. *Could* he ever get past it all?

Did she want him to reach for that with her?

No. Of course not…

Because wanting that would be stupid, Fiona!

Anyway, Brent and his brothers treated Rosa's involvement in their lives as something exceptional and, in truth, what little involvement might they have had with women overall in any caring capacity over the course of their lives?

Could any of them be capable of that kind of love *with* a woman? Be able to learn how to give and receive it?

The thoughts were a little too deep for comfort—

And Brent hasn't given any indication that he is emotionally invested in you at all!

Nor was she invested in him that way. After all, it wasn't as though she loved Brent or anything. She liked him. She was aware of him as a man. Those were enough complications, thanks very much, and they'd drawn their lines anyway, so that was that.

With last words of advice to the man who really did not want to be an invalid but looked as though he needed to take care of himself for at least the remainder of the day, they all left.

CHAPTER NINE

'ALEX recovered without any difficulties, which is wonderful. He was very brave to go in to help all those people inside the building.' Fiona was in a coffee shop in the city with her mother and sisters. It was after working hours, Friday, a regular gathering for the women in her family, though it was a long time since she'd been invited along.

This time she'd invited herself and in a gap in the conversation had started to explain about her new job, her progress now she'd been there a while, how much she was enjoying the work. That had led to an account of Alex's involvement in the warehouse fire, but she'd lost them some time ago, really. The disinterest was on all their faces, and the joy went out of the telling for Fiona.

She had tried so hard during this gathering to make all the right connections, to make it clear how much she loved Mum and Kristine and Judy.

And she had hoped to get something back other than their usual *Who is this alien among us?* response, but she hadn't.

Brent had told her he had work over this way for this afternoon. Fiona had made the decision to try one last time to connect with her family, if Brent didn't mind her taking that final hour out of her working day.

He hadn't minded, of course.

Well, her efforts had been a waste of time so far. Fiona fell silent.

'I heard your old job at the Credit Union might be coming vacant again.' Her mother took a sip of her latte and examined Fiona over the rim of the cup with an expectant expression that was so devoid of any grain of true understanding of her daughter that Fiona stiffened all over before she could stop herself.

'I hope they find someone good to fill the vacancy.' She squeezed the words out somehow. Maybe it wasn't fair of her to feel that her mum and the others hadn't paid enough attention while she'd talked about her job, her employer and his family.

The difference being—your mother is trying to force you back into a mould more to her liking than the one that actually fits you.

Brent would be drumming his fingers if he

were here. Fiona wasn't sure how she knew that, she just did.

Mum looked at her watch and gathered her handbag into her lap. It was a signal that she intended to leave, and Fiona sighed. She'd be standing outside waiting for Brent for a good ten minutes if they left now.

'Before you go, Mum, I brought you a birthday gift.' Fiona reached for the wrapped painting beside her chair and placed it in her mother's hands. She'd put her heart into the painting for her mother. A landscape of soft restful colours that would match the decor in her mother's living room. 'I know your birthday isn't until next week, but I wanted you to be able to hang it on the day—'

'You are somewhat early.' Her mother peeled back an edge of the wrapping. She glanced at the corner of painting revealed—less than a ten centimetre area—and covered it over again. 'Oh, it's one of your pictures. I don't know what I'll do with it…'

Hurt washed through Fiona. The urge to pull the painting out of the wrapping, explain it, point out its meaning and tell Mum the time and effort that had gone into it was strong. But she couldn't *make* her mother appreciate something like that.

Her efforts weren't ever going to be good

enough, were they? Because they *were* different, and no one in her family wanted *different*. Fiona had tried to ignore and gloss over that fact for a very long time. How much more had Brent been made to deal with these feelings over his father? How could Fiona hope Brent would ever reach out for more when he had that hurt to contend with?

And, yes, a part of her *had* apparently secretly longed for that kind of connection with her boss…

Fiona forced a smile and stood as they all stood. She dutifully paid for her lunch at the register with them, and watched them hustle off in their different directions the moment they emerged onto the city street.

Her chest hurt. Right down inside where she'd been trying so hard for so long to ignore the fact that her family weren't exactly warm people when it came down to it. Well, they weren't. Not to her and, in reality, not to each other, either. It was just that they all felt perfectly secure in that emotionally stunted environment, while Fiona felt *in*secure and left out. At least she could now admit that fact to herself.

'Fiona?' Brent's hand closed over the ball of her shoulder and his head bent to hers. 'I'm early. I thought I'd have to wait for you.'

'I didn't see you there.' She hoped he hadn't seen too much inside her in those unguarded moments just now. She didn't want to be caught feeling sorry for herself. She didn't know how to address what had just happened and where it put her in terms of how she felt about him either. 'You finished your business?'

'Yes. It didn't take as long as I'd estimated. I've been window-gazing since then.'

Fiona tipped up her chin and pasted a smile to her lips. 'Well, thank you for waiting for me. I'm ready to go now. Thanks for bringing me over with you so I could do this.'

'It was no trouble.' His voice was deep. Too deep. The kind of deep that said he sensed there was something amiss in her and that he cared about it.

That one grain of caring, not even openly expressed, went straight to that same hurting place inside her, and Fiona felt caught off guard all over again. She turned her head so he wouldn't see the emotion in her eyes. Instead, she started to walk blindly back towards his truck.

They walked the half block in silence and she used the time to try to pull herself together. She thought she'd done all right, too, until Brent spoke.

'So are you going to tell me, or do I guess?' They'd climbed into the truck, but Brent hadn't started the engine. He rested his hand on the steering wheel and searched her face and just... waited.

'Mum took a corner of the wrapper off the painting, glanced at it, covered it back up and made it clear that a more practical gift might have been good.' What was the point of hiding the facts from him? He'd already worked out something was wrong anyway. 'She also wasn't impressed that I pre-empted the actual date of her birthday by a week. Nothing I do "fits" with my family, I'm afraid. I'm too different from them and they can't accept that about me.'

'It was a good painting and it had your heart in it, and early birthday gifts are nice.' Brent's fingers drummed on the steering wheel and his head twitched once, twice before his mouth tightened and he said, 'Your mother should have liked it. She just should have—'

'Like your father liked and accepted all of you?' Fiona glanced towards the street at the small throng of people queuing to enter a nearby restaurant dance club. 'My family are all practical and they have a hard time relating to me because I'm...not, in a lot of ways. My choice of gift didn't appeal. I should have anticipated that fact and chosen something different. Next time, I will.'

She drew a tight breath. 'But, you know, I learnt a lesson just now. There are limits in my family. I have to accept that. It'll be easier for me in the future if I do.'

'That's not a lesson someone like you should ever have to learn.' His mouth was tight, angry and protective for her sake. 'You're soft, kind. You deserve for them to love you like they should!'

'Yet Charles's treatment of you has put you in the same place, only much more so. It's impacted hugely on core parts of your life, your outlook, what you'll—' She'd been going to say *reach for* but stopped herself.

Brent's expression was a combination of surprise, discomfort, comprehension and a certain kind of need that made her want to hold him for ever.

She wanted to bury herself in his touch and hold him and forget all of the world for a while. Because those feelings were intense and based in emotions she felt towards him that were far from safe and that *he* had denied *her* from himself, she did her best to let the topic go. 'Well, it doesn't matter. We should go.'

Brent hesitated before he gestured towards the club in front of them. 'Actually, do you feel like a meal? We're a fair way from home, and Linc's

been to that club. He said the seafood is good.
Fresh as an ocean breeze.'

If there had been even a hint of pity in his expression now or earlier she would have turned him down.

But there was only the desire to prolong their time together, even if he did feel uncomfortable about the need to do that.

And Fiona felt just restless enough to consider his offer, even if it might not be a smart thing for her to do. At least *he* wanted her company!

'Are *you* a seafood fan?'

'Oh, yes.' He nodded. 'Crab, lobster, prawns, mussels, you name it.'

'Then, yes. Dinner would be nice. Just because…we are quite a way from our homes and it'll be late when we get back.' They could spend time together and, no matter how guarded he was, he would never be *cold* like her family. And right now Fiona did long for warmth…

'Then we're agreed.' Brent felt the corner of his mouth kick up as he spoke the words. He was pleased, whether he should be or not.

But he wanted this time with Fiona. Just to be there for her, to be beside her while she adapted to this next step in the road when it came to dealing with her family. Brent could do that for her.

And for yourself? Have you adapted to

Charles's rejection? Or have you just been avoiding it all this time?

Fiona bit her lip as though she wondered if her response had been too enthusiastic. But she'd said yes. Brent wasn't letting her off now.

So what if they ate a meal together? Tonight she needed company. He could be that for her. Why not?

'We're still in our work clothes,' Fiona pointed out, but it didn't matter.

Brent wore tan trousers and a navy shirt, and Fiona was in one of those silky, swirly skirts of hers and a pink blouse that hugged her curves. She looked—

'I guess we'd do, wouldn't we?' Her eyes shone with the beginning of anticipation. 'Unless you'll need a tie to get in…'

'I most likely will.' He reached over her and popped the storage compartment and drew out a navy tie, held it aloft. 'Emergency supplies. It's Linc's. He's always got his eye out—' He broke off and cleared his throat. 'He sometimes borrows the truck.'

He wasn't sure, but he thought Fiona hid a smile before she reached for the tie and gestured for him to lean forward. 'I'll do this for you, if you like.'

Brent liked.

The feel of her fingers against his neck as she

tied the tie and settled it into place, patted it with
an expression of satisfaction and an edge of consciousness of him.

Yes. He liked that, and he liked that she'd done
it without thinking about it, let herself have the
moment because that was part of what was inside
her, a spontaneity and ability to reach for what she
truly wanted.

*You shouldn't be happy if you think she really,
truly wants you, MacKay. You should be worried
about that and backing off.*

Brent's brows drew down. He threw his door
open and got out. This die was cast. They were
going in. He didn't want to psychoanalyse it *or*
overrate it. He just wanted to do it.

Minutes later, they'd entered the club and been
shown to a dining table near the edge of the dance
floor. The floor was empty, but Brent could
imagine what it would be like later with people
dancing. He could picture Fiona there, could
imagine every movement, every motion as she
gave herself to the beat.

'Seafood for two? There's a few different ones.'
Fiona turned the menu to show him.

They bent their heads over the list until a waitress
came along with her pad and a stub of pencil and
her grey apron tied tight over fitted black jeans.

'This one.' Brent pointed to their selection,

adding a distracted, 'Thanks,' as he turned his attention back to his—to Fiona. She wasn't his date.

No? Then what was dinner and dancing if not a date? And since when had he suddenly started to assume there'd be dancing for them?

A small slice of warning actually got through to him in the moment he asked himself that question. His body tightened in reaction to the corresponding tension that formed inside him.

But the reaction settled down a moment later, and he glanced up and smiled at Fiona. She seemed happier. That was the main thing, wasn't it?

Brent's gaze locked with hers and a silent communication passed between them that made Fiona's skin tingle and her breath catch in her throat. She had so many conflicting emotions right now. Disappointment over her family, thoughts about Brent's situation, happiness for being in his company, warning bells because of that same happiness.

He'd drawn back the last time. That night when he'd kissed her. He hadn't wanted…

And if he wanted now? Would she also want? The emotional risk of letting herself care about him when she wasn't certain he truly could feel the same? If he was attracted to her on some level, but in other ways wasn't, did she want to have to deal with that?

As though there's a choice, Fiona? As though you can decide whether you want to have feelings for someone or not.

That system had worked for her until now. She'd thought she was safe. She *was* safe. This was just tonight, a one-off thing. He'd asked her because he empathised over her mother's behaviour, and it was dinner time, and they still had travel ahead of them. There was nothing remotely romantic about any of that.

And, yes, Fiona might like to speak with him about his own situation, try to get somewhere with that, because she was getting more and more convinced that he hadn't addressed it. Not truly.

'You love music, don't you? It's deep down inside you.' Brent's words broke through her reverie.

She realised she'd been swaying in her seat, and smiled and gave a slight shrug. 'I do love music. All kinds from all eras.'

His gaze narrowed as he absorbed this information. Then their meal arrived and Fiona laughed at the sheer size of it, and he gave a wry grin.

'Don't say we'll never get through it. You haven't seen the amount of food I can put away.' His fingers toyed with the lobster-cracking tool at the edge of the tray. 'I don't think you noticed there wasn't a shred of food left by the time we left the house in the mountains after our hiking and painting trip.'

Fiona hadn't noticed. 'You must have eaten some of it during the night…'

'Yes. I'm a three a.m. grazer, I'm afraid.' He popped a Tasmanian scallop into his mouth. 'I get hungry a lot.'

'And eat people's chocolate stash.' The teasing words shot from her mouth and she bit her lip. 'I didn't mind, and I wouldn't have even noticed, except you bought some extras for me…'

His gaze locked on hers. 'I didn't realise what I'd done until the pile of empty wrappers impinged enough for me to notice them.'

'You ate them while you explored my graphics program?' She sipped her wine and wondered if he realised the significance of him discussing the impact of his condition with her this way. 'I should have walked you through the program when I first started there.'

'I enjoyed looking, anyway.' Brent did eat a lot of the food, and they talked while they shared the meal. It felt…good, and she relaxed and stopped wondering about what he might be thinking or not thinking, and just let herself enjoy the moment for whatever it was.

'Come and dance.' He got to his feet, held out

his hand for hers and, when she placed her fingers against his, wrapped her up in the strength of long fingers and led her onto the floor.

Her senses were consumed in that touch, in the way they matched each other in height as they made their way to a space on the floor.

Brent held her hands and they…danced. And, after a while, he rested both hands on her hips and stood almost still as she swayed in his hold with her hands on shoulders that flexed beneath her touch.

Fiona closed her eyes and let one hand slide until it rested over his heart. And she gave herself to the music and his heartbeat.

Only for a moment. That couldn't hurt…

CHAPTER TEN

BRENT'S hands flexed against Fiona's hips and he watched her dance with her eyes closed and all her enjoyment clear to see on her softened features.

She was so beautiful, and he…wanted her so much. He battled his way through some physical twitches that built in his body and lodged in his shoulders, and eventually got those under control and was able to enjoy her touch on him, the sight of her.

Her hair smelled of peaches and fell loose about her cheeks and neck in a glossy curtain. He bent his head just enough to inhale the scent of it and breathe it deep into his lungs. He liked her at the end of the day this way, with her lipstick long gone and a wrinkle or two in her blouse. He liked her dancing for him, and he liked her dancing *with* him.

Somewhere along the line, this evening had progressed away from his core plan and he had to admit he was responsible for that.

He might have stood and casually asked her to dance, but there'd been nothing casual in his need to hold her. He might have wanted to comfort her after her episode with her mother, but he hadn't said a word about that since they'd come here.

When Fiona's hand brushed his thigh as she moved, Brent drew her into the lee of his body. Not touching, not really. Just her hands against his heart and his shoulder, and his hands on her hips and a lot of…closeness.

But they were touching. He felt every movement she made, every sensual twist and sway through those points where their bodies did connect. Her eyes sparkled as she lifted her gaze to his. The rest of the patrons faded from his notice and his focus homed absolutely on the woman dancing with him.

'I like the way you dance.' Fiona spoke the words against his ear. Her breasts brushed his chest and Brent drew a breath and his arms somehow got all the way around her and held her close until they were both swaying to the music and he felt…as though he held home in his arms, even though he didn't know what home was, except for Linc and Alex and survival.

'I like the way you dance better.' His lips brushed her ear, lingered long enough to explore the feel of the soft, shell shape in a butterfly kiss.

Such a fine line. So easy to step over it because it felt so right.

The sigh of her breath brushed his cheek. That whisper was all about her pleasure in his touch, in what they were doing.

He wondered briefly how long it would be before he lost this calm feeling and had to work to keep his movements controlled again. For now he just…was in this moment with her.

It seemed right to hold her so their bodies brushed chest to chest and thigh to thigh as they swayed to the music. So he did. He wanted to close his eyes and feel her movements and just absorb them, so he let himself.

Somewhere between wanting to take her mind off her mother's hurtful behaviour and now, Brent had dropped his guard, had done it thoroughly, even if as quietly as a whisper.

The scariest part was that he couldn't find the concern over that which he should be able to find.

They danced, and Brent never did dance more than swaying his body while she did most of the work, but, oh, it was the best experience of Fiona's life. Because he danced with *her,* with his gaze fixed on her and never looking anywhere else. He danced with all of his focus, just for her.

It was probably inevitable that he held her

closer, that she moved closer. That the songs went from slow to fast and back again without them changing their dancing at all until they were heart-beat to heartbeat with each other and finally, finally he pressed his cheek to her cheek and his hands stroked up her arms and over her shoulders to the dip between her shoulder blades and down to the dip of her waist.

The hurt of her mother's actions, of her own failure yet again to get what she needed from her family, receded to the background as Fiona lost herself in Brent's attention.

Doubts still hovered. They did. Because Brent's acceptance of her wasn't all-seeing, all-knowing and all-encompassing, either. He accepted her artistic side. Understandable, given he shared similar tendencies.

She liked to think he liked her as a person, overall. But he also held back from her. And seemed uncertain of whether he wanted to accept the attraction he felt towards her or not.

For now he was accepting it, and she was letting herself *hope* probably more than she should that he would continue to accept it. But she hoped anyway.

Fiona wound her arms more tightly around his neck. They didn't talk. They didn't say anything at all. Eventually their gazes simply locked and their dancing stilled and he clasped her hand in his and led her off the dance floor while her heart started a slow, deep rhythm in her chest and she couldn't catch her breath any more and could only walk with him into the night, to his truck, and get in.

He reached for her hand once they were on the road. Tucked it against his thigh and held it there.

'I set out to talk to you about your family—'

'Won't you talk to me about Charles—?'

He turned the truck into her apartment complex's car park and they both fell silent. The need to talk warred with other more instinctive needs. Fiona didn't know where to go with either instinct so she fell back on good manners.

'Thank you…thank you for a lovely evening.' Her fingers fumbled as she opened the truck door and climbed out.

Brent had taken advantage of an empty space towards the end of the courtyard parking. It was silent, shadowed, isolated.

He came to her side of the truck, pushed her passenger door closed behind her after she alighted.

'What are we doing, Fiona?' Did he open his arms?

Or did she step into them of her own accord? Did it even matter? Either way, it was inevitable really that she would melt into him.

'I don't know what we're doing.' She looked into his eyes as she said it. 'You hold back because Charles rejected you. You give him power over you through that. It's not only about your autism. That side of you—it's just part of you. It's…a beautiful part of you.' Everything she wanted from him came out in those words—things she knew within herself and things she only knew instinctively.

Brent shook his head. 'The beauty is within *you,* within your generosity and your capacity to see the best in people.' Maybe Brent didn't want to talk about the rest. Maybe he reacted purely on an instinctive level to what she said to him.

Because his arms locked around her and his lips parted on a breath of desire and then there was no space between them, only his mouth on hers, taking and giving, offering and accepting as they both yielded.

Fiona acknowledged her need and held on. Arms around his neck. Body pressed close. Lips soft beneath his, absorbing and responding as his hands traced up and down her back, over the curve of her lower spine, and lower still. It was a kiss of tenderness and pleasure and sweetness, and she took it down into herself and held it there.

It changed so gradually. She was deep into that change before she even realised. Gentle kisses had become demanding, a play of tongues and desire that still somehow managed to coil around her emotions.

The strength of his body against her softness played through her senses and her heart whispered to be careful. Be so very careful because her soul could enter into this and what would she do if that happened?

'I want you closer. Closer.' Brent whispered the words and covered her mouth again, and his arms closed tight and strong about her and she felt safe with him. Safe and hungry and scared and desperate all at once.

She needed to be even closer, not only physically but to all that was within him. That truth was confirmed in each shaken breath she took. She'd sought such closeness from the start as she'd searched for his emotions in his work. Maybe even then something inside her had known she would come to care for him this way.

It was rumoured he was eccentric. Instead, he was brilliant, talented, unique, charming and intense and sweet and strong.

'Fiona. If I keep going with this I won't be able... I can't... I don't know...' He buried his face in her hair and his breath heaved in and out and his shoulders locked as he fought himself, fought what he wanted from her and maybe fought other reactions and responses in his physical make-up as well. 'I told myself this was safe. We're in a car park, for God's sake.'

It impinged on her slowly that they were. Right out here in the car park, which, while admittedly quiet right now, couldn't be guaranteed to stay that way.

And she had forgotten that, had lost all sense of time and place. Had immersed herself so fully in the moment and in his arms that she hadn't given a thought to their surroundings.

She should step away from him. Any moment now she would gather the strength to do that. Because…

Because they needed to talk. Didn't they?

Brent stroked his hands up the length of her spine and his fingers found their way into her hair and whatever reasons there might have been disappeared on the whisper of her breath.

Her mouth softened and her hands bracketed his face and if he had indicated in any way that she wasn't welcome…

A sound rose in the back of Brent's throat as his mouth covered Fiona's once again. She gave herself to the kiss in the same way she did everything—with generosity and openness. When he dipped his tongue into the cavern of her mouth, hers followed him home again, stroked, tangled.

He crushed her close and loved the way her

body fitted his so perfectly. He couldn't get the thought out of his mind of her legs wrapped around him.

How they ended up outside her apartment he couldn't have said, but she had her bag in her hand and he vaguely remembered that ending up on the bonnet of his truck when he'd first taken her mouth out there.

Now she fumbled in the bag for her key while they snatched kisses, and a moment later they were inside her home.

A lamp burned on a corner table in the living room. That circle of muted light was the only thing that even half registered as he wrapped his arms around her and pressed his lips to hers.

Slow down. You have to slow this down.

But it was a train on a downward slope. Gaining pace and out of control.

How could he need this so much? Brent sought the answer in the warm recesses of her mouth, in the press of her lips against his, in the touch of her fingers where they stroked his arms, his chest.

His tie drifted from her fingers onto the edge of the sofa and slipped to the floor. Then *they* were on that sofa, arms around each other, mouths melding together.

He cupped her breasts through the cloth of her blouse, absorbed the softness and the shape of her...

Brent caught one glimpse of warm welcome in her eyes and wondered what she saw in him, and then he couldn't think any more, only experience and feel and need, with his senses and with pieces of himself that he'd worked so hard to protect from the world for so long.

Pieces that had taken the pain of Charles's rejection and buried it so deep that even Brent himself hadn't realised where he'd gone with all of that.

That one thought pushed through until it hit the surface of his mind and the warnings he'd tried to give himself earlier finally took hold. Brent's shoulders tightened as he faced just how much he was letting her in right now—he could not do that.

So totally couldn't do that. Tension crisscrossed his chest and rippled through his muscles and settled in his neck. Tension that he couldn't control. He broke away from her and his head twitched before he got to his feet in a movement that felt uncoordinated, uneven and aching.

He'd wanted to make love to her. It would have ended in that. The truth was in what they'd done, in the blur of blue eyes softened and confused and struggling to comprehend the loss of his touch as she, too, slowly rose from the sofa.

Everything in him ached to take her back, to

hold her against his heart because there was a tension and lost feeling there that only doing that would ease, but Fiona couldn't be his saviour. He had to be that for himself, survive by himself, protect himself the way he always had done. Protect that part of him that Charles MacKay had done his best to crush so many years ago.

Brent had to do all that. Didn't he?

'I'm sorry, Fiona.' God. His voice was raw gravel. 'This…got out of control. I told you I wouldn't go here again. I meant that. For your sake—'

'Yes. You told me. Foolishly, I thought—' She broke off. Drew a breath. 'I should have learned the first time.' She took his tie from the floor, folded it, handed it to him and made her way to the door with steps that weren't as smooth or co-ordinated for *her* as they usually were.

She opened that door. Waited with her teeth over her lower lip and all sorts of defences wrapped around her, even as her arms wrapped around her waist.

'I don't know…' What she meant by her words. Why her dismissal of him felt like a dismissal of herself.

In this moment Brent knew nothing—how did he deal with that?

He hesitated and faced her. 'Fiona—'

'It's all right. You need to go. We both need for you to do that. This…' She hesitated. 'You thought you wanted me, but the reality… And I… It would be too much. I'm not ready.'

To deal with all of him? If not with the signs of his autism, with the emotional limits he carried that went far deeper than dealing with them?

How could he expect her to be ready to deal with such obstacles when he didn't know how to deal with them himself?

Brent crushed the tie in his hand and let his tension focus on crushing the fabric over and over.

And he searched her eyes one last time before he walked away.

CHAPTER ELEVEN

THEY worked. Interacted for the good of the company. Made progress on one project after another. Melded their ideas and their strengths and all they had to bring, combined, to the table.

Winter weather closed in. Chill winds and grey skies and morning rain. Fiona dressed warmly and worked as the consummate professional and told herself she wasn't unhappy, didn't feel unfulfilled, didn't need anything from Brent beyond their relationship as employer and employee.

And she decided she simply was best off just being 'everybody's friend', sticking to her known ground and not stepping beyond it where she couldn't feel safe.

She was good at being a friend. She did great pet minding and pot plant watering and advice to the lovelorn.

At that last thought, Fiona's mouth pulled tight. Some advisor. She certainly couldn't sort out her own issues. They were all still shuffling around in her head over and over.

As for her relationship with her family, she'd made her decisions about that. It would always hurt that they didn't accept her and love her for herself, but she could learn to be a step back from that hurt. She could protect herself.

If she needed to do that, how could she expect Brent to do anything other than protect himself in his life as much as he felt was necessary?

She rapped on the door of Brent's home inside the warehouse and forced herself to draw some deep even breaths as she waited for him to answer.

He wasn't expecting her but she couldn't do anything about that. The manila folder clenched in the fist of her left hand was proof of that. He'd left it in her car when they'd used it yesterday to attend an initial client discussion on site.

The file the client had given them held photos that covered the history of the area and its land-scaping back over a hundred years, and Brent had told her he planned to work on that project, from home, all day today.

So…he needed the file.

And she was fine about delivering it.

Hand it over. Wish him a good day. Leave.

It wasn't her fault he hadn't answered his phone. At least she'd managed to slip in as Alex was going out. As though in response to her first thought, Fiona's phone beeped out a message and she drew it out of the bag slung over her shoulder.

Brent might not have been at home, of course, but he'd said he would be and maybe he had his mobile turned off and had let the home phone battery go flat. His receptionist was always at him to hang his cordless phone at work back on its cradle, not leave it lying on his desk.

Fiona thought she heard the click of a door catch somewhere inside Brent's home and turned her attention quickly to reading her phone message. It was from her mother.

I've spoken to the boss of your old job and she's prepared to take you back. Consider it, dear. Haven't you had enough of playing at this other career? You know it won't get you anywhere.

Anywhere except in love with Brent.
Oh, God.
Of all the thoughts to surface. Not, *It would get her where she wanted to be in her career path.* Not, *It was what she wanted to do.*
Not even, *I'm sorry, Mum, but this is me and I'm over you not accepting and loving me just as I am.*
All those thoughts were valid and real and true.

None of them even compared to the one thought that filled her so utterly.

She loved Brent.

The knowledge hit her hard and deep. This was the reason she couldn't forget those moments that had come so close to a culmination in lovemaking.

'Fiona. Hi. I thought you must have been Alex and he'd forgotten something again...'

Brent's words trailed off and Fiona lifted her gaze from the message on the phone screen and stared with a brand new, shocking, devastating knowledge pulsing through her.

Brent was bare to the waist. That was what registered first. Steam wafted from the open bathroom door behind him. That registered second. Moisture beaded on his chest and his hair was freshly washed and still damp. He had jeans on with the top snap unfastened. She really shouldn't be looking but she had dreamed of him, of seeing him like this, and her heart was in her throat and her pulse and each breath she took.

Her gaze climbed his chest before it reached his face and looking into his eyes wasn't any better. They burned. A deep, slumberous green that sent hot and cold chills down her spine and fire licking along her nerve-endings, and all she could do was let love and need wash all through her.

'Um... Alex drove away.' Right. And that piece

of information was completely vital, of course. As well as being coherent and oh, so eloquently put. She had to get hold of herself. Had to hide these feelings from him!

'Did you have a message for me?' Brent gestured towards the phone. His jaw was clenched. His gaze swept over her, from the hair in a ponytail high on her head, over the cream T-shirt and chocolate-brown pants. And returned to her face, lingered on her mouth, caught her gaze and locked there as though he couldn't stop himself.

Then why do you have to stop yourself, Brent? She loved him. Was *in love with him*. She wanted the opportunity to express that emotion.

Even if he can't give it back to you? Even if, because of his father's rejection, he will always be emotionally unable to give all of himself?

But Brent wasn't asking for that from her…

'It's not a message for you. Mum said she can get my old job back for me.' She dredged up the answer from the part of her that had remained aware of anything other than how much she desired and wanted and…needed him. His arms around her, his mouth on hers. Her love being given to him.

'You're not taking your old job back.' His words were anger and protectiveness wrapped into one. 'This job, working with me, it's right for you. It's the work you deserve, not some clerical ob designed to turn you into the rest of your family. I don't want you to…' He stopped the words there, but his gaze expressed his thoughts.

Not only that he didn't want her to be hurt by her mother's words and behaviour, but that *he* didn't want to lose contact with her.

Because of the work they shared. She told herself this. It wasn't because he loved her, for goodness' sake.

Even so she told him, 'Don't worry. I signed a contract for the next twelve months with you, and I want even longer, a long-term career path with you, if that's possible.'

I don't want to stop seeing you, Brent. Not now. Not in the future. I have no idea how I could cope with that if it happened.

The discovery that she loved him was too new and raw for her to imagine not seeing him, career path or otherwise. How could she have let herself come to this? Have fallen for him so utterly?

Yet how could she have stopped it? She'd responded to his heart, in his landscaping designs that she'd studied, before they'd even met. When she'd met him face to face, some part of her deep, deep down had known that he would come to mean all of this to her. Otherwise, why would she now feel this utter acceptance, even in the face of all her uncertainties and fears?

But she did have those uncertainties and fears and, because of them, Fiona tried to pull herself together so she could deal with the reason she had come here, and take herself *out of here,* where she would have a chance to gather some defences and figure out how to go forward with these new feelings without revealing them to him.

She shoved the phone away into her bag and held out the folder gripped in her other hand. 'Anyway, that's not why I'm here. You left this in my car. You'll need it. I couldn't get you on either of your phones. Obviously you were in the shower.'

She passed her free hand down her thigh. Nervous gesture. She hadn't done that since she first started working for him.

'Thanks.' His hand closed over the folder. 'If I've made you feel awkward because I kissed you—'

'No. Oh, no.' Their kisses had unlocked things in her. She couldn't do anything about that but she couldn't regret it, either. Regret…just wasn't an option she could even consider.

'Good. That's good.' There was relief in his glance—more than relief—and somehow he was tugging on that folder and she still had her hand clenched around it and the momentum brought her through the door and into his home and he closed them in there while her gaze took in the extremely close view of a great deal of tanned male skin.

It was a very beautiful chest, the skin stretched tight over well-formed musculature, a light dusting of dark hair across it and arrowing down.

Not looking down again. That was a mistake the first time.

Brent seemed to become aware of his half-dressed state, too. He gestured towards the kitchen. 'You can get a coffee, if you like. I'll just…yeah, I'll be back in a minute.'

He disappeared into what must obviously be his bedroom and Fiona stood there with the folder still clutched in her hand because he'd left her with it, hadn't he?

What was she doing? What were *they* doing? Coffee while he threw some more clothes on? Would that help her at all, him covering up?

She walked to the kitchen and laid the folder on the bench and made her way towards his front door on wobbly legs, determined to get that wobbliness back to strength somehow. To leave before she did something that gave away how she felt.

Brent stepped into the hall from his room and she walked straight into his chest. Her arms came up, forearms against that chest, which was now, indeed, covered very discreetly with a button-down navy shirt.

That's right, Fiona. You notice that while you're staring stupidly at him and all your feelings are probably right out there for him to see.

'I don't know how to do this. I'm better in the "friend" role,' she blurted, and his hands made this odd *touch her—don't touch her* motion at his sides for a moment before they closed over her elbows.

He could have pushed her away. Maybe he intended to.

She could have used his touch to lever herself away. Maybe she might have.

But the irises of his eyes darkened to a deep, moss-green and his breath drew in on a sharp inhalation. 'I want—'

'Then take what you want.' The words burst from her because it was what she wanted, too, and couldn't he see that? 'Take what we both want, Brent.'

Her heart spoke for her, whether she could handle the fallout or not.

'God, Fiona. I can't fight this again. I just… can't.'

When his fingers tightened on her elbows, she leaned in to his touch, let it become an embrace, and breathed a sigh of relief and pleasure when he drew her in against his chest and cradled her there, heartbeat to heartbeat as his mouth came down on hers.

She had needed this, and her heart ached at the chance to have this. That ache warned her of all she would invest in loving him this way and of how much it could come to hurt her because, for her, it was love. For him...desire, need, perhaps, but those were all.

Even then, she could not turn back.

And Brent, oh, she hoped and prayed Brent would not turn back.

He gave her lazy kisses first. Long, slow, drugging kisses that reached inside her and let her immerse herself in pleasure.

He stroked his fingers up and down her arms, caught her around her waist and held her gently as his mouth took hers. Tremors passed through his body and for a moment he stilled, forehead to her forehead, as he breathed deeply.

This was his condition, and she stroked his back and murmured how much she enjoyed his touch, and he relaxed and the tension left him and he kissed her again.

And again and again.

He must have done this at other times, with other women. Yet she couldn't let herself think of those times, didn't want to think of her own past experiences, of trying to find a connection, only to discover there was nothing there.

With Brent it was all there. For her, it was, and

she didn't think about what he might feel for her.
Surely he must be in a better place within himself
if he could reach for this with her this way…?

'You know what you want, what you're able to
have.' She murmured the words and his gaze
locked with hers and for a moment doubts bruised
his eyes before they were blinked away.

So it was fine. Wasn't it?

They found their way onto his sofa.

Brent didn't know how that happened, only that
he had his arms full of Fiona and his heart was
hammering and when he drew a breath it was filled
with the scent of her and he wanted to press his nose
to her neck and just inhale the sweetness of her.

He did that, and she shuddered and a soft
yearning sound came from the back of her throat
and she tightened her arms around him and held on.

Just held on while Brent held onto her, too, and
his reasons for holding back disintegrated in the
face of his need for her. Was it necessary for him
to try to reason through that, understand it or define
it? Couldn't this moment be enough in itself?

'I need this with you, Fiona. This once, if you
can allow it.' Just once. If she understood that at
the start and he understood it…

Brent's expression showed his concern for
Fiona, his confusion and uncertainty and, over it
all, his need.

If he'd said he wanted this, wanted but didn't need, Fiona might have made a different choice. 'Then we'll have this, Brent.' It wasn't even a decision for her. It was a beat in her heart that matched the beat in Brent's heart. It was all of her that had to do this, to be with him this way.

If a part of her desired so much more than that, well, she was used to having less than she wanted. Life was like that. She would take this moment and immerse herself in it and live it and give all of herself to it, and that would be fine.

Just fine.

Fiona pushed the element of sadness away and focused her attention on the man in her arms. She'd sought his emotions. Maybe, in these moments, if she were very lucky, she would have them, even if they were only hers to keep for a very little while.

Brent took Fiona into his bedroom. His need outstripped his doubts and concerns. They were still there but, even so, he drew her into his arms beside the bed and looked deep into her eyes and let his touch and his reverence tell her all the things that were locked inside him, that he couldn't say and couldn't own and yet they were there.

They drew clothes from each other and tossed

them on the floor until there was just them and the quietness and the sunlight slanting in through the gap at the edge where the curtains met the window.

His gaze roved her body and his hands followed, and he drew her onto his bed and touched every part of her until she took the foil packet from his bedside table and drew him home.

There was an aching need in the centre of his chest. Brent registered this as his body arched into Fiona's and longing and sensation rushed through him.

His throat hurt and he kissed Fiona blindly, emotions wrapped into it, control…lost with all cognizant thought other than to please her, to make this the best for her that he could. Somehow he crossed the line into instinct. The acceptance in her eyes took him there and he pushed back every other thought and made love to her with everything he had to give.

Not enough, his mind told him, and yet his body and his emotions told a different story.

No. Not his emotions. Brent pushed that possibility out, even as his hands worshipped her soft skin and his eyes gazed into hers, letting her in and taking her into himself in return.

At the last moment, she cried out and his control mechanisms fractured.

His body shook and he kissed her mouth and her eyelids and buried his nose in her neck and inhaled her scent. His arms locked around her, all the way around her shoulders and back and he...held onto her and his fingers stroked her damp skin.

Over and over and over.

She wrapped her arms around him, too, and her hands stroked over him and she made a sound that was pure pleasure. 'I love...your touch.'

And though Brent should assess what had just happened, think about his loss of control from the broadest perspective, think about a lot of things, her gaze was dazed and slumberous and he didn't let himself think about any of those things.

Instead, he made love to her again until they lay on the bed with streams of sunlight filtering onto the wall.

Only then did his actions begin, finally, to impinge. His fingers digging into her back in a kneading motion as he held her. Thumbs stroking across her collarbone repeatedly.

Burying his nose in her neck and inhaling the scent of her skin until his body was filled with it. 'I shouldn't have... I didn't expect... That wasn't what I wanted to see revealed.'

All the idiosyncrasies that went with his condition. All the...insecurities about them that

Charles MacKay's words and actions had left Brent with for all these years.

Maybe she finally thought about that, too, about all the ways this hadn't been normal for him and…never would be.

Because she drew her hand away from his chest and sat up, took the sheet from the base of the bed where they'd kicked it and wrapped it around herself. There were shadows in her eyes as she got to her feet and started to gather clothes off the floor.

Brent also stood, pulled on his jeans and felt now even more vulnerable than he had at the height of loving her, when all his defences had been down.

Fiona pressed her clothing to her chest. 'This… I still have to go to work. I have work…'

She turned and shut herself in his bathroom.

Brent dressed and left the warehouse then. Just got in his utility truck and drove away because he didn't know what to say to her and he didn't want to face his thoughts and he wasn't sure where doing that would take him anyway.

He was still the same person Charles MacKay had rejected and he still didn't have enough to offer a woman and particularly one like Fiona, who deserved so much.

That was all still the case.

Wasn't it?

CHAPTER TWELVE

THEY'D made love. For Fiona it had been the most beautiful experience of her life...until Brent had come to himself enough to regret what they had done.

She loved him. Loved him deep inside herself in a way she knew she would never love again. All her life, she had searched the world around her for the emotion she needed.

Now she saw inside her own heart and knew that this was the one and only deep love she would ever have.

But Brent didn't share those feelings. He'd proved that through all the things he hadn't said at the end of their time together.

He hadn't even waited around to speak with her after she'd got dressed.

And she had to come to terms with that silence somehow and know how to go on.

She didn't want to lose his presence in her life.

Did that make her weak? That she couldn't imagine walking away from him, even if he couldn't love her or feel the things for her that she felt for him?

She'd gone straight from his home to work, and then she'd lost her nerve, made an excuse and gone from work up here into the mountains. She'd needed time to think, and hadn't been able to trust herself to do that in front of the others in their office space.

But eventually she was going to have to go back and face Brent. Somehow. Fiona didn't know how.

Oh, why couldn't he admit how much his past had hurt him? If he would accept that, maybe that could be the start of him being able to accept… her.

You're a fool, Fiona Donner. Making love is one thing. Yes, he seemed to enjoy that and seemed to be over any issues he might have had about your generous body size or anything like that, but he's not in love with you. Don't kid yourself into thinking otherwise. That was a one-off experience for him. No doubt he's totally over it already.

Right. And Fiona needed to be 'over it' as well. And just as soon as she got her emotions sorted out and felt she could face others without revealing them, she would be.

For now, cold stung her cheeks. Damp air filled her lungs and the scent of bush land closed around her. Fiona had the walking trail to herself and was photographing flora for a montage she wanted to use as a backdrop for her computer graphic work on one of Brent's projects.

If she focused her thoughts enough, she would make a success of this trip. It wouldn't be wasted. She wouldn't have to admit it had been as much about escaping having to face Brent as anything else.

Fiona worked on and eventually decided she had done all she could with the photography. The light wasn't as good now and there was a heavy stillness in the air that rather matched her mood.

Wetness formed on her cheek and her mouth tightened. She brushed her fingers over it, but other wetness caught on her eyelashes at the same time and she realised she hadn't given way to the emotion she'd been holding back this last week.

Snow was falling.

Unseasonably early, unexpectedly thick and getting heavier by the moment. White, pure flakes of snow that would obscure the trail she'd taken if it continued.

She had to get back to her car. Fiona packed her photography equipment into her backpack, gave thanks she hadn't tried to bring a tripod with her and began to retrace her steps.

Walking through that flurry of innocent-looking white flakes, Fiona told herself she would be back in the car park safe and sound in no time. And, if anything happened, the office knew her location. She didn't have her mobile with her. It was in the car in her bag. She hadn't wanted to carry any extra weight. Well, that had been a poor choice to make, but there was no point worrying about it now.

A bush parrot appeared briefly out of the flurrying snowfall and disappeared again. And Fiona hurried along and thought of Brent. Even now, she couldn't push the thoughts away.

For a short frame of time she had felt she'd held Brent's attention and focus and maybe even…his heart. That he had given all of himself to her, was trusting her with all of him. She had let her own guards down, all the way down, had believed, foolishly, that he could find as much fulfilment in her as she had found in him.

Obviously, that hadn't been the case and she understood his need to protect himself. She did! Within her family she had felt the same way. Not loved for all of herself, not understood. But the whole world wouldn't be like Brent's father to him. Fiona would never be that way to him.

The snow thickened and Fiona realised she could be in real trouble for other reasons. She had to get out of here before she lost the ability to see the trail. She put her head down and walked as fast as she was able and prayed she wouldn't end up lost in the bush…

'Fiona? Fiona!' Brent shouted Fiona's name again, and again received no response. He walked the trail in jerky strides while snow coated his back and shoulders and brushed against his face.

It was cold. The snow had been falling for over an hour. And Fiona was out in it. He had to find her. Already he was struggling to be certain he was still on the trail. If he hadn't walked it before…

Fiona had left her plans at work but Brent had stayed out of the office until well after lunch. He'd dodged making contact with Fiona, and this was the result.

All because he hadn't known how to address the concerns at war inside himself, but now he'd worked that out and he needed to speak to her.

He needed first of all to be certain she was safe!

Brent pushed on and tried not to imagine Fiona lost in this.

Please stay on the path until I find you, Fiona. When the snow covered the path completely he started to call her name again in earnest. He should have called in a search and rescue team, not tried to find her by himself.

He shouldn't have walked away this morning and left her to find her way out of his home by herself, left things unresolved between them.

And do you know what you want now, MacKay? And, more importantly, whether you have the right to try to have it?

Brent didn't know. Not entirely. He wanted Fiona as more than an employee. That much he now fully understood and admitted. He wanted her…as a lover. For however long they could make that work. If they could make that work…

For now, he needed to make sure she was safe.

Brent hadn't imagined this snowfall. Who heard of this kind of snow at this time of year here? It just didn't happen.

But today it was happening.

'Fiona!' His voice echoed. There was no response.

Brent pushed on, decided he would give himself another ten minutes and then get on the phone to Linc, ask him to organise help.

When Fiona hiked out of the snow straight at him, her face pale and anxious, all Brent's well-considered thoughts about the future, about speaking carefully and working things out in some way to buy them some time together and avoid hurting either of them when that time inevitably came to an end fell away.

He simply snatched her into his arms. 'You're all right? I thought you might have gone off the path. It's completely obscured now.'

His arms shook as he held her at arm's length so he could examine her. Brent registered that knowledge and couldn't do a thing about it.

She had a coat on, no hat. Her backpack and hair were covered in snow and, as she stared into his eyes, her mouth trembled for a moment before she pressed her lips together and tried to smile all at the same time. 'I'm okay. I was hoping I wasn't too far from the car park, but I've lost track of where I am.'

'It took me over an hour to get this far.'

'I thought I heard you calling me once, but I thought I must have imagined it because I wanted—' She broke off and shivered.

Brent pulled her in close again to his body. 'You're half frozen. I have to get you out of here.' His head twitched but he managed to hold on to her through it, and then he covered her in the second coat he'd worn for that purpose and started back along the trail the way he'd come.

He had her hand. He wasn't letting go.

He never, ever wanted to let her go.

The thought washed over him right there, closed in with swirling white, and his fingers squeezed hers as he faced what was behind the desperation and concern that had driven him to rush here to find her when he'd heard the weather report for the region. More than the same concern he would feel for *just anyone*.

Because this wasn't *just anyone*. This was Fiona. And Brent had fallen in love with her. Fallen totally and utterly all the way in love with her, in the way people would do who wanted now and forever and a picket fence. The way people would who wanted *normal* and believed they could have it.

Brent had never been *normal*.

How could he have done this? How could he even know how to love her in such a way? *How could he make a success of loving her like that? How could he ever be someone she would be able to love like that?*

'I didn't notice what was happening with the weather.' Her teeth chattered as she tried to speak.

'It doesn't matter. I found you. That's all that matters.' He drew her alongside him and chafed her hand with his, trying to warm her while the knowledge of what was in his heart for her spread through him.

He couldn't live without her. Her safety and

security meant more to him than anything else in the world. The feelings were more intense than the…love he felt for Alex and Linc, the only two people in the world he had ever connected with.

He'd bonded with Fiona on some deep level. He…loved her. But not even just in the way he loved Linc and Alex, which was more than he had ever loved any person.

He loved her man to woman. Wanted her at his side for ever—

Later, that knowledge would burn him as he faced the impossibility of it. For now, he had to get her safe from this storm. He had to focus on that! 'Save your energy for getting out of here, okay?'

She nodded and wrapped her arms around herself.

Brent couldn't have Fiona that way, should never have made love to her in the first place when he knew there was no way things could work between them.

How could he ever expect her to accept all of him? His own father hadn't been able to do that. His father had rejected him so deeply and thoroughly that there'd never been any going back. Going forward, for Brent, had been something he had to do alone when it came to relationships, other than with the two men who'd been through the same rejection Brent had been through.

Brent promised himself he would get her out of here, into safety, make sure she was well, and then he would step carefully back into the role of employer. He'd been tempted. He'd allowed himself to dream some big dreams, but those dreams were not realistic.

The snow got heavier and he was thankful when they reached the part of the track where the trail was hewn out of rock face. Tracking it with their hands slowed them down even more, but it kept them on the path and that was vital.

Finally they climbed the last steps into the tiny car park. Her car was there but he put her into his utility truck with the engine running and the heater on and a blanket wrapped around her. It only took a minute to stick a note inside the windscreen of her car with his phone number and the message that the car's owner was with him at his home. He grabbed her handbag and took it to her, laid it on the floor of the truck at her feet.

'I've caused a lot of trouble.' She glanced at the bag and away again. 'I should drive the car out of here.' But she could barely get the words out, let alone carry out such a task.

'I left a note. We'll get your car later.' There was no way Brent would allow her to try to drive in these conditions. On top of that, his arms ached to hold her; his whole system ached with hat need. He felt out of control and words wanted to push up from inside him and burst out, telling her again how worried he'd been and how relieved when he'd found her and so much more. The *so much more* was the biggest worry of all.

Instead, he strapped her into her seat belt and tucked the blanket around her. 'Hold tight. We need to get out of here.'

The drive that should have taken ten minutes took thirty, but they reached the mountain house and he turned the heating up high and brought out towels from the bathroom and warmed them before the heater outlet.

'I can take the wet things off.' But her fingers wouldn't work.

He brushed them aside and stripped her to her underwear and wrapped her in one of the towels. He took care only to let her feel efficiency in his touch, though he hated the knowledge of her chilled skin beneath his fingers as he helped her.

Brent took her into the bathroom and set her in the shower and adjusted it to slowly get her thawed out. She gritted her teeth against even the lukewarm water at first, but slowly she warmed up.

'Your hands are cold. You must be frozen yourself.' She clasped his hands to stop his movements where he'd been guiding the shower spray over her back and arms. 'Let me get out and you can get in.'

He searched her face for long moments. She had colour in her skin again, a soft flush in her cheeks that may have been from the warm shower or from the intimacy of what they were doing. Brent didn't know which, but the thought lodged in his mind and he became aware then of exactly how intimate this was.

To be bathing her, even if he'd left her in her underwear. Her beautiful body was still revealed.

'I don't need a shower. I dressed for the conditions.' Yes, his hands and feet were chilled but a few minutes in front of the heater would fix that. 'Come out and I'll dry you off.'

She submitted meekly enough to being towelled mostly dry and then she took the towel out of his hands and tucked it around herself and said, 'I hope you have some pyjamas here or something because I'm not staying in this wet underwear.'

And she said it firmly enough that some of his tension and worry about her eased. *Some of it.*

'Right.' He wheeled about and went to his room, ransacked it for something suitable, brought her a pair of drawstring sweat pants, boxers and a flannelette shirt and a thick cable-knit jumper and two pairs of socks. 'Do you need help to dress?'

'No, Brent. Really, I'm fine.' She half pushed him out of the bathroom and closed the door in his face.

Tension built in the base of Brent's neck then. He didn't have the capacity to control it right now. He submitted to the twitchiness and the obsessiveness as he changed into dry clothes himself and then paced the living room floor and told himself that now was the time to back off. To pull this back somehow.

The problem was he had a snowball's chance in hell of doing that. To quote the weather and the drive of absolute need inside him right now…

Fiona emerged from the bathroom just as he turned to pace the length of the floor again.

Instead, he froze in the centre of the room. She looked so beautiful in the borrowed clothes with her face shiny from the shower. She looked healthy, strong enough to fight off any after-effects of being thoroughly chilled.

She also looked embarrassed and there was something in the backs of her eyes… 'I'm sorry you needed to rescue me, but I'm glad you did. I don't know if I'd have been able to make it out on my own. I admit I was starting to get really scared, and I'd left my mobile in the car. That was a huge mistake.'

'You couldn't have known the weather would turn.' He explained why he hadn't known of her plans sooner. Almost, he could tell himself that discussion led them back to a more work-related basis.

Except it didn't feel work-like to want to pull her into his arms and never let her go. 'I shouldn't have walked away this morning, and I didn't do much rescuing just now. I just got in the truck and got on that trail and prayed you'd stay safe until I found you.'

'And put me through the shower when we got back here.' This time she dropped her gaze, didn't meet his eyes. 'I should have done that myself. You didn't need to see me. I know my body is larger—'

'I've seen you.' Every beautiful part of her. 'Fiona, you shouldn't ever feel—'

'We should focus on what happened today. I'm so sorry, Brent.' She tipped up her chin as though a brave smile was as necessary as a change of subject.

He wasn't sure which topic concerned her the most. Getting caught in such dangerous weather or the topic of her appeal. Maybe he should let that issue go, but how could he when he needed her to understand how beautiful he found her? 'Don't ever think you're less than completely—'

'I've caused you a lot of trouble.' She'd heard him. Her gaze admitted that, but it equally told him she didn't want to revisit how he might have formed his opinions. 'And all because I didn't stop to think I should get a weather report before I headed onto that trail. I wondered why it was completely deserted, but the solitude suited me and I didn't think…'

'How could you have known?' Brent left the other topic for the time being and focused on re-assuring her.

He drew a deep breath and realised he was running his fingers repeatedly over the cable pattern on the shoulder of the jumper he'd loaned her. How long had he been doing that without so much as a by your leave?

Brent dropped his hand away.

And Fiona moved towards the door of the house. 'You have chains and four-wheel drive. The snow has stopped falling. It can't be more than six inches deep. We should get back to Sydney. I've caused enough trouble and I want to get back to my work.'

To forget all about them? Wasn't that the con-clusion he'd come to eventually too? So why did his chest ache as though something sharp had been driven through it?

'We'll go.' There was no reason to stay on.

Brent turned off the heater and led the way to the door. 'Your car will have to stay where it is. It can be collected for you.'

'I appreciate that.' Fiona didn't argue with Brent. Her car didn't have four-wheel drive or chains on it. And she wanted to get back to the city.

So they went.

Fiona settled into her seat and pretended to sleep.

Brent might want to reassure her, but that made no difference to the fact that she loved him and he didn't return those feelings.

Well, she had survived today. She would regroup and survive whatever else was ahead of her, too.

CHAPTER THIRTEEN

'DO YOU WANT to tell me what's wrong with you, or are you going to just keep snarling at everyone who moves until you get it out of your system that way?' Linc tossed the question Brent's way while Alex turned his back at the barbecue and focused on cooking the bacon and eggs.

Brent rammed his hand through his hair and started to compulsively straighten everything on the table. It was Saturday morning. They were outdoors in the courtyard area of their warehouse home preparing a cooked breakfast to share.

Yes, it was somewhat cold this crisp morning. Yes, his brothers hadn't entirely expected him to bang on their doors and demand they come out and eat breakfast with him.

Brent hadn't cared. He'd wanted to eat out here where he didn't feel stifled and unable to breathe, and…he'd wanted Alex and Linc's company while he did it.

His brothers had looked at his face, donned jackets and said very little one way or the other.

Until now.

And Brent had deserved Linc's rebuke.

'I'm sorry, Alex.' When Alex turned his head, Brent met his brother's gaze and went on. 'Your company business is yours to run as you please. I've got no right to shove my opinions down your throat or say you don't know what you're doing. Obviously you do. I don't know why I ever got started on that.'

'If I thought your attitude was about me just now we'd have a problem, but I don't think that outburst had anything to do with me.' Alex put the cooked eggs and bacon onto the platter and carried them to the table. His gaze was shrewd, too knowing. 'I'd just like to know what it *was* about. Are you well? If your condition is causing problems—'

'Yes. We both want to know the answer to that, Brent.' Linc joined them there at the same time.

Both brothers stared at the plates, condiments and cutlery lined up like soldiers right along the centre length of the table.

'You haven't done that with the table stuff since that time in the orphanage when we were about eight years old.' Linc shook his head. 'What's going on, Brent? Do we need to be worried about you?'

Both older brothers had borne the strap over

hat performance at the orphanage because Linc
hadn't let Brent take responsibility for it, had said
hey'd done it together, that they'd made up a
game to entertain themselves.

Alex had been too young then. They'd all been
too young, damn it. To be abandoned the way
hey had been, in Brent's case by a man who was
no man at all, because what kind of man dumped
his child that way and never looked back?

'They should have kept us and looked after us.'
He uttered the words and realised Fiona was right
about that. She was so right about that. 'Our
families. They should have wanted us. Loved us
exactly how we were.'

Fiona's family should love her that way, but they
didn't. Why should Alex have been put into a
shopping bag and dumped, or Linc knocked around
and given up on? Why should Brent have been
given up on because he had some perceived *fault*?

People lived with autism and didn't care who
knew they had it. Brent had spent his life trying
to hide it.

Trying to hide *from* it.

Wasn't that what he'd done?

He had, hadn't he? He'd held Fiona in his arms,
had been given the gift of loving her, and all he'd
done was worry about a condition he was lucky
wasn't life-threatening. A condition that didn't

limit his work capabilities, that was compatible with his design work. *That Fiona said only made him appeal to her all the more.*

She saw his autism as a gift, something that made him unique.

So he was different?

Fiona's family treated her that way and her only *crime* was loving deeper and more, living life with her heart open to others.

Brent had loved her in his heart, but he had rejected that love the moment he acknowledged it. He hadn't let her in. And, by keeping that door closed, he'd robbed both of them of any chance of being together.

What if she wanted that? What if he could convince her to take him on? What if the way she had loved him, given herself to him, had come from her heart as well as her senses? He *could* do this. He wasn't Charles MacKay, nor should that man's attitude and behaviour decide Brent's future!

He'd made a huge mistake. Was it too late to try to fix it? How could he fix it? Brent's mind began to focus on the possibilities…

'What's going on, Brent?' Alex's broad shoulders hunched like the boy he'd been not so very long ago. That young-old child who'd got into trouble and needed his brothers so desperately

ad needed to be out in the world with them, not
n the orphanage waiting for Brent to get it
ogether to rescue him.

Brent had done his best, Linc had done his part,
oo, and they'd all made it. What if Brent and
Fiona could make it, too?

Linc leaned forward in his seat and his gaze
earched Brent's. 'Alex is right. You've been a lot
nore off-kilter than usual lately. If you need a
loctor—'

The worry in Linc's tone brought the words
out of Brent when everything else wouldn't have.
The only doctor I need is a "love doctor".' When
iis brother looked at him blankly, he went on.
Relationship advice.'

Brent dismantled the items he'd lined up down
he centre of the table, systematically set them
oack where they should be.

'You fell in love with someone.' Alex made a
statement of the words, as though he wasn't sur-
orised at all.

'Fiona. I'm in love with Fiona.' Brent stabbed
several pieces of bacon with his fork and slapped
hem onto his plate, dumped some eggs beside
hem, then pushed the whole lot away from him.

'If you love her, you should go after her.' Linc
eaned forward across the table. 'There's no
eason why you shouldn't. Not a single reason.'

'What do I know about women or relationships?' What did Brent know about trust, or
whether he could reach out? But he wanted to.
Oh, he wanted to.

'You told us we could work it out if we found
the right woman.' Alex pointed this out and
pushed his hands into his pockets. 'We've had
Rosa in our lives. She's a woman.'

'Rosa's great, but knowing her doesn't exactly
qualify me for loving Fiona and doing a good
job of it.'

'Everyone has to learn how to love.' Linc's words
were surprisingly revelatory. As though he truly
knew what he was talking about in this. 'We've
all…loved each other. How we are hasn't mattered.'

That was true, and Brent had been stupid not to
acknowledge that fully a long time ago. He'd let
Charles's rejection of him convince him that no one
in the world, aside from these two brothers, would
ever be able to give and receive love with him.

He'd told Fiona that he and his brothers would
always be guarded, but with each other they
weren't. So maybe they wouldn't be with other
people. Significant people. People they…loved.

'I never should have pushed you both out of
that part of me. The autism. I shouldn't have
worried about hiding it at all. It's not an indict-
ment. It's just part of me.'

'At least you realise that now.' Alex clapped him
on the shoulder. 'We have tried to show you that.'

'I know.' They'd tried, and he had pushed those
efforts away until they'd given in and pretended
to ignore the whole issue. 'I just didn't want to
see. Now there's Fiona. I have to figure out how
to do this, and then I have to go find her.'

He needed to go shopping. Urgently. And he
knew exactly *where* he needed to shop.

Brent walked away without thinking to say
goodbye.

His brothers didn't seem to mind.

Fiona had been painting in her living room listening to music when she received Brent's mysteri-
ous call to meet him at the lookout on their
favourite mountain trail.

Well, it wasn't *their* anything and she didn't
know where that thought had come from. But
Brent wanted to discuss a new project. Perhaps he
needed to show her some local flora or something
in relation to it. At any rate, she'd made the trip,
had been grateful to see pale blue sky above and
no sign of snow. And now here she was, walking
towards the lookout in jeans, a soft pink blouse,
cream jacket—and with her mobile phone in her
back pocket because she'd learned that lesson!

Brent had come after her in these mountains,

had worried about her safety. He'd been gentle and focused and she'd run because he'd seen her in her underwear and all her old fears and uncertainties had surfaced and she just hadn't been able to take it. She'd loved him too much. And he didn't care for her in the same way.

Fiona took a few more steps and contemplated turning around and leaving. It was Saturday, after all. She didn't *have* to work today, even if her boss had asked her to make an exception and give up this time for him.

Her heart hurt. She loved her boss and she wouldn't turn around because she worked with him, and she needed to be his employee and do a great job of that, just like being a 'friend' was something she did so well, giving out advice about relationships…

Well, she wasn't good at relationships and it was a wonder she'd ever thought she knew anything about them. She would resign from that particular position among her friends. From now on they would just have to work out their problems for themselves, because Fiona was *not qualified* to help them.

Fiona trod the final stretch of path and caught sight of Brent standing at the lookout railing, his face turned towards the view. At the sound of her footfalls, he turned to face her. One hand was deep in the pocket of his brown leather jacket. The collar of his tan shirt wasn't quite straight and he looked…both focused and uncertain at once.

'I wasn't sure if you'd come.' Brent's low words washed over her senses.

'You said you wanted to discuss a project.' Why discuss it here? Her heart couldn't define the answer, could only take in his presence as she joined him at the railing and a deep, strong beat registered in her chest, as though being with Brent had brought her fully back to life when she'd only been existing before.

'A project of sorts, yes. Did I disturb anything important when I rang you?' Brent's gaze searched hers.

Behind them, mountains and valley glowed in gentle winter sunshine. Mist particles clung to tree branches and bushes and hung in the air, turning the panorama a beautiful warm blue-grey. Fiona nervously ran her hands down her thighs and forced herself to stop the motion. 'I was just fiddling with a painting. If I could capture the beauty of this…' She gestured towards their surroundings.

'That's why I chose…here for this.' His gaze shifted to the view, and returned to her. 'I knew at this time of the day the colours…would complement your eyes and that it would be beautiful, like you, and it's quiet here, peaceful and tranquil,

the way you make me feel inside myself.' He
stopped speaking, couldn't seem to find what else
he wanted to say.

Fiona didn't know what to say. His words made
her feel beautiful.

A moment later he cleared his throat. 'Tell me
what you were painting?'

'Nothing specific. I was just seeing what
emotions I could get out onto the canvas.' So she
could get them out of herself. And now he had
said things that brought all those emotions to the
surface once again. Her voice quavered a little as
she went on. 'Why did you ask me to meet you
here, Brent?'

Why here, specifically, as opposed to anywhere
else? He'd said it was because of the colours and
a lot of other things that didn't seem to relate to
business.

And if they didn't relate to business—

'A similar reason to why you were painting.' He
hesitated and his gaze searched deep into her eyes.
'Bringing you my emotions way too late and
hoping…you might welcome them if I brought
them to you here, where we could be by ourselves
with nature and I could focus on you and be surrounded by plants and trees, things that help me
feel calm and centred.'

'I don't understand.' Her heart had leapt at his

words, but she couldn't rely on that particular part of her. It had led her into loving him, but it didn't know how to make her stop.

She didn't think she could stop.

Maybe he was finally ready to speak about his relationship with his father. That was emotional. Maybe Brent needed to unload that and it had nothing to do with…them. If so, Fiona would still listen. 'Charles—'

'Hurt a very small boy deeply, enough that it almost crushed that boy.' Brent drew nearer, reached for her hands, gripped them in his and his thumbs stroked her skin over and over. 'Enough that when that boy grew up, he told himself he couldn't have normal relationships and blamed that on a condition instead of the hurt that was handed out long ago and *blamed* on that condition by the man who abandoned him.'

'Charles walked away because he was too weak to be a father to you.' Fiona's mouth trembled as she spoke the words and her hands gripped his. She couldn't help her reaction. She wanted to draw Brent's head to her chest and hold him. Just hold him. 'Not because he couldn't cope with your condition.'

Brent dipped his head in acknowledgement. 'That's right.'

'There's no reason why you couldn't have…all

sorts of relationships.' She tried not to sound as though she needed him to think about a relationship *with her*. 'You can have whatever you want.'

He dipped his gaze to where his fingers stroked hers, clenched his teeth and stopped the motion. Only to shake his head and start it up again, as though he'd chosen to let himself, or to give her that touch that was uniquely his. 'There's only one person I want to build a relationship with now.'

'Who…who is it?'

'I think you know the answer to that, but I want to tell you anyway.' His voice deepened as he went on and he released one of her hands and pushed his into his trouser pocket. 'I don't know how to tell you how I feel, or what you might feel in return. I'll try to express it. I bought something…I'm hoping you might be able to feel *something* for me. I'm hoping you might be able over time, if we spend a lot of time together and I work to show you how much I need you and love you…'

An insecurity of hers that she'd thought she'd conquered rose unexpectedly. 'My body shape and size… After we made love you didn't like…'

'I didn't like what I'd *done*. Losing control exposing aspects of my autism. Those stroking and kneading motions, the way I inhaled your scent over and over.' His hand rose until it cupped the soft flesh of her upper arm in the most gentle of touches. 'But you…you were so beautiful. You *know* that's how I felt and what I saw. You have to know.'

Fiona looked into deep green eyes and wanted to believe him. Oh, she did. 'I'm large. There's no getting away from it. I'll never be dainty or petite or small. I try to dress in things that suit me, but Mum says—'

'Your mother's got no right to say anything other than how lovely you are, inside and out.' Brent made a sharp sound in the back of his throat. 'I don't want them to hurt you any more, Fiona—your family. There must be some way—'

'There is.' She'd been thinking about that, too, and she'd taken her first steps. 'I've called a family conference so I can tell them they're not…meeting my needs. If they can't hear that, can't respond as I need them to, I'll begin to draw some lines regarding my involvement with them. I've let that situation hurt me long enough.'

'I want to come to that meeting with you.' He wished he could protect her from having to do it, but he understood why she had to. And there was something he could do for her. 'When it's over, we'll have a meal with Alex and Linc. They will love you, Fiona. If you…can be part of us? Of *our* family? If you can let me love you with all my heart and soul?'

He realised he was getting ahead of himself and tried to explain. 'I want…all that with you. For us to be a family. When we made love, I didn't understand the feelings I had for you then, all the need and desire and tenderness wrapped up inside me and welling in my heart.' He stopped and shook his head. 'I lost control—because of the autism. Because I wanted you so much. I thought there was no way you could have…been okay with the repetitive touching, the way I smelled you.'

Brent drew a breath. 'Even when I thought maybe you were okay with those things, I thought back to how Charles had pushed me away. I got…angry. And resentful. All these old hurts that I'd never addressed rose to the surface and I realised I'd pushed them all down.'

'Maybe you should take some steps where he's concerned as well.' Fiona made the suggestion with gentleness in her gaze, with nothing but acceptance and, dared he hope, with total love?

Brent had made the same decision. 'There's no chance of reconciliation and, truthfully, I'm not prepared to open myself to him a second time when I see no chance of him changing at all. For me it's more about putting his rejection in perspective. He had no right to abandon me the way he did; I didn't deserve that. There's a service available for separated family members; it's government run. I'm going to make contact and book an appointment. I want the chance to tell him, that's all—'

'I'll go with you.' The words burst out of her. 'I'll go with you and when it's over you'll come home to me, to be with me. I love you, too, Brent, with all my heart, with all my soul. I spent…my life looking for you. I looked in paintings and artwork and faces and the world around me. I think somewhere deep inside I knew what I'd found when I first looked at your landscaping work. I knew I'd found…what my soul needed.'

Brent squeezed her arm gently beneath his fingers, and his fingers shook as he touched her. His voice shook, too. 'I love you, Fiona. I love you with all my heart. I want us to be together. I want to be at your side for the rest of your life.'

He drew his hand from his pocket and there, at the edge of a lookout in the mountains, with towering trees all around them and mother nature providing a soft background of bird calls and the whisper of the wind rustling through grasses and leaves, Brent dropped to one knee before her.

Between his fingers he held a diamond ring. Behind them, as he glanced from the ring up into her face, the sun brightened suddenly and gilded the mist that filled the air and kissed the treetops until everything turned golden and the ring glittered and sparkled while Fiona held her breath and kept on holding it.

'I went to a jewellery store in the city.' Brent's fingers tightened on the ring and the green of his eyes deepened. 'That day I waited for you to finish visiting with your mother and sisters, I saw this ring in the window and thought how pretty it would look on your finger. The diamond…it's cut and set to look like a particular type of everlasting—'

'Daisy. The one we spotted here, with the golden spiky petals around the outside and the lovely white centre.' Fiona completed the sentence for him. Indeed, they had spotted exactly those flowers when they'd first walked this mountain trail. She'd paused to admire the tiny sturdy blooms that managed to look delicate and yet were so enduring.

'I wanted something that reminded me of you, and that would tell you how I feel about you.' Brent's gaze softened as he spoke the words. 'You're those daisies to me. Delicate and beautiful, steady and strong and I want to be what they represent, to you. I want to give you my love for ever, unfading, everlasting.'

'I love you, too, Brent.' With all her heart—for better, for ever—she loved him. Oh, she did!

'You're a good friend and a beautiful person.' He

took her hand in his and laid her fingers in his gentle clasp. 'Inside and out. To me you are perfect.'

Fiona finally believed it. A soft warmth swept into her cheeks. 'I loved the things you…did when we made love. All those things. You don't need to worry about that because you entrance me. Your focus and all of those things that are unique to you.'

'Then…' He drew a deep breath and his gaze held hers, deep moss-green to her robin's egg blue. His fingers squeezed hers. 'Will you marry me, Fiona? And live the rest of your life at my side in all the ways there are? Will you wear this ring for me and wear a wedding ring for me, and let me wear a ring for you? I don't know how to do marriage. I don't know how to manage even a serious relationship, but I love you and I'll learn.'

'Oh, Brent.' Fiona stayed very still as he took in the expression in her eyes and slowly slipped the ring onto her finger and got to his feet still holding her hand.

She slid her arms up and her hands cupped the sides of his neck and she sighed as his arms closed strongly around her. 'Yes. Yes, I will marry you and we'll learn together.'

The ring caught the sun's rays and reflected golden light from every facet of the diamond, and Fiona knew this was indeed the beginning of their everlasting love. Hers and Brent's together.

LIGHTS, CAMERA...
KISS THE BOSS

BY
NIKKI LOGAN

DID YOU PURCHASE THIS BOOK WITHOUT A COVER?

If you did, you should be aware it is **stolen property** as it was reported *unsold and destroyed* by a retailer. Neither the author nor the publisher has received any payment for this book.

All the characters in this book have no existence outside the imagination of the author, and have no relation whatsoever to anyone bearing the same name or names. They are not even distantly inspired by any individual known or unknown to the author, and all the incidents are pure invention.

All Rights Reserved including the right of reproduction in whole or in part in any form. This edition is published by arrangement with Harlequin Enterprises II BV/S.à.r.l. The text of this publication or any part thereof may not be reproduced or transmitted in any form or by any means, electronic or mechanical, including photocopying, recording, storage in an information retrieval system, or otherwise, without the written permission of the publisher.

This book is sold subject to the condition that it shall not, by way of trade or otherwise, be lent, resold, hired out or otherwise circulated without the prior consent of the publisher in any form of binding or cover other than that in which it is published and without a similar condition including this condition being imposed on the subsequent purchaser.

® and TM are trademarks owned and used by the trademark owner and/or its licensee. Trademarks marked with ® are registered with the United Kingdom Patent Office and/or the Office for Harmonisation in the Internal Market and in other countries.

First published in Great Britain 2009
Harlequin Mills & Boon Limited,
Eton House, 18-24 Paradise Road, Richmond, Surrey TW9 1SR

© Nikki Logan 2009

ISBN: 978 0 263 86981 1

Harlequin Mills & Boon policy is to use papers that are natural, renewable and recyclable products and made from wood grown in sustainable forests. The logging and manufacturing process conform to the legal environmental regulations of the country of origin.

Printed and bound in Spain
by Litografia Rosés, S.A., Barcelona

Nikki Logan lives next to a string of protected wetlands in Western Australia, with her long-suffering partner and a menagerie of furred, feathered and scaly mates. She studied film and theatre at university, and worked for years in advertising and film distribution before finally settling down in the wildlife industry. Her romance with nature goes way back, and she considers her life charmed, given she works with wildlife by day and writes fiction by night—the perfect way to combine her two loves. Nikki believes that the passion and risk of falling in love are perfectly mirrored in the danger and beauty of wild places. Every romance she writes contains an element of nature, and if readers catch a waft of rich earth or the spray of wild ocean between the pages she knows her job is done.

Visit Nikki at her website: www.nikkilogan.com.au

To Mum, whose passion for anything printed
rubbed off on me from an early age.

Thank you to The Bootcampers, I may have been the
first across the line but I know I won't be the last.
Many thanks also to Melissa(s) James and Smith for
your advice and encouragement, to Kim Young for
trusting my voice more than I did, and to the beautiful
Rachel Bailey for…pretty much everything else…
you may never know what a pivotal part you played
in the realisation of my dream.

And to Pete—who's picked up the slack of a woman
working two jobs, and grown accustomed to
the back of my head and to eating dinner solo—
you *are* my hero (sorry about all the vacuuming).

CHAPTER ONE

'Is THAT even legal?'

Ava Lange glared at the row of suited clones flanking Daniel Arnot in his high-rise Sydney office. Smugness fattened their expressions; they were all too used to getting their own way.

Four against one. *Nice.*

'Can they do this, Dan? Mid-contract?' Her use of *they* was no accident. The word demarcated a battlefield, with the network suits on one side and her on the other. Between them stretched a mile of barbed tangles—a very apt representation of Ava's feelings towards all of them right now. Particularly the man in the centre, whose fringed brown eyes stared steadily back at her.

'We can, Ava, yes.'

Ah.

Disappointment bit deep as Daniel declared his allegiance. Then anger surged in like a king wave, swamping any anxiety she had about being called in today. She'd assumed she was here to be fired, not promoted.

The former held vastly more appeal.

She stalled her hands before they smacked down on his desk, settling them instead with deceptive care. Blessedly, they were steady. 'You're telling me keeping my job as landscape consultant for *Urban Nature* is now conditional on me getting in front of the camera?'

Clone Number One eagerly spoke up. 'There is provision in your contract for AusOne to modify the manner in which you—'

Dan looked askance at the man until he fell silent, then he turned and reclaimed her gaze steadily. 'Test audiences loved your brief appearance on the behind-the-scenes episode last season,' Dan said, as though that explained it all. 'We'd like to give you a fly and see what happens.'

It had been a long time since she'd last swum in the chocolatey depths of his eyes. Ava had to steel herself against the urge. 'I have no interest in being on television.'

His jaw tightened, and some perverse part of her delighted to know she was troubling him. That she was impacting on him at all. But he wasn't done yet; those eyes were at their blankest when that mind was working its hardest.

'Ava, this is a once-in-a-lifetime opportunity,' e said. 'You should take it.'

She pulled her hands off the polished surface f his desk, leaving a heat-aura in the shape of her lender fingers. It evaporated into nothing, along vith her words in the face of Dan's blind deter-nination to get his way. Her pulse picked up and he straightened.

'I have *no interest* in being on television, Dan. 'm saying no.'

Clone Number One piped up again. 'You can't ay no. You're contracted.'

Ava's eyes flicked to him, to see how serious e was about that. He had the intense look of a eral dog scenting blood. Ava imagined just how abid he'd be in court, and how many prize horses er father would have to sell to help her mount a egal defence. She swallowed the discomfort.

Seasoned leather protested as Dan settled his urfer's shoulders deeper into his chair. He ilently lifted two fingers and all three lawyers ose as one. If she hadn't been so furious, Ava night have laughed.

She kept her eyes fixed on Dan's dark brown nes as the clones filed past her to the door. It was nly when his posture changed that she knew they vere alone. He ran a carefully manicured hand hrough his hundred-dollar haircut.

Manicures, Dan? Really? The Daniel Arnot she remembered had paid about as little attention to his cuticles as he had to politics. If he couldn't surf it, he couldn't see it. As a girl, she'd dreamed he'd turn that singular focus in her direction—just once. Now he had, she wanted to bolt from the room.

He looked at her from beneath an untroubled brow. 'Ava...'

'Don't!' She shot to her feet, recognising that honey-smooth tone all too well. He'd used it on her half his life when he wanted something. Today was not the day to discover whether or not it still had power over her. She prowled across his office, venting a warning over her shoulder. 'I know where this is going. You sharpened your negotiation skills on me and my brother growing up, remember?'

'Ava, if you say no you'll be breaking your contract with the network and the piranhas waiting outside will pull you to pieces in court. Is that what you want?'

A horribly expensive and public legal case? That was the exact opposite of what she wanted. She just wanted to grow her consultancy business and build herself some kind of financial security. Right now she couldn't afford to fight, or the bad publicity. Heck, she could barely afford the tax are to this meeting! Every cent she earned these days she plunged into her business.

She made a beeline for the ornamental black bamboo in the corner, where it was strangled in its constricting pot. Its roots had nowhere to go.

I can empathise entirely.

She spun around, thick hair swinging. 'Don't you know me at all, Dan? What made you think I'd go for this?'

'Common sense. You don't have a whole lot of options here, Ava.'

Irritation hissed out of her and she crossed towards him. 'I enjoy my job the way it is: behind-the-scenes, designing the gardens, planning the themes.'

'You'll still get to do all that; you'll just be doing it on camera. A handful of set-ups per shoot and the rest is unchanged.' He rubbed his chin and Ava lost her train of thought for a moment, suddenly imagining it was *her* palm tracing over the stubble growing along the square angles of his jaw.

She shook her head and doubled her focus. 'Except that I'll be on set all the time, instead of in my home office working on the designs.'

Long fingers waved her concern away. 'We'll get you a mobile office.'

The speed with which he offered a six-figure

sweetener took her aback. His cashed-up world was a million miles from her carefully budgeted one, but even so it was suspiciously generous. She sank onto one hip and tipped her head to study him.

'What's in this for you?' His jaw set and she knew she was onto something. 'You know I'd never go for something which puts me right in the public eye. So what is it, Dan? Why the pressure?'

'Ava…' *There it was again—that tone.* 'Be reasonable.'

Heat roared through her body. 'You're asking me to give up my home, my business and my life to give you what you want. I think I have a right to know what you're getting out of it. Money? Promotion? A corner office?'

That one hit home. A tic flared in his left eye, but he didn't bite. 'One season, Ava. Thirteen shows. Then your contract expires and you can negotiate freely.'

She snorted. The last time she'd been free had been six months ago, right before she'd signed on with AusOne. Back then, the promise of a year's fixed income and the chance to quadruple her portfolio had been like a siren's song. And it had been going to plan for the most part.

But *this*… After everything her family had done for him. What had happened to him?

Fury and a healthy dose of Lange mulishness

ade her rash. 'This is hardly a negotiation. I
onder what my father would have to say about
ou press-ganging me into this.'

Like a disturbed tiger snake he shot out of his
hair and advanced around the desk, stopping a
ere breath away from her. Ava met his stare and
ltered air in and out through her lips rather than
sk inhaling his intoxicating scent.

Nine years had changed nothing.

'He'd say *Thank you, Dan, for making sure
va's livelihood is secure—that she has food in
e fridge and a future in the industry she loves.*'
rown eyes turned nearly black as he glared down
her. 'Not to mention for the extraordinary boost
e publicity will give your business.'

He radiated furious warmth, and Ava had to
orce herself not to bask in it. Not to look at him
id think about how well the extra nine years
uited him. 'I don't value the publicity and I don't
onsider hosting a gardening show will do diddly
help my career—my *serious* career—in land-
cape design. Quite the opposite, in fact.'

Colour streaked along those sensational cheek-
ones. 'This would be the same gardening show
at has bankrolled your fledgling consultancy,
es? A show you obviously have little respect
or.'

Guilt intensified her heat. She'd used his tele-

vision programme to kick-start her business an
they both knew it. Being a hypocrite didn't si
well with her. She'd always prided herself on he
honesty, too. *Curse him!*

'You might as well put me in a bikini and drap
me over an expensive car,' she said. Heat flared
in his eyes before they dulled to blank, behind
the-desk Dan. 'How many people do you suppos
will want to commission me to design their cor
porate landscaping projects if I'm a poster-girl fo
television? You're bargaining with my profes
sional self-respect.'

Conscious of her shaking voice, she bough
some calm-down time by filling a glass with coo
water from an ornate pitcher and taking a long
slow sip. Then she crossed the thick wool carpe
and emptied the remainder onto the parche
bamboo. The hint of a smile on his face when sh
glanced at him sent her roaring straight back u
the Richter scale to furious.

'What?' she snapped.

'You love your plants. It's part of who you are
Sincerity glittered in his eyes. 'Why not let that er
thusiasm and expertise show for everyone to see
No more getting irritated when a presenter mispro
nounces the Latin or dumps a plant into unprepare
soil. You virtually write the scripts anyway—wh
not simply be the one to deliver them?'

She narrowed her eyes, thinking furiously. She was trapped by her contract; the lawyers knew it and Dan knew it. They were just waiting for her to catch on. There was no way in the world she would be able to match one of Australia's biggest television networks legally, and neither could she afford to resign. In fact, the pay rise Dan was offering meant she could wash her hands of AusOne at the end of her contract and still be on track with her business plan.

Just six months.

'Ava, they have you over a barrel. You really don't have a choice here.'

Her head snapped up. No way was she going to cave just because she couldn't afford a five-hundred-dollar-an-hour lawyer. The days of her just giving in to Daniel Arnot were well and truly over.

'I get to be hands-on,' she said. 'No swanning in for two shots and then leaving assistants to do all the work…'

'Fine. But not at the expense of your designing,' he countered.

'Naturally. And Shannon and Mick stay with me.'

'I couldn't agree more.'

'You'll put it in writing?' she parried.

His lips thinned at that one.

'Come on, Dan, you're not short of a lawyer or three to whip something up for you.'

He exhaled, and shoved his hands deep into his designer pockets. 'I'm disappointed you think you had to ask, Ava. I swear I've tried to make this a good deal for you. It's happening; you might as well just...' He waved frustrated hands.

'Lie back and think of England?'

A phone rang in an office somewhere. His mouth set dangerously. 'Thirteen episodes, Ava. That's it.'

And then she saw it: the tiniest glimmer of the younger man she remembered. Deep in those brown eyes was some fear that she'd take her skills and walk out. This *mattered* to him. That was her undoing. Instantly she was sixteen again, and every protective urge she'd spent years exorcising came bubbling to the surface. It galled her that she was still biologically opposed to hurting him.

'You hold my self-respect in your hands,' she said quietly. 'My career.'

He sighed and held her gaze. 'I know.'

'Give me your word it will be handled tastefully.' *That I will be.*

'You have it.' He stretched out a large hand. 'On your mother's memory.'

Ava glanced at his long fingers, at the tanned hand where it emerged from an expensive cuff. She itched to feel that smooth skin. But she forced herself to remember which side of the battlefield he'd chosen just minutes before. She stood straighter.

'If you had the slightest respect for my mother's memory you wouldn't be screwing her daughter over to further your own career.'

Even after nine years she still had enough residual hurt left in her to be satisfied as the colour leached entirely from Dan's face. Then she turned and walked from his office. It would be too easy to fall back on old times and trust him. She had to remember he was no longer Steve's best mate and her *de facto* big brother.

He was one of *them*.

The enemy.

CHAPTER TWO

'YOU are kidding, right?' Ava looked at her brother in confusion. 'I can't afford this!'

A magnificent home spread out before her, the deep blue of Sydney Harbour reflecting in its many tinted windows. It was sensational. Shooting six days a week for *Urban Nature* meant the ninety-minute commute to her south coast home just wasn't doable. Steve had warned her that city accommodation wouldn't come cheap, but even so she hadn't appreciated how much of her lucrative pay-rise would be eaten away.

He'd offered to scout affordable rentals for her in the week it would take her to pack up her life in Flynn's Beach. They'd looked at three already, but this opulence was by far his most ludicrous suggestion.

'You don't get it all.' Steven Lange took her shoulders and twisted her gently to face the east side of the residence. 'You get that bit.'

'What bit?'

'This bit.' A smooth voice cut in from her right, and Dan walked towards them, a newly cut key dangling from his fingers. She met his gaze evenly, almost defiantly, hoping he'd never realise she harboured the slightest remorse for the way she'd last spoken to him.

He clapped his hand on her brother's shoulder. 'Hey, mate. Good to see you.'

Steve grinned. 'Danno.'

A bad feeling came over her. *Oh, he hadn't...*

'Come on, I'll show you around my humble abode,' Dan said.

She turned and glared at Steve as Dan guided the way to a refurbished arched gate in the large rammed-earth wall that obscured the rest of the house from view. Ava's heart leapt as she stepped through the pretty gate into a small garden space, and her designer's eye immediately started doing its thing. There wasn't a lot of planning evident, but it was lush, flowering and completely unexpected in a house as modern as this one. An ancient birdbath leaned skew-whiff in the garden's heart. It was designer crooked, dotted with clusters of moss, and looked as if it belonged in a home magazine.

She fought to keep her face from betraying how much the whole setting appealed to her. It was precisely the sort of thing she might design.

'Garden and price, you said.' Steve spoke from behind her. 'They were your criteria. This has a garden, and you can afford it.'

Looking at the affluent surroundings, and considering it was in one of Sydney's top harbourside addresses, Ava struggled to imagine how she possibly could.

She lifted her chin and stared both men down. 'It also smacks of a set-up.'

Steve glanced away, but Dan wordlessly led them along a path made of rough-cut stone pavers and into a small guesthouse, which shared one wall with the main building. His tour of the little house ended in an airy bedroom, where he parted timber bi-fold doors and sunshine and fragrance from the garden spilled across the timber floor. Ava caught her breath and had to drag her focus back to her brother before she gave away how beautiful she found it.

Such a shame she wouldn't get to enjoy it.

Steve flopped onto the sofa in the living area. The throw draped so casually across it looked as if it was worth more than her entire budget lounge suite at home. Dan's new life certainly was a comfortable one.

'There must be other places on the list?' she said hopefully.

'Nup. Not with ticks in both boxes. And this

one's close to the city and the waterfront as a bonus. You're not going to see better.'

She didn't doubt that for a second. The wash of the harbour was a tranquil soundtrack with the doors wide open like this, and it was just a ferry ride to the central business district. Lord, it was going to be hard to walk away from this one.

She turned to her brother. 'Come on, Steve, show me the list.'

His hands rose in a *mea culpa*. Dan spoke from behind her. 'Ava, take it. Just pretend you're living next to someone else.'

'It's not…' Lord, how did she begin to explain how she was feeling about all this now it was a reality? Working with him. Sharing a roof with him. *Him.* While she still felt so exploited.

'You're getting mates' rates,' Steve helpfully piped up.

She glared at him. That was a dirty pitch. He knew very well that finances were her Achilles' heel right now. 'How much?'

Steve looked to Dan for the answer, which meant Ava couldn't avoid it any longer. She dragged her eyes to his. He shrugged and said, 'It's part of your employment package.'

Free? This magnificent light and that gorgeous garden and harbour view were gratis? She forced the excitement down deep, visualised the revised contract she'd only just signed and looked Dan in the eye. 'No, it isn't.'

The tiniest hint of colour crept above the collar of his shirt. 'It's sitting here empty, Ava, and I'm hardly ever home. It's no skin off my nose if someone's living here.'

'What if you want to have guests to stay?' she asked.

He clamped his jaw hard. 'It won't be a problem.'

Because he had no friends? Or because most were of the female variety and would share his bedroom rather than the visitor's quarters? That nasty jealous whisper took her by surprise, and she twisted away to cross into the bedroom. Pettiness wasn't like her.

She looked again at the blossoming garden and imagined how it could look with a bit of time and focus. Then she thought about the many ways that her salary could be better spent than lining a stranger's pocket as rent. Just like that, a zero fell off her debt to the bank.

She glanced between Steve's hopeful grey eyes and Dan's veiled brown ones and chewed her lip. Which made her the bigger fool? Taking the guesthouse or knocking it back?

'Does it have its own entrance?' she hedged, desperate to find a valid fault.

'It's completely self-contained. And—' Dan

guided her through the suite and out of the rear door, where a Winnebago barely fitted into the carport —it comes with a mobile office. As agreed.'

Ava stepped past his guarded look and into the twenty-foot vehicle, with Steve following close behind. Her heart missed a beat.

'Courtesy of AusOne, for as long as you're with us,' Dan said. 'You can take this on location and work on your designs between shoots.'

It was ideal. Fully converted as an office space, with a drafting table, desk, filing cabinets and a kitchenette. Every inch of it was modern luxury, and no bigger than the horse-trucks she'd driven without problem for her dad. She was fast running out of good reasons to say no.

She clamped her jaw. 'Wow. When you guys sweeten, you really sweeten.'

'The network was…appreciative…of your situation, and eager to ensure you could work on location,' he said.

She shot him a wry glance. 'A happy host is a good host?'

He smiled, not quite relaxed, but it was the first she'd had from him since she'd seen him a week ago. The smile before that one had been more than nine years ago, before *that* night. She pushed the unwelcome thought from her head.

'You're not the host, truth be told,' he said.

'No?' Steve and Ava spoke together.

'You're the brains of the outfit. Brant Maddox is the anchor.'

'Ugh. Maddox.' Steve stomped out of the trailer in disgust. Ava frowned. Where had she heard that name before?

Dan clarified. 'Maddox is AusOne's latest and greatest.'

Oh, *right*! She grinned as she remembered. Brant Maddox was serious eye-candy. 'That should get you the female half of Australia watching, anyway.'

Dan held her look. 'You'll do all right with the male half, Ava. You forget, I've seen the test rushes.'

With no clue what to do with a compliment from Dan Arnot, Ava escaped the modern trailer office and returned into the world's most perfect guesthouse. Finding an affordable short-term rental in inner-Sydney wouldn't be easy for the six months she'd be here. This was pure luxury, central, a bargain, and she knew the landlord. All major plusses. And, of course, there was the magnificent light and the garden. She chewed her lip and looked everywhere but at the man standing next to her.

Could she do the girl-next-door thing again…?

Dan watched the conflict play out on Ava's face and tempered a smile. When she was young she'd used to have out-loud conversations with those voices in her head. Now it looked as if she'd mastered the art of internalisation.

Somewhat.

She'd walked away from him just now with as much dignity as when she'd marched from his office a week ago. Head high, as if she owned the place. Right now she wanted to. He could tell. The way her eyes had lit up when she saw the light streaming in the bedroom, and when she'd walked through the tiny garden courtyard.

But that light dimmed every time she looked at *him*. Like polished silver instantly aging.

He sighed and carefully closed the door to the trailer behind him, conscious of its price tag. If this season didn't go well, the leased RV and everything in it would be heading back to the dealers.

Bloody AusOne. He'd brought them a string of winners in his six years there, but one little sleeper in a glutted lifestyle market and suddenly they were *sending the boys round*. That meant forty jobs on the line—one of them Ava's.

Another one his. And he hadn't sacrificed a third of his life to give it all away this easily.

He leaned casually on the doorframe to the bedroom, dropped his voice and brought out the big guns. *He knew this woman.* At least the girl before the woman. Her habits couldn't have changed that much.

'Come on, Ava. Just imagine yourself stretched out in here having lazy Sunday afternoon naps, falling asleep to the sounds of the harbour.'

And just like that he had her. The grey eyes she turned on him brimmed with longing. Then, out of nowhere, his gut tightened, and he got a flash of long afternoons in there with her. But it was a different breed of longing in her eyes, and neither of them were napping.

He blinked the vision clear.

Watching her in the soft glow from outside reminded him of her test shots: how the light had seemed to radiate out from her rather than reflecting off her. She'd been on screen for less than five minutes of the behind-the-scenes special, but the test audience had rated her through the roof, responding unanimously to her vitality, her gentle nature and her absolute love of what she did. And it didn't hurt that she had a natural, earthy sexiness that any viewer with a Y-chromosome would respond to.

Dan certainly had. Lucky he was known for complete absorption during previews, or his total captivation might have been noticed. Little Ava was a now a certified knockout. Who would've thought it?

The last time he'd seen her she'd been all legs and teenage angst. A good kid, with a heart as big as a continent, right on the edge of womanhood, but high-maintenance in the extreme. And definitely not comfortable around him. That much, at least, hadn't changed.

'Excuse me.' Grown-up Ava avoided his eyes as she moved to pass him in the doorway.

He almost—almost—made her squeeze past him, but nine years had cured him of viewing her blushes as sport. He straightened and let her through, ignoring the subtle soapy scent that tantalised his senses and focussing on the challenge at hand.

He *needed* Ava on this show.

Urban Nature was practically made for her designs. Her talent for turning heavily urban spaces into green ones was as unique as it was inspired. Her proud brother had all too willingly fed Dan's need to vicariously monitor her progress and every design he delivered convinced Dan more and more that she was the key to a new concept in lifestyle. He'd offered her the designer's role on the pilot version of *Urban Nature* through a go-between, knowing she'd never willingly accept a job from him. Then, once she was well and truly hooked, he'd left it to Steve to break the bad news.

That she was really working for Daniel Arnot, scourge of Flynn's Beach…breaker of hearts.

Destroyer of dreams.

She locked eyes with him from across the suite and then glanced at the door leading to his part of the house. At the spanking new deadlock he'd installed yesterday. She looked somewhat comforted by it.

Dan forced down the regret and guilt at manipulating someone he considered a friend, a mate's sister. He'd worked too hard and sacrificed too much to retreat now. He had a point to prove to his old man and, by God, he was going to sharpen that point until it glinted.

The anticipation pulsing in his chest was all about his career goal suddenly being a heck of a lot closer. It had nothing to do with the woman looking back and forth between him and her brother.

So when she thrust out her hand and said, 'Okay. I'll take it,' the rush he felt could only have been the thrill of victory.

Couldn't it?

CHAPTER THREE

WHAT the..?'

Dan lengthened his strides as he approached the production trailer parked at the rear of the industrial property where they were shooting. More than one crew member had turned his head in the direction of two frazzled female voices—one raised and indignant, the other softer, more urgent. He climbed onto the trailer step with only a cursory knock and flung the door open.

On the periphery of his vision he saw the warning gaze of Carrie Watson, their make-up guru, but his attention was entirely consumed by five foot four inches of Ava.

Very angry Ava.

'Is this your idea?' she blazed, straight at him.

She stood, hands on hips, clad only in low-slung cargo shorts, which revealed a mile of tanned leg, and a brief—make that a *minuscule*—tank top. It was small, white, and disturbingly tight, with a logo for a popular brand of power tool stretched across her full chest. Every curve— and Ava had definitely been standing at the front of the queue when those were being dished out— screamed *notice me*.

'I'm digging a garden, Dan. Not dancing on a bar.'

He forced his eyes away from that logo. The last time he'd seen Ava in anything less than corporate wear she'd been sixteen years old. And this was definitely less. Way less. He sucked in some air.

'I'm not wearing it.' She stood legs apart, ready for a fight. A blistering one, by the looks of her.

His attention snapped back to her face as cold fury seeped in. This was not the outfit he'd signed off on. No, this had network written all over it. It was only the first day of filming and Bill Kurtz was already playing games. He bustled past her to rummage in the small clothing rack in the corner.

'I couldn't agree more,' he said, reaching to pull a crisp pale blue shirt from its hanger.

'That's Brant's shirt,' Carrie hastily warned him. 'We need it for the next set-up.'

Dan fumed and shoved it back on the rack, glancing at Ava's clothes draped over the chair. She couldn't wear her own blouse; it was too

busy for television. But she couldn't wear that...
outift...either. It was completely the wrong image
for the show.

Besides, he'd given her his word, and that get-
up protected no one's integrity. Least of all his. He
prowled around the trailer, looking for inspiration.

'They're going to want that logo in there, Dan,'
Carrie reminded him unnecessarily.

'I know, Carrie. Just let me think.' Frustration
made him short. They were filming in an industrial area, twenty minutes from the nearest
shopping mall. That was a one-hour round trip the
schedule just couldn't afford. The cursed network
would know that.

He swore again.

His gaze landed on a blue singlet that sat
unopened in its packet. On Ava it would be no
better than her tank top, but it gave him an idea.
He tugged his Yves Saint Laurent business shirt
out of his waistband and made quick work of the
dozen buttons.

'Here.' He thrust the still-warm shirt at Ava.
'Put this on over the top.'

It was too large by far, but she slid it on, and
Carrie fashioned the excess fabric into a knot at her
waist. The sponsor logo was still easily visible, but
the result was infinitely less gratuitous.

Dan did his best not to look too closely. 'The

shorts have to go, too,' he said. Exactly how Kurtz imagined those would work when Ava was digging in a garden bed in several shots… Oh, he knew exactly what Kurtz had imagined.

'I have cargo pants for tomorrow, Dan,' Carrie said, reaching to a low shelf.

'Perfect. Wear those,' he barked at Ava, then turned and nailed Carrie with his glare. 'Burn the shorts.'

He yanked the blue singlet from its packet and stalked out of the wardrobe trailer, tugging it on. He knew he'd snapped at both of them, but he was still reeling from his reaction to the skin-tight tank top. That chest. Those legs.

She was practically his little sister, for crying out loud.

He tucked the singlet in, not caring how ridiculous it looked over suit pants. It wasn't a patch on how ridiculous Ava would have looked in the get-up the network had switched to. Thank God he'd been on set today.

He was going to have to watch the filming like a hawk.

'Wow!' Carrie unfroze just long enough to snap her gaping mouth closed. She blinked in the direction that Cyclone Dan had just blown through. The image of that sculpted chest free of its expensive covering burned into Ava's brain like a cheap plasma television. Last time she'd seen it, it had been slick with sweat and barrelling towards her in the dark of night. She swallowed the thought and turned away from the doorway as the warmth of Dan's shirt soaked into her. She met Carrie's eyes for a moment, and they burst out laughing.

'I'm sorry I was being a princess about the tank top,' Ava said. Prima donna was no way to start a working relationship.

'Oh, love—forget it. I wouldn't have worn it either. I'm just amazed you got away with it. He's a *producer*, you know.' Carrie shook her head and went back to placing out the tiny pots and brushes that were the tools of her trade.

Ava had already discovered that the higher up the food chain you got in television the less popular you became, but she felt obliged to defend Dan. For old times' sake if nothing else.

'He's all right.'

'Honey, for what he just did the man's a hero. You know he's going to take some flak for that. I wouldn't like to be a fly on the wall when the network sees the dailies from this shoot.'

Ava ran her hand along the smooth collar of the business shirt and turned partly away from Carrie to breathe her fill of Dan's distinctive cologne.

The rich scent mingled with his own personal smell. How many years had she been as sensitive as a tracker dog to that particular scent? Until she'd exorcised it through necessity.

The fabric was warm, fragrant, and hideously expensive—and she was about to start shovelling dirt with it on. The irony made her smile.

Carrie steered her to the well-used chair in front of the trailer's mirror. 'Sit yourself down, love. If Dan's butt is on the line, let's give it some company.'

Twenty minutes later Ava stared at her reflection. She knew she had a face full of make-up, but Carrie had applied it so subtly it looked as if she was wearing virtually none. Enormous grey eyes stared at her from the mirror, artfully highlighted with kohl, her skin was wrinkle-free—for that alone Carrie deserved a medal—and her honey-blonde hair was restrained in a tight ponytail that managed to accentuate the long curve of her neck while still looking completely effortless. She'd never been one to overplay her strengths. She had a good mind and a good heart and those assets meant the most to her. But for the first time ever Ava looked at her own face and didn't count her flaws.

Her heart lifted slightly.

Minutes later she stepped out of the trailer

shrouded in Dan's shirt and wearing the practical cargos. She tossed the shortie-shorts in the trash on the way out and farewelled Carrie.

An ally. Exactly what she needed on a day like today. She could do with a friend on set.

You have one, a tiny voice reminded her. A friend of many years.

But Dan had chosen the other side in this whole mess. Despite the chivalry of this morning, he was still corporate with a capital 'C'. Still the boss. Inevitably the time would come when he would remind her of that fact, and any shred of friendship they had left would be nothing but history.

It was daunting to be the centre of attention, taking commands from a swag of people with their own jobs to do, trying to follow various instructions while remembering what she was supposed to be there for.

Read this. Say that. Step here and you'll be off camera. Step there and you'll be out of the light.

Her patience was just about shot by the time Dan reappeared on set, his suit jacket slung over the blue singlet. He moved so comfortably through the throng it was easy to see why he was successful at what he did. He still oozed confidence. So much so he made pairing a workman's singlet with suit pants seem almost normal.

Ava glanced away, not wanting to stare.

Slightly behind Dan came a vision she couldn't help but appreciate. His Hollywood smile lit a path straight towards her and she blinked as he turned its full force onto her.

Brant Maddox. Host and celebrity hottie.

'Ava. Such a pleasure to meet you.' Brant's hand closed around hers. Warm, smooth...but empty. Nothing like the sure grip of the darker man beside him. She frowned at the comparison. Before she could return the greeting, Brant's hand tugged her in to kiss her cheek. She stumbled and fell into him, still conscious that the tank top magnified her assets.

Brant seemed pleased with the heat flaming in her cheeks and stepped away. An odd expression flitted across his blue eyes. *My work here is done*, they seemed to say. Had the whole encounter been manufactured for effect? What was his story?

'Ava Lange—Brant Maddox.' Dan's belated introductions were pointless, but Ava appreciated his businesslike tone. It helped her remember why she was there.

'Ava, can I have a word?' He held up five fingers to the director, who then called a break to the crew. She followed him off to one side, smiling an unnoticed farewell at Brant, who was now thoroughly engaged in chatting to his next target. Dan steered her with a gentle hand to her back. Heat soaked through his shirt to her skin where he touched her.

Down, girl...

'You look great,' he said, examining her dispassionately. 'Much better.'

Offence nipped in her belly and her eyebrows rose. 'They don't call them artists for nothing.'

He looked at her more closely then. 'I was talking about the clothes. But now you mention it, yes, she's done a great job with your make-up. Natural.' He scrutinised the whole picture again, trailing his eyes over her face slowly and thoroughly.

Two blushes in two minutes. Even for her that was something. She glanced at the set, uncomfortable with his intense regard.

He cleared his throat, back to business. 'Two things. Your latest design is brilliant—possibly your best yet.'

The glow that warmed her body irked her. She shouldn't need his endorsement to feel proud about this design. She'd channelled all her frustration and anger at being coerced by the network into the most beautiful garden she could create. It had resulted in some of her best work.

'Thank you. I figured that if it's my face, now, as well as my name on it, then I'd better make it a knockout.'

His chocolate eyes studied her closely. They did nothing to ease the warmth in her cheeks.

'You've succeeded,' he said. 'Although I had to lean on our suppliers for better prices to afford some of the centrepieces.'

She smiled sweetly. A pair of massive ornamental *dracaenas* would have added a zero to the budget all by their spiky selves. It felt magnificent to finally get one over on Mr Smugness himself.

Almost too good. Addictive. Her body stirred.

'I'm just looking for an indication as to whether you're planning on maintaining that level of terrorism by design,' he said.

Her laugh tinkled even to her own ears. 'I can give you no guarantees.'

'Just remember it's not the network whose day you're making harder with those little rebellions.'

She smiled and held his gaze. Pure innocence. 'No?'

He smiled, too. A sexy, knowing kind of smile. 'No. And not mine either, although I'm sure that was your intent.' He steered her further away from prying ears. The heat radiating from where his hand closed over her elbow was both comforting and disturbing. 'Tania from Procurement spent a whole day trying to get you what you wanted within the budget she'd been set. She was embarrassed to have to tell me she couldn't do it.

Ava's smile instantly dropped. 'Oh. Not my intention.' Talk about backfire!

'I know. I just wanted to point it out.'

How could he know her so well even after nine years apart? He had the uncanny knack of reaching right into her mind and plucking her thoughts like daisies.

'Okay. Lesson learned,' she said. 'What was the second thing?'

He assessed her for a moment before continuing. 'Brant Maddox.'

Ava's eyes found Brant in the jumble of crew, casually leaning on an upturned urn, chatting to an assistant—although there was really nothing casual about it. Again, he was posing for anyone paying attention. A picture of casual male beauty.

'Speaking of expensive ornamentals…'

Dan laughed quietly and looked at her through those killer lashes. 'Okay, so maybe I don't need to worry about point number two.'

Realisation struck. 'Oh, you were *not*…' He was going to warn her about Maddox? 'You, of all people!'

It was Dan's turn to flush—just slightly, but with no corporate collar to hide it she saw colour steal its way up his tanned throat.

'I'm thinking about the show, Ava. We can't

afford any interpersonal issues that might screw things. There's too much riding on this.'

She straightened, armed and dangerous. 'And of course you automatically assume I would be the screw-up. That I wouldn't have the same appreciation of the importance of this.'

'You said it yourself, Ava. You don't value it.'

'No, but *you* do.' Her raised voice drew a few curious glances from the crew. She dropped it carefully and let her eyes burn into his. 'I wouldn't do that to you, Dan.'

Despite everything he'd done—now and nine years ago—that was true. She had no interest in causing him harm. But…it didn't hurt to remind him that he hadn't been as considerate of *her* needs.

'That's generous of you, under the circumstances…'

It was the first time she'd seen him look uncomfortable. Just when she'd thought he wasn't capable of it. 'I'm a generous woman, Dan.'

Her flippant reply took on a whole new meaning as his eyes flickered to the logo on her shirt. It was such a brief moment she thought she might have imagined it, but her skin tingled all over at the suspicion.

He spoke quietly. 'Thank you, Ava. That's more than I deserve.'

Oh. The man certainly knew how to throw her

off kilter. All the fight drained out of her. She cleared her throat. 'Shall we get to work?'

Dan stepped away so Ava could return to the middle of the ugly concrete rooftop where they had three days to transform it into a world-class rooftop garden. She looked completely in her element, and surprisingly at ease with the attention now centred on her. Attention she'd been loath to accept.

The Ava he remembered from childhood had always been gutsy, a rampant tomboy, until one day around her thirteenth birthday a switch had flipped and she'd suddenly discovered she was female. She'd been ragingly shy from then on, the only female left in an all-male family after her mother died when she was eight. The baby by four years, too, which meant she'd been frequently over-protected.

Looking at her now, smiling up at something inane Maddox was saying, professional respect warred deep in Dan's gut with the blinding desire to protect her. He frowned as the feeling shifted south.

Or was it just plain desire?

She was hardly little Ava now. Grown. Talented. Attractive. Beautiful in this moment, with the television lights shining down on her. But she was still Steve's little sister. Virtually his, too.

But not quite.

Not that he wouldn't have killed to be part of their family for real.

Maddox looked at her and spoke, hitting her with one of those perfect smiles that Dan had seen work so often on women in the network. She tipped her head and laughed. The sound danced right over to where he stood watching, and the urge to protect surged in him again.

Steve's kid sister. He had responsibilities here. Professionally and personally.

He'd have to stay on his toes.

CHAPTER FOUR

THE voices were back. Whispering. Urgent.

Even through the thick veil of sleep Ava knew that couldn't be good. Not again…

No one ever whispered in the Lange household. They did everything at mega decibels. But what were the chances, on the eve of her sixteenth birthday, that secrecy and whispers could mean anything other than a surprise being hatched? She shook the beach sand from her hair and tiptoed, smiling, to the kitchen, then crouched, frozen, by the doorway.

It was Dan. Three years of undivided attention had a way of branding a voice into your brain. And that must be her brother with him but—really—who cared? Gorgeous, talented, spectacular Dan was conjuring up a birthday surprise.

For her.

Did anyone else matter? Her heart kicked up three notches.

'Ava's not twelve any more,' Steve's voice whispered, deeper than usual.

Dan sighed before he answered. 'Believe me, I know.'

Ava frowned. His sad voice didn't make him sound as if he was plotting anything fun. Her skin prickled.

'You should say something—'

'I can't,' Dan said. 'When she turns those beautiful eyes on me…how can I?'

Her heart beat like the wings of a honeyeater. Dan was talking about her! He thought her eyes were beautiful. After so many years of seeing her as a kid, he'd finally noticed she was a woman. Nearly.

Tomorrow.

Ava's legs thrashed painfully amongst her bed-clothes as the dream images morphed into a Flynn's Beach backyard, minutes away from midnight.

The lights were off in Dan's converted games room, but that didn't slow Ava down. She'd chosen her best skirt and blouse—strategically short-buttoned—and practised her speech in the mirror fifty times, so she'd know exactly how to stand when delivering it and exactly how she'd look as she did.

Her empty stomach trembled. Dan wouldn't be able to help but take her in his arms and kiss her until they were both breathless.

She'd practised that too. Over and over while

sequestered away for three years, pining for a young man who was, miraculously and unexpect-edly—going to be hers.

God, would she even know what to do with him? An unfamiliar tightness and an unbearable excitement overcame her.

She was practically part of the furniture in Dan's retreat, so turning the unlocked handle without knocking seemed a perfectly reasonable thing to do...at midnight...in the dark...

The door swung inwards and she whispered his name into the darkness...

Ava forced her eyes open on an outraged shout. Her pulse galloped beneath sweat-dampened skin and she lurched up onto her elbows to force air into desperate, aching lungs.

At least this time she'd woken herself before the worst part.

Before the congealed, nine-year-old montage accented by moonlight: the illicit sheen of Dan's toned buttocks; the long length of female leg bent skywards; the sweat-slicked contours of a grown man's chest as he twisted towards where Ava stood, horrified, in the doorway.

Her own agonised sprint down to the beach with Dan's angry oath echoing in her ears.

Ava's body shuddered with mini-convulsions. *Why?* She'd been dream-free for a year. A whole blessed year. She'd thought the nights of thrashing and trembling were finally behind her. It had been bad enough living through it the first time, without reliving it over and again courtesy of her subconscious.

Damn him.

She swung her legs out from under the twisted wreckage of her bedcovers and slowly put her weight on both feet. It wouldn't be the first time her legs had failed her after the dream, but tonight they held. She pushed upright and picked her way carefully to the guesthouse kitchenette.

Coffee. Now.

Too bad it was only two a.m. There was no chance in Hades that Ava was going to let herself fall back to sleep. Not tonight. Not if it meant going back to the agony of her memories.

She set the kettle to rapid boil.

It didn't take a psych major to work out why the dream had returned. She hadn't counted on working this closely with Dan; hadn't expected him to be so hands-on. It made keeping some distance between them challenging and keeping the memories at bay impossible. They retreated away from shore by day, but surged back like a moontide at night.

She rubbed her closed eyes.

The first sip of coffee helped to settle her churning stomach. The second slowed her trembles. It was hot and strong and so terribly normal it chased some of the demons away. But not all of them. The little guesthouse suddenly felt claustrophobic.

Tiny and crowded and...Dan's.

The man sleeping just metres away. The man who had chased after her that night, still buttoning the denim glued to him like a second skin. Still with an acre of bare chest. Still smelling of a strange woman and sex.

Ava surrendered to the urgent desire to be far away. She let herself out through the bedroom doors and tiptoed with her coffee through the garden, beyond the rammed-earth archway to the water's edge. Harbourview Terrace at two a.m. wasn't too far removed from Flynn's Beach at midnight. Quiet, tranquil, private.

She self-medicated again with a gulp of hot caffeine.

Sixteen. Such a blind age. And so horribly, horribly fragile. There'd been a moment back then—hidden away in her favourite grotto on the beach—where she'd thought she might be able to come up with a credible reason for having appeared at his door at midnight. But the complete fatal understanding in his eyes when he'd found her there had robbed her of that hope.

He'd tried to be gentle with her, but she'd

shrugged him off violently, tears fuelled by excruciating humiliation racking her body.

Every time she had the dream, every time the carnal montage played back in her unprotected subconscious, she relived the mortification as though it were fresh. Her heart tightened until it hurt. From her spot by the water the lights of Sydney were a blurry, incandescent mush through eyes awash with remembered pain.

Sixteen.

For a girl with not a lot of life experience she'd certainly had a finely honed instinct for what would hurt. Demanding to know—as if she'd had any right at all—who the woman in his room was. Knowing before he'd even answered that she was a surfer. The woman's blonde hair, tanned, toned muscles and enormous cartoon breasts had been a dead giveaway.

She remembered crossing her arms protectively over her own pathetic efforts and letting nasty Ava out to play. It had felt good. Given the pain somewhere to go.

'How does she stay upright on the surfboard?' she'd sneered.

The censure in the way he'd clipped her name then had hurt almost as much as seeing him lying on top of someone else. Hearing the hoarse ecstasy in his groan.

'I'm twenty years old, Ava. I can sleep with whomever I like.'

Just not me, Ava thought now—not for the first time. Dan had never seen her as anything other than a child.

But his eyes when she'd angered him that night… They'd flooded with the same passion she'd glimpsed in them in the nanosecond before she'd fled out of his bedroom, and for the first time in her life her teenaged body had responded sensually.

Like a woman.

Ava drained the last of her coffee, shifting on the limestone levy to dislodge the uncomfortable tightening of her nipples that plagued her even now. Back then the feeling had confused her, surprised her.

But nowhere near as much as it had surprised Dan.

She remembered his exact expression as the tightening had drawn his focus to the buttons still undone on her blouse. Confused fire had flashed in those molten depths and he'd ripped his eyes violently away from the lace-covered curve of her young breasts. Breasts that had suddenly been aching.

His eyes had widened. The horror on his face had spoken volumes. It had made Ava's breath catch as she'd fumbled the blouse buttons into their eyelets.

'We're just friends, Ava.'

Lord, that had been like steel wool on sunburn. He didn't love her. Or even want her. Her heart had sunk beneath an ocean of shame. She'd wanted to run out into the dark ocean, make a miserable meal for some shark. But something imperceptible and irrevocable had shifted in the moment that her body had responded to the fire in his.

She'd grown up.

She held her breath now, remembering how close his half-naked body had suddenly felt in her beach grotto, how the frost of her breath in the cold night air had mingled with his. How he'd been both the cause and the only analgesic for the throbbing pain in her heart.

Her lips had fallen open and she'd locked eyes with him. Absolutely nothing on this earth to lose. One hundred percent woman.

One hundred percent deluded.

The *doof-doof* of a heavy bass beat dragged her attention back to the small harbourside park between her and the guesthouse. This might remind her of Flynn's Beach, but she'd do well to remember that it wasn't. This was Sydney. And that was a car full of young men out cruising after a night on the turps.

She let the car pass harmlessly by, then dragged

herself to her feet and turned for the house. She'd been lost in her memories for over an hour out here. They swamped her, refusing to be set aside.

As she returned to the house, she noticed a light on at the back of Dan's side of the house. Awareness bristled on her nape. Why was he up at three a.m.? Was he walking off disturbing vivid dreams too? Was he thinking about that night on the beach? How they'd fought?

The realist in her slapped those thoughts down. He was probably not even alone. A man like Dan was hardly likely to be wandering the halls pining for a woman like her. *Particularly* not her.

He'd been more than clear that night on the beach. He'd recognised her unspoken invitation, had stared at her for eternal moments, and then dragged his focus away—out to sea. When he'd brought it back, his eyes had been hard and empty.

Ava hadn't seen them like that since he'd first come to her family, years before. His lips had paled, his jaw had tightened, and then he'd uttered the words that had burned into her young soul for ever.

'I'll never be with you, Ava—'

She'd failed miserably to disguise her flinch at the cruelty in those words. It had been like being dumped by the biggest, coldest wave conceivable. Air-stealing, baffling, aching pain. She'd scrambled to right herself on the ocean bottom.

'You're a child; I'm a grown man—'

Had he thought she wouldn't understand the cold finality of those words? Had he truly needed to grind salt straight into the gaping wound in her chest? It burned again now, a referred pain from years ago. She'd never been enough for him.

'—with the interests and needs of a grown man. Neither of which you could help much with, kiddo.'

Ava stiffened against what had come next. Her blinding attack. The indiscriminate slashing of a mortally wounded young woman. Anything to hurt him the way she'd been hurting. She closed her eyes. Oh, the poison that had poured from her lips... She'd attacked his intelligence, his integrity, and—she shook her head—his surfing. His only love in the world. By the time she was done, his hands had been shaking.

'I was wrong to think we could get past this.' He'd moved to stand. 'I'm leaving in the morning—'

And just when she'd thought she had no heart left to break, she'd felt it rip completely free of her chest. He was leaving. On her birthday. The terror of losing him had cracked headlong against the hurt of his rejection, giving birth to a bright spark that had ignited the rocket-fuel of anger in her belly.

She'd never again spoken to another human

being the way she'd spoken to him then. Shouting, crying. Dying.

'You *should* leave. You've been like a blowfly hanging around ever since I can remember. Go find your own family!'

Stupid with grief, she'd shot to her feet and pursued him when he'd stalked off, unable to stomach the sight of her.

'Like mother like son, huh, Dan? Running off when the going gets tough.'

The kettle's song interrupted the painful memory, and Ava realised that it was tears, not steam, which dampened the kitchen benchtop. Her heart pounded with the realism of the ancient memory, and her throat ached as if she was still sixteen. She recalled vividly the anger in his eyes as he'd spun around and surged back towards her. She'd never in her life seen him so…dark. She had stumbled backwards, but his words had hit her like a barrage of gunfire.

'I will *never* be with you, Ava. I don't know how to make myself any clearer. I'm sorry if that hurts you, but you need to understand.'

Then he'd turned and stalked out of the grotto. And out of her life.

When she'd woken to her father's gentle touch and his sombre, 'Happy sweet sixteenth, princess,' she'd known he'd already gone.

After the humiliation and agony of that night she'd never let someone get close again. She'd lost her confidence, her dignity. Her friend. She'd trussed up her heart in a lead box and buried it in the deepest abyss of her consciousness. She channelled herself into her schoolwork, then her studies, then her employment, and finally her business.

Daniel Arnot had taught her how to be impenetrable. It was a successful strategy that had achieved its goal perfectly.

Until now.

Now her protective casing had been peeled back, leaving her exposed and vulnerable to the one man who had hurt her more than any other. Not that he'd shown the slightest interest in her other than as an asset to his company. A dollar sign on a profit and loss report.

And probably just as well, because—judging by her feelings tonight, by her body's physical response to events that had happened nearly a decade ago—if Daniel chose to turn all that Arnot charm on her she'd be powerless to prevent her body and her heart from overthrowing her carefully reinforced mind.

And that would be a very bad day.

Ava hugged her coffee close, stared at the brightening clouds of morning, and let a decade of pain stream down her face.

CHAPTER FIVE

DAN'S assistant let Ava into his spacious office and encouraged her to make herself comfortable. She moved towards the window, her arms wrapped protectively around her. She was still raw from her restless night, but more determined than ever, in the cold light of day, to find a way to exorcise Dan from her heart.

His office wasn't on the top floor, but it was close. And it was nearly bigger than the entire guesthouse in Harbourview Terrace. The last time she'd been here, she'd been too angry to really appreciate the tasteful decorations and magnificent outlook. She stared across the water. Somewhere on the other side was his sprawling waterfront house. Her temporary home.

He had certainly done well for himself in the years since he'd walked out on her family.

She'd kept up her awareness at first, through her brother, but after a while it had been easier not to

ask. Not to wonder. It had just hurt too much to
hear about his life. The many girlfriends. The
great city career. She looked around. He must
have worked hard to forge the sort of success that
led to this kind of opulence at his relatively young
age.

She trailed her fingers along the hardwood
bookshelves, full of marketing and commerce
tomes. She wondered if he read them or whether
they were props. It didn't matter what he wore or
how big his office was, Ava had a hard time imagining him as the executive type. She remembered
him as a young man in love with the ocean, not
with the stock market. He'd been all set to become
a pro-surfer.

'We've come a long way, haven't we?'

She spun around, embarrassed to be caught
browsing the contents of his shelves. Her eyes
caught the large indoor ficus now standing where
the bamboo had been a few weeks ago. 'What
happened to your *phyllostachys*?'

'Antibiotics cleared it right up.' She blinked at
him. He moved to his desk and flipped open a
panel covered in buttons, smiling to himself.
'Kidding, Ava. I moved the bamboo out of here a
few weeks ago for some time outdoors. I noticed
you weren't happy with its condition.'

He had? Ava could barely remember looking a

t. Her lips moved of their own will. 'The ficus will do better.'

She fell to silence, but it was a far cry from the comfortable silences they'd once shared. In the good old days. Before hormones.

He waved a disk. 'You did well these past two days. I've got some footage if you'd like to see it?'

Her stomach flipped. Oh, Lord—did she? Standing in front of a camera was one thing, but watching herself played back in close-up was quite another.

'What if I stink?'

He smiled and closed the office door, until only an inch of light streamed in from the outer office. 'You don't stink. Quite the opposite.'

She sank onto the sofa in front of the large screen while Dan loaded the disk. Automatic blinds slid out of nowhere across the window and the lights in the office dropped as the television hummed to life.

'These are only dailies, so they haven't been edited or balanced yet,' he warned.

On screen, Ava looked nervous, glancing around the rooftop set anxiously as the tape rolled before anyone called *action*. A sound assistant shot into frame briefly, to better disguise her radio microphone, and then she was alone on screen again. The camera zoomed right in on her eye, focussed sharp, and then pulled back out.

'You look terrified,' Dan commented through the darkness. 'But wait…'

Ava watched herself glance off to one side for the barest moment, see something there, and then turn her face back towards the camera. The fear and tension faded. She took a deep breath, tugged Dan's business shirt more securely across her front, and smiled.

Dan froze the image and that brilliant smile lit the office. She jumped as his voice sounded right behind her.

'What did you see? Then…when you looked away?'

Ava knew exactly. She remembered it. But no way was she going to tell him.

I saw you.

He'd walked past with the director and given her an encouraging smile just as she was about to start. At the time she'd appreciated the show of support, but had no clue what a difference it had made to her face, her fear. Until now. She looked at the giant eyes on screen and recognised that dazzled expression one hundred percent.

Oh, Ava, girl, you're going to have to learn to cover that up.

'I don't know,' she lied. 'There was a lot going on.'

'Well, whatever it was it was good. It put you

in a different place. Watch how you change.' Dan
thumbed the 'play' button and the first to-camera
segment began. On-screen-Ava introduced herself
and spoke briefly about the inner city roof space
they'd be working on. She dropped a line midway through, paused, and calmly commenced
again from that point, running smoothly through
until Brant walked into the shot on cue.

She was no actress, but she wasn't bad either.
Relief trickled through her body. Dan sank onto the
sofa next to her as the disk played on. There was a
second take of the whole introductory segment,
and then some straight-to-camera pieces of Brant's.
Then there was a two-shot, with herself and Brant
walking through the desolate urban roof space.

'You look good together,' Dan murmured from
the shadows next to her ear.

'That's what Brant said.'

'Hmm…I'll bet.'

Ava smiled, distracted by the scene playing out.
She was going to have to get used to seeing herself
on screen. She understood suddenly why television starlets were so bird-like in reality. The
camera forgave nothing. Well, they'd wanted
'healthy'…

The footage played through, and Ava smiled at
the vaguely flirtatious on-camera interaction of
her co-host. It made for good television, and it

was nowhere near as sleazy on camera as it had felt in person. Brant obviously had a good instinct for what worked on screen.

When the entire disk had played, Dan lounged next to her, his arm slung across the sofa-back in the darkness. Without the monitor casting its sickly glow, the only illumination in the room was a thin shaft of light that spilled in from the outer office. Otherwise it was just the two of them, alone in the dark. Ava stiffened.

'What do you think?' He was disturbingly close. Ava forced herself to ignore the ambrosial scent of his aftershave. Like something mixed especially for her from her favourite things.

Ocean, forest and Dan.

She wasn't used to blowing her own trumpet, but she actually didn't stink! 'I'm happy with it. Are you?'

Dan made a so-so gesture and her heart sank. 'For a first day, yes, it's good,' he said. 'There are some things we need to tighten.'

What he thought shouldn't have mattered so much, but disappointment flooded through her at his less than enthusiastic response. 'It's only the first day...'

'It's also the first thing new viewers will watch. We sink or swim on that first day's shooting.'

He was right, but she struggled to see what was

so terribly wrong with it. Naturally, he enlightened her. 'The lighting wasn't even between shots,' he went on. 'Some of the camera work could have been tighter. Your movements weren't the height of grace...'

Ava's cheeks burned in the darkness. He'd have to feel the furnace cooking away next to him, surely? She put her hands up to dampen the heat as excuses started tumbling across her lips.

'It wasn't the same as the run-throughs. The layout of the rooftop was different in rehearsal...'

I've never done this before!

'We'll be rescheduling to allow rehearsals on location to help with that. So you'll feel more comfortable when we roll.'

Ava felt the bite of his censure—all too like that other time. Thank God for the low light. 'Was there anything you *were* happy with?'

'Sure. Your to-camera work is great. The sound was faultless. And the byplay between yourself and Maddox is fun. That'll sell.'

Ah, yes. Ratings. What would work well on television and what wouldn't. Presumably a clod-footed host stumbling over air-conditioning ducts wouldn't. Ava swallowed her pride and listened as Dan outlined the changes he wanted to make before the next shoot. If she could have separated her brain from her heart she would have recognised they were nothing dramatic or particularly difficult. Nothing that a second day of experience wouldn't fix.

But as she sat in the dark, listening to Dan's honey voice pulling her performance to pieces, she just couldn't be dispassionate about it. His opinion mattered. His disappointment hurt.

'Ava?'

'Sorry? What?'

Irritation tightened his tone. 'Was there anything you wanted to ask me? Anything you don't understand?'

I don't understand how you can have changed so much. 'No. I'm good.'

He shifted in the dark. Paused. 'I've upset you.'

The obtuseness in his voice was the absolute last straw. 'Why would you say that? Just because I did my very best, with no experience and not much instruction?' She surged to her feet. 'This was *your* plan, Dan, not mine. If I'm not quite what you were hoping for then you can talk it over with your network buddies and fire me. I'm all too happy to return to my design work and chalk this up as a really bad idea.' She stumbled to her feet.

'Ava, wait...' Dan's hand closed around hers as she yanked the door open. Light pooled in from the outer office, illuminating the regret in his face.

She knew it must also show the hurt and anger in hers. He pulled her into the office—into him—letting the door swing closed again. The darkness was like a warm cloak around her.

'I'm sorry. I forgot you're new to the idea of critical feedback.'

Ava dropped her lashes, ashamed at her unprofessional outburst, but not ready to *still* not be good enough for him.

'I should have taken more care,' he said gently, his thumb stroking the underside of her wrist. It was strangely comforting. And more than a bit distracting. 'You've always been so tough, Ava. Scrabbling straight to your feet after wrecking your bike. Backing younger kids in a fight.'

He was gentling her now, making good on his mistake, but knowing that didn't change its effect on her one bit. She softened like butter in summer.

'I wanted to do well.' *For you.*

'You did do well, Ava. Did you expect to be perfect?'

She blushed. 'Yes. I hoped to be.'

'Ah. Revenge?'

He understood. She remembered that about him. He always got her. Her voice was wry. 'I was hoping to stick it to the faceless suits at the network by being the best I could possibly be.'

He pulled her close, away from any prying ears

in the outer office, sure that at least one of them was supplementing their income courtesy of Bill Kurtz. 'Your logic is fuzzy at times, kiddo. You want to punish them by proving them right?'

'Don't call me that.' She stiffened. 'I'm not a kid any more.'

'No, you're not.' He kept her wrist in his velvet grip, and the husky tone in his voice had her glancing up at him in the half-darkness. 'I realised that the moment I walked into the wardrobe trailer yesterday.'

His thumb grazed over her pulse-point. She swallowed. Hard. 'I'm fine now, Dan. You can let go. Hissy fit is over.'

He didn't let go. 'What are you doing for dinner?'

The rapid change of subject had her reeling. That or the feel of his skin pressed so perfectly against hers. 'Uh...I hadn't thought about it. Something simple?'

'Want some company?'

The thought of eating in the guesthouse alone with Dan was too much to contemplate. 'I was thinking of trying one of the local cafés.'

'Aardvark is good.'

She couldn't help a laugh. 'The mammal or the venue?'

When he released her hand, Ava felt the loss

keenly. 'It's a waterfront café. Excellent chilli mussels.'

Sheesh, was there a single button that Dan hadn't remembered? The idea of a whopping great bowl of her favourite mollusc dominated her mind the moment he planted it there.

'Okay.' Without even touching her, Dan held Ava in complete thrall. She was powerless to move. She stared at his handsome face and wondered what he was working up to say to her. It looked serious.

'Mr Arnot?' A voice interrupted from the outer office.

Dan tensed immediately, but didn't take his eyes from Ava's. 'Yes, Grace?'

'Mr Kurtz on line one. He says it's urgent.'

A moment went by before he peeled his gaze away and the lights suddenly brightened. Ava blinked. There was not a trace in his expression of the gentle coaxing of barely moments ago.

Had she completely imagined it? Wishful thinking?

He nudged her towards the door. 'After all, we both have to eat. Might as well do it together.' The words were impersonal. Convenient. All business.

I must have imagined it. She sucked in a baffled breath, then walked alone out of the room.

Dan swore and turned to his empty office. It

wasn't often he felt comfortable in his own space, regardless of its splendour. Standing in the dark with Ava he'd felt as close to relaxed as he ever had here.

'Line one, Mr Arnot.' Grace called a reminder through to him. He snatched the phone and punched the blinking light with a brisk greeting.

'How did our new talent go this week?' Bill Kurtz wasted no time with niceties. His questions were usually loaded, and Dan knew the Executive Producer would have seen each day's footage before he had himself.

'Good,' he said. 'Great, in fact. A few tech issues, but nothing we can't iron out tomorrow.'

Kurtz snorted. 'Better than good, I'd say. She's a doll. And she's the perfect accessory for Maddox.'

'She's more than an accessory, Bill. She gives the show its street cred—'

'Course she does, course she does...'

Okay, so you're not looking for conversation. So what do you want?

Kurtz barrelled on. 'She wasn't really dressed the way we expected, though...'

Ah.

'But the whole farm girl thing worked for me,' Kurtz said. 'Fresh-faced. Innocent. That was a good call on your part.' Dan gnashed his teeth. 'The client will be happy, and if the client's happy...'

...*Kurtz is happy.* Dan knew it well. Just as he knew what happened if a client wasn't happy. He thought of Ava, waiting for him downstairs, and how he'd bundled her so rudely out of his office. This was not a conversation he'd want her to overhear. But Kurtz wasn't as livid as he'd been expecting. Which made him immediately suspicious.

'Was there something else, Bill?'

'Just one thing...'

Here we go...

'About Maddox. I like what's going on with them in the dailies. That spark. They work well together. I want you to exploit it, Dan.'

Dan's lips tightened; his tone cooled. 'In what way, Bill?'

'Hell, I don't know. Throw them together more. Give 'em more interplay. Sex it up a bit. You're paid to work that stuff out.'

Dan pinched the bridge of his nose and closed his eyes. 'Sex it up?'

'Audiences love chemistry, Dan. Will they? Won't they? The wondering...'

'We're a lifestyle show, Bill. Not daytime,' Dan said.

The phone almost frosted over in his hand. 'This is not a negotiation, Dan. I want to see sparks flying between those two. You have a reputation as the go-to-guy for brave programming, so let's see a little courage here. Stretch the envelope. Prove that our faith in your choice of presenter was not misplaced.'

As if they hadn't forced his hand to consider using Ava like this in the first place... Dan's jaw ached. His dentist was going to be buying a new Mercedes if he didn't ease up on his enamels.

But he knew when to affect a strategic retreat. The harder Dan leaned, the harder Kurtz would lean. It was a case of pick your battles with the unpleasant senior executive. If it had been just him at risk he'd have leaned harder; it was in his nature. But with forty other employees and their jobs in the mix...forty-one if he counted Ava...he'd have to suck it up.

This time.

Ava and Maddox. His stomach turned over. 'I'll see what I can do, Bill. We'll need to introduce it slowly or audiences won't buy it. Don't expect a Royal Wedding.'

'Not for a moment,' came the insincere response. 'I just expect you to do the best thing by the network. I know how much it means to you.'

The older man rang off, leaving Dan glaring angrily into space. Kurtz knew exactly how important Dan's career was to him, how ruthlessly he'd worked over the past six years to make it to producer. A few more wins and he was on track to be the youngest executive producer Australian elevision had ever seen. What a handy tool to wave around in his face. To threaten him with.

Sex it up.

Dan grunted. There was no question Ava wouldn't tolerate it. Most likely she'd tell him and the network exactly where they could shove their sparks. He hadn't needed to grow up with her to know that. He tugged his suit jacket on over his Hugo Boss shirt. Immediately he flashed back to draping his shirt around Ava's bare shoulders, to her standing between his arms, afire. It was disturbingly vivid.

His body tightened.

He sighed. He'd seen exactly what Kurtz saw. There *was* a noticeable…something…between his two co-stars—a relaxed kind of ease. He tried to imagine how it might be to be on the receiving end of that ease and couldn't. Ava just wasn't comfortable around him.

But there was a connection there with pretty-boy Maddox, and Dan's order—his job—was to play on that connection. His mind raced. He could increase the number of their scenes together, look for opportunities in the editing. Let it evolve…naturally.

That way he would be keeping his word to Ava and keeping faith with the network. Simple.

Right.

* * *

'You sure you didn't miss any?' Dan smiled across the table.

Ava folded her serviette and placed it on her spotless plate with no remorse. She'd soaked up the last traces of chilli sauce with crusty bread. Frankly, she'd almost licked the bowl clean while he watched, gobsmacked. Well, if he'd forgotten what a woman eating looked like, that was on him.

'I grew up around a bunch of men. If you left it you lost it.'

Dan laughed. 'I know. I was there. I did warn you their mussels were good.'

'You weren't kidding.' She patted a hand on her stomach. 'Fortunately I can work it off walking home. Which I should do soon if I'm going to be on set on time tomorrow.'

Dan stood and moved around to slide her chair out. Thank goodness his mood had lifted almost the minute they sat to eat in the crowded café. She wasn't ready for another dose of surly Arnot. Whatever had been bugging him when she left his office seemed to have sorted itself.

'My shout,' Dan offered smoothly, sliding his gold credit card across to the pretty cashier who'd been working hard all night to get his attention. And failing.

'That's not necessary...' Ava reached out and

stalled his fingers with hers, embarrassed. This was hardly a date. Even if her tingling fingers hadn't got that message. She curled them safely into her fist.

'Corporate gold, Ava. It's on the network. It's the least they can do.'

It sure was. Ava laughed and let AusOne buy her a meal. Moments later they were walking away from the busy café strip towards Dan's street. Hers now, too. She risked a glance in his direction. He'd been nothing but charming throughout dinner but was patently preoccupied. Several times she'd caught him looking at her strangely, as though he were just about to ask something. Then he'd drop those killer lashes and when he looked up again the strangeness would be gone and they'd go on talking—about the old days, Steve, her dad.

Even at one point her mum, whom Dan had mourned as if she'd been his own. She practically had been. It was she who had convinced Ava's father to let Dan stay as often as he needed to when he was a boy. So they knew he was at least sleeping in a safe place.

Dan took her elbow and steered her across the street between the cafés and the waterfront walk. A thousand lights sparkled across the harbour and cast a pretty glow.

'I lived for Friday nights back then,' he said, his eyes searching the water. 'Did you know that?'

Ava shook her head slightly. 'All I knew was you'd turn up on a Friday night like clockwork. There was a standing invitation.'

'Dinner at the Langes was the highlight of my week. So normal. I even got to play big brother for a night. I used to wish there were seven Fridays in a week.'

Ava flushed. There'd eventually come a point when she'd no longer been able to think of him platonically at all, and she'd barely been able to tolerate the meals which had grown increasingly frequent and increasingly awkward as her awareness of him had grown.

He kicked a stone to the side of the path. 'I missed those dinners after I left.'

Just the dinners, she told her racing heart. Not her. She mustn't read into it. 'Did you miss the surfing?'

She'd never forgiven herself for attacking his surfing that night on the beach. For sneering about his inability to make the pro circuit. He was still the best surfer she'd ever seen. Fearless. Inspirational.

Just part of the reason she'd been so crazy about him.

He studied her as they turned across a park

towards the waterfront, his brows drawn together in a frown. 'No. If I hadn't given away surfing I never would have gone to uni. And if I hadn't studied business there's no way I'd have found my way here. We all grow up.' He sighed. 'But some days I'd just like to sit at that table again and flick peas at the kid across the table, you know?'

Ava smiled. 'You always missed.'

'You always ducked.' He stepped sideways suddenly and nudged her with his hip, the way he'd used to when they were kids. She laughed to cover the zing that raced through her at the simple contact.

We all grow up.

And apart. The man he'd become was a hundred miles from the almost-man she remembered—the hotshot surfer whom everyone had expected to turn pro; the boy with a father but no family. She wondered whether she'd changed, too. The essential Ava.

'You've done well,' she said. 'Maybe it was all worth it?'

'I'd like to think so.'

'Word on the street is that you're the it-boy in television,' she said.

'"Word on the street"? What, you're hanging out with the boys in construction now?' His sideways glance was warm and close. Her heart kicked over.

Was he flirting with her?

'Okay, word in the catering van. I have ears. And Brant knows a lot about the business.'

He slowed as they approached Ava's little gate. She was happy to slow with him. She was enjoying this rare chance to connect with the *old* Daniel. No strings. No agendas.

'I don't want to talk about Maddox.' His brown eyes didn't quite meet hers.

'You don't like him?' she said.

'I didn't say that. He's very good at what he does, and he rates his socks off.'

'But?'

'But… I just don't want to talk about him. Not tonight.' He stopped under the stone arch which formed the gate to her little garden. His eyes were suddenly masked.

Tonight?

The word hung like a firework in the sky, all bright and hard to ignore. It made Ava suddenly aware of who and where they were: a man and a woman on a warm, moonlit night against the sparkling lights of Sydney. With a whole night ahead of them.

It almost made it possible to forget everything that stood between them.

He rested his forearm on the rammed-earth arch above her head, and it brought his body closer to ers. Her mouth dried as she looked up at him. He was still the best-looking man she knew. Brant might be beautiful, but it was a manufactured kind of beauty. The moonlight accentuated the line of Dan's jaw, his cheekbones and the ridge of his firm brow. The essential maleness of him stirred the same appreciation in her now as it always had.

Long before she should have been appreciating maleness. Her body quivered an alert. Time to change the subject.

'Did you ever sort things out with your father?' She winced as soon as the words were out of her mouth.

His whole body changed in an instant. His voice was curt in the quiet of the night. 'Next topic.'

Right.

'I guess some things don't change.' She didn't mean to say it aloud, and she barely did. Her body instinctively responded to the pain in his clipped words, wanting to heal him.

He looked at her steadily, his gaze softening and flitting over her face and shoulders before returning to her lips. Her heart fluttered helplessly. When they finally zeroed in on her eyes, his own had darkened two shades. Thick lashes swept down over them.

'While others change massively,' he murmured.

'How can I be standing here contemplating kissing the kid I flicked peas at?'

His hand dropped from the archway to rest gently on Ava's bare shoulder, his thumb toying with the thin straps of her summer dress where they crossed her suddenly scorching skin. Her heart pounded against her chest as though desperate for oxygen.

Her lungs certainly were.

This was a bad idea for so many reasons. But for the life of her she couldn't dredge up one.

This is Daniel. Beautiful, gorgeous, talented Daniel. And he was on the verge of kissing her. And she wanted that. Very badly.

How many kinds of masochist was she?

I will never be with you, Ava. His words echoed in her ears, forcing her body into action. She straightened against the little rendered archway and tried to think of something clever to say— something brilliant and witty and diverting—but she came up desperately short.

So she just stared at him, wary.

'God, Ava,' he breathed, dropping his hand. 'I'm sorry. I shouldn't have said that. You deserve more than your boss pawing you at your front door.'

Expensive aftershave mingled with the scent of raw man, seeping into her blood, racing narcotic-like through her veins. Waves lapped on the nearby waterfront. The aged archway pressed grittily into her shoulders. A phone rang somewhere nearby. She forgot to breathe.

I will never be with you, Ava. A voice screamed at her to remember, trying to make a dent in the bubble of awareness suddenly growing around them. She was supposed to move away. That would be the smart thing to do. But, God help her, only one part of her could move—and it wasn't her feet.

She straightened towards him, drawn like a magnet to his heat, and raised her eyes.

He bent cautiously towards her, his dark hair slipping down his forehead. A question burned bright in his gaze, but his lips separated just slightly as he zoomed in on hers. Such beautiful lips.

The phone pealed a second time. *Her* phone, inside the guesthouse. She ignored it. Dan's eyes held hers intently and his hands moved up to frame her face, strong fingers sliding behind her jaw and tipping her mouth towards him. The feel of his skin brushing against hers caused her legs to tremble and an impatient pulse kicked in deep inside her.

For the love of God, kiss me!

The phone shrilled a third time.

His mouth traced along her jaw just a milli-metre above her flesh. He was scenting his way to his target, his breath hot against her skin. The excruciating trail robbed her of what precious little air remained in her lungs. Ava's fists clenched in his jacket to hold herself up.

And…finally…he touched his mouth to hers.

The charge that had built between them for over a decade was expelled the moment their mouths met. At the first caress of his soft, warm lips Ava jerked backwards into the rammed earth. With solid rock behind her there was nowhere else to go but ahead, into him. She closed the distance, sliding her mouth over his with a hungry moan.

Nine years of hunger. More.

'Ava…' he groaned against her lips. One large hand closed around her nape while the other slid to her waist, pulling her tight against him. Her own hands drifted deliriously against his broad chest as she tasted and tested and discovered his lips. Opening her mouth to him was as natural as the night going on around them.

Her face turned towards his like a moonflower straining towards its god. Dan splayed his legs slightly, to fit better against her small frame. Her head fell back as he stroked his tongue in and out of her mouth, tangling with hers, tracing the shape of her teeth on a long, pleasured growl. Every twist, every tangle was an erotic dance, increasing the voltage between them. The earth began to spin. Electricity buzzed, chemicals surged and Ava knew without a shadow of doubt that she would never experience a kiss quite like this again.

Ever.

It didn't matter that her legs gave way, because Dan held her so securely in his arms. Every part of him was rock-hard and, wrapped so close into him, she felt as though the two of them had simply melted into the stone archway.

In that moment she would have quite happily resided there with him for ever.

Dan's head lifted, his brown irises now liquid magma. Colour raced high in his jaw and his breathing was rough against her ear. 'Tell me to stop.'

Ava heaved in deep, ragged breaths, her thoughts jumbled. Why on earth would she stop something that felt this good?

I will never be with you…

Shut up, shut up! She trembled as endorphins surged through her system. She glanced at the door leading to the guestroom. The thought of Dan pressing down over her in the bedroom there, silhouetted against the giant moon was…*perfect*. But the chances of him sticking around afterwards? Of having anything more meaningful to offer her than one night?

Not high.

Still, she wasn't going to get another chance. She was lucky to be getting a second crack at her dream at all. And she was older now, and wise enough to know that there was no such thing as a happy ending. She glanced again at the door and verbalised her decision.

'Don't stop.'

Dan buried himself in her hair and pressed his lips behind her ear. Her legs sagged. He lifted her hard against him on a groan and turned towards the door.

Just then Ava's answering machine finally picked up the call in the guesthouse. Her father's voice carried out to where they stood. 'Hey, brat, it's me. Sorry, I've missed you...'

Dan froze, mid-step. Mid-kiss.

'Steve and I were cleaning the garage and we came across a pile of your old things. We were wondering if you wanted them? The only thing I recognise is your old blue bike, the one with the spokey-dokeys still on it.'

Dan's breath punched out of him. Ava looked into his pained face, his suddenly blank eyes where the fire had been.

No, no, no.... Her pathetic tugs towards the

bedroom failed miserably. He tore his arm away from her and his head sagged towards his chest.

'Anyway, just give me a call and I'll talk you through it. Okay, talk soon. Love you.'

A beep, then silence. The only sound in the garden was them both heaving in a lungful of air. Ava took his hand in hers, her voice artificially, desperately light. She tugged…

But he resisted. Right up until that moment Ava had thought there might be something to salvage. That her chance might not have turned completely to ashes with one phone call.

He lifted tortured cold eyes and she knew.

Daniel Arnot was about to reject her…again.

CHAPTER SIX

EXCRUCIATING.

That was the only word for it. Ava wasn't sure what was worse—the moments where Daniel refused to meet her eyes, or those accidental moments where they did meet hers across the busy set, dark, shuttered, and glaring at her from under thick lashes.

Nice work, Lange. Sleeping with the man who broke your heart. Your boss. The fact she hadn't was only a matter of semantics and a few precious minutes. If not for her father's call…

It was all horribly out of character for her. She'd slept with an impressive total of two men in her whole life—hardly a football team. She'd not had the time or the interest for more. The first time had been all about getting it out of the way, shucking off the virgin label. And the second time… Well, he'd been nice, funny and interested, and she'd thought that might be enough. It had been affection more than attraction on her part.

But she'd sure been attracted two nights ago. She'd never felt such a yearning. Stupid word, but it fitted perfectly.

She could only wonder what she'd be feeling today if the phone had been set to silent.

'Ava?' Brant appeared beside her, and she welcomed the distraction. 'Care to run some lines while they change the set-up?'

Brant knew next to nothing about plants—although he was a quick study—so he rarely deviated from the text provided by the show's writers. The cues were his anchors, and so, for his sake, Ava tried to memorise them. If she was going to go roaming freely off-script to talk about her passion, the least she could do was give Brant his in and out points.

He thrust some crisp, clean pages at her. She took them cautiously. 'What are these?'

'Rewrites.'

'They've rewritten the segments?' She had one to-camera segment today, and Brant had one. Both complicated set-ups. Between that was some serious design time. Now she had to run new lines.

'Nope, merged segments. We're doubling up in each one.'

Both of us? She glanced at the pages and saw

the writers had added a line or two for each of them in the other's segment. At least she wouldn't be standing there like a dunce while Brant presented. 'Why?'

'Orders from our friendly neighbourhood producer. Shall we?' He popped her on the shoulder with his rolled-up pages and smiled.

She sighed. 'Sure. Let's use the stairwell, where it's quiet.'

They were eight storeys high on the roof of a small business block on the edge of the Sydney CBD. A rooftop seething with tradesmen, television crew and assorted *Urban Nature* work crew. She'd designed this rooftop habitat months ago, such was the preparation which went into some of these rehab jobs. To Ava it *was* rehabilitation: turning grey concrete messes into natural spaces with soul. She'd relished the challenge of taking this barren man-made rooftop and softening it with native grasses and succulents, running it through with timber boardwalks.

All day long they'd drawn curious looks from the windows of the factories that overlooked their worksite. Ava wasn't sure what interested them more, the transformation of the roof space into a lush garden, or the cameras and obvious television activity. Or possibly the presence of pin-up boy Brant. She'd like to think the former.

'You sure you don't want to use your trailer?' Brant gave her one of his winning smiles as she hauled open the door to the infrequently used stairs leading from the rooftop. 'It'll only take a second to get there.'

Ava frowned. Was he trying to get her alone in her trailer? The way he was leaning on the doorframe oh-so-casually, smiling down on her, cajoling... But there was something not quite authentic about it. She looked around them. And smiled.

'You don't want to get your trousers dirty.' She knew she was right. The stairs were caked in years of commercial grime.

Brant glanced over his shoulder and then pursued her into the stairwell, pulling the door closed behind them. 'It's filthy in here,' he whispered urgently. 'And Carrie will have my ass if I trash another set of trousers.'

Ava laughed. 'You are such a princess, Maddox.'

He whacked her harder with his script pages. Ava laughed more. It was getting tougher not to like him. 'Fine, we'll adjourn to my office—where we can rehearse in the splendour to which you've obviously become accustomed.'

Brant smiled as they turned to the stairs and slung one arm around her shoulder. 'You're a good sort, Lange. I owe you one.'

'Going somewhere?'

Cool air was sucked in as the rooftop door suddenly opened behind them. Ava twisted to follow the sound.

'Dan.' She cringed at the breathiness of her own voice, and the subtle lift of Brant's eyebrow told her he hadn't missed it. Defensiveness surged through her. 'We're off to rehearse our surprise new lines. Your doing, I understand?'

His chocolate gaze was steady. 'I wanted to try working you two together more this episode. Give you a chance to get to know each other.' He looked pointedly at Brant's arm around her shoulder then looked at Ava. 'Perhaps it was unnecessary?'

Brant dropped his arm, but not in much of a hurry. 'I'm not complaining. I think we make a good pair, don't you, Ava?'

She struggled to muster a smile. The Dan she remembered had never switched it on and off quite so effectively, but he was standing scowling darkly at her now. Two nights ago he'd had his tongue in her mouth.

For the first time since moving to Sydney she felt out of her depth. Was this how things were done in Dan's high-rise world? Treating people this way? She wasn't cut out for it if it was. But she'd be damned before she'd let him see that. She took her cue from Brant, adopted an unconcerned veneer and smiled. Her best TV-host sparkler.

'Absolutely.'

Without a backward glance, she continued down the stairs to the top-floor elevators, below which was the safety of her mobile office. The one place she knew Dan would not enter uninvited. Since gifting it to her it in the first place he hadn't set so much as a foot across its threshold. It was her sanctuary.

She felt his eyes on her until she pushed through the heavy door onto the top-floor landing. She glanced up at him just before she passed through. He stared down the stairwell as dark and gloomy as a storm cloud.

One that was threatening to break.

Yesterday's work had been brutal, but productive. They'd shot all the 'before' segments, showing the scope of the barren rooftop canvas they would be working with, and overnight construction fairies had come in and laid the entire space with a chequerboard of timbers and subterranean drainage to help keep the tonne of introduced soil on the rooftop from becoming waterlogged.

They'd captured that work in time-lapse, so that there'd be no illusions that it was an easy job, but for the production crew the hard work started now.

Dan roamed the set, thinking about how long

it had been since he'd been hands-on in production. Or since he'd worked outdoors. It felt good.

Really good.

The stairwell door opened and Ava and Brant emerged from below, kidding around with a sound technician and entirely relaxed at the start of the day. But the moment her eyes found his they dulled and the gorgeous smile faltered.

Damn. He'd done that. He'd done exactly what he'd promised James Lange he'd never do.

Hurt Ava.

Twice. And now he'd been complicit in setting her up with a lech. The worst possible type of man for her. Okay, the *second* worst possible type of man. Maddox had yet to paw her in her own front garden. Dan glared at the blond pretty-boy and the way he smiled at Ava.

Give him time...

On a curse, he marched over to where Ava poured coffee from the makeshift servery. 'Ava. Can I have a minute?' he barked at her.

She fumbled the coffee she was pouring, and then placed it down carefully before turning to him. Silent. Not giving an inch. He probably deserved at least that. The caterer raised his eyebrows and turned politely away, but Dan knew he wouldn't miss a thing. He drew her away from prying ears.

'About Maddox and you...' The rest hung awkwardly.

Ava raised her eyebrows, clearly impatient. He instantly felt about eight years old, facing his father. The man with a special talent for making a boy feel stupid. But on this occasion he was doing just fine on his own.

'The two of you are...getting on well.' He struggled to pull the frost from his voice

Ava shook her head and took a deep breath. 'Yes, we are. Isn't that what all the rewrites have been about? Building rapport?'

'On screen, Ava. Not off.'

Her sharp mind raced. 'There is no "off screen" with Brant and I. What are you accusing me of?'

'I'm not accusing you. I'm just reminding you. I don't want any interpersonal issues affecting production.' *You stinking hypocrite, Arnot.*

Ava glared at him. 'Brant's not the man you seem to think—'

'I know exactly what kind of man he is. He's not the right sort for you.'

'Oh, really?' Sparks practically shot from her eyes. 'And what kind of man *is* right for me?'

'Someone who challenges you. Someone with half a brain.'

'Only half? You flatter me.' She shot him a contemptuous look and turned to walk away.

'Don't.' He reached out and spun her towards him. The caterer abandoned all pretence of not listening in. Dan pulled her entirely out of earshot. 'Don't look at me like that.'

She blazed at him. 'Like what?'

'Like I've done something to you that you weren't a willing party to. You kissed me back.'

'I thought your plan was just to pretend that never happened?'

'It happened, and my bet is we've both been thinking about it,' he said.

'But not talking about it, apparently.'

'What's to talk about? It was a mistake.'

Doe eyes rounded in her pale face. 'Is that a fact?'

'You're Steve's little sister—not to mention you're the talent on my show. And we have history.' He stacked the excuses so high he could hardly see over them. 'You and I hooking up was never going to be anything but inappropriate.'

'*Inappropriate?* That's a very politically correct way of putting it.'

'You want me to say *mistake* again?'

Colour roared into her face. 'The kind of man that suits me or doesn't is none of your business Daniel Arnot,' she raged. 'My relationship with Brant is also none of your business. AusOne's bought my face and my expertise. Nothing more

Now, if you don't mind, I have work to do.' She twisted free and marched off towards the rest of the crew.

A choice curse crossed his lips.

He'd stuffed that up royally. All he'd wanted to do was warn her, take some of the wind out of Maddox's sails. His gut was festering like an ulcer watching them together. Smiling at each other, sharing private jokes. Sharing private anything.

It galled him almost as much to watch it as it did to know that she was playing right into the network's hands. What had happened to the professional self-respect she had gone on about? He'd barely had to give her a nudge and she was falling right in with a sleaze like Maddox. So easy.

Dan frowned. Ava wasn't easy. The woman was pure hard work.

Despite what they'd shared three nights ago, Dan knew in his heart that it wasn't her style to sleep with someone on the first date—it hadn't even been a date, he had to remind himself—so she wasn't about to go tumbling into bed with Maddox.

Not straight away, anyway.

But later? When she'd got to know him a little? Would she remain blind to the real man beneath the glamour? The man who liked his women fast and free? Who left them even faster? Just the thought of Maddox's hands on Ava's body made his skin burn. He unclenched his balled fists and glanced at the red welts across his palm where his nails had cut in.

Not Ava.

He felt like a fraud. Pushing Ava towards Maddox with one hand and pulling her away with the other. He'd jeopardised his job, just now, trying to warn her off. But he'd underestimated her tenacity and her loyalty. Or maybe he'd underestimated Maddox and his skill. Either way, the result was the same.

Maddox one, Arnot nil.

Damn.

CHAPTER SEVEN

THERE were less than ten minutes to crunch time. The first show of the new season was airing across Australia at seven-thirty p.m. Ava kept telling herself it didn't matter if she did well—that it wasn't important to excel, she only had to be reasonable. Maintaining her professional credibility was what was important, and the designs. Not being the world's best television presenter.

But another part of her wanted to do well. For herself and for Dan, if she was being honest, to help make the show the success he so desperately wanted it to be. She was still mad with him, furious that he'd brought Brant into the stupid mixed-up mess that was their friendship, but despite all that her lingering feelings for him still drove her to do well for his sake.

Lingering, Ava? Or returning?

Dan entered the crowded bar on the ground floor of AusOne and, judging by his suit, he'd come straight down from his office. He scanned the room immediately, until his eyes met hers for less than a heartbeat before he looked away. But his room-scanning ceased. He immediately became engaged in conversation with a few of the mid-level executive types from the network.

She fought her natural inclination to think he might have been looking for her. Probably gearing up for battle. The past few days had been uncomfortable enough—avoiding each other's eyes, the stony silences.

'Nervous?' Carrie, resplendent in a peacock-blue skirt and with the sensational make-up you would expect of a professional, shoved a glass of juice into Ava's hand as she slid into the booth next to her. Ava regretted her choice of a simple summer dress and not even eye make-up.

'It feels weird to be worrying about anything more than how the design comes across on television.'

'The design and you will both be fabulous.' Carrie squeezed her arm.

'I hate this part.' A bright-eyed Brant slid into the booth beside Ava, then waved Carrie around to his other side. 'If we go down in flames then I'd like to do it sandwiched between two beautiful women.'

Carrie laughed and obliged, shuffling over to

Brant's left. 'Nice suit,' she said to him, sipping her drink innocently.

'Spotless, you'll notice.'

Their typical banter helped take her mind off the moment to come. She looked at her watch and swallowed. Two minutes to launch. Dan moved to stand under the widescreen television and called for hush.

'In just over sixty seconds the second season of *Urban Nature* will hit living rooms all over the country,' he announced. 'Advance audiences have liked it, some have loved it, but we've all seen shows rate well on test and then sink on air.'

Ava swallowed. He looked so calm, utterly confident. She knew he had to be anything but, and her heart went out to him. She reined it in.

'This won't be one of them. We've pulled a good show together, folks.' He raised his beer in salute. 'To all of you who've worked so hard, and to what we hope will be AusOne's biggest new hit…to *Urban Nature*.'

The crowd echoed his toast, and the sound of clinking glasses resounded through the stylish bar. Carrie and Brant touched glasses to her left. Ava looked up and met Dan's eyes, and he raised his bottle of designer beer in silent acknowledgement and then brought it to his lips as the lights started to dim. She couldn't get her eyes off those lips. She knew, firsthand, how that bottle was feeling. Only when the room got dark and the titles for *Urban Nature* began to air was she able to drag her focus off his mouth.

She let her breath out slowly in the darkness of the now quiet room. The opening titles finished and the show began. Brant's handsome face, even better-looking on television, beamed out at them. His voice was warm and rich as he introduced the audience to the *Urban Nature* concept and his new co-host and designer, Ava Lange.

Ava saw her own face fill the screen. She looked far more together than she remembered feeling; the editing team had done a fantastic job of placing overlay footage at those places where her composure had faltered. She and Brant worked well together, and it was clear immediately that there was a whole team working on the install.

A load lifted from her as she realised the network hadn't pulled any swifties regarding the true number of people working on the installs. No one would be in any doubt about how many people it really took to create the finished garden. She'd heard on the grapevine that Dan had negotiated ruthlessly to affect those changes with the network this season. *Her* season. Would he have made the same call had she not put such a priority on maintaining integrity?

Her credibility was thus far intact. She settled in to watch, her drink untouched.

Six minutes later the show broke for the first of many commercials. Ava glanced nervously around the room as the lights rose and saw nothing but smiles. Gradually the silence morphed into a murmur of excitement. Then a throng.

'I'd say we're onto a winner, hon,' Brant said, beside her. 'You're quite amazing up there. Completely…' He struggled for the right word.

'Vibrant.' Dan spoke from immediately behind their booth, and Ava leapt at his unexpected closeness. 'You've both come up trumps. Congratulations.'

'We should say the same to you.' Brant tipped his head in courteous acknowledgement.

Dan slid onto the seat by Ava's side, leaned over and clacked his beer against the one offered by Brant. The move pressed his body against hers.

Her blood thrummed. The booth was small, and the addition of Dan only made it smaller. His heat soaked into her and she struggled not to think about the many places where he was touching her. His thigh, his hip, his long muscled arm. Fire rose in her cheeks and she squirmed. *Not* thinking about touching only made her flash

back to the other night. Something she was
trying hard not to do. How those powerful arms
had felt crushing her to him. How his hands had
dwarfed her face as he cupped it. How he'd
spread his thighs to bring his mouth closer to
hers. Oh, that mouth….

'How are you feeling?' Dan's breath tickled
her ear as he leaned in close to speak.

She nearly yelped. The question encompassed
more than just the show; she could see it in the
smoky depths of his eyes. Was this an olive
branch? Lord, she wanted it to be. She missed
him, pure and simple. The kisses had been to die
for, but she wasn't sure they were worth the arguments
or the days of frosty silent treatment
afterwards. The hurtful, lingering silences.

For the first time she began to understand why
he had left back when she was sixteen. The
cleanest cut.

'Pleased so far. It's good, Dan.'

Warmth flashed across his expression and she
struggled to read it. Was it pleasure at her compliment
or that she'd accepted his peace offering?
Whatever, she found it hard not to bask in the hint
of warmth in eyes that had been arctic for days.

'I haven't seen you around at the house.' She
leaned in close, keeping her voice low in the
hubbub. Only a trusted few knew she and Dan

were sharing a roof. The move only increased the number of places their bodies touched. Her nerve-endings sang. 'Where've you been?'

'I've worked late quite a bit this week. End of financial year reports, market analyses.'

Avoiding you, he might as well have said.

But she was no different. How had she known Dan wasn't home? Because she'd worked late every night, tucked up in her Winnebago in the car bay next to his empty one. There was something sad and lonely about that—the two of them burning the midnight oil, working towards the same goal, yet in complete isolation from each other.

'Dan, I—'

The lights dimmed again and a hush fell in the room. He threw her a long look as he slid out of the booth. In the sinking darkness his fingers brushed against hers and then he was gone. She stared at the giant monitor but saw nothing. The tingle in her fingers from where he'd accidentally touched her spread like spilled champagne.

If it had been accidental?

They'd done it. Everyone in the room held their breath until the final name rolled on the credits, and then a rousing cheer went through the bar. The show was good—better than good—and everyone knew it.

Drinks flowed and the conversation grew deafening as excited people tried to talk over other excited people. The energy in the room quadrupled, and Ava got caught up in the maelstrom of sheer goodwill. After the first couple of shouted compliments—which she struggled to accept without flushing—it became easier to smile, to receive the good wishes with grace.

The editing team were the heroes of the night, their work being the major contributor to the pace and atmosphere of the programme. They'd lifted it from the realm of commercial lifestyle television to somewhere higher, and they'd taken everyone involved in its creation right along with them. It was nothing like their competition.

Ava didn't realise she was searching the room until her eyes found their target. Across the bar, Dan flipped his cell open and answered. He turned half away and plugged his other ear with a finger, as if that would lessen the cacophony. Ava watched him closely, trying to guess what he was saying. His eyes widened, and then closed briefly before he lowered the phone. But he didn't snap it shut.

He called again for quiet, and had to employ the help of several others when he was roundly ignored by the masses. Eventually the noise level reluctantly dropped. He spoke quickly to his assistant producer and turned away.

'Preliminary figures have us at eight!' the assistant whooped.

Another cheer, more whistling and clinking of glasses, a second round of backslapping. Brant had warned her anything above six on the rating scale was good news. An eight was fantastic news. She looked around to congratulate Dan, just in time to see him slipping out of the bar, the phone still glued to his ear. She pushed towards him, but not fast enough.

In the end her whispered congratulations smacked against the door he disappeared through.

'Say that again, Bill?'

Dan slumped against the wall of the lift, his pleasure at rating an eight short-lived.

'They were every bit as popular with the real audience as they were with the test one. We want you to ramp up the Ava/Brant thing. Put some spin on it.'

'Spin.' The word was like a curse.

'Maddox has made some bad choices in his career. Not in terms of his work, God knows, but his personal life. The number of times the network has had to bail him out of one seedy bar or another, or pay off some skank who's trying to make the headlines… Someone like Ava could be the best thing for his reputation. Put a bit of distance on those bad choices.'

Who cares about Maddox? Dan closed his eyes. 'She won't do it.'

'Persuade her. Convince her. Lie to her for all I care. Just make it happen. I want apple-pie Ava Lange and bad-boy Brant Maddox firmly connected in people's minds this time next week. I don't care if they're out buying milk—you make it look like they're scouting for a home.'

'And if I say no?'

The silence was ugly. But Dan could play that game; he'd been raised on it. He waited Kurtz out.

'I'm giving you first refusal here, Dan. Out of respect. But if you won't do it I'll task it to the spin department. I don't care who gives it to me just as long as I get it. Lange and Maddox are the next it-couple on the East Coast.'

Dan thought furiously. He'd seen what the sharks from PR had done before. No way was he throwing them Ava. But that meant he had to work her over himself. Kurtz was counting on that. This stank of a set-up.

Kurtz had just declared war.

Was this how evil did its thing? No shadowy horned creature standing at a crossroads at midnight. Just a whole series of moments like this one, with choices that could be justified if you talked long enough. When someone asked him to compromise just a little piece more of his soul.

On those occasions, Dan just looked to the thing inside him that surged in his gut and drove him like a wild-eyed racehorse. A vivid memory of a sneering voice and a brutal hand and the damage that both could inflict to a young boy.

But under no circumstances was he throwing Ava to the PR sharks. He took a breath and ripped off another chunk of his soul. 'I'll take care of it.'

'Excellent.' Kurtz didn't even bother to disguise the gloat. 'Let me know if there's anything I can do.'

Dan slammed his phone shut on the mirrored wall of the lift, his mind racing. Publicity was essential to a programme's success, and it would naturally focus on the two hosts to some degree. His job now was to make sure that he could spin the pin.

Control the beast.

But that meant controlling Ava. Good luck with that! If she found out about this, there was every chance she'd end up hating him. If she didn't already hate him for running out on her the other night.

She'd never believe for a second that both were for her protection.

He shook his head. Was there really that much difference between him and Maddox? His father had always said he was as faithless as his cheating mother, and in this at least good ol' Pop might have been on the money. He visualised Ava's beautiful face in the bar downstairs, the trust that had flowered so easily after a few days of hostilities between them. Then he imagined betraying that trust.

If this was going to work he'd have to depersonalise things. Sever those golden rare threads of attraction that had started to string between him and Ava. It was an all too seductive luxury that he just couldn't afford.

He swore under his breath and sent the lift to the foyer.

'Want to share a ride home?'

Home. The word sounded so comfortable coming out of Dan's mouth. Almost possible. Ava let herself be guided out of the bar by the hand at her back, squeezing past the still celebrating crew and network personnel. The warm night air kissed her skin as they emerged onto the street. Dan glanced around for a taxi.

'How do you feel about the ferry?' Ava asked, waving onwards the taxi that had spotted them. ') could use the walk.' *And some uninterrupted time with you.* Ten minutes to Circular Quay, fifteen crossing the harbour, and another ten strolling home from the Neutral Bay pier. Plenty of time for what she was hoping to say.

It was time she laid a few demons to rest. And established a few boundaries.

Dan set off on an incomprehensible route towards the quay, through bustling night streets lit mostly by the fluorescent shop-fronts and fast-food signs which lined them. It wasn't yet ten o'clock, and the city still bustled with diners, shoppers, sightseers and late workers heading home. He cut confidently through all the passers-by just a step ahead of her, making her path effortless. He was so comfortable in this city, such a natural part of it.

'Okay, Ava?'

The man could sure read her. 'I was just thinking that I could drive a tank through the main street in Flynn's Beach this time of night and not see a soul.'

His lips quirked at the memory. 'Different world. Each has its merits.'

They emerged onto George Street and turned towards the Sydney Harbour Bridge in all its glory against the night sky. They moved with the crowd surging towards Circular Quay, where a fleet of large green ferries came and went like a rapidly changing tide, taking people across the harbour and up-river.

Dan slowed and stepped in beside her. 'It took me a while to get used to Sydney time. It works differently to the rest of the country.'

Ava looked at the throng of people around her and shook her head. 'I'm struggling with the idea of six months, and you've been here six years.'

'You get used to it. It gets in your blood.'

'I thought you'd have picked a beach property? To be close to the surf?'

His glance flicked to the bridge. 'I needed a clean break from surfing. It wasn't something I could just do casually. But I couldn't face the idea of watching other people do it out of my window.'

A clean break. He seemed to have so little difficulty making that kind of cut. She visualised his favourite surfboard and wondered if Old Faithful felt as strongly about his amputate-the-limb approach.

Surfing. His father. *Her.*

The throng paused momentarily at an intersection, and then surged ahead as the crossing lights changed. Dan directed her carefully, with a hand at her lower back. As warm as she already was on the typical Australian summer evening, his palm seared its print on her skin through her light dress.

At the quay, ferries came and went, servicing the many luxury properties along Sydney's extensive waterfront. Dan and Ava broke away from the general crowd and crossed to where the Neutral Bay ferry sat waiting for passengers travelling across-harbour to the ritzy suburb. The lights of the Opera House cast an eerie glow.

Dan led the way to the enclosed upper deck, close to an open window. Fresh salty air streamed in as the massive engines roared to life and they rumbled out into the harbour.

Ava settled in for the fifteen-minute trip and did her best to ignore the heat surging from the man next to her. It wasn't easy. He'd shrugged off his jacket so only the thin cotton of a designer shirt stood between her and the hard expanse of his chest.

That chest. Two deep breaths were barely enough to get her composure on an even keel.

'Feeling okay?' he asked.

'I'm just…puffed out from the walk.'

'Yep. No one strolls in Sydney.'

She shifted uncomfortably on the green plastic seating. 'Why did you come here?' she asked.

'This was where the work was.'

'There was work at home.'

His eyes darted to the lights of the city, receding behind them. 'I couldn't be who I needed to be in Flynn's Beach.'

'Who was that?'

Waves crashed relentlessly on the ferry's bow. 'Someone new. I needed to reinvent myself.'

'What was wrong with your old self?'

'Nothing. He's still in here somewhere. But to

do what I wanted—want—to do, I needed a blank canvas. I needed to be anonymous.'

She looked at the city where he must have known practically no one six years ago. 'You certainly got that. Did you not feel that old Dan could make it here?'

His fists clenched and unclenched on his lap. 'I was barely more than a kid, Ava. Dan-the-Man— king of the small town waves. How seriously was that guy going to be taken in Sydney?'

'So you just killed him off? Cut him off, just like surfing?'

Just like me?

His jaw clenched. 'Having nothing, knowing no one, helped me focus only on my goal. My career.' His eyes found the blinking lights of the far shore and home. 'I wouldn't have any of this if I hadn't taken the risk.'

'It doesn't mean you'd have nothing. You'd just have had different things. Why do you want this particularly?'

He spun round to pin her with his eyes. 'Same reason you do. To be the best. To be the first. You create gardens; I create television shows.'

'I design landscapes because I want to help change people's attitudes to nature. Why do you want to create television shows, specifically?'

She couldn't fault his drive or question his

success. Even if some of his methods didn't seem ideal, if the gossips were to be believed, Daniel Arnot was on the fast track to running his own network one day in the not too distant future. That sort of success didn't come without a cost.

But did that have to include his soul?

'Because I want to be…' He dropped his eyes and his voice. 'Because it's important to me to succeed.'

'I get that. But why the mammoth drive? Why do you burn with it?'

He nailed her with his gaze. 'Because I want to be better than *him*.'

A tiny light came on in her mind. His father. Mitchell Arnot owned a small chain of garages along the southern coast. He was one of Flynn's Beach's leading businessmen.

She frowned. 'I think it's safe to say you've eclipsed his success ten times over, Dan.'

'Eclipsing is not enough. I'm aiming for total annihilation.'

Well! That was a conversation-stopper. If not for the agony in his eyes she'd almost be afraid of the hate also burning there. Ava had wondered what had driven Dan away from his father, but her parents had never shared. She'd gleaned a few things from the town gossips—a hippy mother who left him when he was barely walking, and a difficult relationship with his father ever since—but nothing that warranted that level of response.

Lord, a public ferry was so *not* the place for this discussion. She leaned forward and lowered her voice. 'What did he do to you?' she whispered.

'That's none of your business.'

He might as well have slapped her in the face.

He swore and barely met her eyes, speaking softly. Pained. 'I can't talk about this with you, Ava.'

She willed herself to be patient. Not to react to the hurt. 'Have you talked about this with anyone?'

The silence stretched. The ferry chugged. 'Your father. He helped me to...moderate...my feelings.'

This bruised, vicious drive was *moderated*? What on earth had Mitchell Arnot done to his son? Ava covered her shock. 'That explains a lot. You two were always so close.'

Dan just nodded.

'Do you miss my dad?' she asked.

'Yeah. I do. I tried to stay in touch for a while, but it got...hard.'

She remembered how worried her father had been when Dan had moved to Sydney. When he'd dropped out of all contact. How hurt. Trying to disguise it from a still-grieving Ava. 'Too hard to pick up the phone?'

Dan glared at her. 'You were just a kid, Ava. You don't understand.'

'What?' Her eyes burned into his. 'What don't understand?'

He seemed to pick his words carefully. 'Not everyone got to have a fairytale childhood.'

'Fairytale? I watched my mother die of cancer when I was eight years old.'

Dan swore. 'I know. But you had your father and Steve. I had no one.'

I *have* no one. Was that what he meant? 'You chose to go. Nobody forced you,' she pointed out.

He burned to say something more; it was in the tightness of his lips, the intensity of his eyes. But he turned away and stared down at the watery depths passing by. They ploughed onwards in silence, and Ava grew hypnotised by the wash of the waves against the bow, the smell of the salt water on the warm night air. The rush of her thoughts.

She'd never got anywhere with her questions about Dan's family, so eventually she'd just stopped asking. Stopped thinking about it. She'd accepted Dan as part of the furniture—part of the family. Even now. No matter how much time had passed. No matter how he'd hurt her.

Or that they'd kissed.

But he still wouldn't share himself with her. Not as he'd shared himself with her father. She'd wanted to talk about the kiss tonight, to boldly go… But he suddenly seemed further away than ever, though he was only inches from her.

And so she sat, listening to the whoosh of the waves as it melded with the steady thrum of blood past her ears.

She'd waited nine years. She could wait a little longer.

As they swung against the pier at Neutral Bay, Dan stood and offered Ava his hand. She placed hers tentatively in it. As he pulled her up, the ferry lurched against the row of tyres mounted to the jetty and he caught her as she stumbled, wrapping one arm across her protectively.

Immediately her senses thrilled. Images, memories and feelings from the other night rushed in, exalting at being released. His lips. His warmth. The hungry press of his body. She slid one hand between them and braced against his chest to steady herself, hungry to feel again the particular hard softness that was Dan. She suddenly realised the whole night had been leading to this moment in her mind. She peered up at him through a veil of lashes.

Holding her breath.

He watched the boat's docking with interest, and his arms dropped from around her as soon as the ferry's turbulence eased. She straightened.

frowning and not a little disappointed, and followed him to the exit.

He was entirely unaffected. More fascinated by the boat landing, apparently, than by the woman in his arms.

Ava trailed desolately down the stairs to the gangway. They crossed the pier and walked out into the quiet, late-night streets of Neutral Bay. Three or four others disembarked behind them and then dissolved into the darkness of the night, heading for their own homes.

Dan hooked his jacket over one shoulder and buried the other hand in his trouser pocket. *No chance of further accidental contact there.* Or intentional. Ava's lips tightened. She wondered if her carefully rehearsed speech would be wasted. He hardly seemed eager for a repeat performance of the other night—perhaps her boundary-setting would be unnecessary. But home, their separate dwellings, was only a few more minutes away.

It was now or never.

'Dan,' she began, risking a glance at him, 'about the other night…'

He slowed fractionally—all the evidence Ava got that he'd heard her. His eyes remained silently fixed on the luxury street they walked along.

Frustration leaked out between her words. 'Are we never going to discuss it?'

Silent seconds ticked by before he sighed and pulled his fingers from his pocket to drag them through his thick hair. 'It shouldn't have happened. It was inappropriate in so many ways.'

Ava's lips tightened. *There was that word again.* 'Because you're my boss?'

'And a friend of your brother's. Your father's. I'm practically a brother to you.'

Her head snapped up at that. How long was he going to hide behind that one? She scoffed. 'You don't think they'd approve?'

'*I* don't approve, Ava. You and I getting hot and heavy is a bad idea all round.'

Ava nursed the tiny hurt his words caused and forced herself not to dwell on just how hot and how heavy he might be, towering over her. Her blood rushed.

'Then why did we?' His shrug was no answer. It irritated Ava enough to make her careless. 'You started it, Dan.'

He hissed at her choice of phrase. 'Can you hear yourself? You might as well be wearing plaits and braces. Not exactly an image I find attractive at my age.'

At any age. She'd been there the first time. 'You're hardly an old man, Dan. And I'm twenty-five. All grown up.' She clamped her jaw hard.

'Physically, maybe—'

'Emotionally as well. I'm a different person to the girl I was then.' Belatedly, Ava remembered she was supposed to be arguing him *out* of any further physical interaction between them. But the sheer injustice of what he was saying stuck in her gut. 'If I'm able to separate boy-Dan from man-Dan, then why can't you separate the girl I was from the woman I am now?'

He stopped hard and blazed dark eyes at her. 'You had a head start, Ava. I was already a man and you were always just a kid.'

The old hurt surged to the fore. 'You're overlooking one important point, Dan. *You* came on to *me*. *You* kissed me. No one held a gun to your head.'

His lips tightened, then parted in an almost-snarl. 'You want me to say it, Ava? Fine. You *have* grown up. You have a fantastic body and you know how to use it. You were using it on me that night, in all that moonlight, and just for a second I thought why the hell not?'

Ava sucked in an outraged breath to protest but he bullied onwards.

'Hey, I never pretended to be a saint. I got carried away in the moment, just like you did. Thank God your father called when he did, or we might be having a very different conversation right now.'

Outrage shook her hands, and she tucked them

behind her. Unfulfilled tears ached in her throat. 'I did not get carried away—'

Sharp eyes challenged her. 'You meant for it to happen, then?'

'No!'

'So you got carried away.' He loomed over her. 'Put away the righteous indignation, Ava. We were both curious and we tested the waters. End of story.'

Suddenly what they'd shared sounded so… *filthy*. She blazed silently at him, determined not to let one angry tear spill over. She wouldn't give him the satisfaction. She turned and stalked off along the leafy street.

His quiet challenge followed. 'Or were you hoping for a second go-around?'

She spun around to face him. 'You must be joking!'

'Wasn't that where this was going? *Can we talk about it, Dan?*' His impersonation of her was insulting.

'No!' She moved off again, furious.

'Then where's the problem? You were going to tell me it won't happen again. I certainly don' want it to happen again. I think we're actually o the same page here.'

She turned with dangerous deliberation and marched straight towards him, fast enough that h

ctually faltered back a step when she poked him
n the chest.

'What happened to you, Dan? What happened
o the clever, troubled young man who used to
atch me up when I fell off my surfboard? The
oy my mother opened her home to?'

The boy I gave my heart to. He didn't answer,
taring at her with intense heat. Well, if he had
othing to say, then, by God, she was going to
ave her turn.

'I thought I'd lost him that day on the beach,
when you ripped my heart out without a second
hought, and then in your office, when you
rought in your legal muscle to force me into accepting your stinking deal. But then the other
ight I got a glimpse of the young man I remem-
ered, and I wondered whether he wasn't just
uried, deep in there—' she poked his chest hard
—under six years of loneliness.'

He stepped back again.

'But that Daniel—my Daniel—would never
peak to someone the way you just did. Not
omeone they once called a friend.' Impotent rage
hook her voice and she swiped at a single tear that
ad leaked out, furious with herself for allowing
to escape.

'That's the problem, Ava. I was never *yours*.
nd you always did have me on too high a

pedestal.' He flung his arms out wide. 'Welcome to reality, honey.'

'Your reality, maybe. Not mine.' She heaved in an angry breath. 'I'll stick out my six months because I said I would, and because, unlike you—' she poked him again '—I still value the integrity my father raised me to have.'

'Leave your father out of this.'

She started retreating from him, eager that he wouldn't miss her parting words. 'I hope it's worth it, Dan—your success, your high and mighty career. Because I know Dad would be ashamed to see the man you've become. *I'm* ashamed of you.'

With that, she spun around and sprinted off into the night rather than shed one more tear in front of him.

Coward, coward, *coward*.

Dan cursed himself all the way into his immaculate home. Spotless, expensive and empty.

I was never yours. Such lies. He'd been hers the moment she stood up to him and his lawyers in his office. But he'd said the one thing he knew would force some space between them. And it had worked. For a few minutes there, on the ferry he'd felt her drawing closer, felt the threads of attraction strengthening and tangling. He'd been crazy to think the two of them could have any kind of normal relationship.

She was too much a part of his history. She knew all his buttons. And he wore down too quickly with the distraction of her closeness, her smell. Relating to her more like lovers than friends.

Almost-lovers.

For a few tantalising minutes on the ferry he'd let his guard relax, cracked the radiator cap and let some of the incredible pressure he'd been holding onto out into the atmosphere. But Ava was the one person in the world he couldn't afford to get close to.

What the hell kind of choice was that? Between the girl he'd promised to protect and the career that was his whole reason for being.

But then the ferry had sent Ava crashing into his arms, and one glance at her flushed face and parted lips and he'd *known* he was in trouble. It had taken all his will-power to keep his own face impassive, to give nothing away.

To take his hands off her.

She'd been braver than he was, broaching the subject of the kiss directly, and with such an accent of hope in her voice. One gutsy woman— but still entirely transparent. He'd had no choice but to come out swinging.

Dan reached into his stainless steel fridge and

snatched out a frosty beer, twisting the cap off and hurling it across the room into the gleaming sink. He downed one-third of the bottle in one miserable swallow and then slammed it onto the bench, his eyes watering.

He hadn't worked himself halfway into the grave for six years to throw it all away now. He would not rest until his father knew exactly how successful his son had grown up to be.

Without him.

Mitchell Arnot was a big fish in a small pond. A pompous, ignorant fish, with all the parenting skills of a sea-jelly. Being able to get a transient hippy pregnant did not a good parent make. And Dan had paid his whole childhood for the sins of his free-spirit mother, who had skipped out when he was barely out of nappies.

He might have been beloved by the folk of Flynn's Beach, but Mitchell Arnot was loathed by his son and the feeling was entirely mutual. He'd got more love and understanding from the Langes than he'd ever got from either of his real parents.

The only useful thing his father had done was taunt him about being a beach bum. That had sparked a passionate desire to succeed that had quickly flared into an all-consuming bushfire. And he was going to ride this train to the end of the line if it killed him. To show Mitchell Arnot the true definition of success.

He had a job to do. And today's compromise, as much as it clawed in his gut, was that he needed to throw some logs under Ava and Brant, to kindle the illusion the network wanted. But he couldn't do that while Ava's attention was on *him*.

And, man, did he want her attention on him. He closed his eyes, letting all the feelings and mental pictures that had occupied his nights lately flood through him. It was as though she'd stained him with her essence wherever she'd touched, kissed.

She quite literally haunted him—day and night.

He pushed away from the kitchen bench, swallowing back another third of the beer as he paced. She'd invaded his life. Snuck up and taken it over. The level of cruel he'd just been to her was directly proportional to amount of hold she had over him.

And that made him nervous. Getting attached to someone had never been part of his ten year plan. Particularly *that* someone.

He set the bottle on the bench and ran his hands roughly through his hair with a grimace. He'd been brutal. Intentionally. Gnawing off the last sinews of friendship so that he would be free to manage this situation unencumbered. He couldn't think straight when Ava was near, let alone act decisively.

She hated him now. It had been written all over her flushed face as she'd let him have it with both barrels. She'd handed him the opportunity to put some distance between them on a silver platter. And he'd ripped her heart out with it.

His particular speciality.

He took a final swallow of frigid beer and relished the ache of it freezing in his gut. The pain was no less than he deserved. A sudden flash of grey eyes, bright with accusation and confused hurt, trebled the size of the rock in his gut.

Ashamed of me, Ava? He pitched the empty bottle into the trash and turned towards the hall. *Nowhere near as ashamed as I am of myself.*

CHAPTER EIGHT

WHERE is everyone?' Brant suavely squired Ava
through the restaurant doors, scanning the room
for any sign of their colleagues.

She glanced at her watch. 'It's just after seven-
thirty. Where are they?' She looked at the name
emblazoned on the wall. Scarparolo's—right res-
aurant.

'Here comes Dan.' Brant said it so casually,
oblivious to the effect the simple words had on
Ava. She steeled herself not to turn and look.

'Maddox.'

'Arnot.' Ava knew Brant well enough now to
spot his very subtle use of sarcasm as he mirrored
Dan's unfriendly greeting. She turned casually
and met Dan's eyes. Or would have if they'd been
rained on her. He looked flustered. Distracted. He
crossed to the *maître d'* and had a quick conversation. When he returned, with a black-clad

waitress in tow, he addressed them both briskly, his gaze barely acknowledging her.

'I'm just heading out to the car. I forgot my phone. You two go ahead and take a seat.'

He departed, sparing only the briefest glance for her. His brown eyes were dark with anger. She sighed. Hostilities had resumed, then.

She turned her attention to the table she and Brant were being directed to. By the window, candle flickering, beautifully set.

For two.

'Uh..?' Brant looked as confused as Ava felt. Their waitress stared at him, dazzled, but remembered to slide Ava's chair out. Brant caught his lapse of manners and took over, gliding the chair in as Ava sat.

'Excuse me?' she queried, finally drawing the woman's eyes off her co-host. 'We should be part of a larger group? The AusOne booking?'

The waitress looked nonplussed for a moment, before flashing her previous perfect smile. 'One moment, I'll just check.' She drifted over to the *maître d'*. A furious whispered discussion behind a stack of menus ensued.

Brant smiled gallantly at Ava, his public face firmly in place. He took her fingers in his. 'Looks like you'll have the pleasure of my company to yourself for now. Try not to swoon.'

Ava laughed and glanced out of the window. In that instant a car turned onto the dark street, spot-lighting the road ahead with its headlights. In the distance, beyond the glare, Ava thought she saw Dan in conversation with a shadowy figure on the sidewalk. It didn't look like a relaxed conversation. She frowned.

Brant raised her hand to his lips. She restrained the impulse to pull it free, conscious that there was more than one pair of speculative eyes in the restaurant. Whatever Brant's game was, he was a friend, and she owed him the courtesy of playing along in public. But later…

She spoke through the careful smile plastered on her face and tried to disentangle her hand, worrying that Dan could probably see them from his position out in the street. Not that he would care. 'Oh, please, you've had me to yourself prac-tically all day. I swear the network must not trust me in a scene alone.'

His face lost some of its slick. 'You're doing a great job, Ava. Has no one told you that?'

She squeezed her fingers gratefully around his and lowered them decisively to the table. 'None so sincerely. Thank you, Brant.'

The puzzled waitress returned and said brightly, 'There does seem to have been an error. You're seated over on the large reserved table. Your booking was for eight p.m.' There was no blame, only confusion in her voice.

Ava frowned. 'My call sheet said seven-thirty.'

Brant's surprise mirrored hers. 'Mine, too. The call sheet never lies.'

Just then Dan walked through the door of the restaurant, phone in hand, colour high. His eyes connected with Ava's immediately, then dropped to where her fingers were still gently clutched in Brant's. She slid them free as he approached.

They followed the waitress to a table at the rear of the restaurant set for more than a dozen.

'Looks like even executives can have scheduling malfunctions,' Brant said casually. 'We're not due until eight.'

Ava's nape prickled. Good point.

'Don't let me interrupt your earlier conversation,' Dan said, deftly changing the subject. 'Pretend I'm not here.'

Oh, would that she could!

Brant looked at him, eyes narrowing. 'Actually, I was telling Ava what a great job she's doing. It seems she's been made to feel...inadequate.'

Ava studied the embroidered tablecloth furiously, but felt Dan's eyes on her.

Brant went on. 'A little more praise might be in order from the higher end of the food chain.'

Ava hadn't heard this steely tone from Brant before. Her eyes rose, but Brant's gaze was locked firmly on Dan's. Tension surged between them. Then Dan's heated focus shifted to her, pinning her like a butterfly in a museum. She immediately regretted speaking, coming out tonight at all. When would she learn?

'My apologies, Ava. You didn't strike me as someone who needed constant reinforcement.'

Desperate to move the conversation away from her, she parried, 'I don't, but I was curious as to why I'm yet to be trusted with a scene by myself.'

A tiny crease appeared between Dan's brows. 'Those decisions have nothing to do with your abilities—'

'So you say,' Brant risked from across the table.

Dan fixed him with an irritated stare. 'I do say. Let's order some drinks, shall we?'

Ava was intrigued at the by-play between the two men flanking her. It had all the hallmarks of a peeing contest. Brant had dropped all pretence and looked as if he was thriving on the chilly encounter. For his part, Dan was matching him head-on. Brown eyes locked with blue ones.

Brant looked away first. He picked up the menu, and in an instant the charmer was back. He smiled winningly at the dazzled waitress and ordered an expensive bottle of wine. Ava occupied herself with filling each of their water glasses from the carafe in front of her, used the moment to steady her hands. Though she steadfastly avoided Dan's eyes, she was conscious of them, narrowed and glancing between herself and Brant. The air was thick with unasked questions.

She discreetly peeked at her watch. A quarter to eight.

Oh, please let someone be early.

'I'm done, Bill.'

Dan tossed the early edition on the desk in front of Bill Kurtz without bothering to sit. He wasn't staying long. 'It's not working for me, and its not working for the show.'

The older man smirked, not glancing at the newspaper. He'd already seen it, then.

'Ava-ricious!' the headline called her, claiming she'd wasted no time in snaffling her pretty-boy host for herself. There was even an incriminating picture—Ava Lange and Brant Maddox in a romantic candlelit tryst.

'Give it a chance to work, Dan. We've only just started.'

Dan pressed his thumbnail into the flesh of his index finger hard, and concentrated on the dull pain. It was an old trick he'd developed when he was a kid. To manage the anger. To control it.

Possibly the only practical life skill he'd taken from his relationship with his father.

'This show can succeed on its own. You've seen the dailies—it's coming up beautifully,' Dan said. 'We don't need this.'

'Everything needs a boost.'

'This is my show. My concept. We're doing this my way.'

Kurtz glared at him. 'You don't want to get yourself a reputation, Dan. Reputations are career hurdles.'

Dan snarled. 'Lucky I'm so athletic.'

There was something in Kurtz's thin smile. Something predatory that reminded him of his father. How long had Kurtz been waiting for this moment? How disappointed must he have been every time Dan had acquiesced to the network on one ludicrous demand or another. Just waiting for the time bomb that was Dan to explode.

For the first time he saw himself through Kurtz's eyes. The young gun, rising fast, rising straight towards Kurtz's job.

The older man narrowed his gaze. Mentally reviewing Dan's contract, looking for a weakness, most likely. There were none. Dan had checked.

'I had that photographer primed,' he said. 'He knew exactly what kind of a story I wanted. This—' he flicked his fingers at the paper '—is not it.'

Someone had undermined him. Someone with really bad taste in suits.

'Since when have you ever heard of paparazzi working solo?' Kurtz said.

Son of a... There'd been a second photographer. Dan had kept the first one occupied, ridden him until he'd fired off a few simple shots and departed on a mouthful of muttered abuse. But Kurtz must have known Dan would try to control the publicity stunt and he'd arranged a second snapper.

'Tell me where the value is in portraying Ava as a scheming gold-digger. What happened to your desire to link Brant with a fresh-faced innocent?'

Kurtz didn't answer.

'You don't really care how she's portrayed, do you?' Dan suddenly realised. 'As long as she's on the second page.'

'Nor should you, Dan. This is outstanding PR, and that's our primary objective.'

Dan's lip curled. 'This is not outstanding anything. It's tabloid pap. Have you forgotten that Ava's not just the face of *Urban Nature* but she's the designer? I need her to be credible.'

For the show and for her self-worth.

'That's your problem, Dan.' A distinct chill had entered Kurtz's voice. 'You seem to have lost track of where your loyalties lie. With AusOne. The network that put you where you are today.'

'There will be no further PR relating to Ava Lange and Brant Maddox.' His voice was granite.

'Not your call.' Kurtz tried to shut him down. 'You don't want to run this yourself, fine. We have specialists to take care of this kind of thing. People who've worked this industry for a lot longer than six years.'

Dan rested his palms on the edge of the desk and leaned towards the older man. Icicles could have formed off his words. 'This is my show. Nothing happens without my authorisation.'

Kurtz glared, but leaned back. 'I have a half-a-million-dollar production bill that tells me it's the network's show, Arnot.'

'And you pay me fifty percent of that to make it the best it can be. And best doesn't include discrediting the talent.'

'That's a matter of opinion.'

His fingernails bit cruelly. Dan calculated his next move, then casually spoke. 'How good would your picture look on the front page of the *Standard* with the headline "AusOne exploits female personnel", Bill?'

Kurtz surged to his feet, dragging his belly past the desk on the way up. 'Don't you threaten me, boy. Don't you dare. This network made you, and we will break you if necessary.'

Oh, just like his father.

Dan stood his ground, steel in his voice. 'I calloused up amongst the best, Kurtz. I don't break easily.' He turned for the door. 'I will not be playing this particular game. And I'll be watching production frame-by-frame to make sure no one else does.'

'You do not control what this network does!' A spray of furious spittle fell short of Dan's side of the desk. Kurtz's raised voice earned a hush in the outer office.

Dan walked to the door before turning. He forced his body to relax. There was only one coronary in the making in this room. He pinned the blustering man with his steeliest gaze. 'Do your worst, Bill. I'll be ready for you.'

He turned and walked out of the office, mentally reviewing the coming month's filming. You didn't wave a red rag at a bull and then go and sit at your comfortable desk. He'd have to keep an even closer eye on production in coming weeks. Control things from the inside. Minimise the potential for Kurtz and his cronies to go to town on Ava. He had enough contacts in the PR department to stay across whatever disasters the executive producer was probably already conceiving.

He marched past Kurtz's gaping assistant, glancing at the garish furnishings. Some days it was hard to remember why he wanted all this so badly.

Then he visualised his father, conjured feelings from twenty years ago. Never being good enough, talented enough. Being too much like his mother to bare tolerating. The liquor. The abuse. The crushing grief of a parentless boy; one parent who abandoned him literally, and one who abandoned him emotionally. When he wasn't thrashing the living daylights out of him.

Until eight in the morning, when Mitchell Arnot suited up and went out into the public world. Popular, respected, adored by all. The town rep for Eyes-on-the-Street, for crying out loud. There was only one other living person in all of Flynn's Beach who'd had any clue what kind of a monster his father turned into behind closed doors.

James Lange.

The man Dan respected above all others. The man he'd shared his fear with. The man who had taken him in. The man who, eventually, had asked him to go.

The man whose only daughter Dan was helping to screw over.

The innocent lift button bore the brunt of Dan's fury. At Kurtz. At his father. But above all at himself.

He rubbed his eyes, breathing slowly. He couldn't tell her. She'd never forgive him if she found out he'd been any part of it.

But how would she? If he stopped now.
How would she?

'Ugh, this is awful,' Brant murmured in Ava's ear, when they paused for a moment between appearances. 'If not for the intravenous latte I'd be desolate.'

As publicity exercises went, this was one of the network's better ideas. Ava felt a thousand times more comfortable here, amongst her friends the plants, than at last week's shopping mall debacle. Or the inner city appearance before that.

Bad enough to have to endure the claustrophobic crush of shoppers pressing in on them to see exactly what celebrity *du jour* the mall was offering. Bad enough that some grunted and walked away when they saw it was just the cast of a new lifestyle programme. But to spend the entire day under fluorescent lights smiling and waving, without one single breath of fresh air all day... Intolerable.

Today, in the dappled light of a leafy boutique garden centre, Ava stood elbow-deep in potting mix, demonstrating to two dozen wealthy would-be horticulturists how to re-pot a root-bound fern. The smell of the earth, the feel of the living roots, the waft of the fragrance rich air. And this time the audience had a genuine interest in what she was doing and what she had to say. They were plant people.

Her people. Good people.

She laughed and tucked her face close to his, so there was no risk of their hosts or audience overhearing. 'Tell you what, from now on you do all the malls and I'll do all the garden centres. Deal?'

'Woman, you have yourself a deal. Sadly, I doubt the maestro over there would let us do anything independently…'

Ava followed his gaze to where Dan stood, monitoring the day's activities. Just as Ava had finally accepted that she and Brant would share just about every scene, the PR personnel had finally accepted Dan's presence at every event. He was senior to them, after all. They could hardly tell him not to come. But it was still hard to believe how hands-on he was. Did he really trust her so little in public?

How stupid did he think she was?

'God forbid we should be seen without each other,' Brant continued. 'It might cause some kind of irrevocable breach in the space-time continuum.'

That drew Ava's glance back to Brant. 'You know, one day you're going to slip up and expose yourself as quite an intelligent man.'

'Perish the thought.' He winked at her, then spun around to face his adoring public shouting flamboyantly, 'Who's next for an autograph?'

She watched him with affection. There was little question in her mind now that Brant Maddox was a far better performer than any of them knew. He had the public and the network completely fooled. He was amazing.

'Careful, Ava, you're going to give the tabloids fodder for another story, gazing at him like that.'

Her stomach dropped and she spun round. Not that she needed to. Her tingling senses had told her exactly who it was before he even spoke. Just thinking Dan's name made her sigh.

'I doubt I need to give them anything. They seem quite capable of fabricating what they need,' she said.

There'd been two more stories published about her and Brant since the restaurant debacle. Not quite as offensive as that first one, but both complete with made-up content and carefully edited images from the PR trail. She swore the photographers must have waited, without blinking, for her and Brant to share a single up-close moment. Next thing she knew they were gracing the inside pages again—although no one had invaded her privacy quite like that first time. She wondered if the network had read the riot act to the press.

'No smoke without fire, I think the tabloids would say,' he growled.

'They'd be wrong.'

Ava was tired of Dan's ever-present attention. His constant fixation on how she presented herself with Brant. Once she would have been thrilled to be the centre of his attention like this. But now it was hard enough enduring the public frenzy, without the added pressure of him monitoring her every move. Judging. If not for the steady thrum of her heart whenever he was close she'd have thought she was finally over him.

'You carry on as though Brant and I manufacture these things intentionally. The kind of press exposure I was hoping for was related to my skills. My talent. Not my love-life. Or my supposed love-life.'

'He was kissing you in the restaurant, Ava. Hard to misinterpret that.'

'It was my *hand*, Dan. Who cares about that?'

He locked eyes with her. 'We're talking about the press. All it did was whet their appetite. From that moment you two had a paparazzi price on your heads.' He ran an agitated hand through his hair. 'Just...be careful. Don't give them any more than you have to.'

She wasn't in the mood for a fight, but it seemed the fight was finding her. 'What's that supposed to mean?'

'I thought your professional reputation meant something to you.'

'It does!'

'Then take care, Ava. This isn't Flynn's Beach. You can't wear your heart on your sleeve in this industry.' He looked furious. But he sounded concerned. 'Just…take care. That's all.'

'Here's a crazy idea,' she said, glaring at him. 'Why not stop putting Brant and me together in front of the cameras so much? Stop feeding the frenzy?'

He considered her words and visibly discarded them. 'I think you enjoy spending time with him.'

She threw up her hands in frustration. 'Yes, actually, I do. He's the best part of this whole circus. At least he understands how I'm feeling.'

'I imagine that's part of his appeal.'

'I can't speak for all womankind but, yes, it *is* nice to have an ally on this battlefield.'

He stared steadily at her. 'When did I become the enemy?'

Ava swallowed. 'You know very well when. And that was your choice.'

An age passed before he nodded. 'Then I have nothing to lose by warning you not to get too involved with Maddox.'

Outrage warred with frustration. 'I'm *no*. involved with Brant. Lord, Dan, you're as bad a: the tabloids.'

'The camera says otherwise.'

'Oh, please. As if *you* can tell. I had a crush on you for years and you had no idea—' She sucked he words back too late.

Smugness settled across his features, infuriating and entirely seductive. 'I had an idea, Ava. More han an idea, actually. And long before that night on the beach. I have a radar when it comes to you.'

His eyes gleamed hazelnut and she forced herself to ignore his use of the present tense. Did he seriously think that she would go from kissing him to being with Brant in a few short weeks? 'Then your radar needs recalibrating.'

For the first time in an age he laughed. Loud and genuine. Ava blinked her astonishment and her heart squeezed hard. The laugh instantly made her think of home, and warm fires and safety.

And it made her blood thicken.

She shook her head. She *had* to get a handle on these feelings. The man had made it perfectly clear he wasn't interested. Beyond their charming little experiment in the garden, of course. And, more relevant, she wasn't interested either. Daniel Arnot was too much work. Too career-driven and too complicated. She needed someone simpler in her life. Or at least someone she had a hope of understanding.

A perverse little demon raised its head. Why not? They got on well enough. Maybe attraction would grow between them? He was certainly handsome enough. She'd worked with less in the past.

'What makes you think you have the right to tell me what to do anyway? If I choose to see Brant Maddox then that's no one's business but my own.'

Silence crackled. 'Yours and the entire country.'

'If I'm damned-if-I-do/damned-if-I-don't, then I might as well enjoy the journey.'

Dan braced his feet and crossed his arms. His suspicion burned her. 'What are you saying?'

Ava looked over to where Brant was busy flirting with the women in the crowd and still signing endless autographs. *Don't do it, Ava…*

'He's a good-looking man. We get on. Besides, I don't know many people in town. So, why not?'

'Ava…'

That manipulative tone again. Just like that first day in his office. Fury simmered in her veins. 'We're spending all our time together anyway— thanks to you.'

'I just warned you—'

'That's the thing, Dan. You don't get to warn me about anything. I'm a big girl. Just because you can't see that, it doesn't mean Brant can't.' She prayed to the angels of understanding for forgiveness on that one.

Dan's nostrils flared.

'It's win-win, Dan. You get all the on-screen togetherness you want, and I get all the off-screen togetherness I crave.'

Just not with the right man.

'Until he breaks your heart,' Dan said quietly. A man like that won't stay interested in a woman like you for long.'

Ava froze. Did he have no survival instincts whatsoever? 'A woman *like me*?'

'You're too white bread for him, Ava. Look at the women he's dated in the past. Wild, racy, sexy women.'

She swallowed hard on the insult. Her voice was arctic when she could finally speak past the lump of pain in her throat. 'Well, I may not be sexy, but at least you finally agree I am a woman.'

She turned and marched away from the man who had so much power to hurt her, ignoring him as he called her name. Ahead of her, Brant was finishing with the autographs. She grabbed him by the sleeve with shaking hands, pulled him over to a stand of indoor palms, turned, and slammed straight into him.

'You owe me one, right?' she warned, reaching up behind his bemused face. 'I'm calling it in.'

Then she kissed him.

To his credit, he didn't flinch—just stood frozen while she plied him with her most convincing kiss on his stunned mouth. The crowd went wild behind them. To them it must have looked as if she'd had enough of Brant flirting with the women in the crowd. Her lips ground into his, and Brant recovered enough to slide his hands around behind her and pull her even closer to him. And then he kissed her back.

That got her attention.

The anger suddenly drained right out of her and she pulled away, deflated. What was she thinking?

'I don't know what we're doing,' Brant murmured against her ear, panting slightly, 'but I thought you'd want it to look good.'

'Let 'em talk about *that* in tomorrow's paper,' she ground out bitterly, glancing over to where Dan had been standing.

He was gone.

'Ava, honey, are you crying?' Brant shifted slightly so he was between her and the rapt crowd, providing a little privacy. He stroked her hair from her face.

'No...' She swiped at her eyes, dragging dirt across her nose. She glanced at the exit gate swinging open. Brant's gaze followed hers. 'No.'

CHAPTER NINE

BRANT'S face was serious as he entered the Winnebago. 'For what's about to happen, I'm truly sorry.'

That was all the warning Ava got as a whirlwind shoved past him to invade the sanctuary of her office trailer. Brant locked the door firmly behind him as the black-clad, pale-skinned woman came to a halt a few feet in front of where Ava sat, bemused, behind her drafting table.

She glanced nervously from Brant to the heavily made-up woman. The other woman glared, uncomfortable and angry, but did not speak.

Brant finally found speech. 'Ava, this is Cadence, my—'

'His girlfriend!' The woman jerked her thumb in Brant's direction, and Ava knew immediately that Cadence was much angrier with him than she was with her.

And why.

Cadence was young and slim—that much fitted Brant perfectly—but there it ended. She had dark red hair piled messily on her head, an ancient, torn rock band T-shirt, a long layered black skirt, Doc Marten boots, full Goth make-up, and at least a dozen piercings that Ava could see.

Probably a dozen more she couldn't.

Brant's girlfriend? This woman? Self-preservation kept her silent. She moved out from behind her desk and extended her hand respectfully, testing the waters. 'Nice to meet you, Cadence.'

Cadence blinked twice, then pushed out long fingers tipped with black nail varnish. No, no black, Ava noticed as she shook the death-pale hand. It was darkest red, like Cadence's hair. Snug PVC wrist gloves fitted over elegant wrists and were laced back past her elbow. The work on the gloves was stunning.

'They're gorgeous!' Ava said, one hundred percent sincere, touching the sensual material lightly.

Cadence glared at her a moment longer, then thrust the other one out for Ava to compare.

'She designed them herself,' Brant piped up from his corner. Peacemaking, no doubt, but Ava could still hear the pride in his voice. She looked again at the young woman before her, still glowering unhappily. Bull by the horns time.

'You've come about yesterday?'

Cadence didn't answer, but her lips tightened. Brant flapped around uselessly in the background. This wasn't some casual, recent thing, Ava realised, reading the body language between the two of them. How long had they...? Oh.

Oh!

Time to fess up. 'Yesterday was my fault, Cadence. Brant had nothing to do with it.'

'That's not exactly how he tells it.' Blue, blue eyes didn't waver, blazing out at Ava from a thick smudge of charcoal.

Ava lifted her hands helplessly. 'He owed me one. And he's a good actor.' She saw uncertainty flash across Cadence's face. 'And a really good friend.'

That did it. Cadence's blue eyes blinked furiously. Ava yanked some blotting paper from her table and thrust it urgently at Cadence. 'Don't— you'll wreck your make-up.'

Cadence took it gratefully and carefully folded an edge against her eyelid to absorb the tears. 'Are you kidding? Goths kill for that look.'

Brant relaxed visibly, but didn't leave his post as guardian of the door. Ava glared at him with an open question in her eyes. What had he been thinking, telling her about the kiss?

He shrugged and said, 'I tell her everything.'

Cadence sniffed. 'I find out everything. It's in his best interests to tell me first.'

Ava smiled, and guilt nibbled at her. She'd kissed Brant selfishly, with no thought for who else it might affect.

'I'm so sorry. I didn't know Brant had a girl-friend.' This was to both of them.

'You wouldn't. I'm the Anne Frank of the tele-vision world—hidden away in the attic of ano-nymity.' Cadence had mopped up the worst of her tears and blew out a steadying breath. 'I don't really fit the mould.'

Ava glanced at the anxiety marring Brant's handsome face. 'How long have you two been together?' she asked.

'Since high-school.'

Years? 'But all the other—' She cut herself off. Too late.

Cadence waved her concern away. 'Women? Go ahead, say it. It's not like I don't know about them.'

'Props,' Brant clarified from his corner. 'Or a smokescreen, more rightly. It's a network thing. Keeps people guessing. Makes it easier on Cadey.'

Ava found that hard to believe, and looked at the younger woman sceptically.

'He thinks he's protecting me.' Cadence spoke with such a mix of pride, fury and frus-

ration, Ava knew their feelings for each other
ran deep. Very deep.

A nasty little green-eyed monster reared its
head. When would she meet someone to defend
her that loyally?

'But he hadn't kissed any of them,' Cadence
went on. 'Until yesterday.'

A small groan escaped her. Some friend. She'd
really messed things up for Brant. 'That was me,
Cadence, I swear. I...um... Well, I used him to
make a point, actually. I'm so sorry.' The last bit
she directed straight to Brant. He shrugged, and
it saddened Ava how blasé he'd become about
being used by other people.

Cadence's barked snort contrasted wildly with
her sombre appearance. 'That would be a nice piece
of karma, then! Who were you trying to get back
at?'

Heat roared up Ava's neck.

'That's Ava's business, Cadence.' Brant spoke
in a way Ava had never heard, and Cadence
dropped her eyes. She knew immediately who
truly wore the pants in this relationship. Never
mind startling appearances to the contrary.

'Right. Sorry...' Cadence trailed off awkwardly.

Ava chewed her lip. It was fair penance, after
all. She had some damage to undo. She sighed
and spilled the beans. 'Dan Arnot.'

The avenging angel in front of her nearly squealed, completely intrigued. 'Maverick? Really?'

'Maverick?'

'Oh, that's what I call him. The top gun in the industry and all that. Good looking. Cocky. Danger zone. You know...'

As nicknames went, it was strangely apt. Dan had always been so fearless as a younger man. Did he still have that quality now that he was older? Enough to get a nickname like that? How had she missed it? Her heart squeezed again. She was getting used to the sensation.

'Anyway,' she fumbled on, clearing her throat, 'the kiss wasn't about Brant. He was just the nearest handy male. An innocent bystander.'

'Innocent?' Cadence snorted. 'Yeah, I'm sure he didn't enjoy a second of it.'

Awkward silence descended. Ava felt some heat rising. Saw it echoed in Brant's face. Time for a subject change. 'So, you design fashion?'

Cadence shrugged. 'Goth stuff, mostly. Punk.' Her eyes strayed to Ava's shambolic workbench. 'I guess we have something in common. Designing.'

'I guess so. Want to see?'

The two women pored over Ava's most recent design, and she showed Cadence how she worked

n layers from the bare schematics of the space
he was renovating.

'I watch all the shows,' Cadence murmured,
ot looking at her. 'I really like what you do. And
ow you present. Can't say I'm crazy about how
ou and Brant come across…' Ava looked at her
bout to apologise again. Cadence waved her
concern away with a quick flash of the PVC
gloves. 'No, I get it. All must bow down before
he mighty ratings god. No wonder they've been
hrusting you guys together so much.'

Ava blinked. She knew her rapport with Brant
vas good for the show, but it hadn't dawned on
er that it was so…engineered. She spoke the
vord aloud.

'Right. Exactly. I know it's not real, my family
knows, our friends know—sort of. But, still, it's
ard to watch.'

She nodded, empathising completely. It was hard
nough hiding her feelings about Dan from Dan
imself. She couldn't imagine how hard it would
e keeping a secret like this from the whole country.

Or being deemed sub-standard just for being
ourself.

The thought must have filled the air, because
uddenly Brant moved away from his station by
he door and came to stand right behind Cadence.
he fitted perfectly under his chin as his arms

came around her. He rested it lightly on her head and tucked her into him.

As odd a pair as they made, it was achingly sweet. And perfectly right. Brant looked like a different man when he was with the love of his life. And Cadence quite obviously was.

She felt more than a pang of jealousy. Not for Brant, but for the love.

'What if I *had* kissed him?' curiosity made her ask. 'With intent, I mean? What would you have done?'

Cadence didn't hesitate. 'I would have fought for him.'

Looking at the determination in the young woman's eyes, she didn't doubt it for a second.

Cadence stared at her for a moment, her mind ticking away behind expressive blue eyes. 'Can I ask a favour?' she suddenly said, full of determination.

Ava nodded and laughed. 'After yesterday, you can ask for a few!'

'No, just one. It's a big one. Chalk this up under "Better-the-devil-you-know", but…would you continue to hang out with Brant? I'd feel much better knowing it's you he's with than some of those other…*women* the network finds.' The way she spat the word spoke volumes about exactly what Cadence thought the women really were.

Ava considered quickly. She hadn't lied when

he'd said she enjoyed Brant's company, and now he knew he was happily in love with Cadence ny vestige of concern that he might form an at-achment to her thoroughly evaporated. And it vasn't as though Ava had her own relationship to rotect.

'I'd be happy to, Cadence.' She looked at Brant, oo. 'Until my contract's finished.'

'Thank you.' Relief filled Cadence's pale-owdered face and showed Ava the young woman s she really must look beneath the layers of make-p. The slim hand she wrapped around Ava's was varm now, and unhesitant in its squeeze.

Cadence apologised for bursting into the RV, nd Ava laughed her concern away. Then Brant udged Cadence and pointed to his watch. They aid reluctant farewells and Ava hinted that she'd e happy to tag along if the two of them ever vanted to hang out. Do a movie. Anything.

Maybe Cadence could be a good friend, despite heir disastrous start. And Ava sorely needed riends here in the city. Cadence led the way out f the RV and marched off to the right. Brant shot Ava a grateful glance over his shoulder as he tarted to turn left.

The manoeuvre hit her in the solar plexus. How ard for them to constantly need to pretend the ther didn't exist.

'Brant?' Her soft voice stilled him. He turned his handsome face to her. 'She's perfect for you.' It wasn't lip service. Ava could no longer remember the type of woman she'd thought was right for Brant. Only crazy, gothic Cadence.

His heartbreaking smile was full of love. 'I know.'

Ava sighed as the door closed behind them and they went their separate ways. There went a woman who had every reason in the world to give up on her love and crawl into a hiding place to die. But, no, she stayed, and worked hard behind the scenes to reinforce her relationship. And she fought for her man.

There was a lesson in that.

Something had changed between Ava and Maddox. Dan couldn't quite define it, but there was a level of comfortableness that hadn't been there before. He didn't know where it was coming from, but he knew that he absolutely did *not* want Ava getting comfortable with Maddox.

He didn't want her doing anything with Maddox.

Too late for that, a dark little voice reminded him. The mental image of Ava kissing the vapid pretty boy, his hands sliding down over her body was seared into Dan's mind.

He swore.

He wasn't having much luck keeping her on th

afe side of the line he'd drawn in the sand. If she
vasn't stumbling over it herself, then he was
manufacturing unconscious ways to drag her over.
And what did it say about him that he'd been
villing to exploit Ava to give the network its way.

Not very much.

Another image of Maddox bending to Ava,
:issing her enthusiastically, flashed through his
nead. It only served to fire him up more.

Dan knew he'd handled that one badly—had
virtually pushed Ava into Maddox's arms yester-
lay. He remembered too late how prone she'd
ilways been to doing the exact opposite of what
:he wanted if it happened to be what *he* didn't
vant. Or her brother or her father. Or anyone who
vas telling her what to do.

So much for having grown up!

Flash. Ava's lips on Maddox's in the moments
)efore Dan had walked away in pained disgust.
Then—*flash*—the feel of Ava's lips on his own.
Pliant. So addictive. So unquestionably adult.

Get a grip.

Dan shook his head as he waited for the lift to
ake him to the rooftop they were working on this
veek. Not a true roof, more of a giant outdoor
.pace about halfway up a thirty-storey high-rise.
When they'd first scoped out this site it had been
. bare tiled space with a few tip-burned potted

palms abused as a convenient ashtray by smokers in any of the three hundred offices on nearby floors. Today it was a half-finished tranquillity garden, filled with wind-tolerant species suited to an exposed location this close to the coast.

It was going to make magnificent television.

His eyes found Ava the second he emerged onto the set. She was talking through some design features with one of her offsiders, Shannon. He knew the moment she sensed him by the sudden stiffness of her back and the way her fists curled into little balls. Her assistant noticed as well, and glanced around to see what had caused it.

'Hey, Mr Arnot,' Shannon called, oblivious to any undercurrents.

He returned her greeting casually and walked straight by, without acknowledging Ava. It took some doing when he really wanted to grab her and drag her away somewhere private to talk. More than talk. But she didn't so much as glance at him, so he kept walking, furiously trying to fabricate some errand on the far side of the set to justify arriving there.

Maddox's knowing eyes met his halfway across the rooftop. Dan's narrowed. What the hell was he looking so smug about? Instantly his hackles rose. It was bad enough imagining those slimy hands all over Ava's perfect flesh without having to endure his gloating, too. He hadn't realised how much pleasure he'd got from knowing he'd tasted Ava, touched her, felt her body against his…while he hadn't shared any of that with Maddox.

Now that the playing field was more even, he didn't like it one bit.

His smile was tight as he reached the First Assistant Director on the far side of the set and asked a few vaguely salient questions about the day's shoot. Not that he heard a word of the answer. His focus was across the roof with Ava. She'd finished her dealings with Shannon and was scanning the crowded rooftop. Her eyes landed on Maddox.

The smile she gave the man made Dan's abs tighten.

He forced his eyes down, to maintain the illusion that he was listening to the AD. When he looked back, it was in time to see Ava move up next to Maddox and rest her hand lightly on his arm, laughing easily at something he said. It killed him that Maddox could inspire such warmth in Ava and all *he* inspired was pain. His foot ground into the gravel that had just been introduced to the rooftop.

A moment later his distinctive ringtone pealed out across the roof, drawing all eyes, including Ava's. He dragged his focus away and snapped his mobile open on a curse.

He was in no mood for anything more challenging than his stock update.

Kurtz started in with one of his monologues. The only blessing was that it didn't require Dan to listen particularly hard. He glanced over at Ava, where she was joking around with Maddox as they prepared the next shot set-up. Kurtz droned on about ratings and broadcast numbers.

'Anyway, I wanted to pass on the good news personally.' The unusual tone in Kurtz's voice brought Dan's attention back to the phone call. 'It's official. *Urban Nature* is a nominee for an Australian Television Award. Best New Lifestyle Programme.'

Dan sucked in his breath.

'The first time a programme has been nominated this early into its first season—'

'This is its second season, don't forget,' Dan said, irritated that they could so easily overlook a whole season of television. A year of his life.

'Everyone has forgotten the first season, Dan. It's *this* season they're all talking about. The whole Ava/Maddox thing is working a charm, as is our new no-bull format.'

Our... Dan knew how many meetings it had taken to lock down a bit of verity in television. AusOne had haemorrhaged steel filings over the simple idea of showing the construction as it truly

vas. The real size of the team. The actual amount
f work. The true price tag.

'The odds are in our favour, Dan. But the
etwork is keen to capitalise on the exposure.'

'In what way?' Dan's neck hairs prickled. They
vere already running a PR extravaganza on the
ide—what more could they expect?

'The short PR pieces have been great, but we're
ooking for something longer. More substantial.
n-depth. We're thinking print. Feature article.
A-day-in-the-life type thing.'

Dan cringed. How had someone whose taste
vas so firmly implanted up their butt risen so high
n AusOne's ranks? His teeth ground together.
And I assume you want me to broker this?'

'Not in a million years, sunshine. You had your
hance. Although I'd have thought you'd be all
ver this, Dan—a chance to get a nice high-profile
aperweight for your desk. Runs on the board.
Generate some real interest in the public.'

The network weren't yet aware of the very
eal, very public kiss Ava and Maddox had
hared the day before. Kurtz's PR stooge
ad been inside on the phone when Maddox
nd Ava had tangled tongues. There'd only been
ne photographer there, but Dan's investiga-
ions had revealed he was a stringer for a
umber of magazines. If the photo appeared in

one, they could guarantee real interest brewing in the public.

The network would be delighted.

They'd be the only ones.

Now they wanted a full-on journo to be given access to Ava. Potentially the sort who could take a kiss like that and turn it into something far more sordid. Dan knew any number of that calibre. And a few who weren't.

An idea began forming.

'Let me know when they're coming.' He signed off, any pleasure about the unprecedented award nomination floundering beneath his concern about the feature article.

He could try and swing it to Tannon or Larks, both good journalists from competing papers and tending towards the more moderate side of their business. One of their papers was likely to be thrown the exclusive. If he could swing it, either of those writers might actually stay focussed on the show rather than the private life of its hosts.

Lives.

Dan swore. Even he was linking Maddox and Ava together in his mind now.

It was worth a shot. It was the only way he could think of to keep things from escalating. He looked through narrowed eyes to where Ava and

Maddox now stood talking by the coffee station, heads dipped in some confederacy. He'd have to talk to them both. The amount of time they spent with their heads bent might alert the rawest of journos. And that was the last thing they all needed.

Dammit. What had changed between them? It was driving him crazy.

And yet a big part of him really didn't want to know the answer.

Are you serious?'

Brant's voice rose an entire octave. He scooped Ava up in a massive bear hug and spun her round while the faces all around them broke into big smiles and murmurs of congratulation. She clung on for dear life, laughing.

'An ATA this early in a season is an Australian first,' Dan said. 'We can all be really proud. More than other programmes, this one truly is a team effort.'

Ava glanced at Dan. It felt good to be smiling at him again. Meeting Cadence had put a few things in perspective. It wasn't his fault he didn't have feelings for her, would never look at her like Brant looked at Cadence. Or think of Ava the way she thought of him. But she had no idea where to start with putting things right.

This news provided exactly the sort of introduction she needed.

'We'll be hosting a journalist on set in a few days,' he continued, 'for some pre-award coverage. There's interest in a full story on the show and its inception.'

Not entirely true, but it would be if he got his way. He released the gathered crew for a spontaneous coffee break and retreated to examine the latest part of the garden. Ava grabbed her chance and drifted up behind him.

'Congratulations, Dan. You must be so pleased.'

He turned slowly. Appraised her with those bottomless brown eyes. Her heart did its familiar squeeze thing.

'When the network's happy, I'm happy,' he said.

'You don't look all that happy.' As openings went, it wasn't bad.

He considered her, his eyes dark. 'In some ways I'd rather we'd got there the traditional way. Rather than trading so heavily on the chemistry between you and Maddox. The show has plenty of merit on its own without that.'

That mirrored Ava's own feelings almost exactly, but coming so hard on the heels of meeting Cadence, she suddenly saw the opportunity to make good on her promise to her two friends slipping away.

'Maybe the audience is responding to both? It certainly hasn't harmed anyone.'

'Hasn't it?' His dark eyes swept the set.

Could he not even look at her? She persevered, intent on trying to salvage something of their friendship. 'Give yourself a break, Dan.'

He looked at her then. Hard. 'You've changed your tune. A week ago you loathed the publicity stuff.'

Ava's essential feelings hadn't changed. But her promise to Cadence made the publicity more bearable. Gave it a purpose. 'I've come to terms with it. I know it's important to the show. To you.'

His eyes narrowed. 'Me?'

'I know how important success is to you—successes like this one. Awards and little blue numbers on a printout. If me getting on well with Brant helps that…why wouldn't you use it?'

Ava was startled by the bouquet of curses that Dan thrust at her. He pulled her further out of the way of prying ears, yanking her around behind a large ficus, and spat out a question. 'Does your perfection have no end?'

She stared at him, shocked. 'I don't mind—'

'Oh, give me a break. You don't *mind* your face being splashed all over the newspapers? Your relationship with Maddox?'

'There is no relationship.' She was tired of defending herself. But knew she only had herself to blame. This time.

'Your *thing* with Maddox, then.'

Exasperation made her short. 'It's not a thing, Dan…'

'Oh? You go around kissing just anyone, then? Oh wait, yeah—I guess you do. You kissed me not so long ago. Should I be putting an alert out to all the male members of the crew?'

Mortification streaked through her. Heat raced into her cheeks. 'That was different.'

'Why? Because you have some latent childhood crush thing going on? Time to get over that, isn't it, Ava?'

The heat fled. 'Don't! Don't ridicule what I felt.' *Feel.* Her voice broke slightly.

Dan sighed and tugged exasperated hands through his hair. 'You should be furious with me, Ava. I've treated you appallingly, and yet you stand here trying to make me feel better about what I've done. Why is that?'

There was no way she could answer that question honestly. Not now. 'Because you're my friend, Dan. And friends look out for each other.'

'Oh, grow a spine, Ava. If you're going to make it in this industry you can't let people walk all over you like this.'

Hurt gnawed through her chest cavity, aiming

for her heart. 'That's what you don't get about me, Dan. I have no interest in making it in this industry. And I don't *let* anyone walk over me.' At Dan's sceptical expression, she barrelled on. 'I'm going along with this charade because it helps someone I care about—despite not particularly liking the man you've turned into. You were part of my family growing up and you filled an important place in my life.' She dropped her voice. 'And so if it helps you to have me seen in public with Brant, and it helps him to be seen with me, and it doesn't hurt me...' *terminally* '...then why not? That's what friends do for each other, Dan. Or have you been alone so long you've forgotten the concept of loyalty?'

Pain, confusion and anger all warred at once in his hard brown eyes. Ava's heart thumped high in her throat, squeezing around the icy lump that spread steadily in her chest. 'If there's something you need and it's in my power to do it, then I will.'

'Why, Ava?' It was a half-whisper.

Because I love you.

'Because that's who I am, Dan. I may not win any prizes for street smarts, or survive very long in this piranha pool of an industry, but I will at least still be me. And I happen to like who I am.' She straightened her shoulders and forced the words out before turning back to her work. 'Even if you don't.'

CHAPTER TEN

SINCE the day she'd moved in, Dan had virtually disappeared. Ava had all the privacy she wanted and more. It had been days since she'd seen him for longer than a few seconds. Which meant she was stupid not to have expected the knocking at her front door. She answered it.

'Are you insane?' Her brother stood on her doorstep, pressing a copy of a gossip magazine under her nose.

Hi, Sis. Good to see you. 'It's not quite how it looks, Steve.'

'Oh? You *don't* have your tongue down Maddox's throat?'

She sighed, knowing she'd brought this one on herself, and stood clear to let him into the guesthouse. 'It was just a kiss. It didn't mean anything.'

'Just a kiss in front of a hundred people? On every magazine stand in the country?'

'Okay, not my finest moment.'

Steve must have seen the anguish on her face because he eased off. 'Maddox, Ava? *Maddox?*'

'What does everyone have against Brant? He's been nothing but lovely to me.'

Steve snorted and flopped onto the sofa. 'He's trying to get in your pants. It's in his best interests to be lovely.'

'He is not, Steve. Don't be so crude.'

The look Steve gave her spoke volumes. 'Oh, so *you* were kissing *him* in this photo, yes?'

Yes, actually. 'Lord, if its not you, it's Dan,' she said. 'What do you both have against Brant?'

'Maddox is bad news. He's constantly in the papers with his latest piece of—'

'That's not the man that I see every day at work.'

'It wouldn't be, would it? You're in his sights,' Steve said.

Hashing this out wasn't going to undo Steve's prejudice. She changed tack. 'How's Dad? Has he seen this?'

'No. But he will eventually. Someone will show him.'

So much fallout from one stupid moment of thoughtlessness. It didn't matter whether it was real or not. In fact her father would be just as mortified to know that she'd used Brant to score points. That was not the daughter he'd raised.

'Can you explain?' she pleaded. 'When you go

home this afternoon? Tell him it's not what it seems?'

Steve shook his head. 'I'm not going back until tomorrow. I'm heading out with Dan tonight.'

It was irrational to feel a jealous pang at that news. Just like when they were younger, and he'd got to hang out with Dan all the time and she hadn't. Maybe Dan was right? Maybe she hadn't matured emotionally at all. 'Tomorrow, then? Will you explain to Dad?'

'You want me to tell him that you've been photographed swapping saliva with a man you're *not* involved with?'

Ava rubbed her aching temples. How had this all got so complicated? 'Please just tell him…that I'm losing my way. Six months is such a long time, but I'm doing the best I can.'

Steve pulled himself to his feet and crossed to the sofa, then dropped next to her and wrapped a big-brother arm around her. She sagged into his familiar warmth. Some of her anxiety soaked away. 'Things are…complicated. I should have known they would be,' she said.

She could almost hear Steve's eyes narrow to slits with his next words. 'Is this complication Dan-related?' he asked, dangerously neutral.

She straightened carefully. 'Why would you say that?'

'Come on, Ava. I was there. I saw how you felt about him.'

Ava pointed at the magazine on the coffee table. 'That photo is doing the rounds and you've somehow drawn a connection to Dan?'

'It may surprise you to know that I believe you when you say there was nothing to that kiss with Maddox.'

Relief washed through her. 'You do?'

'But that's not you, Ava.' Shame sliced through her. 'Something had to be driving you to those lengths. It doesn't take a genius to eventually arrive at Dan's doorstep. You've always done stupid things when he's around.'

Ava took a deep breath. She glanced at the bed just a few metres away, where Dan might have made love to his best mate's little sister. The one he was supposed to be watching out for. She could make things really difficult for him with just a few sentences.

'Dan's not the problem, Steve.' *Oh, such lies.* 'I'll just be happy when this contract is over and I can go back to being me.'

'You're still you, kiddo.' He glanced at the magazine and cleared his throat. 'At least most of the time. Just don't let them suck all the goodness out of you.' Such displays of emotion were rare in her brother, and he didn't look entirely comfortable. He nudged her sideways. 'I'd hate to have to assume the role of the good one in the family.'

Ava laughed. 'I'd have to fall much further from grace for that to happen.'

The teasing continued for the next hour, and Ava let herself enjoy having family with her. Unconditional love. They chatted and joked over a constant supply of fresh coffee.

'What are you guys doing tonight?' she eventually asked.

'Dan's got some club in mind. The waitresses serve food off their bellies.'

Her eyes shot wide. She had a sudden flash of Dan's tongue circling a chilli mussel out of a delicate belly button.

'Kidding. Don't look so horrified—jeez. We'll probably hit the waterfront, catch up.' He shrugged. 'Guy stuff.'

Guy stuff. That encompassed a lot, and none of it wholesome. Suddenly the nightclub didn't seem so unlikely.

It was nearly midnight when Ava returned from her movie with Cadence. What an unexpected delight to find someone willing to indulge her passion for classic cinema. She'd managed to put the disasters of the past month well and truly behind her as she fell enthusiastically into a rich European saga of love, betrayal and intrigue. It had been a blessed three hours of pure escapism. Plus trailers.

And some good old-fashioned girl time with her unconventional new friend.

Her answering machine was flashing when she walked in from the ferry. She kicked off her shoes and tossed her handbag onto the sofa as the first message started to play. Thirty seconds later she was sprinting, barefoot, for Dan's front door.

Please, let them be home.

Her father's voice had been full of concern, desperate to get in touch with Steve. James Lange didn't usually *do* desperate. She rang the doorbell twice, then, impatient, followed it up with a brisk knock. There was not a sound inside. She glanced at her watch. Would they be home by now? *Damn!*

She turned to sprint back to her place and then spun round, eyes wide, as a light came on in the imposing portico.

'Ava?'

She rushed past Dan into his house. She could apologise for her rudeness later. 'Where's Steve?'

'Gone.'

That stopped her in her tracks. 'Gone where?' Panic rose in her voice.

'To Flynn's Beach. He got a text message from your father.'

Relief flooded through her. Steve was already on his way home. 'Oh, good. I got this call…' Her hands started to shake. Dan steered her to the tall leather stools lining a granite-topped breakfast bar. 'Not sure what was going on, but Dad sounded urgent. He never sounds urgent.'

Her heart was thumping a tattoo. Ava told herself it was because of her fright, and not because Dan was standing before her in nothing but a pair of silk boxer shorts. She glanced down the darkened hall to where light spilled from a doorway. She finally noticed his messed-up hair and her hand shot to her mouth.

'Oh, you were sleeping!'

A slight flush stained his jawline. 'Not exactly.'

She gasped as understanding flooded in. What had he done? Hit his little black book right after waving Steve off? 'You have someone here. I'll go…' She stumbled off the stool towards the front door.

He stopped her with two hard hands on her shoulders. 'I was in bed—alone—but not yet asleep. Relax, Ava. You've interrupted nothing important.'

Oh. Then why did he look so distracted?

'Weren't you supposed to be having dinner off a stripper or something?'

His harsh laugh barked through the silence as he moved into the kitchen. The powerful topography of his back shifted as he reached into an overhead cupboard for coffee. Ava studied the nearby microwave intently.

'That'll be your brother's fertile imagination at work, then!' he said. 'We went for a beer, and then he got your dad's message. He left straight away. Lucky he'd only had the one.'

'Oh.' She nibbled her lip. 'I wonder what happened.'

'Something about his stud stallion and an alteration with a *post-n-rail* fence.'

'Oh, no—Vasse. Steve loves that animal!'

'He treated the call with the urgency it obviously deserved. I dropped him at his car and he took off immediately. He left you a message on your machine.'

She blushed. 'I didn't stick around to hear the second message.'

They fell into silence and, with crisis averted, Ava was suddenly embarrassed by her dramatic arrival and conscious of everything that had gone on between them earlier in the week.

And that he was near naked.

She cleared her throat and slid off the stool until her toes touched the cool slate floor. 'I'm sorry I pushed my way in here. I'll let you get to bed.'

'Ava, wait.'

She paused midway across the room, dreading what was coming next.

'I owe you an apology,' he said.

Her face snapped up and her breath hitched. Not what she was expecting!

He watched her warily from behind the kitchen bench, a thousand uncomfortable miles away. 'What I said yesterday. It was unnecessary and rude. And I'm sorry.'

Apologies clearly didn't come naturally to him. Not the new Dan. 'Which part?' she asked.

He grimaced. 'All of it, but particularly about what you and Maddox have going. It's none of my business. I was just...concerned.'

Ava blinked cautiously, then returned slowly to her stool. The sight of his naked torso in the kitchen had her imagining that the rest of him was naked too. Naked and making her coffee. Suddenly she couldn't think of a thing to say.

Or how to speak.

He filled two mugs with piping hot water from an elegant spout fixed to the wall. He stirred one sugar into hers, then slid it over to her, black.

'Hope you don't mind instant.'

She was too amazed that he'd remembered how she liked her coffee to care. The last coffee he'd made her had been nearly a decade ago.

'I'll be right back.' He padded up the darkened hallway.

She took a deep, steadying breath, then pulled
the aromatic brew towards her. Her cold hands
shook slightly from the fright of the past ten
minutes. She warmed them on the expensive
ceramic mug.

Dan returned a moment later, a navy blue robe
providing considerably more modesty. It was still
creased from where it had been folded, and a price
tag swung off the collar. Ava stepped towards him
and reached her hand around behind his neck.

He froze on the spot. His eyes fluttered shut.

She broke the tag free and stepped away,
handing it to him. 'You don't get around in this
much, then?'

His smile was sheepish. His blush endearing.
'I'm not used to putting more clothes *on* when
there's a woman in the house.'

I'll bet. Just another reminder of the world he
now mixed in. And how she didn't fit.

With less hard flesh on display, she could think
again. She didn't want to be angry with him. He
was her friend—someone she wanted to like and
respect. There were things he'd done that she
wasn't crazy about, but it was hardly his fault that
she couldn't think straight when he was around.
That he drove her to do stupid things.

Like kissing Brant.

'We're not involved. Brant and I,' she said on a rush. Dan raised a single expressive eyebrow. She took a deep breath and raised her chin. 'You made me angry. That's why I kissed him.'

'It's none of my business.'

Lord, what was worse? His infuriating excessive interest in what she was doing, and with whom, or this new lifeless disinterest.

'You were judging me based on nothing but the speculation of a bunch of tabloid reporters. It made me mad,' she said.

'And do you always express your anger in such physical terms?'

Ava blushed. 'The only person I owe that explanation to is Brant. He was most immediately affected.'

'Oh, I saw how affected he was.'

His gaze strayed down to her bare feet, twisting awkwardly on the footplate of her stool. Not wanting to show how nervous he was making her, Ava consciously arched them, elongating her ankle where a delicate silver anklet rested. His eyes snapped back to hers, flaring briefly.

'Brant is not the man you think he is,' she risked.

Dan's jaw clenched. 'I'm fairly sure we've covered this already.'

'I just want you to understand…'

'Why is it so important that I understand?'

There were a number of answers to that, and none of them good. The nervous breath Ava blew out lifted her fringe. 'Because he's a good person. And he's being unfairly judged. Having had a taste of assassination by media myself, I can empathise.'

His eyes flashed and darkened, and she knew that was too low a blow. It was hardly Dan's fault that the media were suddenly crucifying her.

'That doesn't answer my question,' he said. 'Why is it so important to you that *I* understand?'

'I'm trying to explain…about Brant.'

He surged to his feet. 'I'm so sick of talking about Brant bloody Maddox. Everything revolves around him. He isn't even here and he's dominating the conversation.'

Ava let her mouth snap shut, realising at last that she was on dangerous ground. She glanced at the door and considered her escape. He moved into her line of sight, blocking her exit.

'Too late, Ava. You wanted to know what happens when I get mad? Well, you're about to find out.'

He closed the space between them in one fluid movement, stepping effortlessly between their stools. One arm slid around her while the other burrowed into her thick hair to hold her face still.

Then he hauled her towards him. His lips pressed into hers, angled and possessive and his tongue charmed its way inside her mouth. Ava stole a lungful of air in the split second that he realigned his mouth to fit his lips more perfectly against hers. The oxygen did little to ease the spinning of her mind, and her protest came out more of a moan than a squeak. She battled the carnal desire to lean into him, fighting the seduction of his personal scent until finally he noticed. The bruising pressure of his lips instantly eased. His mouth brushed rather than consumed. The iron bars of his arms relaxed their hold and his kisses gently nipped where only moments ago they'd crushed so violently.

'Ava.' It was more a breath than a word. He lifted his head, gazing through molten eyes, his voice thick and hoarse. 'I can't stand knowing that my kiss wasn't the last one on your lips.' Large hands framed her face.

A single kiss. Another.

Soft, now, and seductive. Hands stroking. Ava felt her tension melting. Wait—she was still angry with him. Wasn't she? She held firm. His lips grazed back and forth over hers. Tempting. Healing. Erasing any memory of the harsh treatment of moments ago. He bit gently at the fullness of her lower lip. Tasting and exploring.

Until she burned to kiss him.

Muscles deep inside her tightened and her udas body swayed towards his. The smell of him seduced her, eddying around her as she fought the desire to taste him all over again.

His lips stopped moving against hers. He didn't pull away, but let bare millimetres open up between his stilled lips and her pulsing ones, offering her the next move. Giving her the choice.

She took it.

It was nothing like their first kiss. And everything like it. She pressed herself into Dan's hard warmth, increasing the contact of her lips on his. It was easy—easy and natural—to open her mouth to fit better over his. To let her tongue steal out and engage his in a flirty dance. The moment she pressed her lips to his all the tension flowed out of him. As if he'd been expecting her to push him away. Those silk-covered arms, all muscle and warmth, dropped away, leaving just their mouths clinging together.

He slid his palms up her thighs, ruching her dress higher, then nudged her knees apart with his hips. Ava gasped at the startling intimacy of the move, at his boldness and what it meant, but she didn't clench them shut. Without taking his mouth from hers, he stepped further between them, and then gently closed her knees against his thighs, trapping him inside her grip. Then he tangled his fingers into her hair.

She tore her mouth from his and sucked in a deep breath in the brief seconds before Dan reclaimed her. It was no prelude to something more racy. He just wanted to be closer. *To her.* Her heart tumbled, lost, into her love for him as their kisses burned on.

Her voice was breathless when she finally lifted her head, tempering the flames with gentle humour. 'Wow. What do you do when you get mad with Steve?'

She hadn't meant to put the brakes on entirely, but his burst of laughter took care of that. He held his position between her thighs, but let his kisses drop away until the only part of him moving were his magic hands, stroking through her thick hair.

'I didn't mean any of the things I said,' he whispered, hot breath chasing across her skin. A shiver of delight followed every word. Just as well she was already sitting, because her knees went completely to liquid. 'You have to know that's not how I really think of you.'

He kissed her eyelid. Her earlobe. She whimpered at the sensation.

'You think of me as a little sister,' a breathless sexy voice said. Lord, was that her?

He smiled and pressed closer to her body. 'Yes, because this is exactly how the average brother and sister spend their free evenings.'

She couldn't laugh when his answer meant so much.

He took pity on her, pushing her hair clear to stare intently into her grey depths. 'Ava, I stopped thinking of you of a kid the moment you walked into my office.'

'But…'

'I was lying to myself. Using that old excuse to keep some distance between us. I didn't want to get involved.'

His use of the past tense was all that kept her in her seat. 'Why?'

'Because I made a promise a long time ago. Not to hurt you. And I thought not getting involved was the easiest way to do that. But all I've done since then is cause you pain.'

'Who…?'

He stared at her long and hard. 'Your father.'

She straightened. 'My father? When? You haven't spoken to him for—'

'Nine years.'

'He warned you off me way back then?'

Dan kissed the confused creases she could suddenly feel in her brow. 'He saw the writing on the wall. Knew that you weren't getting over your...thing...for me. He asked me to take more care.'

Oh, he didn't! Heat flared in her cheeks.

'He did it because he loved you, Ava. And I left because I cared for all of you too much to stay.'

A cold dread came over her. 'You left because of me?'

'I thought it would be easier on you to make a clean break,' he said.

Easier? She'd cried herself sick for a month solid. 'But you gave up your only family. For me.' Tears sprang into her eyes.

He stroked away the tears with his thumbs. 'You were just the catalyst, Ava. I needed to leave. Needed to step out from under James's protection. It was time.'

Ava stared at him. 'Did my father ask you to go?'

Dan smiled. '"Ask" is a subjective word. Let's just say a serious talk in the kitchen one day planted the idea very firmly in my head.'

Her eyes widened. That had been her father— the hushed conversation she'd overheard. God, if only she'd stuck around to hear more of it. She never would have... *Oh, so much...*

'Why did you never call him?'

'I called once. You answered.' He traced her lips with his finger and she sighed. 'Then the next time I got your father, but he was so busy trying to convince me you were fine I knew that meant you weren't. It just made things strained between us. Either way I'd hurt you. In the end it was just easier to drop out of contact.'

Ava thought about that. 'Will you tell him that one day? So he knows? He was hurt when you left.' *Too.*

Dan looked at her, kissed her nose, her lips. His eyes held such sorrow. 'I will. If he'll speak to me.'

'Just try and stop him. He never stopped caring about you.' *Neither did his daughter.* 'So all this…hedging…was about keeping a promise you made nine years ago?'

'I owe your father a bigger debt than you can ever imagine. I figured the least I could do now was never hurt you again. Yet that's all I've done since you irritated the stuffing out of my lawyers.'

'I'm not hurting now…' She pressed her lips to his. Although she might be later. Based on their history, that was a distinct possibility.

'No?' His smile was easy.

She shook her head, side to side. Pressing her aching breasts into him. Her tongue slid so easily across his teeth, stole into his mouth to taste him, finally on her terms. She leaned into his strength and let her love steal out through that kiss. As though he would somehow taste it. She crossed her ankles behind him.

His eyes flared wide. 'Ava, you have to be sure. This is not something we can undo. Is this what you really want?'

Am I who you really want? She knew exactly where this was heading. She met his look with more control than she presently felt, and let him see the truth of her words. 'I really do, Dan.'

'This will change everything. I don't think I can go back after this.'

Back to being friends. No, that was not somewhere she wanted to go either. She stared at him, felt the blood still pumping into her aching lips, chest heaving, legs trembling.

'I don't want to be your friend,' she whispered. 'I've been your friend for a lifetime. I want to be something else.'

His next word was cautious. 'What?'

She tightened her leg-hold on him and looked him dead in the eye.

'I want to be yours.'

Warm lips murmured words close to her ear, tracing light kisses along her collarbone. Butterfly fingers stroked the flesh of her naked belly.

Ava awakened to all these things one by one.

'Ava, are you okay?'

Concerned brown eyes found her. She blinked her confusion. A husky laugh chuckled out of her. She nestled in closer to his furnace of a body. His beautiful, hard, ex-surfer's body. 'That was…'

Gravel rumbled in her ear. 'Everything I imagined.'

She tilted her head to look at him. 'You've been imagining?'

Dan laughed. 'You have no idea. Did you think you'd cornered the market on unrequited lust?' He looked down quickly.

Ah. *Not love, then.*

Ava allowed the tiny heart-bleed, even though she hadn't gone into this expecting anything more than the fulfilment of one of her own lifelong dreams. It should have been easier to swallow her disappointment after a lifetime of practice, but she got there. She stretched in his arms, lazy as only a highly satisfied woman could be.

'I've been wondering what you'd feel like,' he said. 'Since that night at the guesthouse, actually.'

'Really? So you'd been working on it? This seduction?'

'Not working. Hoping,' he said.

She eyed him seriously. What was he saying? 'Then this isn't—wasn't—purely spontaneous?'

He met her look with his own level one. 'I don't do spontaneous.'

'So the last time...?'

'Not entirely unplanned,' he granted. 'I'd been watching you shuck mussels all night, and wondered how I could get you to use those lips on me.'

She feigned outrage and went to push him off. He wouldn't budge. Her eyebrows lifted as colour piped into her cheeks.

He answered with an endearingly smug smile. 'I'm not done yet.'

She pressed her lips to his sweat-slicked shoulder, then his mouth. Their kisses forestalled conversation for some time.

Finally, his breath burned against her ear. 'So no more Maddox?'

'I thought you were sick of talking about Brant?'

'I don't want to talk about him; I just want to hear you say it. You guys are through, right?'

Ava turned her head on the feather pillow to study him. There was no point denying it yet again. It wasn't what he wanted to know. 'We'll always be close friends.'

'Just not too close.'

'Don't you need us to...seem close? For the show?'

Dan closed his eyes, and when he opened them they were pained. 'No.'

Ava knew better. 'Yes.'

'The network needs it.'

'And you are AusOne's creature.'

He kissed her long and hard, fingers punishing her with a pinch on her still sensitised flesh. Pleasure had her muscles clamping hard around him.

Dan hissed.

'Serves you right.' Her laugh was lusty.

'I'm *your* creature,' he joked gently.

She grazed her lips across his and closed her eyes to appreciate the moment. How much would she give to have him mean that? 'I'll do whatever you need me to, Dan. I know how important this is. Maybe we could just keep it simple?'

'That didn't really work the first time. The papers have a way of turning simple into scandal.' He moved against her and they both sighed.

'Not all of them, surely? What about this one who's doing the full-length feature?'

'I've called in a few favours. Got a good journalist assigned who'll favour an angle other than what you and Maddox get up to between takes.'

Ava laughed, thinking of the games of cards, old wives' gossip and many, many cups of very unexciting coffee she and Brant had shared between shots. 'They'd be seriously disappointed with Brant and me. You and me, on the other hand…'

She pushed hard against him. His eyes fluttered shut. She kissed each lid. When they opened

again they were umber. Funny how many browns
there were, and how she'd learned to read them.
Like a secret code.

'We can't let anyone know about this, Ava. You
understand that, right?'

Ava thought about Cadence, and how many
years she and Brant had kept their relationship
under wraps. 'If Brant can do it, we can too.'

His head jerked back as he looked at her. 'What
do you mean?'

This little titbit would have made a lot of difference to their relationship earlier. She'd
withheld it intentionally. Self-defence. She took
a breath. 'Brant has a long-term girlfriend who he
loves desperately.'

Dan laughed. The movement caused delicious
friction inside her. 'Maddox wouldn't know love
if it bit him on the butt.'

'I was at the movies with her tonight. She's
lovely—in a spooky kind of way.'

Dan stopped moving. Confusion and realisation filled his face. 'You're serious! But the
network...the papers?'

Ava nibbled her way across his chest. 'Looks
like they don't approve of Cadence. She's not TV
royalty material.'

She looked at his frown and wiggled into the
thick quilt. Had he truly believed that Brant was

serial sleaze? Was he as much of a victim of the
network's game-playing as she was?

'The women?' he asked, bemused.

'Set up by Kurtz. Brant loves Cadence.'

Dan's mind got busy dissecting that new information. Ava snuggled closer, happy to see that he
wasn't afraid of re-evaluating. 'And here's something else to blow your mind. He's smart too.'

His snort told her she'd pushed the limits of
Dan's belief too far on that one. 'But he's not
interested in you?'

'Only as a friend.'

'Then how smart can he be?'

He rolled suddenly, taking Ava with him so she
ended up lying on top of him, her hair swinging
in thick waves around her shoulders. His gaze
swept appreciatively over every part of her
exposed to him from this angle. She fell forward
and found his mouth with hers.

'Dan?'

'Mmm?' He managed between kisses.

'Can we not talk about Brant while we…? It's
kind of creepy.'

He smiled against her lips.

'My pleasure.'

CHAPTER ELEVEN

'DIONE LEEDS, *The Standard*.'

The tiny woman with cropped bleached blond curls made a beeline straight for Ava. She dusted the dark soil off her hands and shook the offered hand. Designer outfit, overly thin, overly tanned, overly gymed, Leeds was one hundred percent yuppy. The woman couldn't have looked any more out of place amongst the earth, shrubs and flowers on the set of *Urban Nature*. Dan had chosen her because she was a journalist he trusted, but Ava didn't get a trusting vibe from this tight-faced woman.

Far from it.

'Thank you for the opportunity, Ms Lange.'

Ava smiled out of pure manners and saw the cavalry approaching. 'Don't thank me. Here comes the man who arranged it all.'

The woman stiffened, and then turned briskly and introduced herself to Dan before he could get a word out. 'You're not Lindsay Tannon,' he said

'I'm not, no. Lindsay is ill. I'm subbing or her.'

If it was a lie, it tumbled effortlessly off Leeds' ongue. Ava would have bought it, but Dan didn't. The exclusive was offered to Ms Tannon. 'erhaps we should reschedule—'

'No need. I'm more than qualified to stand in er place, and my substitution has been okayed y AusOne.' She met his gaze directly. 'Unless here's a specific reason you wanted Lindsay?'

Dan's lips pressed together and Ava knew they vere in trouble. There were no legitimate grounds o forbid a journalist from covering the story in er colleague's place. His hands were tied. Ava vas sure she could hear the sound of Dan's teeth ;nashing. But outwardly he was smooth as a good ed wine. If she didn't know him so well…

'Have you been briefed?' he asked.

Leeds smiled, bright and completely empty. Fully, thank you. Congratulations on the ATA iomination. That must be very exciting?'

'Save it for the interview.'

Ava gasped at Dan's rudeness. Surely even he vould have better sense than to wave a red rag at bull? Judging by the flash of annoyance on Dione Leeds' face, she wasn't used to being challenged.

'You have one full morning on set to observe ind record, then private interviews with Ava,

Maddox and myself. That should give you every thing you need.'

'I may need to ask other—'

'Out of the question. Your access is exclusive not unlimited. Ava, Maddox and myself. And we have expectations that this piece will rise a little higher than some of the exposure we've had so far.'

Leeds' face tightened in genuine offence. 'We're the *Standard*, Mr Arnot.' As though that said it all.

'I'm sure your ratings have benefited directly from that exposure, so it's a bit late now to cry poor.'

Ava swallowed nervously. Dione Leeds was every bit a match for Dan. Aggressive, on the ball, and she knew her stuff.

Damn.

Dan signalled to one of the production assist ants and the man wandered over. 'Finn, this is M. Leeds. She'll be on-set today, researching a feature article on the show. I'd like you to stay with her, provide any assistance required, and make sure she's comfortable.'

Don't let her out of your sight. The message was clear. To all of them. He threw Leeds a tight smile.

'Ava. Can I have a word about today's schedule, please?'

They excused themselves, and Leeds go straight to work observing the set-up for the day. Her human watchdog stuck to her side.

'This is not what I had in mind.' Ava could see Dan was more agitated than he'd let on. He pushed a hand through his hair. 'I know Leeds' work. She's in a different league to Tannon.'

'That's good, isn't it? For the quality of the finished article?'

'She's an investigative reporter. A real Rottweiler. If they've sent her they must be after something bigger than we pitched.' He tore his anxious eyes off Leeds' retreating form and looked at Ava. 'I'm sorry. The interview might be harder than we expected. I'll need to warn Maddox, too. Lord only knows what he'll say.'

'Brant might surprise you. But, yes, he should be told.' She feigned a calm she really didn't feel. But Dan was agitated enough for all of them.

He swore. 'She'll almost certainly try and dig for information on you and Maddox, and it's too late to back away from the exposure we've already had. You'll have to tread a careful line with her.'

'In what way?'

'Tell her enough that she thinks she's getting somewhere, but not so much that she'll start sniffing a scoop.'

Ava had no real media training, so the idea of trying to best a professional like Leeds didn't appeal. It must have shown on her face.

His eyes softened. 'Just be yourself. Don't

answer any direct questions about Maddox, but try not to evade them too obviously either.'

Oh, God. Nausea washed over her.

'You'll be fine, Ava.' His gaze caressed her. 'You can talk me in circles with your logic, so just use that.'

She wanted to touch him. To feel the reassuring pressure of his hand on hers. But her first safe opportunity was hours away yet, safely behind closed doors. After her interview slot with the Rottweiler.

Brant's secret loomed large in her mind. If even Dan hadn't known about Cadence then it was unlikely that Leeds would sniff it out, particularly if the network had gone to so much trouble to cover her up. But Ava felt the pressure of being keeper-of-the-secret. She'd need to play on the supposed romance between herself and Brant a little. But not too much. *How much was that?*

The nausea increased. How on earth had she found herself hosting a television show, being pursued by an investigative reporter and protecting someone's deeply held secrets. Three months ago she'd just been Ava Lange, country girl and landscape designer.

How much time changed things.

Brant emerged from his interview in Ava' mobile office looking slightly green around th

ills and more than a little harassed. He headed
traight for Ava and the coffee and doughnut she
eld ready for him. His hands trembled slightly
vhen he took them from her. That worried her
nore than anything, because *nothing* fazed Brant
Maddox. He practically downed his coffee in
ne.

'Cadence…?' she asked.

'No. But she's very thorough. Quite relent-
ess, in fact.'

'What did she ask you?'

'Heaps about the programme, my vision for it.
My interest in plants, for crying out loud!'
Another deep sip. It must have burned, but he
howed no sign. 'She wanted to know about Dan,
nd a heap of questions about you. Nothing par-
icularly controversial, but still…'

As the supposed love interest for Brant, she
vould be a hot topic. She suggested as much to
Brant. He shook his head.

'More than that. It's as if she was talking
round the subject of me and my love-life. We
alked about everything but that. And she never
sked outright about you. She's too good.'

Ava's nausea increased.

'It was like the eye of the storm—like the real
neaning was in the centre there, hiding inside ev-
rything else we talked about. But if you read a

transcript there'd be nothing wrong with the ques
tions.'

He took a deep breath and released it with a
slow hiss. Then he blinked and refocused on Ava.
'I'm sorry, I'm scaring you to death. It wasn't all
that bad, just…watch yourself. Go in knowing
that she's got some kind of agenda.'

Great! 'I'm terrified she'll spring a surprise on
me. That she'll know about Cadence and I'll panic
and blow it for you.'

Brant balanced the doughnut on top of his
coffee and put his free hand on hers. 'Hey, if that
happens it won't be because you stuffed up but
because she's a good journalist. Cadey and I know
that we can't get away with this for ever. Don'
compromise yourself to keep my secret.'

'What secret?' The Rottweiler had appeared
silently behind them, a glint in her beady eyes.
Where the heck was Finn, her watchdog?

Brant went seamlessly into charming mode.
'Shameless doughnut addiction,' he said, and took
a healthy bite. He held the remnants out to admire
it. 'I love these things.'

The crumbs exploding from his mouth as he
spoke did the job of distracting Leeds. She looked
away, disgusted. 'Ava. Are you ready?'

No. Not nearly. God, she wanted Dan by her
side for this. She took a breath and smiled. 'Sure.

A few minutes later they were in the comfort of Ava's office trailer. They'd talked niceties about the weather, the building they were renovating, the credentials of the crew. To her credit, Leeds had taken detailed notes of all the relevant discussion and politely listened to the rest. Then she got down to it.

'So, quite an amazing journey you've been on these past months. From behind-the-scenes designer to out-the-front presenter.'

Leeds' smile actually seemed genuine this time, and Ava relaxed a little. 'I still design the spaces. I consider myself a designer first.'

'The network would have to disagree with you, wouldn't they? They've invested quite a bit in you as screen talent.'

'In terms of time, I suppose. The risk of going with someone new…'

'I meant the pay-rise. The RV.' She looked around the comfortable trailer.

Ava faltered for a moment, but then remembered Dan's advice. 'This is my office. It's so I can work between takes on designs. And the pay-rise is because I'm effectively doing two jobs at once. It's not unreasonable.' Ava realised she was defending herself. Not a good start.

Leeds recovered smoothly. 'No, no—of course not. It's quite flattering when you think about it, that they felt strongly enough about you as a presenter to go to all that trouble.'

Had she ever felt flattered? Nope, not once. 'I suppose so.'

'I have to say you don't really strike me as the usual television starlet type.'

Ava forced a smile to her lips. 'I'm not. I'm a landscape designer who happens to be on television.'

'You come from…' Leeds consulted her notes. '…Flynn's Beach, yes? Must be hard, being the new kid on the block in the big city, mixing in the television industry, nominated for an ATA only three months out. Pretty heady stuff—'

'The *show* is nominated.'

'And Brant Maddox.'

'He is?' That was news to Ava. Her smile was immediate and sincere. 'Oh, that's fantastic!'

Leeds looked curious. 'It was announced this morning. I'd have thought, of all people, he would have told you.'

Ava's guard shot up. 'The Brant Maddox you see and the Brant Maddox I see are quite different people. My Brant is modest enough not to brag about something like that.'

She grimaced at her own choice of phrase, and Leeds didn't miss it. Her smile was twitchingly alert. 'Your Brant?'

Despite Dan's advice, Ava couldn't bring herself to stumble through a half answer. 'If you want to ask me, go right ahead.'

Leeds didn't hesitate. 'Are you involved with Brant Maddox?'

'I'm close friends with Brant Maddox. Anything else is nobody's business but mine.' *And Dan's.*

'And Brant's?'

Ava dipped her head and conceded that point.

'Still, I would have thought that he would share his exciting news with a *close friend*?'

Ava chewed the inside of her cheek. What was the right approach here? Saying yes would be a lie, and saying no would undermine the image they'd been portraying and risk exposing Cadence.

'Perhaps he's being sensitive. Since I wasn't nominated.'

Leeds laughed. It was the most genuine thing he'd done all day. 'Sensitive? Right.'

Ava's blood boiled. Poor old Brant was going to be crucified again if she didn't speak up. She widened her eyes, all innocence. 'Oh, I didn't realise you knew Brant. He didn't mention it.'

The smile faded from Leeds' face, leaving a cold blank canvas in its place. 'I don't.'

'Well, you'll have to take it as given from someone who *does* know him that he would definitely put my feelings ahead of his own.' She managed a fair impersonation of Dan, staring Leeds down.

The woman dropped her eyes. 'Ain't love blind?' she muttered, saccharine-sweet.

Ava didn't bite. She had Leeds' number now.

Leeds shifted tack. 'Let's talk about Arnot.'

Or not. The change of subject surprised Ava. She stiffened immediately.

Leeds barrelled on. 'You seem really relaxed in his company. He must be a decent boss?'

'Because I'm relaxed around him?' Ava asked.

'And because he personally signed off on this RV.'

'Are we back to that?'

Leeds' stare was steady. 'You tell me.'

'Dan's a producer. By signing me to this deal, he got a presenter and a designer in one. I imagine it actually cost the network less, even with the pay-rise. I'd call that doing his job.'

'You defend him quite loyally.' Beady eyes grew keen.

Ava bristled. 'Why not? He deserves a little loyalty. He's been good to me.'

'Good? Feeding you on a plate to the tabloids?'

Ava's confidence stumbled, but she kept her eyes carefully screened. 'It's a producer's job to arrange publicity.'

'No, it's not, honey.' Condescension fairly

ripped from Leeds' too-red lips. 'That's the publicist's job. Why is a high-level producer getting so personally involved in *your* publicity, do you suppose?'

Ava knew when she was being provoked. What was Leeds trying to imply? Her frown was genuine. 'Perhaps he's very hands-on?' she suggested.

Leeds smiled and scribbled in her notepad. 'Perhaps. You don't seem too upset about it?'

'I'm a paid employee of AusOne. If they want me to undertake PR, I'll do it. You can't imagine I'd be here with you if I wasn't required to be.'

Leeds' eager expression turned frosty. Then she struck. 'Are you involved with Daniel Arnot?'

Ava's heart stopped. She struggled valiantly to keep her expression even. When her heart started up again, it thumped so painfully in her chest she thought the journalist would surely hear it. 'Exactly how many of the men in this show am I supposed to be involved with? Perhaps you could give me a checklist to save some time? I'll just tick all those I've slept with.'

'You live in his house.'

Ava's stomach dropped. She should have predicted that one. *Stupid, stupid.* Her pulse hammered. 'I *use* his guesthouse. His completely separate guesthouse.'

'Convenient!'

'Not particularly—especially if I want to ge
away from work for a while.'

Leeds studied her intently. Ava met her stare a
nonchalantly as she could. 'Still, not the kind o
offer high-powered TV execs usually make t
their employees.' Innuendo saturated the question

Feed her a bit, but not too much. Ava had n
choice. It was this or admit there was somethin
between her and Dan. She hoped Steve woul
forgive her. 'It is when he's friends with th
employee's brother. Her enormously over
protective brother, who wanted someone to kee
an eye out for her in the big city.'

The wind billowed from Leeds' sails most ef
fectively. She'd been completely unprepared fo
that answer. Her research hadn't extended t
family members and their backgrounds, obvi
ously. Ava had to fight to restrain a triumphan
grin.

'Oh, I see. Okay.' Leeds cleared her throat an
glanced at her notes. Silence ticked by in excru
ciating seconds. Then she looked up again. 'Bac
to Maddox.'

Too good to be true. Ava sighed. But at leas
they weren't talking about Dan any more.

'It occurs to me that—' Leeds picked her word
carefully '—should someone want to disguise
relationship with someone…let's say someon

ontroversial, then a high-profile work romance vould be a great way to do it.'

Cadence. Ava's heart started thumping again. She was growing to hate Dione Leeds so much it vasn't hard to affect coolness in her answer. 'Is here a question in there somewhere?'

Leeds studied her closely, patently deciding vhether to risk her next question or not. This eemed to be dangerously close to the defamation ine. Ava held her breath.

'No. I guess not. Let's move on to the designs.'

Ava let air out slowly and silently, consciously rying to slow her rampant heartbeat. That had een too close for comfort. She settled in her eat and reminded herself she was in her office. Her domain.

She lowered her shoulders, quelled her hurning stomach, and looked coolly at Leeds.

Bring it on.

I guess we shouldn't be surprised she knew about ou being in the guesthouse. Even Tannon would ave done some homework.'

Ava was spread half across Dan as he lay on the luffy covers of her bed—his bed, technically. She sighed. 'I hated lying.'

'What lies did you tell? Sounds to me like all ou did was hedge.'

'Lying by omission.'

'That's not lying. That's politics.'

Ava muttered, realigning herself to lie next to Dan. He sounded so sure of himself. She mentally shook her head. She'd never get used to the kind of world he moved in.

She kissed the soft pads of his fingers. 'What did she ask you?'

'I think my cryptic answers frustrated her. She asked about my career, my professional pedigree—yadda-yadda. All public record stuff so I think she was warming me up.'

'Then what?'

'Super-fast rise, string of successes. Most people compromise their integrity along the way.'

Ava knew how she would have reacted to such an insult. Integrity was as important to Dan as it was to her. 'Like *she* can talk! What did you say to that?'

'I told her that the secret was in remaining honest to your roots. That keeping close to my childhood friends was the key.'

Her lips stilled on his hands and she looked at him. 'Friends, plural?'

'No, singular. Thanks for the heads-up about Steve. Mentioning him directly took the bite right out of Leeds' attack.'

She tucked his hand into her chest. His finger lazily traced the under curve of one breast. Tiny hivers raced across her skin. 'I didn't know what else to say,' she murmured.

'It was the right thing to say.' He gazed at the light streaming in the window and idly stroked her naked shoulder. 'I'm sorry that you have to be cagey at all—it's not how I'd like it to be. In a perfect world we could be out and proud right now.'

'Right now?' She smiled seductively.

He twisted free of her hold. 'Keep giving me that smutty little smile and I *will* be out and proud.'

His mouth found hers, putting conversation on hold while they feasted hungrily on each other. Finally he pulled free, sprinkling little kisses across her jaw before lifting his head. 'I have something to ask you.'

Dan's uncertainty intrigued her. She'd never seen him lost for words.

'Tomorrow night.' *The ATA Awards dinner.* 'I'd like… Would you…? I realise you're going anyway, but would you go with me?'

It was hard to keep the confusion from her voice. 'But don't we have to—?'

'Maddox, yes. But you and I will know… secretly…that you're with me.' Dark eyes held grey ones.

You're with me. The three most seductive words in the universe. Ava felt their impact deep in her gut, in a primal place. They entirely eclipsed those other words from her past. *I will never be with you.* She breathed deeply before answering, reminding herself that in a few months her contract would be over and she'd be returning to Flynn's Beach. She wouldn't get this chance again.

'Yes, Dan. I'd love to go with you.'

His features softened and his eyes darkened and intensified. Tension she hadn't even noticed he held drained out of him. He trailed the back of one hand over the curve of her neck. He leaned in close to her mouth and his words were almost lost in his kiss. 'Thank you.'

Every kiss just got better and better. How did he *do* that?

She sighed into his mouth and tried not to let her love show. Surely this would be enough? He didn't have to give her for ever. He laid his hand gently at her nape and shifted over her.

This would be enough.

'It's not enough!' Carrie examined Ava's flushed face critically. 'This is the Australian Television Awards, Ava. Red carpet, cameras, claws at the ready. If ever there was an occasion to break the make-up rule, it's tonight.'

'I think it's perfectly fine—'

'Perfectly bland is what it is.' Carrie bustled Ava

nto the bathroom, where a large mirror was rimmed
vith bright lights. She yanked open the marble
vanity and groaned at the paucity of its contents.

'Honestly, Ava. A dress like that needs comple-
menting, not contrasting. You're going to have to
rust me on this one, okay? Do you even have
mascara on?'

Ava sighed heavily, knowing it was a lost cause.
The network limo wasn't due for twenty minutes;
he had time to indulge Carrie. A little. 'Okay, but
lon't go crazy.'

There was nothing crazy about the end result.
t was more make-up than she had ever worn
pefore, but the deep slashes of copper across her
eyes, the way the kohl fringed her lashes, the
rtful application of colour to her cheeks and jaw
complemented her loaned dress perfectly.

The network had sent a rep from a fashion
lesigner round the day before to measure up. She
nadn't recognised his name, and had been duly
esigned to wearing whatever minuscule mon-
strosity they demanded of her. But the designer had
peen astute, and the dress he'd sent was stunning.
Exactly what she might have chosen for herself—
f she'd had a choice. Modest, simple, earthy.

That last point, particularly, brought a lump to
ner throat. Maybe the network was finally
getting her.

Moss-green fabric melted across her body, with the subtlest traces of a leaf motif, depending which way she turned in the light. A tiny clutch of embroidered leaves across one shoulder held the dress up. A mastery of hidden internal suspension held the rest of her up.

It was the most beautiful thing she had ever worn. And Carrie's magic fingers had given her a face to match. Except now... She gnawed her lip and said, 'Hair?'

Carrie glanced at her watch anxiously. 'We have time.'

They didn't, but they worked quickly together to trap Ava's locks in a creation worthy of any wedding. Forty hasty hairpins and a spritz of hair spray later, and her honey-blonde tresses finally did justice to the rest of her.

Carrie nodded with satisfaction. 'I'm going to have to sit with someone else now. So as not to be the dull one.'

Ava laughed. Carrie's plunging fire-engine-red dress was anything but dull. 'You have to sit with someone else anyway, don't you?' she teased. 'Somewhere in the cheap seats...?'

Carrie feigned outrage, her fingers reaching for the pins. 'That's it...'

Both women emerged, laughing, into the living room. Ava had left the front door open

waiting Brant's arrival, and they saw him perfectly framed in the doorway, pulling up and
clambering out of his car.

Cadence was driving.

Ava held her breath and glanced at Carrie, who
looked curious but not fascinated as Brant
stretched over and kissed the shadowy figure
goodbye. She probably figured it was just Brant's
latest pair of legs. He loped towards them across
the lawn. Her heart went out to Cadence, who
shouldn't have to sit out such an important
occasion in Brant's career. Ava knew she must see
her, standing illuminated at the front of the guesthouse, and waved subtly, trying not to draw
Carrie's eye.

She knew the little toot Cadence gave as she
took off was as much for her as Brant.

The man in question checked out both women
thoroughly. 'You both look amazing,' he said,
swooping in to kiss Ava's cheek and then Carrie's.

'Don't mess the make-up!' the women shrieked
together, then burst out laughing.

'Been on the champagne already?' a familiar
deep voice asked.

Ava's heart flip-flopped. She turned as Dan
emerged through the side gate from his property
and strode towards them between the gardenias
she'd been training up since she'd moved in. Her

throat constricted. She'd seen him in busines:
suits plenty of times, but in a formal tuxedo—an
not a cheap one—he was completely...

'Breathtaking.' Dan spoke for her, as his glowing
eyes drifted over her from her gravity-defying hai
to her perfectly painted toenails. She knew what
picture she must present, golden tresses piled high
neck and throat bare, figure-hugging dress and the
highest of strappy high heels. There was no disguising the longing in his gaze. Not that he looked t
be trying particularly hard.

'Hi, Dan.' Carrie's welcome was pointed.

Ava had to force her eyes away from Dan's
and she blinked to clear them. But not quickly
enough. Carrie's eyes rounded in astonishment as
the penny finally dropped. Her mouth fell open.

Brant, always attuned to the vibe of a crowd
broke the awkward silence, flattering both womer
and moving things along nicely with his usua
panache. He looked fantastic himself in his
designer tuxedo. His moss-coloured tie was
perfect match to her dress—no accident, she was
sure. The network was still at it. They'd beer
dressed to impress, or at least to leave an impression.

Of togetherness.

You and I will know... Ava remembered a week
of lazy afternoons—and late nights—and thrille

to hold that secret between them. In a room full of celebrities they would have eyes only for each other.

'Practised your acceptance speech, Maddox?' Dan said, relaxed.

'Practised yours, Arnot?'

Some of the frost had chipped off Dan's attitude since Ava had told him about Brant and Cadence. The four of them had even been to dinner together. Being public, Cadence had necessarily 'partnered' Dan. His expression on seeing her in full Goth regalia had said it all, but within the hour Cadence's amazing mind had won him over completely. He'd relaxed into an easy repartee with her and—astonishingly—she'd even blushed clear through her pale make-up at something he'd said.

Not one to hold a grudge, Brant had accepted Dan's improved attitude towards him gracefully. But still…boys would be boys.

Dan practically growled Brant away from Ava.

An enormous gleaming vehicle materialised out on the street, surprising them all. How something that large moved that quietly Ava didn't know. Brant was the first to the door, followed closely by Carrie, who appeared completely blasé about their transport. So did Dan.

Ava sighed. Was she the only one never to have ridden in a limo?

'You guys go on ahead,' Dan said quietly. 'I need a quick word with Ava.' He nudged the door partway closed behind Carrie.

Ava turned to him, a question on her lips, but Dan silenced it by pressing his mouth to hers. He didn't mash—sensitive, maybe, to how long it had taken to put on her awards face—but he held her tightly to him as he kissed her breath away.

Finally he raised his head. 'We can't go.'

'Why not?' Oxygen depletion robbed her of sense.

'Because I need, very badly, to kiss you again. Right now.' His lips hovered just above hers. 'You look sensational. Did I tell you that?'

Ava smiled, not so secretly pleased. 'In a manner of speaking.'

'I picked that dress personally. I love it on you.'

She should have known. It was truly perfect.

'But I'd love it even more off you.' He kissed her again, walking her backwards towards the bedroom door. 'Except the killer heels. You can keep those on.'

She laughed against his lips, twisting reluctantly out of his grip. 'The car's waiting.'

He scooped her towards him, his hips pressed firmly against her. 'Let them wait.'

She knew he wasn't serious. He couldn't be,

with two of his staff and the company limo waiting only metres away. Could he?

'Later.' Her huskiness surprised even her.

'Promise?'

She turned and teased her lips across his. 'I promise.'

A quick mirror-check later they were out through the front door, hurrying towards the idling limo.

The excitement, the glamour, the dress, Dan's closeness.

As long as she lived, she'd remember this fairytale night.

CHAPTER TWELVE

AVA didn't recognise the stocky man waiting inside the limo, but she recognised the expressions on the faces of her friends. Carrie's was pale and horrified. Brant's was furious as he stared at the newspaper in his hand.

'Bill?' Dan's voice was instantly suspicious as he pulled the door closed behind them. This man was not expected.

'The evening edition just hit the stands,' the older man said, a fevered excitement barely disguised in his eyes.

Dan reached over and took a newspaper from the seat opposite and started to read it.

The man turned to Ava. 'Bill Kurtz, Ms Lange. It's nice to finally meet you.'

Kurtz. The man who'd been making Dan's life a misery. The man who'd deemed Cadence below par. The man who'd been setting her up with the media. She took his hand reluctantly, distracted by

he fury banking in Dan's eyes as he scanned the
ewspaper. She looked across at Brant, who was
lso still reading.

'That bitch…' Brant said.

Carrie reached out and put her hand on Ava's
eg, sympathy etched into the sudden creases on
er face. Ava's stomach plummeted.

The feature article.

'What the hell happened?' Dan exploded in the
onfines of the vehicle, his intensity completely
ocussed on Bill Kurtz.

'You tell me,' the older man said, a nerve
ounding high in his jaw.

Brant threw his copy of the paper onto the
mpty seat in disgust, and Ava read the headline
pside down.

*'Unlikely starlet's success proves it's not
hat you know…'*

She sucked in a breath. Oh, no…

'This is more than assassination, Bill. This is
ibel.' Dan scanned the remainder of the long
rticle quickly.

'I imagine *The Standard*'s researchers have
een all over it,' Kurtz said.

She reached for the paper and Brant stilled her
and. 'You shouldn't read it, Ava… Not tonight,'
e said.

Carrie jumped in. 'She has to, Brant. She's
bout to walk into the lions' den.'

Ava's confused glance swung around to Dan. He raked an agitated hand through his hair and shook his head.

'I'll read it—' Kurtz offered eagerly. Dan virtually snarled at him.

'I'll read it!' Brant said, and threw Ava an apologetic glance. He lifted the paper and cleared his throat. Twice. '"Just when the status of women in media appeared to be reaching new heights, along comes a nobody from the sticks—"'

'Cow,' Carrie interrupted.

Ava blinked. Offensive, but not the end of the world. She noted Dan's pale face and Kurtz's smug satisfaction. What was she missing?

Brant read on. '"Ava Lange appeared out of nowhere onto our screens and seemed, at first take, to be a strike for real women on television. Heavier than most of her peers—",' Ava repressed her instinctive wince at that and Brant flushed red '"—but smarter and every bit as talented, she looked like a new breed in female presenters."'

Ava could feel it coming. *But…*

'"But one day in the company of Ms Lange and her sycophantic collective of supporters and it becomes clear what's really going on behind the cameras on the set of *Urban Nature*."'

Ava met Dan's eyes and held them. Agony filled his.

"'The show reeks of nepotism, dirty secrets and spin-doctoring.'" Brant skipped ahead, touching only on the worst parts. The parts she had to hear. "'Lange is an old friend of hot-shot young producer Daniel Arnot, proving that jobs for the boys aren't restricted to those with testosterone. Arnot himself admitted to practically writing the show for Lange…'"

Ava's hands began to shake, and nausea washed through her. But her eyes never left Dan's. In her periphery, Kurtz's glare was trained in the same direction.

"'It took *The Standard*'s researchers only minutes to discover the extent of Lange and Arnot's past, and just one visit to the south coast to lock it down.'"

Ava's heart froze. They had gone to her home.

Brant paused, and skipped over a paragraph or two before resuming. "'While Arnot's past smacks of unconfirmable child abuse, Lange's was comparatively idyllic. Yet more than one Flynn's Beach local raised a question mark over the appropriateness of a teenaged Lange spending all her time with a much older Arnot. Whatever their relationship in the past, it's definitely not history…'" Brant's voice cracked as he read "'…with confirmation this week that Lange and Arnot are considerably more than friends.'"

Ava closed her eyes, frozen in her spot. She could only imagine what that confirmation was.

Dan swore. Kurtz looked at him hard.

"'Which must be a surprise to the romantically challenged Brant Maddox, who has been seen all over town with his buxom co-host… One wonders whether the gormless Maddox is aware he's being used as a cover by his apple-pie co-host, to hide a more unwholesome relationship.'"

'Enough,' Dan rumbled in the confines of the limousine.

Not Cadence and Brant. *She and Dan.* That was what Leeds had been digging for with her questions about smokescreens and inappropriate relationships. Ava's hands trembled under Carrie's where she held them tightly. A thousand thoughts rolled through her mind, but only one was clear enough to be vocalised.

She begged Dan with her eyes. *Why?*

He swore. 'You were an easy target, Ava. I should have known better. I should have thrown her off set the moment she arrived.'

Kurtz spoke. 'That would have only stirred more suspicion and damaged AusOne's relationship with the *Standard*.'

'Screw AusOne's relationship, Bill. What about the damage to Ava?'

'That's something you should have thought about before hiring your old childhood sweetheart and moving her in under your roof!' Kurtz face glowed red with smugness. 'This disaster is all on you, Arnot.'

Dan bit back, but Ava barely heard their argument. She thought about all the work she'd done over the past few years to establish herself as a leading name in her field, to carefully build a base of credibility and goodwill. It had all disintegrated into dust. Her body started to go numb from the inside out. It helped—marginally—to keep the tears at bay.

What helped more was that in less than ten minutes she'd be getting out of the limo in front of dozens of cameras and the who's-who of the entertainment industry. The thought of doing that with a face full of shamed tears was...unthinkable.

'Stop the car. We can't go.' Carrie was definite, her focus on Ava.

Kurtz pulled rank. 'We're going.'

'If we don't go it proves Leeds right.' Brant still sounded furious.

Ava groaned and put her face in her hands. 'She *is* right.'

'She's not right, Ava,' Dan said. 'Don't give that bottom-dwelling hack the satisfaction.'

'What part of what she's written wouldn't stand up to scrutiny?' Ava pleaded with him. 'We *do* go way back. You *did* create the show around my designs. You *did* promote me to presenter unexpectedly. We *are* sleeping together.' Her voice rose almost to hysteria on that one. She looked at Brant. 'We *were* an item as far as the rest of the world was concerned. Regardless of the real facts, how exactly do you imagine we'll find the high ground here?'

The car dropped to frosty silence for the next kilometre. Everyone was thinking furiously as the Milana Hotel appeared in the distance. Ava's throat ached from holding the tears at bay, and from the advancing pain that had crystallised around her heart. Dan buzzed through to the driver and spoke quietly into the speaker. Almost immediately the limo slowed.

More time. As if that was going to change anything.

'What else does it say?' Her voice sounded as hollow and dead as she felt. She didn't look up, but Dan knew the question was for him.

'More of the same. She has a few things to say about my ethics. Brant gets it a few times.'

It stunned Ava out of her fog the tiniest bit to hear Dan call Brant by his given name. She met his blue eyes with a silent question.

Cadence?

Brant shook his head almost imperceptibly, but enough to let Ava know she'd managed to keep their secret. That tiny glowing light was something, at least.

'Okay,' Dan said, swinging into damage control mode. 'We can play this two ways. Close ranks. Present a united front and ride out the speculation.' He looked at Brant. 'They'll be expecting you and me to be at each other's throats, so we make sure we're the best of mates tonight.'

Brant nodded and Dan continued. He leaned over and took Ava's icy hand. 'Ava, you flash that smile and keep letting it shine. You stay close to one of us at all times. Don't let anyone get you alone. Even in the Ladies' Room, you take Carrie. Someone's bound to be sniffing around for a response. We give them nothing—understood?'

'No comment,' Ava murmured. Did that actually work in the real world?

'What's the other option?' Brant asked.

'We don't go,' Dan said.

'Not an option!' Kurtz nearly choked on his own outrage.

Dan shot him a venomous look. 'If Ava wants out, I'll be with her.'

'Me too.' Brant and Carrie said together.

Kurtz turned purple, and eventually dragged

his eyes to Ava. Disempowerment was clearly no
somewhere he spent his summer holidays!

She considered the options. Turning around
and going home was the most attractive one, bu
it would only delay the inevitable. She closed he
eyes and took a deep breath. Walking into tha
crowded function room was going to be the
hardest thing she'd ever had to do.

When her eyes opened the first thing she saw
was Dan, the steadiness of his expression. A quie
confidence had replaced seething fury. Brant, too
looked different, his features hardening into a face
that said *don't mess with me*. For the first time she
recognised why Cadence leaned on him.

The limo crept along. The hotel drew closer
Ava sat taller on the plush leather seat. 'If we're
going to do this, then let's do it.'

Kurtz sagged with relief and looked every bi
the old man that he was.

She glared at him hard and gave him an order
'Tell the driver to put his foot down. I want thi
over.'

Ava's hands still shook, and she had nowhere to
hide them. As they stepped out of the limousine
Dan and Brant took one hand each, as though by
arrangement. It was a dangerously provocative

thing to do, under the circumstances, virtually confirming the article's claims.

Yet at the same time it screamed *we have nothing to hide*, and was a clear signal to everyone watching to back off. It was a gift to have two men so experienced with the media flanking her. Gratitude for their unspoken solidarity stole a bit more of what strength she'd been able to muster.

She squeezed Dan's hand tight, drawing courage from his solid determination.

'Smile, Ava,' he whispered as they reached the edge of the dense media throng. She tried. As soon as they were spotted the cameras went crazy. The sudden barrage of flashes made the entrance of the Milana Hotel glitter like a giant diamond. Ava worked harder than she ever had to keep a brilliant smile on her face, even managing to copy a gesture or two from Brant's public repertoire.

It helped. A lot.

'You're doing great,' Dan muttered through his own tight smile. She was close enough to see fury still darkening his eyes. She knew how she looked, escorted by two burly men, and suddenly felt very much like Dorothy approaching the gates of Oz, flanked by the Tin Man and the Scarecrow. Or maybe she was the Cowardly Lion. She sure felt like it right now. She giggled weakly, entirely overwrought.

Brant threw Dan a concerned look.

Ahead, the red carpet bottlenecked into a gauntlet of television and radio presenters interviewing the beautiful people as they arrived. There was no going around it and, judging by the keen interest from the few who glanced their way, their arrival was eagerly anticipated.

'Follow my lead, hon.' Brant broke away from their defensive line and walked directly over to a tanned male presenter representing one of AusOne's major competitors. Straight into the line of fire. Dan stepped her quickly past the distracted journalist, effectively screening Ava with his wide shoulders and preventing the journalists on the other side of the gauntlet from catching her eye. It worked—for a moment.

'Ms Lange?' A young woman from an independent radio station thrust her microphone out in front of Ava so that it was virtually impossible not to stop. Dan released her hand and gently brought her to a halt in front of the woman, whispering her name to Ava. Six other microphones suddenly populated the small space between them.

'Ms Lange, are you looking forward to your first ATA awards?'

Ava knew the station by its reputation: indepen-

dent music, young, switched-on presenters, philo-
sophically resistant to commercial gossip. She
realised Dan had stopped her there strategically.

She played to her strength. Directness.
'Remarkably—yes, I am, Corrine.'

She hadn't broached the subject, per se, but
she'd shown she wasn't shying away from it either.
The young woman smiled and pressed her luck.

'Got a battle plan this evening?' she asked.

Ava laughed lightly, practically high on adrenaline. 'First order of business is to get in there,'
she said, indicating the crush ahead. 'Then to
avoid any and all newspaper journalists.'

Next to her, Dan stiffened perceptibly, but the
radio journo and her peers within hearing range
all laughed. There was no love lost between print
and broadcast media in Australia. Even Ava knew
that.

'Good luck, Ava.' The woman smiled and
stepped back so they could move on.

And just like that she survived her first skirmish
with the media. She glanced around, risking eye
contact with some of the fans in the throng. There
was certainly a whole heap of interest in the stars
of *Urban Nature*, and some speculation, but less
judgement than she'd feared.

Much less. Her lungs loosened a little and the
smile felt less forced. She paused long enough for

Brant to catch up, and then proceeded, flanked again by her two bodyguards, through the press pack.

'Ms Lange…' A dozen voices juggled for supremacy. 'Mr Arnot…'

Someone screamed Brant's name from the rear of the throng, and Ava's laugh was genuine. This was her first taste of hard-core fans, but Brant played them like a Stradivarius. If she were ever to survive something like this again, she'd need lessons from the Maddox School of Media Training.

She stumbled slightly on the thought. Since when was she even considering sticking around long enough to do this ever again? Was the adrenaline affecting her judgement?

'Nearly there.' Dan guided her with a steady hand, and she saw the red carpet widen out ahead, and then the gaping entry to the Milana's glamorous function room beyond it. His hand burned against her bare skin and he softly stroked his thumb across her hip. She would never have managed this without him. She owed him—owed them both. Except Brant's thank-you would be more in the order of a good bottle of wine, whereas Dan's…

She chuckled. Then laughed again when Dan's eyes narrowed. He probably thought she was losing it.

He wasn't far wrong.

They stopped twice more, bypassing certain journalists and favouring others. Brant stole the show, gracing the press with his full attention and taking the heat off Ava. He brushed aside the few tactless comments made by less courteous media, and easily shepherded the interviews into less awkward territory. Since he was the one supposedly scorned, they were more careful with him than they would have been with her.

It baffled the heck out of all of them that the three were being so supportive and friendly with each other after what they'd read in *The Standard*.

Ava didn't get off completely, though she found herself able to answer questions more easily now that she knew the throng wasn't out to lynch her, specifically. Her heart-rate slowed to a steady thump, then spiked when a gorgeous-smelling Dan bent close to her ear.

'Last stop, Ava. Get ready.'

An honest-to-goodness supermodel—now a key presenter for AusOne's rival network—stood at the top of the sweeping stairs leading to the doors of the hotel function centre. Ava realised with a rush what was coming up.

The fashion corral.

She'd watched this part of the ATA ceremony in her pyjamas a hundred times. All the beautiful people passed through the corral, showing off their designer creations and answering questions

Live to air.

Her mouth dried and she scrabbled around in her muddled brain for the name of her designer Reluctantly Dan released her hand and dissolved into the background, leaving her to face it alone She felt bereft at the tiny betrayal. Then suddenly Brant swept in beside her and took her arm.

Better than nothing. His grin was wide and flashing enough for both of them as he greeted the supermodel.

'Ava, Brant. Lovely to see you both this evening.' The model plied her trademark smile generously. Ava blinked in the bright light from the camera pointing at them. She didn't want to think about it being live to air. If this woman chose to say something shocking, she'd have no hope of covering her reaction. Brant slid an arm around her and tucked her closer to his side.

'You both look fantastic. Who's your designer?' A microphone was thrust towards her. Ava opened her mouth and prayed something intelligent was going to come out. Lord, who *was* her designer?

'Glenn Lo.' Oh, thank the stars! 'I think he's picked the perfect dress for me.' She sucked in a nervous breath.

'You look magnificent,' the presenter said. 'And what a lucky girl—a gorgeous man on each arm, and a third one gifting you fashion.'

Allusions, but no direct attack. In fact there was a strange glint of solidarity in the super-model's eye. Ava scrabbled in her memory banks. Wait—was this the woman whose ex had put a video on the internet...?

The model turned to the camera and winked. 'We should all be so lucky! Speaking of luck—all the very best, Brant, for your category tonight.'

Seconds later, miraculously, it was over. The three of them stood patiently for the compulsory publicity shots in front of the sponsor's signage, and then were shooed into the darkened auditorium.

Ava's legs began to weaken as soon as they were in the shadows. The adrenaline dissipated, leaving her wobbly. 'I think I should sit...'

'Hang on, Ava.' Dan was right there beside her, his hand sliding around her waist. He signalled to Brant, who snagged an elegant chair from nearby and placed it deep into the shadows of a recess. She sank gratefully into it and the two men closed ranks in front of her, facing the crowd, bodies relaxed, as though they were having a casual conversation.

Dressed as she was, putting her head between her knees was out of the question. She settled instead for letting it sag while she sucked in great a lungful of designer air. *I can't do this.* Impossibility washed over her. Who would notice if she tiptoed out now? As long as Brant stayed for his award, Dan, too, for *Urban Nature*'s… couldn't she go?

No, someone would make it their business to notice. And to speculate.

United front, Dan had said. And not just for her sake. They'd all been tarnished by Leeds' shameful article. She should remember that.

Child abuse. Leeds' allegation suddenly came into clear focus in her mind. Dan's father…

Her heart ached for the frightened, lonely little boy Dan must have been if it was true. There was no way she was going to repay his courage by leaving now.

She flexed and un-flexed her fingers, noticing their tingling for the first time. Had she been numb since getting out of the limo? The natural chemicals zinging around her system had made her oblivious to anything but survival. Like getting through the media pack in one piece. Now that she had, her body's defences were easing off and pain was returning. Her jaw ached from its rigid smile and her rib muscles were tender from being held so tight.

'Ava?' Dan's voice was loud enough to carry to

her, but not so loud it would draw any attention. She sighed, knowing she couldn't stay here all night, expecting them to cover for her. It wasn't fair to them. They'd been amazing to get her this far.

'I'm ready.' She stood and stepped into the gap that opened between them.

The function room was exquisitely decorated, and filling rapidly with Australian and international guest celebrities as well as producers, film-makers, crew and their partners. Ava scanned the room but saw no sign of Leeds. Maybe the press were still caught up out at the front.

She relaxed a little, shaking off her nerves and smiling shakily at Dan. 'Shall we find our table?'

The first part of the evening wasn't being televised. Ava was embarrassed to discover they'd arrived well after the earliest awards were read out. She felt affronted on behalf of those people who'd worked hard for their place on the awards list but whose achievement was barely acknowledged by the handful of assembled guests. There seemed to be a category for everything—theme music, catering, costume, make-up, even commercial risk finance.

None of them sexy enough for broadcast, apparently.

She paid particular attention to every one as

penance for her late arrival, and in solidarity for the little people. As far as she was concerned she was still a behind-the-scenes person at heart. Dan smiled when he realised what she was doing and patiently sat with her, attending to the activity on stage with just as much focus as she.

How could she ever have thought him disloyal?

For another thirty minutes other distinguished guests continued to stream into the venue, upstaging the award presentations onstage. The later the arrival, the higher the standing in the industry, it seemed. Ava was too exhausted to care as some big name Hollywood types strolled past them just minutes before the start.

Carrie caught up with her briefly and pointed out where her table was. Just as Ava had joked, it was right at the back, near the restrooms. The mere thought of the word had Ava thinking about her bladder, and she excused herself quietly.

'Take Carrie,' Dan ordered.

Although one or two seemed to consider it, no one actually approached—thanks largely to Carrie's excellent impersonation of an Alsatian. Every time someone came too close, she swung her body around and glared at them.

'You'll be growling next,' Ava laughed, soaping her hands.

'This whole business has me so mad,' Carrie

whispered fiercely under her breath. 'Of all the people, Ava. *You?* There couldn't be a nicer person to work with in this entire industry. You make coffee for the crew, for goodness' sake. Who else does that? I just don't understand it.'

Carrie's rigid defence thawed a bit more of Ava's frozen heart. She'd really lucked out finding this woman as a friend. She squeezed Carrie's fingers with her own lavender-scented ones.

'I'm so pleased I met you, Carrie Watson. I hope we get to work together for years.'

Years? Ava shook her head to banish the thought. *Not years...months...weeks.* She was going home in a few months.

They stopped by Carrie's table so Ava could say hello to the rest of the *Urban Nature* crew present. Most gave her a supportive smile, but one or two had clear speculation in their guarded expressions. Ava sighed sadly, then turned to Carrie. 'You might as well take your seat. I'm hardly likely to get accosted between here and our table.'

Carrie started to argue, until she saw the determined look on Ava's face. She relented, saying, 'Fingers crossed for both awards, then?'

The awards. Ava had almost forgotten the whole reason for being here tonight. Nervous butterflies launched in her belly. She wondered how Brant was feeling. And Dan. It was an important

achievement for them both. She moved smoothly
and quickly towards her table, avoiding eye
contact with everyone just in case. The last thing
they needed was some kind of public incident.

Another public incident.

Dan sat at the table next to Bill Kurtz. Brant's
seat was still empty while he was off schmooz-
ing. Ava frowned, and the hairs on her arms
prickled. There was something about Dan's
posture… He sat rigid in his seat, and Kurtz
leaned into him like a vulture picking over a
carcass. With their backs to her, neither man
noticed her approach. There was a momentary
lull in the music blaring over the PA system and
she heard Bill Kurtz's booming voice distinctly.

'…never mind your own reputation. I don't
give a toss about that. You put the network at risk,
the shareholders, for a piece of skirt.'

Dan's body language turned from frigid to
fiery in a blink. 'You couldn't help yourself,
could you, Bill? You haven't shared a limo in ten
years, but you were willing to make a concession
if it meant a ringside seat to watch the fall-out of
your handiwork first-hand. You're nothing but
an ambulance-chaser—'

Ava couldn't see Kurtz's face, but his entire
body stiffened. 'Then what are you, Arnot? A
man willing to sell his woman out to the media

ven while you were sleeping with her? Have you
old her yet that it was *you* that sold her out, or is
ll this holier-than-though crap just lip-service?'

Dan surged to his feet. People at neighbouring
ables turned to look.

Ava stumbled to a halt. Her heart struck cold.
he instantly recalled Dione Leeds' snarky
omment about Dan arranging the various PR in-
idents. And then an image came—Dan outside
n the shadows on the night the restaurant photo
ad been taken, the incorrect call sheets, the ones
)an had handed them personally, Dan speaking
vith the *maître d'* just before she and Brant were
ccidentally seated at the wrong table, a romantic
able for two by a bright open window. Where a
hotographer had just happened to see them. The
irst photo that had started it all.

Worse, Dan had been at every publicity event
ince she'd started on-camera with *Urban Nature*.

Her skin prickled into tiny bumps. What was it
he had said about the publicity? *Engineered.*
Crystals of ice immediately encased her heart.

'Is that true, Dan?'

Both men snapped around, but only one looked
ppalled to find her standing there. Bill Kurtz just
ooked smug. Ava ignored him entirely; her
larrowed eyes were fixed in despair on the
landsome face in front of her, on the man who

had always had the power to hurt her. The ma
who looked one hundred percent guilty a
charged.

'Ava…' Dan started towards her as another son
started on the massive PA system. It was a sogg
love-song that any other night she would hav
hummed happily along with. Now she'd foreve
associate it with the feeling of her heart being tor
from her body.

She flung two hands in front of her, stoppin
him. They shook with the effort of keeping he
voice level. *'Is. That. True?'*

He glued a phony smile to his face and steppe
towards her.

'Don't do this, Ava. People are watching,' h
muttered through the grimace, grabbing her arr
and steering her towards the half-empty danc
floor. It was about as private as they would ge
with all these industry types around.

She went into his arms as comfortably as a sac
rifice went unto death, and then looked at hin
through a wash of unshed tears. A giant fis
squeezed her heart and stole her ability to speak. Sh
didn't need to; he knew what she wanted to know

'Hold on, Ava. There are a thousand eyes here.
He pulled her slowly around the dance floor an
Ava struggled to regain some composure. Finall
he spoke. 'I should have told you. I'm sorry.'

Ava didn't know whether to be grateful he was holding her up or horrified to be touching him. Every word he'd ever said to her suddenly turned to ash. She forced sound over her frozen lips.

'What have you done?'

He sighed. 'It was part of my job.'

'To sell me out to the media? Part of your job?'

She saw him wince, but her heart had no room left for pity. A deep-seated coldness spread outwards from the dying organ. 'You kept forcing me and Brant together.' It wasn't a question and it didn't need an answer. He didn't give her one. The restaurant. Was that you?' she grated.

He didn't nod. But he didn't deny it. His eyes were fixed over her shoulder. His grasp tight.

'All those other stories?' Unshed tears choked her throat.

He shook his head. 'No. But I started the feeding frenzy. I made that choice.'

Sharp hurt roiled deep in her belly.

'The first one was really all that was needed,' he said quietly. 'It whetted the public appetite for more. Then Kurtz took over.'

She took a deep breath and spoke through the hurt. 'You let them do this to me? To Brant?'

'No, Maddox knew.'

Wham. A double hit of agony. 'Brant knew. You knew. The network knew. Seems like the only chump not to know was little ole Ava from the sticks.'

'Ava, don't…'

She wrenched free, unable to stomach his hands on her for a second longer. 'Is he that powerful, Dan? Your father?'

He paled and looked away. 'He has nothing to do with this.'

'He has everything do to with this. You chose him over me. You made revenge on him more important than what we have.' She caught herself. Her chest heaved. '*Had*. Past tense.'

The romantic music played on. Dan struggled to keep his composure. 'You don't mean that.'

Ava straightened her spine, amazed it didn't snap under the strain. 'Completely.'

'Without even letting me explain?'

'Oh? You can explain? Go ahead.' She stared at him hard as he moved her automatically around the dance floor. His mouth opened and shut several times until finally his eyes dropped away. 'How did you expect me to react?' she whispered.

Dan sighed and tucked her in closer, as though she might break away. It was hard to know if the lights overhead were spinning or if it was just her.

'Like this,' he sighed. 'You have every right to be angry.'

'I am so much more than angry.' She curled her hands into fists. Wanting to hit him. Wanting him to hurt as much as she was hurting right now. 'I'm broken, Dan.' Her voice cracked.

Bleakness streaked through his eyes. 'Ava, please understand the position I was in. Wanting to do the best thing by everyone. I swear on your mother's grave, I was trying to protect you—'

'A wise man once told me to grow a spine. Well, how about doing the same and standing up for someone you love?' A tear escaped down her cheek just as a booming voice came across the public address system, announcing the commencement of the televised portion of the awards. Guests streamed towards their seats. 'Oh, that's right. It's only lust, isn't it? I doubt you're even capable of love. Look at the role models you had.'

She turned to go. Dan held her wrist and dragged her to him, eyes glittering. 'Nine years ago you accused me of being just like my mother. Of running out when the going got too tough. Well, what are *you* doing now, Ava?'

She stared at him in horror. Apparently even at sixteen she'd known enough to strike exactly where it would do most damage. And it had, if he'd hung onto it all this time.

'I can't understand why hurting him is so important to you,' she whispered. 'Tell me. Help me understand.'

The plea hung between them. Agony filled his eyes. Then his voice was quiet. Hard. 'I don't have room for anything else inside me, Ava. There's nothing left in there except raw hatred for that man and what he did to me. It has sustained me for years.'

She stared at him, appalled by the emptiness in his eyes. No wonder he'd had a string of meaningless relationships. No wonder he was so driven to succeed. It was all he had.

'No, Dan. It has sustained *itself* for twenty years. Like a parasite sucking all the worth out of your life. It's consumed everything you loved.' She twisted her wrist from his hand. 'First you fed it surfing. Now you're feeding it me.'

His eyes glassed over. Toughened as she watched. 'I don't have anything more to offer you, Ava.' He released her away from him. 'I'm empty. I don't know how to be any other way.'

The lights started to dim and the room hushed. She stumbled behind him to the table and grabbed her seat for support just as Brant slid in next to her. She was directly opposite Dan. No coincidence. After all, they were supposed to be giving each other secret cow-eyes across the table all night.

What a joke.

The pain of betrayal sliced through her in the gathering hush. She sensed Brant's confusion when she gave him the cold shoulder, too. The evening stretched interminably ahead of her, seated at a table full of men who had either betrayed her or were using her.

Or both.

The lights dimmed, the glitterati hushed, and a booming voice burst over the crowd. 'Ladies and gentlemen, welcome to the forty-sixth Annual Australian Television Awards gala dinner…'

Ava looked around at the excitement, the anticipation of those seated on other tables. It should have been like that for her. Seated across from the man she loved, celebrating his success, knowing she had contributed to it.

Instead, here they were. Dan's eyes cold and remote, staring away from her. The slimebag Kurtz savouring his victory. Her own heart bleeding out onto the expensive carpet.

It physically hurt to breathe. Was the tug-of-war between loving someone and hating them what made hearts break?

Brant won his category—Best Male Talent in a Non-Drama Role. She might still be mad at him, but it was impossible not to feel some happiness for him. Despite everything people said or thought about him, Brant Maddox was adored by the voting public. The applause from the public seats was thunderous testament to that.

Ava met Brant's eyes a split second before he stood from the table, suddenly unable to punish him further for something he couldn't control. It just felt wrong. She smiled encouragement at him and the sheer relief in his expression only served to intensify her guilt. This was his night and she was blowing it for him. What Cadence wouldn't give to be here in her place...

Brant casually moved to the stage, stopping to shake a hand or two and slap a shoulder or three on the way. His acceptance speech was short and to the point. And one hundred percent loaded for those in the know.

'And to my heart,' he finished, pulling his statuette against the left side of his chest, 'only you know what this really means to me, and only you really know me. Thank you.'

He hadn't looked at anyone in particular, but half the room glanced at Ava. Onstage, Brant blew a kiss to the camera as though it was for his fans. But Ava knew better.

She blinked away tears and glanced up, only to find Dan's burning regard on her. She forced her eyes back to the stage.

Kurtz and a nameless AusOne executive were congratulating themselves on their achievement. Ava's stomach turned. As though their intensive meddling at Cadence's expense had *anything* to do with Brant's own success. He'd got his nomination *despite* their involvement, not because if it.

Brant left the stage via the wings as the show broke for its first commercial break, and then appeared across the room through a backstage door. Out of nowhere, a roving camera appeared at their table and was thrust into Ava's face. She was entirely unprepared. Dan stretched forward, too late to ward it off.

'Ava, that was quite a speech. How does it feel to be so publicly affirmed?'

Exhaustion, misery and anger all warred within her—but all she could think about was Cadence. How she must feel, sitting in her living room watching all this happen without her. Watching the man she loved face his biggest career moment alone. Watching another woman seated in her rightful place.

Ava swallowed her pain and spoke from the soul, the weight of Brant's secret an extra strain on her weary heart, hoping that Cadence was still watching. She turned towards the camera shoved in close to her face, knowing her eyes would be glittering dangerously from the unshed hurts of the evening. 'There's not a woman alive who wouldn't be moved to tears at having her love so publicly validated.' The tiniest of pauses. 'If it was directed at her.'

She threw Brant a watery smile as he arrived at the table, gold paperweight in hand. The cameraman and the presenter exchanged confused looks at her cryptic answer, then turned their attention on the man of the moment.

Ava let Brant enjoy the spotlight. He'd earned it. She glanced briefly across the table to where Dan studied the tablecloth intently. Then his eyes jerked up and locked with hers, blazing and sharp.

Rib-spreaders couldn't have done a better job of baring her pulped heart.

Dan rose suddenly from his seat and walked away, just as the lights dropped again for the next televised segment. Brant watched her watching Dan go.

'What did I miss?' he whispered over the introduction to the next segment.

She shook her head.

'Ava…?'

She spun around, hurt. 'Why didn't you tell me about the publicity? That Dan was behind it?'

'Ah.' He considered her for a moment. 'What would it have changed?'

'I would have known.'

'And that would have been better how?'

'Because then maybe I wouldn't have found out his way.' Her voice was tiny.

Brant dropped his eyes. 'True. But none of us could have predicted this.'

She looked at him. His judgement and his industry savvy were solid. 'You don't think all this was part of Dan's plan?'

He looked shocked. 'No. Do you?'

Ava hesitated at his certainty, and then shrugged.

'Hon, I saw his face in the limo,' Brant said. 'It was not the face of a man who knew what was coming. He was as pole-axed as the rest of us.' He nodded towards Kurtz, who was watching the proceedings on-stage with interest. 'That face, on the other hand…'

Ava considered. 'You think Kurtz knew which way the story was going to go?'

'Dan believed I was a womanising git, remember? And Kurtz is threatened by him.'

She couldn't join the dots. Her mind was too jumbled for any more puzzles. 'So?'

'It means the network didn't fill him in—didn't tell him all the women were a screen for Cadence. They didn't trust him, Ava. I think Kurtz did this whole thing to stick it to Dan, primarily. To establish his dominance.'

The layers of deceit were baffling. It was

almost impossible to sort out who meant what. She'd even indulged in a little spin of her own, covering for Cadence. She'd been a willing participant in most of the PR, made it all too easy for Dan to arrange what the network wanted. She'd put up no resistance at all.

'*Please understand the position I was in,*' he'd said. '*Trying to protect you.*' Maybe he'd been working from day to day with what information he'd had at the time. Trying desperately to control the outcome. While Kurtz had worked behind the scenes screwing him over, too.

With sudden insight she began to see everything from Dan's perspective. Wangling her the pay-rise and the RV to compensate for forcing her hand, supporting her refusal to wear the skimpy outfit, constantly on set to keep control of things; trying to negotiate a decent reporter for the feature article, his absolute fury when that hadn't come off.

Trying to spin the spin. All the while trying desperately to hang on to the only thing that meant anything to him on this planet. His career.

She stared blankly at the stage as the facts slotted into place. Then she looked around for him, suddenly desperate to speak with him alone. To get more answers. To listen. To trust. She saw the big double doors open a crack and a set of broad shoulders slip out into the foyer.

Dan.

Before Brant even knew she was gone, she was threading quickly through the crowded tables towards the exit. She ignored Carrie's signal to her and pushed through into the foyer alone. She glanced around. Empty, save for a few waiting staff doing their thing, bussing dirty dishes out to the kitchen. Surely he wouldn't leave? Not before his category? Her heart lurched at the thought. She hurried to the entrance of the auditorium and peered around outside.

Then she froze as she heard the one voice she'd been avoiding all night.

'Well, well. If it isn't the country mouse.'

[faint offset text from facing page, illegible]

CHAPTER THIRTEEN

DAN slid into his chair and tossed his rolled-up napkin at Maddox, who looked around in surprise in the dark. 'Where's Ava?' he hissed over the hubbub from nearby tables.

Brant shrugged and mouthed the words *ladies' room.*

Why wasn't Maddox keeping an eye out for her? That was his job! *No, it is your job*, a tiny voice reprimanded. He'd lost his cool for a moment—had to get out before he did or said something he'd regret. The pain in her body language had nearly killed him.

He'd left Ava alone and unsupported while she was still desperately struggling.

She was beyond angry—any idiot could see that. She was confused and hurting, and all because of him. His gut had warned him to tell her about the PR stunts earlier. To explain on his own terms. There'd even been a time or two where the conver-

ation had naturally lent itself to a full confession,
but he'd chickened out. He'd been afraid she'd
walk away, tell him it was over. As she just had.

And that possibility terrified him.

Not that he didn't understand. Ava had been
stretched about as far as any human being could
go tonight. He hoped in his heart she'd spoken
only from anger and hurt, and that both might
pass once he got a chance to talk to her. To explain
every detail.

Every humiliating, painful detail.

She deserved at least that. And, frankly, he was
tired of carrying it all by himself. He'd told her
he was empty, had no room for her. But the
weeping hole left now that she'd walked away
from him proved that wasn't true.

Somehow, some time over the past few months,
Ava Lange had worked her way into his heart and
staked a claim. Displaced some of the darkness.

He wasn't going to lose the only constant love
he'd had in his life.

He craned his neck to monitor both sets of doors
leading from the auditorium. Where was she?
Onstage, the presenter ran through the nomina-
tions for Best New Lifestyle Programme and short
snippets of each were played on the giant screen
behind him. Dan's heart gave a lurch to see Ava,
one hundred times enlarged on the massive

screen, looking so fresh and beautiful. The con
trast with how he'd seen her moments ago wa
marked.

A gnawing feeling settled into his gut.

'And the winner of the Best New Lifestyl
Programme is…'

Dan twisted his neck and stared at the exi
doors. What if she hadn't gone to the ladies' room'
Where was she?

Ava pushed past Dione Leeds and headed for the
restrooms, not trusting herself to speak. Leeds
followed her into the ladies' lounge, where
number of comfortable seats and a viewing monitor
were set up so guests could keep track of what wa:
happening on stage as they used the facilities.

'Nothing to say now, Ms Lange? That's cer
tainly a change from our interview.'

Ava spun around to face her nemesis. 'Is tha
what this is about? You didn't like the way
spoke to you?'

The journalist laughed. 'Oh, please, don'
flatter yourself.'

'Then what? What exactly do you have agains
me, particularly? You don't even know me.'

Dan's voice came to her. *We give them nothing*
But she couldn't do it; there was too much figh
in her. She was a pressure cooker ready to blow.

'I know your type.' Leeds glared at her coldly. I had to work damn hard to get where I am, and had to scrabble my way over the corpses of women like you who slept their way into cushy positions and then couldn't pull their weight. It fell to the rest of us to pick up the slack. Meanwhile we got overlooked time and again for advancement because we were too busy covering someone else's ass.'

Ava heard the desperation behind Leeds' words, but she was incapable of compassion. That was a first. She gathered all the hurts, fears and disappointments since she'd climbed, innocent and excited, into AusOne's limousine and pushed them out at an unsuspecting Dione Leeds. A woman who had probably figured her for an easy target.

'And is this the kind of story you hope will bring you advancement? A sleazy story about the private lives of people who work in television? This is what passes for ace reporting at *The Standard*?'

Leeds greyed at the gills and was finally speechless. Strength surged through Ava, uncontrolled and wild, but she was determined that Leeds was about to reap exactly what she'd sown.

'You could have written a great business story about Australia's youngest executive producer in waiting. Or done a serious piece on the real issues facing communities who are living their lives in natureless urban environments. Instead you went for a cheap shot, thinking you were onto some sordid scoop. And you signed your name to it like it was something to be proud of!'

She careened on like an out-of-control train. 'After tonight everyone will remember you for a trashy piece you did on some lifestyle presenters. They'll forget all the meaningful articles you've ever written in that long, hard climb to the top. And, worse, your paper's hardly going to reward you when AusOne sues you for defamation— because, although you got some basic facts right, you've put them together wrong. Bill Kurtz might be a powerful man, and he might have promised you the earth, but Daniel Arnot is the future of that network and he has silent support higher up the food-chain than Kurtz or he wouldn't have come this far. What you've printed is fundamentally lies, Ms Leeds. And we'll prove it.'

Ava's voice was clear and unwavering, and that, more than anything, was Leeds' undoing. The woman paled even further, and then pulled herself up to her full tiny height, turned on her heel and marched out without saying another word. She pushed past Carrie, who stood, agog, in the doorway.

'You were fantastic, Ava!' she squeaked.

Ava felt the rush of a crisis passed, and sank into one of the comfortable armchairs in the lounge, trembling. She felt as if that was all she'd done all night.

'Are you okay?' Carrie slipped a warm hand over her cold one.

'I will be,' Ava said with certainty. 'If I survive this night, I can survive anything.'

The two of them sat in companionable silence, staring unseeing at the television until Brant and then Ava's face appeared briefly on screen, along with the presenters of three other popular lifestyle programmes.

Carrie gasped. 'It's our category.' She deactivated the mute button on the remote just as the announcer spoke.

'And the winner of the Best New Lifestyle Programme is…'

'…*Urban Nature!*'

Before his boss could do more than button his blazer Dan was on his feet, striding toward the stage. He didn't need to look behind him to know Kurtz would be livid. There was an unspoken rule at AusOne. The staff did all the work. The executives took all the glory.

Dan took the steps to the stage two at a time, and moved straight into an air-kiss with the gorgeous starlet who had presented the category. He accepted the award statue, and then waited for the courteous applause to settle.

'Thank you, on behalf of AusOne and the hard-working cast and crew of *Urban Nature*.' Someone yelled *woo-hoo* way up at the back. 'It's my absolute pleasure to accept this award for the network that gave me my start in this business.'

More polite applause, then the audience fell to silence. Dan looked at the shiny gold statue in his hands, and then squinted out into the lights that obscured most of the avid faces. It wasn't hard to forget they were there, such was the hush in the room. He visualised his father sitting in the front row, a knowing smirk on his face, having waited for empirical evidence that his son really was a loser.

Not any more, Dad.

'There's a reason I chose to work in lifestyle television instead of drama. I much prefer reality to the kind of constructed fiction others thrive on.' His heart pounded so hard it hurt. 'However, recent events have made my very successful, very enjoyable, very *credible* lifestyle programme seem more like daytime television.'

Someone coughed out in the dark. No one else so much as shuffled.

'Dione Leeds would do very well over in your drama department, Marcus Croyden—' Dan turned towards the right, where he knew the head of a rival network with a stable of highly success-ful soap operas was seated '—such is her talent for stretching a few basic facts into a work of sen-sational fiction.'

A gasp from the crowd this time.

Dan's nostrils flared. 'You think that's a bit bold? I'm only getting started.'

He had time. The floor manager of this broad-cast would lose his job if he cut to a commercial or played the wind-up music now. This was the stuff ratings were made of. Dan could practically feel the cameras zooming in. After all, how often did someone commit career *hara-kiri* live on stage?

'Tonight, part of my job was to help perpetu-ate the idea that Ava Lange and Brant Maddox are involved—caught up in a great love affair which has blossomed since the show started production. It's something the network has been eager to promote. The trouble is Brant and Ava aren't in love. At least, not with each other. Somewhere out there in the suburbs, watching this broadcast, is a sweet and unconventional woman who would lay down her life for Brant Maddox. She already has, in agreeing to virtually disappear because she doesn't fit the mould of celebrity accessory.' All his affection and admiration for Cadence was revealed in his wide grin. 'She is the love of Brant

Maddox's life, and he's paid a huge personal price trying to protect her from the sharks of this industry. I hope next year you'll see her, sitting there at the AusOne table, looking surly and frightening people.'

Brant laughed loudly from his seat. There was approval, relief and gratitude in that laugh.

'Cadence.' Dan's eyes found the camera with a red light on and he looked down its barrel. 'For my part in what's been done to you I can only apologise, and hope you'll forgive me.' He turned his head in Brant's direction. 'I could learn a lesson or two from Brant Maddox about loyalty and about love.' He let that one sink in with the audience. 'And Ava Lange? Well, she's in love, too. *With me.* Or at least I hope so, because I'm absolutely crazy about her.' This earned a chuckle from the crowd. 'It's true I've known her for half my life, but here's a quote you won't have seen on today's newsstands...'

He swallowed hard.

'Ava Lange did not get involved with me to get this role. In fact, she did everything she could *not* to take on the hosting role. I manipulated her into taking the job—just like I manipulated her into participating in this façade with Brant Maddox. Both of which are things I'll have to live with. As it happens, Ava also did everything she could *not* to be with me, but fortunately I prevailed.'

Gentle laughter grew, moving like a Mexican wave through the audience. Dan felt their loyalty shift. He scanned the sea of dimly lit faces in the room until his eyes stumbled upon a lone female figure silhouetted against the light from the foyer streaming in the open door behind her. He would have recognised that stubborn, proud, vulnerable stance anywhere. He stared hard across the hundreds of heads and swallowed nervously. In his periphery, he saw a camera swing one hundred and eighty degrees to see what had grabbed his attention.

He took a breath and took a chance.

'Ava Lange, every time you smile a monkey is born in a forest somewhere. When you're sad, oceans ice over. When you laugh, flowers burst into bloom. You are so intrinsically linked to nature it responds to your moods. And I'm so intrinsically linked to you I can't imagine a life with anyone else. Or a life without your beauty in it.'

Every female in the room sighed.

His energy reached out to find hers. 'I put some really dark emotions ahead of you, even after vowing to protect you for ever. That's on me, and I swear I will do everything I can to fix the damage I've caused. If I hadn't been so blinded by ancient anger I might have seen your radiance sooner. I'm done with proving myself to someone who means nothing to me. I'm moving on to proving myself to someone who means everything to me.'

He shifted more firmly on his feet and cleared his throat. 'You deserve your design spot on *Urban Nature* because you have a unique talent and a world of professional integrity. You deserve your spot as presenter because the public respond so magnificently to your passion for wild things. What you don't deserve is what's happened to you today. For doing nothing less than helping out a friend—' he looked at Brant '—and putting my needs ahead of your own—' then at Kurtz '—you've been judged and publicly executed.'

Dan rounded on the audience and held up the golden statue. 'So, thank you again to the people of Australia who responded to all the good things about our programme. I hope you keep watching. Not to see what the latest scandal of the day is, but to see us give derelict spaces back their soul. And to everyone here tonight I'd ask you to put yourselves in the shoes of a sweet and gentle woman from the southern coast who was crucified in the interest of ratings and newspaper sales. Because it could just as easily be you next. Thank you.'

The applause started slowly, but as Dan

marched down the steps of the stage the ovation grew. A few in the audience even leapt to their feet. It seemed there were more than a few people present who were happy to see a network—and some aspects of the media—called to task for their game-playing.

Dan's eyes sought out the lonely silhouette, and he triangulated the fastest route to her through the crowd.

He paused at the AusOne table only long enough to meet Brant's approving gaze briefly and to dump the prized statuette in front of Bill Kurtz.

'I quit!' he shouted over the noise.

'No need,' Kurtz snarled. 'You're fired.'

As exits went, it wasn't particularly dramatic—he had to weave in and out of tables—but it did mean he passed a number of other network tables. At one, a slim, greying man reached out to shake Dan's hand and subtly pressed a business card into it. Dan glanced at it—X-Dream Sports, the biggest cable sports network in Australia. The largest broadcaster on the surfing circuit in the world.

'I assume you're on the market?' the man mouthed over the din as Dan passed.

He tucked the card away safely.

More and more of the audience turned to follow him with their eyes, until they were all facing the rear of the auditorium. An excited

murmur rose beneath the applause as they recognised the woman standing at the exit. It felt like
surfing, the way he was carried towards her on a
wave of her name on strangers' lips. She stepped
forward into the light. So serious and beautiful.
His eyes held hers as he approached, agonisingly
slowly.

Carrie tactfully disappeared from behind her with
a sisterly squeeze of her arm, leaving the two of
them to be the absolute centre of public attention.

He didn't care. For once in his life the only thing
driving him was the woman standing before him.

Finally she was close enough to touch, and he
stopped in his tracks. Most of the crowd around
them hushed.

She raised a hand towards him…

…and punched him in the arm.

Hard.

'Ava!' Dan rubbed his bruised bicep, his eyes the
mocha colour of surprise.

'What did you do?' She punched him again and
he dodged out of the way. Her heart squeezed so
hard she could only suck in tiny breaths. 'Did
you just throw your career away?'

'I did what I had to, Ava. I had to choose. And
I choose you.'

Tears threatened, but she fought them back

You threw your whole career away—everything you've worked for…'

'Which is meaningless if I have no respect for myself.'

'For me?' The words barely squeaked out. Her throat couldn't do much else, tight as it was with unshed tears. Love welled dangerously close to the surface.

'No,' he said. 'For us. I couldn't ask you to stay with all that hanging over you. I had to set the record straight.'

'It was so…' She groped for the right word. Tears brimmed.

'Stupid?' he smiled.

'Spectacular.' She stepped forward and fell into his arms, his kiss. The people at the tables nearest to them cheered. A lighting tech high in the rig spun the spotlight away from the stage and towards the doors, to bathe them in glorious luminescence. It had the added effect of making most of the audience vanish into shadow. It was a strange, ethereal kind of privacy.

Dan broke away and set Ava back a step. Her overwhelmed chest heaved as she struggled for breath. He glanced at the spotlight and sank onto one knee in front of her.

Oh, God. 'Get up!' It was half-sob, half-plea.

'Ava Lange…'

'Dan, please. What are you doing?' Panic had her clenching icy fingers together. Her wild eyes flicked around the room.

'I just committed professional suicide rather than lose you. Declared my love for you live on national television. Can you possibly *not* know what I'm about to do?'

'Say yes, Ava!' someone shouted from beyond the light.

Her heart flipped into her throat.

'Ava Lange. Will you marry me and let me spend the rest of my life loving you and apologising for what an idiot I've been?'

She sucked in a breath, speechless. Completely petrified. *Love!* Facing Dione Leeds had nothing on this moment of absolute terrifying fantasy-come-true.

He took her hand. 'If you say no, you'll be condemning me to a lifetime of meaningless miserable encounters with Brant Maddox cast-offs. Is that what you want?'

She wanted desperately to laugh, to lighten the moment. But she couldn't find it in her. 'No.'

Dan blinked. Shocked. 'Wait...is that a no?'

The room went suddenly quiet. Or was it in her mind? 'No. It's not a no.'

A huge, sexy smile spread across his face. 'So it's a yes?'

Ava looked into those dark eyes, burning with such intensity, and—*sigh*—there it was…the melted-chocolate colour of love. Promising the world. Promising for ever. The man she'd loved for half her lifetime.

Was there any question? Relief washed over her. And joy. Her face split into a brilliant smile. 'Yes.'

Someone whooped at a table nearby, and in the control booth someone hit 'play' on a loud piece of music that took the broadcast to a well-overdue commercial break.

Dan surged to his feet, hauling Ava close, and wrapped her in the protective circle of his arms. It was as close to privacy as they were going to get as his lips found hers. The kiss went on for eternity, leaving her oblivious to everything but the feel and taste of the wonderful man in her arms.

'People are watching,' she gasped as soon as they broke for air.

'Don't care.' He kissed her again.

She laughed against his lips. 'We've made such a spectacle.'

'Do you think anyone will remember the other story now?'

Ava pulled free and looked at him, fingers of fear skimming over her. 'Is that why you—?'

He silenced her with his mouth, then walked her backwards, out into the bright foyer, and let the huge doors swing shut on the rest of the world. He grabbed her hand. 'Quick—before they all start streaming out for the break.'

They sprinted, hand in hand, for distant doors that revealed a long hallway leading to the hotel's kitchen. Ignoring the surprise of the chefs and serving staff who glanced up, Dan scanned the room and then tugged Ava towards a comfortably large linen store.

'Perfect,' he said, barring the door behind them with an ornate candlestick across the handles.

'Dan, we can't—!'

'Shut up and kiss me.'

This kiss lasted minutes rather than seconds. She was breathless and tingly when Dan reluctantly withdrew his lips from hers and lifted his head. Everything felt like a fuzzy dream.

'I won't hold you to it, Ava. You can pull out if you want to.'

Pull out? Was he mad? Marrying Dan was everything she hadn't known she wanted. She snuggled closer in his arms. 'I wouldn't have pegged you as someone to breach a verbal agreement, Mr Arnot.'

He smiled a little nervously. 'I put you on the spot in there, Ms Lange. I wouldn't blame you.'

'I would. I'm not pulling out. And I won't let you, either.' She reached up and dragged him close for another searing kiss. When she spoke again she was decidedly breathless. 'It's taken me too long to catch you.'

'Did you hear everything I said?' He pulled her into a strong hug, his hands roaming over the low-cut back of her dress.

'The whole country did.'

'I meant it, Ava. I will do whatever it takes to undo the damage I've caused.'

'I was coming to find you,' she whispered against his ear. 'Right before your award was read out. But Dione Leeds found me first.'

Dan pushed her away to look deep into her eyes, concerned. 'What happened?'

'Well… I seem to have made rather a good speech of my own.'

His smile fairly dazzled her. 'That's my girl.' He kissed her again, before remembering. 'Why were you looking for me?'

'I wanted to apologise. I overreacted on the dance floor—didn't give you a chance to explain. Brant helped me to realise you've been trying to protect me and your job at the same time.'

'Brant did?'

'He knows better than anyone how fine a line deception is to tread. I think he knew what you were trying to do. I should have too, and I'm sorry I doubted you.'

Dan thought that through. 'Maybe he *is* as smart as you say.' His eyes grew serious. 'I'm sorry I've kept you at arm's distance, Ava. I've held onto my hatred for so long it's become part of me.'

'Can you share it with me? Can I take some of it from you?'

He closed his eyes and rested his forehead against hers. 'Would you?'

'In a heartbeat.'

He was silent for moments. 'He was a miserable man, my father. Literally and figuratively. When my mother left he took his anger towards her out on me. I reminded him too much of her. When I was smaller he used words—emotional blackmail, verbal abuse. I'd already lost my mother, and he threatened every day to leave me, too.'

He cleared his throat and took a deep breath. Ava's hand tightened on his.

'It worked for years. That and the denigration. When I got bigger, and the words bounced off, he started in with the physical abuse. That's when your parents stepped in. Sometimes my dad didn't even notice I hadn't been home for days. He called me a no-hoper. A loser. As faithless as my mother.'

'Oh, Dan…'

His arms tightened around her. His voice was pure gravel. 'Hating her nearly killed me, Ava.

But hating him saved me. It gave me purpose and courage. I channelled that into my surfing, and later my studies. I burned to prove him wrong. It was like air for me. I lived with him, so I understand why she had to leave. But I'll never understand how she could have left her little boy behind with him. Unprotected.'

Ava buried her face in his neck.

'Hey…' He stroked her hair. 'No tears. I just want you to know what kind of competition you were working against then. Even now. That nothing I did was done lightly.'

Ava dragged her mouth over his, tasting her own tears. 'I understand. I'm so sorry.'

'It was never my intention to portray you as you have been. To impact on your credibility. I know how important that is to you. Kurtz didn't like it when I refused to play along. Unfortunately, you bore the brunt of his fear of me.'

'Fear?'

'I'm better than he is. I'm better than all of them. And they know it.'

Ava smiled. 'Lord, I love that confidence.' She looked him right in the eye. 'And I love you.'

He crushed his mouth to hers and groaned. 'I never want you to stop saying that.'

'I said it nine years ago,' she mumbled against his shoulder, where she rested her head.

'Nine years ago I was so deep in the abyss I couldn't see past my own selfish needs. But even back then I recognised your feelings. I thought it would hurt less ultimately.'

She nodded, remembering how very, very much it had hurt. 'The severed limb.'

'Except you were more like a phantom limb. Even after I'd gone I still felt you. Your complete, unwavering love. It was in every story Steve told. It was in every conversation I didn't have with your father. I grew to hate that love because of what it said about me. That I could walk away like that from someone who'd offered me their heart.'

She stared at him. Resolute. Steady. 'Do you remember what you said to me that night?'

He winced. 'Which part of it?'

'"I will never be with you."'

His eyes dropped. Clouded.

'I took that with me everywhere I went, Dan. For years.' He opened his mouth to speak, but Ava pressed her fingers to his lips. 'Knowing how that one comment affected me for years after, I can't even imagine how an entire childhood of putdowns and abandonment must have impacted on you. It's a miracle you've come out a decent human being at all.'

'You can thank your father for that.' He kissed the top of her head. 'And yourself.'

'Me?'

'I may have been staggering around in my own personal morass, but I knew exactly where my light sources were. You. Your father. Even Steve. And your mother, for the short time I had her.'

Ava tucked her arms around him, holding on tight. 'You've lost two mothers.'

'But I've found true love. Not a bad consolation prize.'

Ava's hand flew to her mouth. 'You proposed to me.'

He smiled, pulling her close. 'I sure did.'

She pushed away, her hands on his chest, and looked at him meaningfully. 'Dan, listen. You proposed to me. We're getting married.'

He blinked at her, and she spelled it out for him in small words.

'My father *is* your father now.'

All the blood drained from his face, and then flushed back up in a rush. His jaw clenched and his eyes glittered with sudden moisture. Ava had never seen someone handed their dream before. Her heart exploded for him.

'That's not why I—'

She cut him off by stretching up to his lips, pressing them firmly against his, giving him a second to recover his composure. 'I know. But it's another consolation prize, huh?'

His answer was to sweep her into his arms and kiss her until they were both trembling.

Minutes passed with absolutely no distance between them, until Ava surfaced, rumpled and smudged. 'Do you think there's a fire escape somewhere close by?' she said.

Her eyes must have given her away, because Dan smiled, long and seductive. He dragged his thumb along the lower ridge of her lip, repairing the evidence of his mouth's assault. 'I have no intention of leaving.'

Her stomach clenched. 'We can't possibly go back in *there*.'

He removed a dozen pins from her dishevelled hair and let the heavy locks fall naturally over her shoulders, disguising the worst of his onslaught. 'No, I think we'll leave Kurtz to talk his way out of this one.'

'Then what?'

'I was thinking…' His hands roamed her body. 'I just got engaged to the most beautiful and brilliant woman I know, and we're standing in the linen store of the best hotel in Sydney.' He kissed her throat softly and whispered into her ear, 'And it appears my schedule is now unexpectedly clear.'

Ava giggled. 'Dan, I have no clothes with me!'

'You won't need them.' His lips trailed over

her shoulder. 'Except those shoes. You'll need to keep those on.'

Her laugh turned sexy, and she dragged one of her three-inch heels up the length of his calf. 'Gosh. What would my father say?'

'He'd say *about bloody time*.'

EPILOGUE

'SHE'S loving it! Look at her.'

Ava snuggled into Dan's chest as they lay sprawled on his enormous couch, watching the widescreen TV across the room. On it, Brant and Cadence hammed it up for the cameras at an official AusOne party across town, celebrating the launch of the third season of *Urban Nature*—still Australia's most popular lifestyle programme. Brant looked gorgeous, as always, tall and tanned, and flirting shamelessly with the female half of the crowd.

Cadence—resplendent in a black creation with torn shards of PVC all over it, and three-storey buckle boots—glowered and pouted and brought new meaning to the word *surly*. The cameras ate it up.

'I just thought it would be nice if they could go to the movies together from time to time,' Ava laughed. 'I didn't expect her to become the media's darling.'

'She's a born extrovert.' Dan chuckled against her nape before pressing his lips to it. 'You don't dress like that if you're hoping *not* to be noticed.'

Dan and Cadence had established a strangely warm friendship, considering Dan had outed her on national television. She was every bit as sharp as Brant, and her quick mind and good business sense had struck a chord with Dan. Besides, he'd found himself with a vacancy for the position of honorary little sister.

'She looks happy.'

Dan laughed outright. 'What do you get that from? The freaky stare, the grim mouth, or the hostile body language?'

'Come on—look at them. He hasn't left her side. Look how he's letting her shine. Only a man deeply in love would take a back seat to his woman. She's waited a long time for that chance…'

Dan moved against her, his lips pressing harder against her nape. 'Speaking of waiting a long time…'

Ava switched off the remote and Brant and Cadence vanished. 'Don't you have some work to do?' she laughed. 'Come on, Mister Executive Producer. You owe X-Dream Sports. They saved your butt, putting you in charge of their surfing channel.' *Programming that Dan had pushed to* *number one in Australia.* She glanced over to where Old Faithful was propped in the hall. Back in the water after a decade. Where they both belonged.

'And you saved my butt by marrying me.' He reached around to stroke her. She wriggled against him, scrambling free.

'Seriously. You have a deadline, and so do I. I have to finish the Becher's design by Wednesday. I've got three more on the wait-list.'

Dan sighed. 'Okay. But not an all-nighter, eh? I want to watch you sleep.'

'Stalker.' Ava straightened her skirt and blouse as she stood.

'Tease.' Dan scooted out of her way, heading for his den.

Ava opened the door that joined the two parts of their home. Predictably, AusOne had repossessed her Winnebago almost immediately following the debacle of the awards night. Fortunately Steve had had the good sense to strip it of everything of Ava's while she and Dan were holed up in the Milana, on their five-day retreat from the world.

Thank goodness for big brothers.

The entire guest house was now Ava's office space. Stunning designs littered the surfaces, decorated the walls—all commissions which had come in since that disastrous story went to print and Dan's spectacular proposal at the awards.

All publicity *was* good publicity, as it turned out, and there'd been no lasting damage done to Ava's design reputation. Thanks to Dan. He'd taken a huge risk, but it had paid off. He truly was savvy when it came to the fickle entertainment industry.

Ava stretched, then sat at her angled drafting desk and pulled a blank sheet of paper over to try some new ideas. She'd barely lifted a pen before she heard the door open behind her. A moment later large, warm hands slid around her middle and soft, firm lips found her ear.

She smiled. 'What happened to working, Mr Arnot?'

'I missed you, Mrs Arnot.' His hands gently brought her to her feet. Ava's eyes fluttered closed as she felt Dan's lips move against the side of her throat, his hard body pressed against hers from behind.

'But X-Dream…?'

Dan slid his hands down her arms and took her hands in his. He whispered against her ear. 'X-Dream get me for ten hours a day. You get me for the rest.'

Ava felt the rush of excitement that always came when Dan was close. Followed closely by

the deep, satisfying bond they shared. She twisted
in his arms, slid her hand up under his shirt, and
loved him.

ROMANCE 2-in-1

Coming next month

OUTBACK BACHELOR
by Margaret Way

Ranch hand Skye grew up dreaming of dating Keefe, heir to a famous cattle empire – and way out of her league. Now a highflying lawyer, Skye's back to win the cattle king's heart!

THE CATTLEMAN'S ADOPTED FAMILY
by Barbara Hannay

Cattleman Seth sets Amy's nerves jangling and not just because he's stop-and-stare gorgeous. Amy's come to Serenity Ranch to tell Seth he's the father of her late best friend's baby girl!

OH-SO-SENSIBLE SECRETARY
by Jessica Hart

Note to self: Summer, get a grip! Phin might be delicious but he's also your boss, and he's completely impossible in every way! You're totally incompatible…

HOUSEKEEPER'S HAPPY-EVER-AFTER
by Fiona Harper

This Cinderella's carriage to happiness awaits…in the unlikely form of hot-shot music executive Mark Wilder's *Housekeeper Wanted* advertisement! Dare Ellie take Mark's hand and jump aboard?

On sale 5th March 2010

Available at WHSmith, Tesco, ASDA, Eason and all good bookshops.
For full Mills & Boon range including eBooks visit
www.millsandboon.co.uk

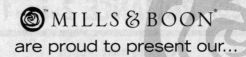

MILLS & BOON

are proud to present our...

Book of the Month

Pure Princess, Bartered Bride
by Caitlin Crews
from Mills & Boon®
Modern™

Luc Garnier has secured the ultimate prize –
Princess Gabrielle – a pearl beyond measure.
But will Luc be able to break through her
defences to make this not just a marriage
on paper, but of the flesh?

Mills & Boon® Modern™
Available 15th January

Something to say about our
Book of the Month?
Tell us what you think!
millsandboon.co.uk/community

MILLS & BOON

MODERN

proudly presents

DARK-HEARTED DESERT MEN

A kingdom torn apart by scandal;
a throne left empty;
four smouldering desert princes…
Which one will claim the crown – and who
will they claim as their brides?

March
WEDLOCKED: BANISHED SHEIKH,
UNTOUCHED QUEEN
by Carol Marinelli

April
TAMED: THE BARBARIAN KING
by Jennie Lucas

May
FORBIDDEN: THE SHEIKH'S VIRGIN
by Trish Morey

June
SCANDAL: HIS MAJESTY'S LOVE-CHILD
by Annie West

Available at WHSmith, Tesco, ASDA, Eason and all good bookshops
www.millsandboon.co.uk

millsandboon.co.uk Community

Join Us!

The Community is the perfect place to meet and chat to kindred spirits who love books and reading as much as you do, but it's also the place to:

- **Get the inside scoop from authors about their latest books**
- **Learn how to write a romance book with advice from our editors**
- **Help us to continue publishing the best in women's fiction**
- **Share your thoughts on the books we publish**
- **Befriend other users**

Forums: Interact with each other as well as authors, editors and a whole host of other users worldwide.

Blogs: Every registered community member has their own blog to tell the world what they're up to and what's on their mind.

Book Challenge: We're aiming to read 5,000 books and have joined forces with The Reading Agency in our inaugural Book Challenge.

Profile Page: Showcase yourself and keep a record of your recent community activity.

Social Networking: We've added buttons at the end of every post to share via digg, Facebook, Google, Yahoo, technorati and de.licio.us.

www.millsandboon.co.uk

MILLS & BOON®

www.millsandboon.co.uk

- ◎ All the latest titles
- ◎ Free online reads
- ◎ Irresistible special offers

And there's more...

- ◎ Missed a book? Buy from our huge discounted backlist
- ◎ Sign up to our FREE monthly eNewsletter
- ◎ eBooks available now
- ◎ More about your favourite authors
- ◎ Great competitions

Make sure you visit today!

www.millsandboon.co.uk

2 FREE BOOKS
AND A SURPRISE GIFT

We would like to take this opportunity to thank you for reading this Mills & Boon® book by offering you the chance to take TWO more specially selected books from the Romance series absolutely FREE! We're also making this offer to introduce you to the benefits of the Mills & Boon® Book Club™—

- **FREE home delivery**
- **FREE gifts and competitions**
- **FREE monthly Newsletter**
- **Exclusive Mills & Boon Book Club offers**
- **Books available before they're in the shops**

Accepting these FREE books and gift places you under no obligation to buy, you may cancel at any time, even after receiving your free shipment. Simply complete your details below and return the entire page to the address below. You don't even need a stamp!

YES Please send me 2 free Romance books and a surprise gift. I understand that unless you hear from me, I will receive 5 superb new stories every month including two 2-in-1 books priced at £4.99 each and a single book priced at £3.19, postage and packing free. I am under no obligation to purchase any books and may cancel my subscription at any time. The free books and gift will be mine to keep in any case.

Ms/Mrs/Miss/Mr_____ Initials _____

Surname _____

Address _____

_____

_____ Postcode _____

Send this whole page to: Mills & Boon Book Club, Free Book Offer, FREEPOST NAT 10298, Richmond, TW9 1BR

Offer valid in UK only and is not available to current Mills & Boon Book Club subscribers to this series. Overseas and Eire please write for details.. We reserve the right to refuse an application and applicants must be aged 18 years or over. Only one application per household. Terms and prices subject to change without notice. Offer expires 30th April 2010. As a result of this application, you may receive offers from Harlequin Mills & Boon and other carefully selected companies. If you would prefer not to share in this opportunity please write to The Data Manager, PO Box 676, Richmond, TW9 1WU.

Mills & Boon® is a registered trademark owned by Harlequin Mills & Boon Limited.
The Mills & Boon® Book Club™ is being used as a trademark.